Praise for *No Other Darkness*

"Last year, Sarah Hilary's *Someone Else's Skin* was acclaimed a superb debut. It was no fluke. *No Other Darkness* is just as excellent, and DI Marnie Rome is a three-dimensional character of an emotional depth rarely encountered in the world of fictional cops." —*The Times* (London)

"At the center is a queasily equivocal moral tone that forces the reader into a constant rejigging of their attitude to the characters. And did I mention the plotting? Hilary's ace in the hole—as it is in the best crime thrillers."

—*Financial Times*

"Unnerving and compelling." —*The Lady* (London)

"Riveting . . . Sarah Hilary delivers in this enthralling tale of a haunted detective, terrible crime, and the secrets all of us try to keep."

—Lisa Gardner, #1 *New York Times* bestselling author

"An exceptional new talent."

—Alex Marwood, Edgar Award–winning author of *The Wicked Girls*

"Truly mesmerizing from its opening page to its thunderous denouement. A haunting, potent novel from a bleakly sublime new voice."

—David Mark, author of the DS McAvoy series

"Sarah Hilary cements her position as one of Britain's most exciting and accomplished new writers. Complex, polished and utterly gripping, this is a book to make your heart pound." —Eva Dolan, author of the Zigic & Ferreira series

Praise for *Someone Else's Skin*

"Fans of Val McDermid and Ian Rankin will love this tremendous debut. *Someone Else's Skin* puts Sarah Hilary and DI Marnie Rome squarely on the map. A gripping, disturbing examination of domestic violence with gravitas in spades, this book haunts you well after its finish."

—Julia Spencer-Fleming, *New York Times* bestselling author of *Through Evil Days*

"A truly engrossing read from an exceptional new talent. Hilary writes with a beguiling immediacy that pulls you straight into her world on the first page and leaves you bereft when you finish. Intelligent, emotional, and totally unexpected in terms of where it goes. I truly loved this book."

—Alex Marwood, Edgar Award–winning *author of The Wicked Girls*

"I briefly interrupt my Internet detox to say thank you for sending me *Someone Else's Skin*. Finally finished it this morning. So brilliantly put together, unflinching without ever being gratuitous . . . and I love the way Sarah writes—every other page has a line I wish I'd thought of myself. It's the best crime debut I've ever read and deserves to be MASSIVE."

—Erin Kelly, author of *The Poison Tree*

"If this first entry is anything to go by, Hilary's sense of plot and subtle character building will make the DI Marnie Rome series one to watch."

—*Shelf Awareness*

"[Hilary] skillfully interweaves multiple viewpoints on the way to the mystery's unsettling conclusion."

—*Publishers Weekly*

"Gripping and full of graphic details about the lives and psychology of her characters, both abusers and their victims. You might be surprised at the end to learn which is which." —*Mystery Scene*

"A supurb debut and an impressive new cop-heroine, modern, passionate, and mixed-up." —*The Times* (London)

"A tense, deep, and dramatic tale of domestic violence." —*The Independent* (London)

"An intelligent, assured, and very promising debut." —*The Guardian* (London)

"What an entry on to the thriller scene Hilary has made with *Someone Else's Skin*. She writes deftly, unobtrusively, subtly drawing her readers in. . . . It's the story that really drives this novel, though, and this is a corker: twisty, tricksy, and, on occasion, seriously scary. This is an extraordinarily good debut." —*The Observer* (London)

"There's an accomplished writer learning her trade here, and it richly deserves to succeed." —*The Daily Mail* (London)

ABOUT THE AUTHOR

Sarah Hilary lives in Bath with her daughter, where she writes quirky copy for a well-loved travel publisher. She's also worked as a bookseller, and with the Royal Navy. An award-winning short story writer, Hilary won the Cheshire Prize for Literature in 2012. *No Other Darkness* is her follow-up to *Someone Else's Skin*.

NO OTHER DARKNESS

SARAH HILARY

PENGUIN BOOKS

PENGUIN BOOKS
An imprint of Penguin Random House LLC
375 Hudson Street
New York, New York 10014
penguin.com

First published in Great Britain in digital format
by Headline Publishing Group 2015
Published in Penguin Books 2015

ISBN 978-0-14-312619-5

Printed in the United States of America
1 3 5 7 9 10 8 6 4 2

Set in Meridien

For my mother, the best in the world

Five years ago

Fred's crying again, a snotty noise with a whine in it, like the puppy when she's shut outside. Archie's the oldest so it's his job to take care of Fred when Mum and Dad aren't around, but he's fed up of drying Fred's tears and wiping Fred's nose. Most of all, he's fed up of telling Fred it's going to be okay. Archie doesn't like telling lies, especially not to his little brother.

Fred's only five but he's got a way of looking at you like the puppy when he knows you're lying. 'No more scraps, girl. All gone,' but Budge always knew Dad was lying and she started whining even before he shut her outside. There's a smeary spot on the sliding door where she put her nose when she looked at you, begging to be let back in.

'I want Mummy,' Fred hiccups. 'Where's Mummy?'

He's twisted the sleeping bag so that Archie can't see the zipper. There's a long dirty streak up the side of the bag where the cement floor's rubbed. The sleeping bag smells bad, like everything else down here. Fred smells bad, and so does Archie.

He says, 'You've got to lie still. It's night-time, go to sleep.'

'It doesn't feel like night-time,' Fred whines.

There are no windows down here, so Archie can't show Fred the dark outside, the way he would at home. He shows Fred the watch face, even though Fred's only just learning to tell the time. 'Little hand's on the eleven, see? That means it's eleven o'clock.'

'I want a banana,' Fred sobs. 'Elevenses I have my banana.'

'That's eleven in the morning. This's eleven at night.'

'Then I want Mummy to tuck me in.'

Archie's skin's too tight around his neck. 'You are tucked in,' he says. 'I tucked you in.'

He rolls away so that his back's turned to Fred. It's mean, but it's what Archie does at home so he thinks maybe Fred will take the hint and go to sleep. After a bit, he decides it must've worked because Fred's gone quiet, except for a couple of sniffs, and that whistle in his chest. His face is white but it's a hot white, like when the sun's gone behind clouds.

The whistle in his chest means something's wrong inside.

Fred's sick.

Archie knows his brother's hungry, because he's hungry too. If he was back home he'd say, 'I'm starving,' but he's scared to say that here, in case it's true. In case they really are starving, him and Fred. Archie won't tell lies, and he won't say things – terrible things – that might be true. In case it makes them come true, like a jinx, or a dare.

When Fred says, 'Mummy's never coming, nor Daddy,' Archie tells him to shut up. It's the only time he gets angry with his brother. 'Of course they're coming. Shut up.'

Archie blinks his eyes open in the dark. He doesn't need to pretend for Fred, not right now. Even if he's awake, Fred can't see. He saw the watch because it's got a little light in the side, but it's too dark for him to see Archie, and anyway,

Archie's turned away. He could pick his nose or cry – he could cry for Mum and Dad, as long as he cries quietly – and Fred won't know. He can't see Archie's face, just the back of Archie's T-shirt where the label sticks up.

Archie should've put on pyjamas at bedtime. He made Fred put on pyjamas, but it was hard work and by the end of it Archie was too tired to be bothered with his own, so he's gone to bed in his T-shirt and shorts. It's the first time he's done that: broken the rules. He should've brushed his teeth, too, but he didn't. He made Fred brush his teeth and then he pretended he'd done his, when Fred was using the bucket.

It scares Archie that he's started breaking the rules, but it also makes him feel brave, like when he stood up to Saul Weller at school. Instead of hitting Archie harder, Saul gave him a brofist. Sometimes it pays to break the rules.

The T-shirt label tickles. Archie's neck is bony, and every bit of him hurts. He's cold all the time. If he was at home, he'd pull the duvet higher. The sleeping bag won't be pulled. It's sweaty inside, and it stinks. Archie hates the stink almost as much as he hates the dark, although he'd never admit it, not to Fred, not even to himself.

At home, their bedroom's at the top of the house and Mum used to say she'd put up special curtains to block out the light, but she never did and Archie's glad because he doesn't like the dark and besides there's a tree outside their window where a blackbird nests. They couldn't see the bird if the curtains were special.

Archie wishes there was a window down here.

But all he'd see would be earth, packed and black.

Even if the window was in the roof, like the one in Saul Weller's house, all he'd see would be earth.

They're buried, underground.

The thought makes Archie sick, makes his wrists skip like

he's run a race. A sour taste leaks into his mouth, like puke coming up. He doesn't want to think about it. He screws his eyes shut and thinks of the blackbird, its yellow beak and blinking eye, watching through the branches of the tree at the top of the house where the light comes in and puts stripes across the foot of his bed, and Fred's.

Fred murmurs in his sleep, 'Mummy. Mummy . . .'

He has to keep quiet. They both have to keep quiet. That's the first rule, and the most important one. They promised to keep quiet.

Archie curls his hands and fits a fist into his mouth to stop him from hushing Fred, from saying, 'It's all right. She's coming, it's all okay,' because it's wrong.

It's wrong to tell lies, especially to your little brother.

PART ONE

1

Now

DS Noah Jake watched Debbie Tanner swinging between the station's desks with her cake tin, like a burlesque dancer collecting big tips. DS Ron Carling dipped a hand into the tin with his stare on DC Tanner's chest as if someone had stuck it there: googly eyes. Debbie had a stupendous chest; it managed to make her plain white shirt look like a basque.

'Muffins,' she said. 'Home-made.'

Carling took a muffin from the tin, making appropriate noises of approval. He'd put on three pounds since Debbie joined the unit.

Noah's phone buzzed: a text from Dan. Not work-safe, not remotely. Noah wiped the text with his thumb, holding in a smile. The cake tin landed under his nose.

'Take two,' Debbie said. 'Unless Dan doesn't have a sweet tooth.' She gave a conspiratorial smile. 'But he's going out with the best-looking DS in London, so I'm guessing he does.' She proffered the tin. 'I made them fresh this morning.'

'Thanks, but it's a bit soon after breakfast for me.'

What time did she get up, to bake a tin of muffins before 9 a.m.?

'I'll leave one for later.' She plucked a muffin and placed it next to Noah's keyboard, where it pouted at him from its paper cup. 'Next time I'll make a Jamaican batch. Banana pecan. Maybe your mum has a recipe?'

'DS Jake, a minute?' DI Marnie Rome beckoned from the doorway to her office, looking pin-neat in a charcoal suit, her short red curls tidied back from her face.

Noah got to his feet, pocketing his phone.

DC Tanner followed him into Marnie's office, swinging her tin. 'Muffin? I make them with courgette. It's much better for you than butter. Not that *you* need to watch your figure.' She patronised Marnie's flat chest with a sympathetic smile, reaching her free hand for the pot plant on the edge of the desk, feeling with her fingers for the soil packed around its roots.

Marnie sat behind her desk, nodding at Noah to take the chair on the other side.

The plant was a cactus which, when it was in the mood, gave out spidery white flowers. It was giving them out now, but Debbie checked the soil anyway, as if someone as busy as DI Rome couldn't be relied on to look after a cactus. Noah winced at the familiarity, but Marnie simply said, 'How's the paperwork going, detective?'

'I'm right on top of it,' Debbie promised. She turned on her heel and wove her way back to her desk, prow and stern swaying dizzily. No wonder Ron Carling and the others stared.

Noah didn't stare. He was watching DI Rome. She had her case face on: a new line, thin as a thread, at the bridge of her nose. 'What's happened?'

'Bodies,' she said. 'In Snaresbrook . . .'

'How many bodies?'

'Two.' She held his gaze steadily and with a measure of sympathy. 'Young children.'

His first case with dead children; well, he'd known it would happen sooner or later. 'Snaresbrook, that's . . .'

'Out east, past Leytonstone . . . Not our usual stamping ground.' Marnie put back her chair and stood, waiting while Noah did the same. 'But it's under the Met's jurisdiction and I know this place, or rather I know the street. So they put the call through to here.'

'What place? I mean, how do you know it?'

'Blackthorn Road.' Marnie picked up her bag. 'I headed up an investigation there eighteen months ago.'

Before Noah's time with the major incident team. 'What was the case?'

'Domestic, with complications.' Clipping the words back, her eyes already in Snaresbrook, working this new case.

'Complications?' Noah echoed.

'A missing child. For a while it looked like an abduction, or worse.'

'But it wasn't?'

Marnie shook her head. 'We found her safe and well. There's no obvious connection between that and . . . this.'

The way she said *this* made Noah's skin creep. 'Except it happened on the same street.'

'Four houses down. And some time ago, judging by what they've found. And where they found it.'

She read his look of wary enquiry. 'Underground. This was a burial, but not in the usual sense. I don't know much more than that. I've asked DS Carling to take a first look at Missing Persons. You and I need to get over there.'

Noah's imagination was conjuring images, each worse than the one before.

A burial, but not in the usual sense . . .

Marnie touched his elbow briefly before she nodded at the door. 'Let's find out.'

2

Sweat made Marnie's shirt cling to the small of her back. Instinct pinched shut her nose in protest at the smell: sweet and bloated by rot. A bluebottle brushed at her wrist and she flinched through the latex glove. It hadn't hatched down here; if it had, the whole place would be foul with flies. A solitary bluebottle had followed her down, seeking the source of the smell, sweeping the dark with its droning before it settled, as she had, by the side of the bed. Useless to bat it away; it had found what flies like best: dead meat.

Every one of Marnie's muscles screamed at her to get out, away, her blood flooded by adrenalin, skin twitchy with distress. She stayed where she was, crouched by the side of the makeshift bed. She couldn't leave them, not yet; it was scary down here in the dark.

The bluebottle had gone quiet, crawling. She made no attempt to knock it away, grateful at some level for the sound it made, an almost human sound. It was too quiet down here.

High overhead, the sky squatted.

A small square of sky, too far away for warmth or light. Marnie had to rely on a trio of police torches, their focus turned to flood, burning at intervals around the room.

If you could call it a room. Thirty feet by fifty of cemented walls and floor, bruised by damp, the ceiling supported by two cement pillars.

Twelve feet underground.

It was a pit.

A burial, but not in the usual sense . . .

Marnie had instructed Noah to stay with the family who'd found the pit, up in the clean air of the garden at number 14 Blackthorn Road. Then she'd climbed down, because she needed to see what they were dealing with.

You entered the pit from a manhole, by way of a rusting ladder. The rungs of the ladder had bitten her gloved palms, shedding sharp flakes of orange iron.

White torchlight burned on the raw walls, and on the makeshift bed.

Marnie couldn't look at the bed, not properly. She wasn't ready.

Instead, she looked around the floor, at the mess of tin cans and clothes, picture books and toys. Keeping very still out of respect for the crime scene, waiting for Fran Lennox and Forensics. Her eyes scanned the dark, making a mental inventory ahead of the official one.

Two small pairs of black trainers with Velcro fastenings stood at the foot of the bed. Two blue anoraks, camouflage-patterned, hung from a nail knocked into the wall. A handful of picture books lay on the cement floor. The books were swollen, the way a telephone directory swells if it's left in the rain on the doorstep of an empty house. Ink had run across the covers, making monsters of ducks and puppies and robots.

A low pyramid of food cans was stacked against one wall. Damp had stripped the labels away and eaten into the tin. The cans had ring-pulls in their lids, tricky for small fingers. The soft toys – a monkey in a striped T-shirt, a squirrel with a red tail – sagged with damp. An abandoned jigsaw puzzle had peeled into pieces of green card. The lid of the box showed a busy farmyard under a blue sky. The jigsaw was simple enough for pre-schoolers, but thanks to the damp, its sky was indistinguishable from grass, its corners gone for ever.

Marnie's eyes burned, looking at the jigsaw. How cruel would you have to be to put a picture of grass and sky down here where there was only grey cement and creeping damp?

She listened for sounds from the garden overhead, but it was quiet. The cement was thick, with three feet of soil above it, stopping sound from getting in, or out.

The river ran not far from the foot of the garden; she could smell it. Had it flooded down here then drained away? Was she looking at death by drowning? She didn't think so.

Not poison, either. The bodies were too . . .

She struggled for the right word. Peaceful? Relaxed? Neither word was right, but poison would have looked different. The bodies on the bed were curled together. Sleeping, except that they weren't. A watch hung off one little, brittle wrist. It had long ago stopped ticking.

What was she seeing? A slow starvation? Sickness? Suffocation?

Probably not suffocation; damp and mould meant the air had been getting in, by accident or design. Design, she guessed. This was a bunker, most probably intended for storage, although she couldn't rule out Cold War paranoia. It'd been built for the living, not the dead.

Which hadn't stopped someone doing . . . this.

She touched her hand to the side of the makeshift bed, even though it made no difference now. She was too late. By her best guess, some years too late. Four, five years? Fran Lennox would know. She was on her way with a full forensic team. The trail was cold, too cold for twenty minutes to make a difference. Soon Marnie would start bagging and tagging. She'd be a detective. Right now, she wanted to be a human being. An appalled human being, sitting in silence with two other, smaller ones. Just for a minute; Fran would be here soon.

Marnie murmured it to the little bodies on the bed: 'She's coming. She'll be here soon.'

She looked away from the bed, to the wall where the food cans were stacked. The bunker was organised like living space: the food kept as far as possible from the corner where a bucket was covered with a mouldy towel. The bed was segregated from the play area by a space for getting dressed and undressed. The degree of organisation said this was a long-term arrangement. Permanent, the way a life sentence is permanent. Pitiful.

She tried to imagine bagging and tagging the contents of the bunker. Most of it would fall apart the second it was touched. Rust had eaten under the ring-pulls on the tins, growing ghostly green flowers. The tins touched a memory, frail, in the back of her head. Steel wants to be iron oxide. She'd learned that at school, remembered the teacher telling the class, 'We dig it up and beat it into steel, but it doesn't last. Steel wants to be iron oxide.' Kettles, cans and cars, the foundations of a thousand high-rises, all with the same ruddy heart lusting to be iron oxide again, to corrode or collapse. It was happening down here, in the dark. She could taste the iron on her tongue, its flavour like blood.

She shone her torch on the nearest of the cans, to check whether any attempt had been made to open it, and to see what kind of food it contained.

In the wreckage of one peeling label she read: *Peaches*.

She must've eaten tinned peaches as a child. Syrupy, slippy, a pink taste although the fruit was orange. She reached out and touched a fingertip, just a tip, to the nearest can. Rust whispered under her gloved touch, like feathers.

They wouldn't get fingerprints from anything in here.

In which case, how would they find whoever did this?

She needed to know who was responsible for what she couldn't look at, not yet.

Her mobile phone pressed hard into her hip as she crouched by the side of the bed. The torchlight didn't make a difference, not really. It just stirred at the shadows, like a stick stirring at mud. She looked around for child-sized torches. Surely they weren't expected to get dressed in the dark, or to use the bucket in the dark, and why allow them books unless . . .

Under the pillows.

They'd put the torches under their pillows, to keep them safe and close at hand. They'd cuddled together because of the dark. Scared . . .

Scared.

The word wasn't big enough.

She eased upright, far enough to stop the phone bruising her hip.

She'd invited Noah Jake to this party; his first case with dead children. She felt a pang of regret. She'd attended plenty of crime scenes. They were never pretty. But this one was up there – *down here* – with the worst. Her body was cramping, sending a scramble of distress signals to her brain. She should go up, back into the fresh air.

You can't leave them alone down here.

She couldn't. Not until the forensic team arrived.

The family up there – the family who had found the bunker – how much did they know?

The pit was in their garden, where their kids played. Marnie hadn't met any of the kids, but she'd met their dad, Terry. He'd been digging a new vegetable patch when he found the pit, was still grey with shock when Marnie and Noah arrived, his spade abandoned, its cutting edge silvered by contact with the manhole cover.

'We only moved in a year ago.' His voice was knocked to

the back of his throat. 'There was nothing on the searches to suggest anything like this. I checked the survey for soil contamination, sewerage pipes. There was nothing. It's why I thought it was okay to climb down . . .' He kept wiping his hands on his jeans. His eyes were blown wide, his nose pinched shut. A handsome man, grey with shock. Terry Doyle.

He'd waited in the garden for Marnie and Noah. His wife, Beth, had stayed inside the house, a long way from the bodies, thanks to the length of the garden. Marnie had caught a glimpse of the woman's face, a toddler at her hip, his thumb wedged in a wet mouth.

'How long . . .' Terry had whispered to Marnie and Noah as they stood at the side of the pit. 'How long have they been down there?'

'We'll find out. Mr Doyle? Please wait with your wife in the house. DS Jake will take care of you.'

'I couldn't . . . I didn't like to leave them.' His eyes were all pupils, struggling to adjust to the light after being down in the dark. 'It didn't seem right, to leave them. They're so little . . .'

'I understand. DS Jake?'

Noah had taken the man's arm, unobtrusively, steering him back towards the house, where his wife was waiting. Marnie had climbed down into the pit, rigging police torches to break up the blackness. At the foot of the ladder, she'd listened for the sound of the two men walking back up to the house. It was just possible to hear their footfall overhead, which made her wonder whether anyone might've heard crying, or calling, from the bunker. Not the Doyles, who only bought the house a year ago. Before that, for years, it was all fields.

She'd been in Blackthorn Road when the houses were brand new, eighteen months ago.

The bodies had been here a lot longer than that.

Terry hadn't wanted to leave them. Marnie liked him for that. Most people would have been revolted, by the smell apart from anything else. He was distressed, but in the same way Marnie was. He didn't try and run, even though he'd seen what she was seeing.

How far down had he climbed before he realised what he'd found? They'd need to swab him for DNA, just in case. Fran would be able to answer his question about how long the bodies had been here. She'd be able to answer Marnie's questions too, about how they died. If they got lucky, Fran would find evidence of who had done this, so that Marnie could start doing her job properly instead of crouching here, knowing she was too late . . .

A shadow fell on her from above. It climbed the walls for a second, as if scared by the torchlight, before settling on her neck. Where it settled, she burned with scrutiny.

She looked up, blind, at the open square of the manhole.

When her eyes adjusted, she saw the shape of a head and shoulders.

Not tall enough for Noah, or Terry Doyle.

A boy?

A teenage boy, his face blotted out by the sky.

Marnie's skin shivered.

Memory snatched her, for a second. From the dark that stank of death and the pitiful little huddle she'd first seen in Terry Doyle's eyes, to another place where she'd crouched, afraid to look and afraid to leave. The bluebottle, buzzing at her wrist, brought her back.

She blinked, and when she looked again, the boy was gone.

Just the ghost of him, a retinal imprint, against the squatting sky.

3

Inside the forensic tent, it smelt green. Not of death, more like compost.

To Noah's right, the open manhole sent up a solid column of curdled air. The ground was spongy under his feet. He was glad he'd left his jacket in the car; the polythene walls of the tent were starting to sweat, and so was he.

'You're looking at penicillin. It loves to grow on dead meat.' Fran Lennox sent a grim smile across her shoulder. 'This's the stuff they feed you when you're sick.'

'Nice.' Just looking at the narrow manhole made Noah dizzy; he couldn't imagine how Marnie had felt down there in the dark with the bodies.

After Fran's team arrived, Marnie had gone into the house, asking Noah to oversee the perimeter of the crime scene; a test for his resolve, he assumed.

Forensics had brought the bodies up, taking special care, carrying the children so carefully the penicillin was still intact, whiskers of mould reaching from the shrunken nostrils of the small faces. The bony shape of both skulls showed white and round through ruined scalps of skin.

'The bunker wasn't airtight?'

'Good thing too; airtight would've rotted worse than this.' Fran hadn't taken her eyes off the bodies. 'I had to open a sealed casket one time . . . Like soup in a satin bowl.'

Noah watched in silence as she took charge of preparations to remove the bodies to the pathology lab. His head was hurting. Not physical pain, more like the steady punching of a pulse. Sometimes in this job it felt like an affront to be alive.

The dead children were six, seven years old. Just little children. Mould had made them into old men with frail white beards.

A member of Fran's team bagged the clothes from the bunker: trainers and jumpers. Navy anoraks, printed with camouflage. On the smaller body: the patchy remains of what looked like red plaid pyjamas.

'Are they boys?' Noah asked.

'No way of knowing,' Fran said. He heard the hurt in her voice, under its protective layer of morbid humour. 'They're pre-adolescent. No sexual dimorphism to speak of.'

Both bodies fitted in the single bag, with room to spare. It was too risky to try and separate them here. Fran would tackle that task back at her lab; her turn to keep vigil.

'How long do you think they were down there?'

'Who knows?' Fran rested her hand lightly on the body bag. 'I'd say they've been dead four years, maybe longer.'

The children had curled together, their bodies making a tight comma, the bigger child hugging the chest of the smaller one, an elbow reduced to a pitiful knot of bone that made Noah's eyes ache. When Fran drew the zipper on the body bag, he blinked and felt the throb of tears behind his eyelids.

Outside the forensic tent, the Doyles' garden was a bright assault of colour. The house had the surprised, scrubbed look of a new-build. Three floors, a pantiled roof ruined by solar panels, a pair of green drums collecting rainwater. The garden had been dug over either side of a long lawn. For vegetables; Noah recognised the leaves of potato plants, radishes and beetroot.

'Isn't it awful?' Debbie Tanner picked her way across the lawn to join him, her face mottled with dismay. 'How old do you reckon they were? Six, seven? Little mites . . .'

'Is there anything from Missing Persons yet?'

'Ron's still looking. Nothing from five years ago, but we haven't much to go on yet.'

'How's the family holding up?'

'Paramedics are checking them for shock, the dad especially. He says he's just glad *she* didn't see what was down there. Poor bloke's in a bit of a state, been crying his eyes out. The boss is with them, working her magic.'

'What magic?' Noah knew what she meant, but he was intrigued to hear her describe what DI Rome did.

'You know. Making them feel like there's no one else that matters in the whole world but them and what they've seen. She's brilliant. Most DIs don't go near witnesses, or victims come to that. Not unless there's been a complaint. *I* certainly never worked with one who did. I suppose she's got a special empathy, after what happened.'

Debbie had found out details of Marnie's past that Noah hadn't known until she started sharing her knowledge around the station. He'd been with Marnie's team less than eighteen months. Debbie's stories dated back five years. Noah had warned her to be careful it didn't reach DI Rome – the things she'd uncovered, or the fact that she was sharing the information freely with her colleagues – because no good could come of it. Marnie was entitled to her privacy, and even if she wasn't, Noah knew she'd fight to protect it, the same way she'd fight to uncover the truth of what had happened to the children they'd taken from the bunker.

'Any sign of the press yet?'

'Not yet, but you know what they're like. The OCU's on his way.' Debbie hugged her arms under her chest. 'Kiddies are always headlines.'

Not these children, or not five years ago, otherwise Missing Persons would have given them names by now.

So who were they? And why had no one reported them missing?

4

The dirt from the Doyles' garden had been trodden into the house, a dark trench from the garden through to the kitchen. The same dirt was under Terry's fingernails, and his wife's.

'We're putting in a vegetable patch, encouraging the kids to be self-sufficient.' Terry wiped his hands on his jeans. They were raw, as if he'd washed them more than once since finding the pit. 'I was on my own out there, thank God.'

Marnie needed to take his boots, and maybe his clothes, depending how close he'd been to the bodies. 'You said there was nothing on the survey to suggest a bunker?'

'Nothing. It's why I thought it'd be safe to lift the manhole.'

'How easy was it to do that?'

'It wasn't hard. I've lifted flagstones that weigh a lot more.' He cringed, as if he was afraid she'd interpret this as machismo. He was a shade over six feet tall and slim, in good shape for a man in his early forties. 'If I'd known what was inside . . . As soon as I saw them down there, I called the police. But I disturbed a crime scene.' His mouth wrenched. 'I'm so sorry. If I've made it harder for you to find who did that . . . I'm so sorry.'

'It can't be helped.' Marnie picked up the mug of tea he'd made, asking the next question as gently as she could. 'How far down did you climb?'

'Four, maybe five rungs?' His voice was ashy at the edges, fierce tears in his eyes, the kind you fight to hold in.

'Did you – I'm sorry – did you touch anything, other than the ladder?'

He flinched. 'Absolutely not.'

'Good. I'll have to take your boots, to rule out anything that might've been dislodged.'

He nodded his acceptance and she waited a beat, to let him know that this part of the interview was over. 'You've done a lot of work out there.' The earth had been dug over, more than once. 'Is this the first time you've found anything unusual? I don't mean the bunker. Other things, maybe clothes or jewellery?'

'Nothing like that. We've been digging for a few months, getting it ready for the planting. The soil wasn't worth much when we started. We've managed to make it better.'

'How do you do that?' Marnie asked. 'Make soil better?'

'It was mostly sand when we moved in. I guess it's a cheap base for the developers to use, but it's no good for growing anything. No nutrients, for one thing, and it won't hold water. I had to put a lot of compost down, keep turning it during the winter.' He mimed the action. She could see the strength in his wrists. 'By spring we had a halfway decent bed for the veg.'

'Terry's a great gardener,' Beth said. 'He does most of the gardens in the street.' It was the first time she'd spoken since the three of them had gathered in the kitchen. 'It's good for the kids to have a sense of permanence, and to be self-sufficient.'

'Will we have to move out?' Terry asked. 'While you're investigating?'

'I'm afraid so. It'll be for the best. Things are going to be busy here for a while. You won't get much peace.'

The press were coming. She could feel the heat of their curiosity at her heels. OCU Commander Tim Welland was on his way too. In his words, 'To check the fan's working before the shit hits.'

'If you can find us a place big enough to stay together as a family,' Terry said. 'I know we're not conventional, but it matters. We've worked really hard for this.'

Not conventional?

Beth said, 'Tommy's sleeping. I managed to put him down for a nap.' The toddler she'd held on her hip earlier. 'Carmen will be home from nursery soon. One of the other mums brings her. I take her little boy in the mornings . . .' She glanced at the clock on the wall. 'Then there's Clancy . . .'

Terry reached for Beth's hand and held it. 'We're new foster parents.' He forced a smile. 'For our sins. If you could find us somewhere we can stay together . . .'

Marnie knew what Tim Welland would say. Her priority was protecting the crime scene; she owed her first duty to the dead, not the living. 'How new?'

'Since we moved here. It's one of the reasons we wanted a big house.'

'How many kids are we talking about?'

'Just Clancy, for now.' Terry squeezed his wife's hand. Marnie would've missed it, if Beth hadn't turned the flinch into a smile. 'Clancy Brand.'

'How old is Clancy?'

'He'll be fifteen in a couple of months.'

'He's not in school?'

'He's not . . . a hundred per cent at the moment,' Terry said.

'We kept him home today,' his wife added. 'In case it's catching.'

The lie stained her neck dull red.

Some people could lie without colouring, but Beth Doyle wasn't one of them. She was pretty, in a passive way. You'd struggle to remember her face when it wasn't right in front of you. Soft mouth and eyes, the kind of fair hair that looks grubby unless it's just washed.

'So with Tommy and Carmen . . . Clancy makes three kids in the house?'

'Four.' Beth put a hand to her stomach. She wasn't showing yet, the bump hidden under a denim smock.

'Congratulations,' Marnie said.

'It's a big house. It needs children. Everyone says we've too much love for three kids . . .'

They'd put their stamp all over the big house, judging by the kitchen: comfortable and chaotic, cup rings on the table where it looked like a grenade had gone off in a jar of Marmite; fall-out from the family breakfast. Children's drawings were Blu-tacked to the walls, next to dirty thumbprints at toddler height. Marnie wasn't a fan of mess, but mess meant living – risk, courage and failure, all the things that mattered.

A noise in the street brought Beth to her feet. 'That'll be Vic, with Carmen.' She headed in the direction of the front door.

Terry stood and started clearing mugs from the table. Marnie helped, taking an abandoned plate of wrinkled orange segments to the pedal bin. 'Compost.' Terry intercepted the plate with a grimace. 'Thanks.' He deposited it in a green plastic container with a slatted lid.

He washed the cups, running hot water sparingly at first and then for longer, scrubbing at his already raw hands, strong wrists wringing repeatedly under the flood from the tap until they turned first white then red from the heat.

'If you need to talk,' Marnie said, 'I know someone in Victim Support.'

'Thanks.' Terry stopped washing and reached for a towel to dry his hands. 'I'll be okay. I'm thinking the fewer strangers in the house the better, at least for a bit.' He blotted at the wet between his fingers, his eyes blank and grieving.

The paramedics had given him the all-clear, but Marnie was familiar with the tricks shock could play, how it went into hiding only to jump out at you, repeatedly. 'The person I'm thinking of is very good. He won't ask questions. He'll listen, if you need that. You've got a lot on your plate here. I can't see you wanting to talk to Beth about what you saw.'

'Not in her condition,' Terry said mechanically.

'I saw it too,' Marnie said. 'I know how hard this is.'

He nodded. 'Thanks. If you could leave a number for Victim Support, I'll make the call a bit later, when it's quiet here.'

Marnie wrote down Ed Belloc's name and number, handed it to Terry.

He folded the slip of paper once, and then again. 'When you find out who they are . . . will you tell me their names?' He folded the paper a third time, scoring the fold with his thumbnail. 'Please. I'd like to know their names.'

Marnie nodded. 'Yes.'

Beth came back into the kitchen with a scowling three-year-old in a pink duffle coat, yellow hair in fraying plaits, small mouth shut above an obstinate chin.

'Carmen's home,' Beth said. 'Here's Daddy, see. Say hello to Daddy.'

Carmen marched across the kitchen to her father, buried her face in his shins and started to howl. Terry didn't pick her up, squatting instead on his heels. 'Did you have a hard day, honey-bee?' He put an arm around her shoulders and stroked her hair in a steady rhythm.

Carmen wept into his chest. Tears of outrage, Marnie guessed, from the angry noise she was making. Terry looked a question across at Beth, who shook her head defeatedly. He kept stroking the child's hair. 'Honey-bee, it's all fine now. You're home now.'

Beth said, 'Let's you and me go for a walk, yes? Let's put our wellies on and find some puddles to jump in . . .' She reached for the boots that Terry had taken off.

'Sorry,' Marnie reminded her. 'I have to take those.'

'Oh. Yes.' Beth looked around for another pair of wellingtons.

When she tried to take the child from Terry, Carmen stiffened and started to scream, the kind of noise that made car alarms sound sweet.

She was still screaming five minutes later, when Marnie left the house.

5

In Blackthorn Road, Noah was making small talk with a PCSO, who was describing in forensic detail how much better crime-scene tape used to be, back in the day. 'Wouldn't wipe my arse on this new stuff . . . '

When Marnie came out of number 14, Noah headed in her direction.

'How're they doing? How's Terry?'

'In shock, trying to cope . . .' She turned to look at the Doyles' house. 'I left him Ed's number. What did Fran say?'

'That she'll call as soon as she has something. They're too young for her to tell if they're boys or girls.' He paused. 'I think from the clothes, they're boys. What'd you think?'

'Boys,' Marnie said, 'but I may be wrong.' She was studying the house.

Noah had done the same. The back of a house was only half the story; they needed to see the face it showed to the street. Houses are among the biggest lies we tell ourselves, hadn't he read that somewhere? Most weren't about the necessity of living; they reflected money or taste or aspiration. Mortgages meant you didn't have to *have*, you just had to *want*.

Number 14 Blackthorn Road was bland and unsmiling, its broad shoulders shrugged up against the house to its left. It was an end-of-terrace, where the weight of the other houses rested. The front door had been painted white, ruined by the weather. Fingerprints stained the area around the lock. A trio of wheelie bins was parked to the left of the door. As lies went, number 14's was a modest one. The terrace was aggressively uniform, in the manner of most new-builds. Seven houses on each side. Number 14 was a little larger, but not by much. Every house had three floors, the third being a faux attic conversion. They didn't look like they'd been standing more than a couple of years.

'What was here, before the houses?' Noah asked.

'Fields,' Marnie said. 'And beech trees.'

The beech trees had survived, flanked at the foot of the Doyles' garden. The houses weren't built when the children were buried in the bunker.

Noah said, 'You were here, eighteen months ago . . .'

'When the houses were brand new, yes.'

'Did you meet whoever was living in number 14?'

'No one was living here. It was the last house to be sold.'

'The last?' Noah looked at her in surprise. 'It's a good size. End terraces usually go first. Was it a lot more expensive?'

'No, just a lot less finished.' Her voice was dry. 'It was the developer's show home. They cut corners to get it ready in time. Then someone noticed the ventilation pipes weren't connected. The overflow fed into the walls instead of outside. Little things like that.'

'That and the bunker in the garden . . . You think the developers knew about it?'

'Someone did.'

'They built the houses . . . *over* the boys?'

'If they're boys,' Marnie said. 'Yes.'

A movement at the window on the third floor made them look up, too late to see anything other than the curtain dropping back into place.

'Clancy,' Marnie said, in the same dry voice as before. 'The Doyles are fostering him. He was watching me in the bunker, too.'

'Yes, I saw him at the house . . .' Noah hated the feeling of being watched. He imagined Marnie felt the same.

They looked at the window for a minute, but the curtain didn't move again.

At his side, Marnie shivered. 'Come on. Before the ghosts get the better of me.'

She started walking in the direction of the squad car, carrying the wellington boots she'd taken from Terry.

Noah followed. 'Ghosts?'

'This road,' she swung back to look at him, 'is full of ghosts. Can't you feel them?'

6

Lawton Down Prison, Durham

The ghosts are out in force today. I can smell them. Sweet and biscuity, like just-washed hair before bedtime. I want to tuck them in and lie down beside them, breathe their sweet smell, bury my nose in their little necks and whisper through the dark.

I daren't, of course.

For one thing, Esther would hear.

The ghosts are scared of Esther. They won't come close when she's here, no matter how wide I spread my arms. It's as if she's still killing them, over and over.

She can't stop. I don't think she ever will.

It's who she is.

Everyone is scared of Esther, even grown men, policemen.

She's a special kind of monster.

My kind.

7

London

OCU Commander Tim Welland looked like an avalanche waiting to land, his big face fisted in a frown. 'Where're we up to, detectives? And don't sugar-coat it.'

'Two small children,' Marnie said, 'dead and down there at least four years. Fran's doing the post-mortems as a priority.'

Welland looked the length of Blackthorn Road. 'Who found them?'

'Terry Doyle. It's his garden, but four years ago there weren't any gardens, only fields. We're looking for someone who knew this place before the houses went up.'

'Missing Persons haven't turned up any names, is that right?'

'Not yet.'

'Four years ago . . .' Welland pulled at his lower lip.

'At least four years.' Marnie glanced at her watch. 'Fran should have some answers for us soon. Nothing definitive perhaps, but she'll have something. And Missing Persons; two small children can't have vanished without someone reporting it. Not even in London.'

'Right . . .' Welland leaned on the word until it buckled.

He sniffed. 'I smell scumbag . . . The media's en route. You'll want to field that, detective.'

'I've got it.' Marnie nodded. 'Press briefing at the station in a couple of hours.'

'Have you spoken with the Finchers?' Welland said next.

'Not yet.'

'And that neighbour of theirs, what was his name? Dougal . . .?'

'Douglas. Doug Cole.'

'Right, gutless Douglas . . .' Welland curled his lip. 'Have you spoken with him?'

'Not yet. I don't want to waste time. We're looking for someone who was here four or five years ago. Cole and the Finchers have lived here less than two years.'

'You're not looking for someone who was *living* here, just someone who knew about the bunker down there.'

'And you think Mr Cole might have known that?'

Welland tipped his face to the sky. 'What do I think about Mr Cole?' He brought his stare down to Marnie's face. 'I think gutless Douglas is exactly the kind of freak who'd buy a house close to where he buried bodies years ago.'

Marnie was silent for a second. Then she said, 'Okay. I'll look into that.' She made it sound like a dead end. 'Maybe someone will remember the bunker being built.'

Welland sniffed again. 'And find the bastard who put houses over it. We'll hit him with a planning violation, if nothing else.'

Noah said, 'There's a housing estate a couple of streets away, built in the sixties by the look of it. Someone there should remember any building that went on.'

Marnie nodded. 'We could use some extra hands,' she told Welland.

'Let's hear how loud the press yelp first. That usually gets us attention in high places.'

'You don't want to try for a pre-emptive strike?'

'On this budget? The only thing I'm pre-empting is an overdraft. You've got a good team.' He nodded at Noah. 'Stretch it.'

Movement at the upstairs window of number 14 made him frown in that direction.

'Who's the ghoul?'

Same curtain as before. It fell back into place when they looked up.

'Clancy Brand,' Marnie said. 'The Doyles are fostering him.'

'How old?'

'Fourteen.'

'Terrific.' Welland wiped his nose with his fingers. 'Try and keep his teenage hormones clear of our crime scene.'

After Welland had left in his car, Marnie and Noah walked up to number 8.

Douglas Cole's house was a mid-terrace with the same unsmiling face as number 14. Marnie knocked on the door and they waited, but there was no answer. No car parked in the resident's space. Empty bins outside; Noah checked.

'Bin day,' Marnie said. 'I asked the Doyles. He's probably on his way home. Come on.'

They headed back to her car.

'Did you speak with Clancy?' she asked Noah. 'When you saw him at the house?'

'Not really. I asked if he was okay and he grunted at me. I'd say he's a typical teenage boy. Not that I'm an expert on typical teenage boys . . .'

'You've got a younger brother,' she remembered.

'Sol.' Noah nodded. 'He's more typical than me, I guess.'

'Typical is overrated . . . So you asked Clancy if he was okay.'

'I tried to. He wasn't exactly communicative. I'd say he's not a fan of the police.'

'You think he's been in trouble with us?'

'Possibly. Could just be an authority thing. You said he was off school.'

'Beth says he's sick, but I wonder if he's been excluded.'

Marnie put the wellingtons into a forensic bag in the boot of the car. 'There's something going on with him, something they didn't want to talk to me about.'

'I'll check,' Noah said again. 'Clancy Brand, right?'

'Yes.' Marnie worked a crick from her neck with the heel of her hand, smelling the bunker in her clothes. 'I met Carmen, their three-year-old. She looks like hard work. Tommy's a toddler, and Beth's pregnant again. We'll need to be careful.'

They got into the car.

'Four kids . . . That's not a family,' Noah objected as he fastened his seat belt, 'it's a recruitment drive.'

'You don't believe in too much love?'

'Not without a lot of alcohol involved. But what do I know?'

'The Doyles must be doing something right for the system to let them foster.' Marnie pulled out into the traffic headed back into town. 'I like them, him especially. He was kind about the kids, didn't want to leave them alone down there . . .'

'Someone did,' Noah said. 'Otherwise how did it happen?' He looked grim.

Marnie knew he was trying hard to treat this case like any other. Knew, too, how impossible that was. Dead children changed everything.

'Do you think they're brothers?' Noah asked.

'Perhaps . . .'

Hard to detect any physical resemblance between the

children. Nearly impossible to detect any resemblance to anyone who'd once lived or laughed, or kicked a ball around a yard, or called for his mum when he fell and scraped a knee, fought with his brother at bedtime. Only the way they'd looked when they died, so tightly curled together, hinted at how they might have been, alive. The older child protecting the smaller one, or simply sharing body heat, trying to keep warm.

'Ron wants to look at child sex offenders in the area,' Noah said. 'I told him to go ahead.'

'Make sure he understands we're talking at least four years ago.'

Noah nodded. After a moment, he said, 'Who *is* gutless Douglas?'

'He's an accountant, a friend of the Finchers.'

'Commander Welland likes him for this . . .'

'We'd all like a short cut to finding whoever put those children down there.' Marnie didn't want to raise Noah's hopes. 'Mr Cole rubbed Welland up the wrong way, it's true. But you and I know how easily that's done.'

'You don't fancy Cole for this?'

'Not remotely.' She paused. 'But I've been known to get things wrong. I've got his number. We'll talk with him as soon as he's home. And we'll talk with the Finchers.'

'The family with the missing child . . . But that ended happily, you said.'

'People have long memories, and it was messy for a while. I'll brief the team about it. We should lean on Missing Persons. The sooner we have names, the better.'

'Ron's on it,' Noah said.

Someone was missing the dead children, whether or not they were siblings. Perhaps Marnie should hope for brothers; only one set of parents to be broken by the news. Assuming they didn't already know what had happened. Assuming they weren't responsible for making, or letting, it happen. Sooner or later, they were going to have to entertain that possibility.

'They looked like brothers,' Noah said. 'The way they were sleeping . . .' Sadness thinned his face. 'I think they were brothers.'

As they reached the station, Marnie's phone played Fran Lennox's tune.

She swung into the car park and picked up. 'Fran, you've got something for me?' Her eyes went to Noah. 'For us?'

'You're not going to like it,' Fran said, 'but yes. Not much, not yet, but something.'

'I'll be right over.' Marnie ended the call.

'News?' Noah asked. An edge in his voice; on his guard against this case.

Marnie wondered in what way Sol, Noah's brother, had been a more typical teenage boy. Less sensitive, perhaps, or more content with easy answers to life's worst questions.

'Stay here. Organise the house-to-house at the flats, and keep an eye on the team.' She could sense their frustration already, like too much static. 'I'll get back as soon as I can.'

'What about the press briefing?' Noah asked.

'Stall it. Tell them we're doing real police work and remind them it takes time. If we're lucky, some of them might even appreciate that.'

8

Fran said, 'They're boys. Neither is older than eight. It's not infallible, but going by the length of the molars and the chin span, I'd say we have two boys, one about eight years old, the other between four and five. I'll know more when I've done the proper tests.'

Marnie pulled out a chair and sat the other side of Fran's desk. The office was tiny, barely enough room for one person, let alone two. 'What else?'

Fran had a plate of toast, and two big mugs of tea. Marnie had never seen her eat proper food. It explained how ravenous she always looked, a starving pixie with a spiky blond crop. 'I think they're brothers. I can't confirm it without tests, but you saw the shape of their skulls. Too similar for it to be a coincidence. And the short shin bones, narrow shoulders . . .' She folded a slice of toast and took a bite. 'Of course some of it's due to malnutrition, and light deprivation. I'd say they were down there a good few weeks before they died.'

'And how long afterwards, how long since they died?'

'At least four years, maybe as many as five.' Fran folded a second slice of toast, still eating the first. 'No wounds on their bodies, nothing obvious in the airways and no evidence they were constrained. No sign of a struggle, all bones intact.'

Marnie processed this in silence. 'So . . . how did they die?'

'I'll know more after the autopsy, but if you're pressing me for a gut feeling, I'd say they slowly starved.'

Marnie's throat griped in protest. 'There was food in the bunker. Tins . . .'

'Maybe they'd got too weak to open them. Maybe it was the cold, exposure. Lack of light, rotten air . . . They were down there a good while. It's possible they just . . . got sleepy, cuddled together for warmth and didn't wake up.' From the way she said it, it was clear Fran meant this to sound peaceful, a gentle death.

To Marnie, it sounded monstrous. 'Who would do that, leave them down there to die?'

Fran dusted crumbs from her shirt. 'That's your territory. The only way it would be mine is if I find the bastard's DNA on their bodies, or *in* their bodies, which I sincerely hope I don't. Sorry not to be more optimistic.'

'We've swabbed everything we could down there. One thing . . . do you think the bunker stayed shut the whole time after they died?'

'I'd be guessing, but yes. If it was airtight, that would be different.' Fran chewed for a minute, thinking it over. 'They were pretty well preserved. If the manhole was disturbed, I'd have expected more evidence of decay. And bugs, rodents. You name it. Forensic fauna, as we're encouraged to call it. There was nothing like that.'

Forensic fauna . . . Rats, she meant. And flies, like the one that had gone down into the dark with Marnie. 'So the chances are, whoever put them down there left them and didn't come back? Not even to check whether they were dead.'

'You wouldn't need to check. Whoever left our boys down there knew exactly what they were doing.'

Our boys.

'Except that they left food and water, blankets . . . Maybe they meant to come back.'

'And what – got distracted?' Fran shook her head. 'We're not talking about a dog in a hot car. These were little boys, buried underground without daylight, getting weak and sick.'

'Maybe they *couldn't* go back for them,' Marnie said, 'because something happened.'

'You think the murderer's dead?'

'Not dead, necessarily. But he or she could've been arrested. If our boys weren't the first children they'd taken . . .'

'Or our boys *were* the first, but he or she went after more?' Fran wiped her mouth on a piece of paper towel. 'It's possible. But if we're talking about an arrest, why didn't they tell the police about the bunker? These boys didn't die quickly. There might've been time to save them, which might have meant leniency.'

'True.' Marnie had only half believed in the idea of an arrest or an accident. It was too neat, and much too convenient. 'You say they didn't die quickly . . . Is there any way of knowing how long they were *alone* down there? We're assuming they had company to begin with.'

'The food, and the bucket.' Fran nodded. 'Traces of bleach in the bucket suggests it was cleaned not long before it was last used. If they'd been down there a long time, unsupervised, I'd have expected more waste, and more mess. Two small children in an enclosed space . . . I'd say days, rather than weeks. Not long, in the scheme of things.'

She reached for her mug. 'Of course, we don't know for sure that they died alone. Whoever did it might've stayed down there to watch.' She sipped at the tea. 'Perhaps they only left when it was obvious the boys were dead, or dying.'

'Stayed to watch?' Marnie shivered. 'Jesus. That's cold.'

'A whole new level of nasty, but I wouldn't discount it, at least not quickly. Whoever did this, however it was done, it was wicked. You can't always slice that into degrees.'

A photo cube on Fran's desk was filled with Polaroids of her and her brothers. She came from a big family: seven brothers; Fran was the only girl. The boys doted on their little sister, the police pathologist.

'You're ruling out poison?' Marnie said. 'And smothering?'

'Smothering, yes, unless the post-mortem throws up any surprises, but plenty of poisons are hard to trace after even a day or two. We're talking four or five years, maybe a bit longer than that. I can't rule it out. In any case,' Fran picked crumbs from the desk, one by one, dropping each crumb into the plastic bin at her side, 'our boys wouldn't have needed a serious dose of anything dangerous. Too much Night Nurse would've done the trick, sent them to sleep with no chance of waking up, given how weak and malnourished they were.'

She cleaned the ends of her fingers with a tissue. 'I can't be sure, but I think . . . I *hope* . . . it would have been a quiet death.'

A quiet death.

Marnie didn't believe that. She could see and taste and *hear* the noise of their dying, alone and scared. Her ears rang with outrage at the noise. 'So I'm looking for brothers who went missing up to five years ago. Any other clues to where they might've come from?'

'Not yet. The clothes and the torch batteries were from Asda; hundreds of those all over the country. The books were UK editions, in English. The jigsaw was printed in China. The tins of food are odd . . .' Fran pulled a notepad towards her. 'Peaches and sweetcorn, but not a brand I've seen on sale in any supermarket where I shop. There might be something in that.'

Marnie made a note. 'British?'

'The boys? Not necessarily. We might need bone chemistry to narrow it down.'

'I'll look at the labels from the tins, see what we can turn up.'

Fran held a mug of tea between her hands. Long hands, their bony fingers delicately strung. Gentle hands. She'd be careful with the boys.

'I'm guessing there's nothing from Missing Persons yet,' she said.

'Not yet. Soon, I hope, especially now you've given us something to work with.'

Someone had been missing two small boys for four years, maybe longer.

It was time to take them home.

9

Noah was queuing in the local café for the team's coffee order. He'd wanted the fresh air; his clothes smelt of the Doyles' garden. The team was twitchy because they had a cold case on their hands. Decent coffee would help.

'No. No, that's enough. Put that down.' At a table by the window, a man was struggling to placate a shrieking child, without conspicuous success.

'Can I help you?' It was Noah's turn at the counter.

'Thanks. Two lattes, one with an extra shot, one skinny, three Americanos and two flat whites.'

The father–son tableau reminded Noah of his brother's childhood tantrums. Sol was in his twenties now, had long since worked out how to get what he wanted in more devious if sometimes still noisy ways. Back when Noah was ten and his little brother was four, Sol had thrown tantrums on a daily basis, making the whole house spin around him.

In the café, the boy's mother reappeared, quelling the child with a look and a handful of words that Noah didn't catch. Her husband sat with his shoulders curled in defeat. Every so often he risked a glance at his son, as if trying to work out where the fury had come from, or distrusting the quiet, waiting for the next outburst. Noah's father, Dylan, hadn't put up with tantrums from either of his sons, but he had worked long hours, and late. Whenever he was out, Sol would start on their mother, Rosa, who responded by taking his temperature, feeding him pink medicine, baby stuff, unlikely to do any harm but unnecessary all the same. The fact that Sol never had a tantrum in front of their father told Noah, at the age of ten, that his brother was fine, and smart, and manipulative. He'd been wary of Sol ever since.

Back at the station, he handed round the coffees, earning a 'Cheers, mate' from Ron Carling.

Carling was unhappy about the case they'd brought back from Snaresbrook. 'If we can't catch this bastard, it's going to be months of work and nightmares . . .'

Ron had two young boys, Noah remembered. 'Let's hope we catch him, then.'

'Have you even looked at the statistics for solving a case this cold? You saw the bodies, you know what I'm talking about. No sleep and effing nightmares, for months.'

'How's it going with Missing Persons?' Debbie asked.

'How do you think? We don't even know if the poor little sods were boys or girls . . .'

'They're boys.' Marnie was in the doorway. 'Probably brothers. The elder was about eight. The little one was four or five. We don't know their nationality yet, but the clothes and books were bought in the UK, so let's start here, in London. Fran says they died four, maybe five years ago. She's sending over her initial findings. DC Tanner will make copies. Make sure you read them.'

She nodded at Noah. 'DS Jake will be in charge of exhibits. We need to look at the labels from the food tins. Fran hasn't seen the brand before. It's the best clue we have right now.'

Ron said, 'So we're on this, then. Even though it's so cold it's going to give us frostbite.'

Marnie turned her steady gaze on him. 'A cold case is something we've investigated and failed to solve. We haven't investigated anything to do with these boys' deaths yet.'

'You know what I mean. Five years, for fuck's sake . . .'

Marnie glanced at the family photos on Carling's desk. 'Someone's been looking for these boys – *missing* these boys – for at least that long. Let's see if we can't bring them some peace.' She nodded at the flat whites. 'Is one of those for me?'

'Yes.' Noah carried the cup to where she was standing. 'I'll get on to the labels, see if I can find a match online.'

'Good.' Marnie nodded at Ron. 'Try Missing Persons again now that we've got an approximate time frame and an idea of their ages. If Fran's right, it could give us a match quite quickly. There can't be many young brothers who've gone missing together in the last five years.'

She paused, looking at the team. 'They're our boys, but I want names. DS Jake?'

10

Noah closed the door to the office and waited for Marnie to sit behind her desk. She didn't, standing with her back to him, her eyes on the brick-wall view from the window.

What was she thinking?

He'd always liked her silences, trusting her need to not always be talking, but now he wondered what she thought about when she went quiet like this. Debbie Tanner had told him about the day five years ago when Marnie's foster brother had taken a kitchen knife to her parents before sitting on their stairs, waiting for the police to come and wash blood and tissue from his fingers so they could take prints at the station.

Noah couldn't start to imagine what madness like that did to a person. Ever since Debbie had shared the story out around the station like so many home-baked biscuits, he'd wanted to say something to Marnie, to express his sadness and the pain he felt on her behalf. He couldn't say anything, of course. For one thing, it would expose Debbie to more trouble than she deserved. Not that Noah liked the easy way she'd shared the tragedy, but she didn't mean harm; she cared for Marnie in her way. Noah doubted she was capable of deliberate malice.

Of course that didn't mean she wasn't capable of what Tim Welland called 'malicious ignorance', hiding behind the refusal to acquire facts, or tact, or both.

Marnie sat at her desk, nodding for Noah to sit too.

'What else did Fran say?' he asked. It would be in the report Debbie was copying, but he wanted to hear it from Marnie.

'No wounds, nothing in the airways. No evidence they were constrained. No sign of a struggle. No broken bones.' She dropped her hands into her lap. 'Fran thinks they starved, slowly. She called it . . . a quiet death.'

'A quiet death.' He wanted to throw something. 'But there were tins of food down there.'

'Fran thinks they got too weak to open them.' Marnie's voice hardened; her way of focusing, keeping emotion in its useful place. 'I don't remember any searches five years ago, for brothers. I'd have seen a picture if they went missing in London, but I don't remember any search for missing boys.' Her eyes went to somewhere Noah couldn't see but which he could imagine, thanks to Debbie's lack of discretion. Five years ago, there was enough horror in Marnie's life without looking for missing children.

'I promised Terry Doyle I'd take him their names, once we know who they are . . .' She drank a mouthful of coffee. 'What've you got for me?'

'The houses were built by Merrick Homes. I had a shufti on the internet and it looks like the development was due to start nearly six years ago, but it got stalled because of funding issues, or permissions. They didn't go on-site until late in 2011. Blackthorn Road's unusual in that all the houses are three-storey, built tall to take advantage of the views. They called it Beech Rise, after the trees that Merrick Homes thoughtfully preserved and incorporated.' He paused. 'That's a quote from their website.'

'It's what else they preserved and incorporated that concerns me,' Marnie said drily.

'I have an address, and a name. Ian Merrick, owner and managing director.'

'Good. Let's pay him a visit.' She checked her watch and stood, dropping her empty cup into the bin. 'It'll have to be tomorrow now. Get some rest while you can.'

'I was going to swing past the refuge,' Noah said, 'and see how Ayana's doing.'

Marnie scanned his face. 'Are you sure?'

'It's just a visit. I know she's fine, because she called me. I'd like to see her, though. I haven't seen her since we got her out of that flat, away from her family.'

Into a witness protection scheme. Ayana was giving evidence against her brother, Nasif Mirza. A man had died after Nasif attacked him with a scimitar. An earlier attack, with a different weapon, had left Nasif's sister Ayana blind in one eye. She was one of the most courageous people Noah had met, and he wanted to tell her so, in person.

'Give her my best wishes.' Marnie was tying her hair away from her face, working blindly; no mirrors in here.

Noah had never seen her consult a mirror. For someone so habitually neat, that was surprising. 'We're a team.' Like Terry, he needed to know the boys' names, and he wanted to be part of the effort that took them home. 'What about Gutless Douglas?' he remembered.

'I've been trying his number, still no answer. He'll have to wait until the morning too. I'll brief the team first thing.'

Marnie nodded at Noah. 'Get some rest while you can. I don't agree with DS Carling's pessimism regarding this case, but he's right about one thing. It's going to be a nightmare for the next few weeks.'

11

Marnie had no plans to move in with Ed Belloc, but sometimes you didn't need a plan.

They'd been sleeping together for six months, at his place since hers was too much like a hotel suite; she'd caught Ed tidying the pillows. His flat was better, messier; lived-in. Hers could've been sprayed with plastic for all the impression she'd made on it. She'd liked her flat once, for precisely that sterile neatness, its estate-agent readiness, the sense of impermanence. But recently it had started to unnerve her, as if *she* was part of the mess it was trying to repel. Ed's place, never neat, felt like home these days.

Ed was in the kitchen, stirring something red in a saucepan. 'Pasta,' he said. It smelt good. 'I thought if you were late, it wouldn't matter.' His eyes gleamed. 'I have Tupperware.'

She leaned into him for a second. 'You're getting domestic, Belloc.'

'You should've seen how long it took me to find a clean saucepan . . .'

He abandoned the stirring and turned to look at her, searching her face the way he did whenever she came back here, as if it was a new miracle each time. Steam had stuck his brown curls to his forehead and freckled his nose. 'Tough day?'

'Dead kids . . .' She wanted to shut her eyes when she said it, but she didn't, letting him look at her because it mattered to him. 'So yes, not the best day . . . How was yours?'

'Nothing as bad as that. Do you want to talk about it?'

She unstuck a curl from his forehead. 'Later. You've got pasta to make. I'm going to take a shower. There's hot water, right?'

Ed nodded, letting her move away. 'Take as long as you like. This'll keep.'

In the bathroom, she undressed awkwardly, clumsy with fatigue. It was frightening how tired she was after one day on this case. Perhaps Ron Carling was right and she'd brought them all a thankless task. Six weeks from now, they might be no further forward, no nearer finding out what had happened to the boys. It bothered her that she couldn't remember hearing about a manhunt four or five years ago. Missing children lit flags across the Met's systems, pulling in people from across forces. How could she not remember? But she knew how.

Five years ago, she'd been trying to deal with the huge hole torn in her life by Stephen Keele. She'd thrown herself into work, couldn't remember details of any of the cases she'd taken on. She hadn't cared enough, that was the trouble, only interested in the solve rate, in scoring points with Tim Welland to earn her another case, harder and faster than the last. The human cost hadn't registered. Or if it had, only as an echo of the bigger pain, fresh pressure on the bruise she was safeguarding. It had taken her years to rebuild the part of her brain that connected her compassion to her intellect. She was a better detective now. She didn't solve cases as swiftly, but nor did she miss tricks because she failed to look where it mattered most: in the hearts of the people damaged by the crimes she was investigating.

She put her clothes aside for the dry cleaner's. Maybe they'd be able to get the smell of the bunker out of her suit. Luckily, she had a change of clothes in Ed's wardrobe.

She should talk with Ed, let him take custody of her tiredness and in return take custody of his. It was what couples did. Once, she'd have taken refuge in work, pulling its layers over her until she was numb. Even now, she was conscious of a nagging sensation in her skin, like an addict's itch for caffeine or worse. Numb had felt so good, once.

She removed her wristwatch, concentrating on what mattered. Ed, and this new case.

Tim Welland was right, she had a good team. Debbie Tanner would make family liaison look easy. Ron Carling, once he was past his gut response, would work harder than anyone to find who did this. And Noah Jake was shaping up to be the best detective she'd worked with: compassionate, inquisitive and unsatisfied with easy answers. She was lucky.

She stepped into Ed's bath, pulling the shower curtain carefully along its pole; like everything else in Ed's flat, you treated it with respect or it fell apart. At her place, the water pressure was like a jet-wash, but Ed's shower was gentle, serving the water softly, as if conscious of her skin's sensitivity, the rawness she'd brought back from Blackthorn Road.

The Doyles had been playing and working in the garden for a year, digging a vegetable patch directly over the bunker. The developer, Merrick Homes, had planted the beginnings of the garden, but hadn't bothered to add nutrients to the soil, deciding sand was good enough.

What other corners had they cut?

She imagined Merrick's team unrolling cheap turf, tamping it down. Had they found anything, before they laid the lawn? Would they have cared if they had?

She didn't see how they could have missed the bunker. It was only underneath three feet of soil. But if they were up against a schedule and a budget, perhaps they were told to ignore anything which got in the way of that. Sand instead of soil, the wrong sound under their boots when they walked across the hollow foot of the garden . . .

She was towelling herself dry from the shower when her phone buzzed: the station.

'DI Rome.'

'Boss?' Ron Carling's voice was ripe with disgust. 'You're not going to believe this.'

12

University Hospital, Durham

They're all in the dark, each and every one of them.

The man sitting two seats down from us, he's in the dark. The police who brought him here: in the dark. The man's nose is broken and there's blood down the front of his shirt, black under the lights. He's holding a cardboard bowl. He's been sick into it twice. The vomit is ninety per cent proof, its paint-stripper stink making our eyes water.

Esther's sitting very still. I'm usually the fidgety one, but tonight I'm copying Esther and keeping like a statue, not wanting to be spotted. Too much is new, tonight.

It's generally a lot quieter than this, which isn't how I remember city life. Last time I looked, the city got lively after dark, dancing and dodging the night away before spilling its guts come morning. Things have changed. It's been years since I saw a city after dark.

We've been away a long time, Esther and me. That's why they think they can play games like this in a public place, somewhere we have no right being, even if we are keeping quiet, pretending to be statues sitting here.

It is nearly 2 a.m. and all's quiet, except the man puking in the cardboard bowl. How long before the bowl soaks through and he's sitting with a lapful of sick? Once upon a time they gave you a stainless-steel dish. Now it's all cardboard, disposable, recycled. He's probably puking into last year's bedpan.

Clock's chiming somewhere: 2 a.m.

I think I hear Esther murmur, 'Bring out your dead,' but I can't be sure.

It wouldn't be like her to say anything at all in a place where we might be heard, or seen. Sometimes she sits so still and quiet, I swear I'm the only one who knows she's here.

The man ignores us, groaning self-pity through his broken nose. I wonder, briefly, who he is and why he's here, but the train of thought requires too much energy and runs the risk that I'll start thinking beyond this place and out into *there*.

Far safer to stick with these four walls, although counting them I see there are seven walls and one is made of glass. Safety glass, I bet. If I ran into it, or threw something – this plastic chair, for instance, which is crucifying my spine – it wouldn't break easily, or usefully. No shards, or dangerous edges. Even so, it's a hell of a lot less safe than the place we've come from, where they'll return us before dawn and the arrival of the hospital cleaning crew. This experiment is risky enough. It makes me wonder what other risks they are willing to take. Do they really imagine we are ready for this, just because we've been good for so long?

Do they think it means we're mended, that the bad we did is back in its box?

I don't see how they can think that, not of me, certainly not of Esther.

The man with the broken nose is breathing thickly. I don't

like the sound of it, phlegmy, and wonder whether Esther is hearing what I am, if memory's playing the same trick on her. It's like the sound of a puppy whining, deep in the pit of its throat.

This is a waste of time, a *criminal* waste of time. Sitting us here, to see who sees us and what reaction it provokes, if we're recognised any longer.

It's been five years.

At least I think it has. I've lost track of time, thanks to the pills.

The self-pitying pisshead two seats down couldn't care less. We could be invisible for all the signs he's giving. Maybe we are. Invisible. Maybe after all the needles they've stuck in us and the answers they've sucked out of us and the pills they make us eat, endlessly, like sweets – maybe we're so empty we can't be seen.

Stranger things have happened.

The woman behind the desk (I don't think she's a nurse, just an agency worker paid to pick up the phones) isn't interested in us. I don't blame her. Personally, I'm sick of the sight of us. Me and Esther, sitting here in our borrowed clothes, trying to be normal, or *pretending* to be trying to be normal, in Esther's case. She was always a sneaky one.

No, I don't blame Ms Agency Worker, not even when she yawns and points her eyes at the clock, wanting her shift to be over so she can go home – to what, I wonder?

A husband? A family?

I bite my tongue to stop myself thinking any further down that dead end. Just the tip, where all the nerve endings huddle. The tip of my tongue is lumpy with scar tissue, from being bitten too much. I'm not as bad as Esther, whose mouth is full of sour, watery ulcers.

I look away, down the corridor to the glass wall that can't be broken. Most people who come here are sick or scared, worried for themselves or someone else. That isn't us. We're not ill, or not in any normal way. Of course they say Esther was sick, very sick. But they also say she's better now, and that's why we're here.

Esther was famous once. They think maybe the people who come here, sick or scared, will recognise us. Not that they'd know me; at least I doubt it. It was Esther's face all over the news. But I'm not sure we're all that different – same eyes, same size – although I'm an inch shorter and less skinny, at least than Esther used to be.

A hospital porter comes to collect the pisshead and I stiffen in panic. I'm the only one who does; not much can panic Esther. She has less to lose, of course, from this experiment.

I could lose everything.

Esther's already lost that.

I should stop ascribing my emotions to her. That's what the therapist, Lyn, says. 'It's good,' she says, 'that you feel empathy. Empathy is important.'

So now I scrabble after empathy, like I scrabble after forgiveness. And mercy too, except I shouldn't expect too much of that, and so I don't.

Believe me, I don't.

You don't do the things we've done and look for mercy.

13

London

In Westbourne Grove, the flat smelt warm and starchy, of rice boiling. Dan was cooking paella. Noah dropped his keys into the bowl in the hall.

He'd done a fair job of disguising his day when he was with Ayana at the women's refuge. Her recovery was inspiring, and exhausting. Just for a second, he wished for a normal job, something that didn't demand either humility or courage to get through a day's work.

In the empty hall, he did what he hadn't been able to do all day: stood with his head bowed and his shoulders shaking, not hiding any of it. Then he straightened and put the anger away, heading for the kitchen.

Dan was frying shrimp at the stove. He'd tuned the radio to tinny pop, moving his hips in time to the beat, an easy rhythm. Noah watched from the doorway until Dan's dance moves had him smiling. 'Hey, sexy disco man.'

Dan didn't hear, over the radio and the wok. He was

wearing jeans and a red T-shirt, bare feet on the tiled floor. Steam had stuck his blond hair to his forehead.

Noah moved noiselessly, slipping an arm about Dan's waist and another around his shoulders, baring the back of his neck to a biting kiss.

'*Ow.*' Dan shook his hand, its thumb branded by hot oil. 'Noah, you maniac . . . Get off.'

'Mmm . . . Or I could do this.' He lifted Dan's scalded hand and sucked the burnt thumb between his lips.

'You're meant to use butter . . .' Dan turned under his touch, until the small of his back was against the edge of the stove. His eyes were a dazed blue.

Noah leaned in to kiss him, for a long time, before he reached for the freezer door. 'Butter leaves a scar.' He found a tray of ice. 'Better use this.'

Dan watched him crack the tray over the sink. 'How was your day?'

'Over.' Noah filled a mug with ice and held it out. 'How was yours?'

'Quiet.' Dan buried his burnt thumb in the ice. 'Until now . . .'

Noah picked up the spatula to stir at the paella. 'What're we having with this? Beer?'

'In the fridge.' Dan took the spatula back. 'You had a phone call earlier.' He started serving the paella on to plates. 'Sol.'

Noah took two bottles of Beck's from the fridge. 'What'd he want?'

'He didn't say. I told him he could come to supper. He said he might do that.'

Noah took the tops from the bottles. 'I don't see a third plate.'

'This is Sol we're talking about. I didn't take him seriously.'

'That probably means he'll turn up just to be awkward.'

'Good. I made enough paella for three. And that's why we have a sofa bed, so your jailbait brother can crash here whenever he needs to.'

'My jailbait brother . . .' Noah tossed the bottle-opener back into its drawer. 'That makes me so proud.'

'You can't blame him,' Dan said. 'You stole all the big brother brownie points when you joined the police. He *had* to go off the rails, just to get a look-in.'

They sat at the table and started eating.

'You like him,' Noah accused, with a smile.

'Like him?' Dan repeated, with a mouthful of paella. 'I bloody *love* him. He's a wicked version of you. Without the great taste in men . . .'

'Without *any* taste in men,' Noah amended.

'Yes. But is the West End ready for gorgeous gay gangsters?'

Noah's response was reflexive. 'He's not a gangster.'

'Not yet.' Dan speared a shrimp on his fork. 'Give him time.'

'Me and half the magistrates in Notting Hill,' Noah agreed, 'when his luck gives out.'

Dan laughed. 'Your jailbait brother,' sketching a toast with his beer bottle. 'Have you introduced him to your boss yet?'

Noah shook his head. 'She'd eat him for breakfast. Sol's only a hard man in his imagination. DI Rome, on the other hand, is the real deal.'

14

'Un-fucking-believable,' Ron Carling said. 'Two kids go missing for five years and no one reports it? No one looks for them? No one looks for whichever bastard took them?'

'I agree it seems incredible,' Marnie said. 'But we're looking now. And Missing Persons haven't given up; they've only just got started. We know how many children go missing every year. One every three minutes, isn't that the latest statistic? We know this sort of investigation is tough. Every aspect of it is tough. We need to focus on what we have.'

Noah understood Ron's frustration. The dead boys didn't match anyone in the national missing persons' database. It should have been impossible, but it wasn't. There were all sorts of explanations, from illegal immigration to child trafficking. Officially, there were no circumstances under which children were allowed to vanish unreported or unnoticed. But it happened, more often than the public, or even the press, knew.

Marnie waited until the room was quiet. 'DS Jake and I are going to ask Ian Merrick how much he knew about the bunker. House-to-house are getting started this morning. We're hoping someone on the housing estate will remember

Beech Rise before the houses went up. I'm going to handle house-to-house on Blackthorn Road, because I know some of the residents there: Carol and Nigel Fincher at number 10 and Douglas Cole at number 8.'

She held up a hand. 'Don't get excited. It's not a lead, at least I don't think so. Eighteen months ago, Mr and Mrs Fincher reported their daughter Lizzie missing. She was five at the time. According to Mr Fincher, his wife had taken the child to a hotel and was hiding her there. According to Mrs Fincher, he'd murdered Lizzie and disposed of her body.'

'Murder,' Debbie echoed. She was making notes.

'Domestic,' Ron folded his arms, 'with knobs on.' He was reading Marnie's face; knew her tells. Like Noah, he'd not been in her team eighteen months ago.

Marnie nodded. 'DS Carling gets the big clock. It was a domestic. Lizzie was alive and well. She'd been left with a friend of her mother's. Doug Cole.'

'At number 8?' Debbie checked her notes.

'At number 8. On the day we were looking for Lizzie, Mr Cole was travelling around the Underground with her. He said it was her favourite game and of course he had no reception on his phone to answer the calls we made during house-to-house.'

'So it was the mum,' Ron said, 'winding Fincher up.'

Marnie shook her head. 'She always denied that. She said Lizzie was friends with Cole and that she told him a fib about her mum wanting him to look after her for the day. Cole insisted it'd been agreed with Mrs Fincher.'

'He was shagging the mother, right?'

'Both of them denied that, Cole in the strongest terms. Mrs Fincher seemed to find the idea ridiculous. She described her friend Doug as "sexless and safe".'

'Meaning what?' Ron looked sharp. 'That he's a perv?'

'She didn't elaborate, but there was no evidence that Mr

Cole had abducted Lizzie. The little girl was happy in his company. There was certainly no evidence he'd harmed her.'

'He could've been saving that for another time . . .' Ron picked up a marker pen. 'I'm putting him on the board.'

He wrote 'Doug Cole' on the whiteboard and underlined it.

Debbie said, 'Did we charge the Finchers with wasting police time?'

'No. The press got involved. It was considered tactically inappropriate to charge them.'

'Tactically inappropriate,' Ron echoed. 'You mean Welland handed you the shitty end of the stick to keep the press quiet?'

Marnie shut him up with a look. 'These boys died at least four years ago. Doug Cole wasn't living in Blackthorn Road then. Neither were the Finchers.'

'So we find out where he *was* living. Unless it's suddenly *tactically inappropriate* to call bullshit on coincidences.' Ron capped the marker pen in his fist. 'Missing kids, abducted kids, it goes on the board.'

'All right,' Marnie said patiently. 'You look into that. You've checked the sex offenders' register from five years ago?'

'Yeah. They're competing with Misper for the Shit-All Information gong.'

'Fran didn't think they were abused . . . All right. Let's get on. DS Jake and I'll do the house-to-house on Blackthorn Road after we've been to see Ian Merrick. DC Tanner, I want you to check in on the Doyles, see how they're settling into the house you found.'

Ron said, 'I'll put a steel toecap up Misper as soon as they're answering the phones. Those kids must've been reported missing.'

'Unless it was the parents,' Debbie said. She pulled a face. 'Sorry, that's a horrid thought, but the parents could have covered it up, not reported it . . .'

Noah shook his head. 'They were school age. The school would've reported any long-term absence.' They hadn't let Sol bunk off longer than two days before they got on the phone, issuing absence agreements and, when that didn't work, threatening exclusion. Not much of a threat, under the circumstances.

'They could've been home-schooled,' Ron put in. 'There's a couple of kids like that at my boys' school . . . Mind you, they get more red tape than the rest of us, as far as I can tell.'

'Or maybe they were immigrants?' Debbie suggested.

'Fran will be able to tell us more after the full PM,' Marnie said. 'Later today, with luck.'

'Or foster kids. They fall through the cracks, don't they?'

Debbie was right; they saw it all the time. Clancy Brand was lucky to be living with the Doyles. Too many kids his age didn't know what a stable family life looked like.

'Not little kids,' Ron objected. 'Not as young as our boys.'

They all looked back at the whiteboard.

Boy 1 and Boy 2. No names yet. No faces.

Doug Cole's was the only name on the board.

'All right.' Marnie nodded. 'Let's work those angles. Foster kids, school records. And keep at Missing Persons. I want to know they've done every search possible before they tell us for certain that they have nothing. DS Jake? Let's see what Ian Merrick's got for us.'

'Shonky bloody builder . . .' Carling uncapped the pen. 'He is *so* going on the board.'

As they walked to the station car park, Noah asked Marnie what theories she had about the bunker on Blackthorn Road.

'Plenty, but that's all they are. Theories. It could be industrial, 1930s, or later. Cold War, maybe. I want to know who knew it was there, and who had access to it before the

Doyles bought the house.' She unlocked the car and they climbed in. 'Someone knew it wasn't airtight. They knew they could put two kids down there, with books and toys and a bucket, and they wouldn't die. Not until whoever did it was good and ready.'

She started the ignition but didn't pull out, letting the engine idle for a minute.

'I was thinking,' Noah said, 'if it was fields, before they built the houses . . .'

'Big fields,' she agreed, 'lots of acres.'

'So who builds one bunker in the middle of a big field? That size, I mean. It wasn't large.'

Marnie cut the engine. She turned in the seat to look at him. 'You think . . . there's more? More bunkers?'

'Maybe. It would make more sense than one. Wouldn't it?'

'Lots of bunkers. And the developer missed them all?'

'He missed the one in the Doyles' garden,' Noah pointed out. 'Or he knew about it and kept quiet, reckoned it was in the garden so it wouldn't disturb the foundations of the house. A row of bunkers would play hell with his planning permission.'

'A row of bunkers,' Marnie repeated. 'One per garden?'

Noah turned away while he fastened his seat belt. 'We should check. The neighbours are going to start asking questions once the story breaks. How long before one of them decides to go digging in his garden, just to make sure?' He looked back at her.

Marnie cursed softly, her eyes a hot blue.

'We could issue a statement,' Noah suggested, 'let them know we're organising an extended search . . .'

'For what, more bodies? You think there's a chance we'll find that?'

'No. No, I hadn't thought of it like that.' He thought of

it now, and his skin grained with goose bumps. 'I just thought one bunker in a field was . . . odd.'

'All right, let's look. Put in a request for a GPR team and let the neighbours know we're expanding the search. If it stops some of them digging around and getting a shock like the one that floored Terry, it'll be worth it.'

GPR: ground-penetrating radar.

Noah searched his phone for the number.

Marnie restarted the engine. 'Let's see whether Ian Merrick deserves that space on Ron's whiteboard.'

15

Merrick Homes had set up base on the Isle of Dogs, an almost-island in London's East End.

A temporary base, Noah guessed, going where the scent of money was strongest. The Isle of Dogs had been a real island, bounded on three sides by the Thames, before part of the river was filled to create a dock. Even now, three of the four ways to reach it were by water.

Marnie and Noah took the fourth way, approaching the temporary offices by car, across a potholed site where a mobile office sat in the shadow of a half-built high-rise.

Polythene wrapped the steel shell of Merrick Homes' latest development. Bad weather had ratted at the polythene; unless it was real rats, up from the Thames in search of food or shelter. The polythene was filthy, months old. Investors losing their nerve? This part of London was a rash of glass and steel. It was hard to imagine room in the market for another office development. Everywhere was puddled by shadows from the building work.

They followed a route of greasy duckboards and gravelled ditches to where a mobile office was set up on concrete slabs. The office had chicken-wired windows and a conspicuous burglar alarm. Soot had put black stripes up its sides. A string of oversized fairy lights dangled off one end like a stripper's feather boa.

Inside, they were back-slapped by the smell of egg sandwiches and armpits.

Ian Merrick was a balding middleweight wearing a high-vis jacket with the look of someone who wished he was less visible. He grimaced when Marnie produced her ID. 'If this's about health and safety . . .'

'God forbid,' she said. 'It's about a double murder.'

Merrick's jaw dropped. Yellow egg yolk was trapped between his teeth. He put his hand over his bald spot, self-consciously, as if he missed his hard hat.

Noah looked around the office, seeing the inevitable girlie calendar: a strawberry blonde spilling her chest across the bonnet of a Porsche. The windows were filthy. One side had a bird's-eye view of the chemical toilet. A pair of filing cabinets took up too much space. Shoved between the cabinets was a red nylon sleeping bag. Did Merrick camp here sometimes? Or was the sleeping bag for the on-site security crew?

Merrick flicked a glance at the girlie calendar and wetted his lips in embarrassment, shuffling papers noisily. 'I don't understand. The site is secure. Are you saying you've found something?' He looked sick. 'Bodies? Here?'

Marnie didn't put him out of his misery, not right away. 'You'd know, wouldn't you, if dead bodies had been found on your site? Or isn't the site secure?'

'Of course it's secure, but you said—'

'It doesn't look very secure. There was no one to stop us walking right in.'

'We've had trouble with kids breaking in. We're fitting new locks today. You said . . . murder?'

'I said double murder.' Dry ice in her voice and in her

eyes, making them smoky blue. She was being Detective Inspector Rome. 'How *is* your on-site health and safety?'

Merrick covered his bald spot again. Noah nearly handed him one of the hard hats. DI Rome had this effect on men. Not all men, but plenty.

'Good,' Merrick said, not quite stammering. 'All the paperwork . . . the paperwork's up to date.' He took his hand from his head and gestured at the filing cabinets before flopping the hand down to his side. 'Everything's up to date.'

'How long have you been based here?'

'Nine, ten months . . .' He tried for a smile, missed and managed a grimace. 'Since November . . . You probably saw the fairy lights? We dressed the crane for Christmas, but it encouraged trespassers, kids coming to take pictures, so now we keep it low-key.'

'You specialise in new homes, is that right?'

'I wouldn't say *specialise*, no one can afford to do that in this game, but yes. Some of our best places have been brownbelt developments.'

'Beech Rise,' Marnie said. 'That was one of yours, wasn't it?'

Merrick nodded. 'Houses, in Snaresbrook. But this isn't about that? We finished there years ago, without accident, one of the cleanest jobs I've worked on.' He was either an excellent liar or he had no guilty conscience where Beech Rise was concerned.

'Cleanest. Meaning what? That no one was hurt during the construction?'

'That's right.' Merrick sat a little straighter behind his desk, as if he was sure of his ground now. 'If you need the paperwork . . .'

'I need the paperwork. Do you have it here?'

'Not here, but I can get it for you, of course. It was a clean project. The only sticking point was moving the gypsies out.'

'Gypsies. You mean travellers?'

Merrick nodded again. 'They'd turned the place into a mud pit. The locals were scared to go there. Everyone was happy when we bought the land and started building.'

'Everyone except the travellers, presumably,' Noah said. 'What happened to them?'

'God knows. They're ruining someone else's field now.' Merrick looked from Noah to Marnie. 'Can you tell me what this is about, please?'

Marnie turned her face in profile, as if she was tired of looking at him. 'Planning permissions, you have those?'

'For Beech Rise? Yes, of course.'

'You had all the necessary permissions? All the building consents.'

Merrick nodded. 'Of course.'

'So you knew about the bunker.'

From out on the Thames: the blast of a boat's tannoy.

Merrick covered his head again. 'Bunker?'

'In the garden you put down at the end of the terrace. Number 14 Blackthorn Road. The show house you rushed to finish, cutting corners in the process.'

'A bunker?' Merrick echoed again.

Marnie turned her head back to look at him. Noah saw how hard she was holding to her patience, and how little of that patience she had left. 'In the garden. A bunker, under three feet of what you passed off as soil. Are you saying you knew nothing about it? Because I don't know much about planning permissions, although of course I know plenty of people who do, but I'm thinking you can't possibly have been allowed to erect houses over ground that wasn't solid. Over a concrete pit, twelve feet down.'

'Oh,' Merrick said finally, 'the bunkers.'

Bunkers plural?

A blunt pain in Noah's chest. He hated that he'd been right.

Marnie said, 'You knew, then.'

'Well, yes.' Merrick looked confused. 'We knew there'd *been* bunkers there, once. But it was a long time ago.'

'How many bunkers?'

'Six or seven, I'm not sure. Cold War, they said.' He shook his head. 'But the ground was solid. The local authority had filled them in, long before we started building.'

'How long before?'

'Years! In the mid eighties, I think. I have the paperwork to prove it.'

'Really,' Marnie said. 'Because I have the corpses to prove it never happened. The bunker at number 14 was never filled in. Mr Doyle, who bought that house shortly after you finished it, yesterday found a manhole cover under his vegetable patch, and since there was nothing on the survey you provided to explain what he'd found, he lifted it and looked inside. His garden is now a crime scene.'

Merrick shook his head, looking sick. 'What . . . what was down there?'

'Two bodies,' Marnie said. 'Two little bodies.'

'Kids?' Merrick abandoned his bald head and spread both hands on the surface of his desk. If he was faking it, he was a good actor. 'Oh God . . . No, no, no.'

Marnie said immovably, 'Yes.'

'But how . . .? Who . . .?'

'Ask me *when*. I can answer that, in broad terms.'

Merrick's eyes were swimming with shock. 'When?'

'Four, maybe five years ago, long after you say the bunkers were filled in.'

'I have the paperwork,' Merrick insisted. He looked at the filing cabinets, as if by producing the planning permission he could undo the fact of the dead children.

'Good for you. I have the bodies. Who told you the bunkers were filled in?'

'The local authority planning people when they sold me the land! I'd never have bought it otherwise.'

'You've never cut corners, on any of your building projects?'

'Of course not . . .' He pushed at papers on his desk, colouring, but it could've been indignation rather than guilt.

'You cut them at number 14. You failed to connect ventilation pipes in the kitchen and bathroom.'

'That's . . . It's allowed, in a show house. The gas supply wasn't switched on, it was the summer. We finished it before we sold it. Of course we did.'

'Tell us about the travellers,' Noah said. 'Who were they?'

Merrick moved his eyes away from Marnie, in relief. 'Women mostly, a bit of a commune everyone said. The council moved them on.'

'Did you see any of them, to talk to?'

Merrick looked confused, as if he'd been asked whether he'd ever had a conversation with a zoo animal, or a cardboard box.

'They can't have been happy,' Noah said. 'Did you speak with any of them?'

'No. No, that was all dealt with by the council, and the police.'

'The police were involved?'

'I should think so. They usually are, aren't they? These people never move without a fight. And there'd been trouble, the usual thing. Burglaries in the area, car theft.' He appealed to Marnie with his hands spread. 'You know what they're like.'

'Do you think the travellers knew about the bunkers?' Noah asked.

'I don't know. I shouldn't think so. The way they were living, there wasn't any room for them to go digging around. It was all caravans.' Merrick made a sound of distaste. 'Not the romantic gypsy kind, either. I'm talking top of the range, more than I could afford.'

'And the police moved them on. When did that happen?'

'A month or so before we went on-site. I can get you the exact date. It'll be with the rest of the paperwork.' He straightened himself out. 'I thought you were here about the bomb.'

'The bomb?' Noah echoed.

'There are UXBs all over this part of London. The Germans bombed the hell out of it. It's why the site was closed for a couple of months.' He glanced out of the chicken-wired window at the half-built high-rise. 'You think it looks like a bomb site now . . . They keep finding the real thing all over here. This new development I'm talking about has German backing. You should've seen their faces when we told them about the delay. Blame the Luftwaffe, I said. That went down a storm, I can tell you.'

He stopped speaking at last, pulling his hands from the desk as if he was rescuing them from quicksand. The light winked on the bald dome of his head.

Noah felt sorry for Merrick. He'd got up this morning thinking it would be a day like any other, not thinking the police would come to his mobile office and look accusingly at his wall calendar, quiz him about planning permissions, bring dead children to his door.

'So you have no idea,' Marnie said, 'who had access to the bunkers five years ago?'

'None at all. I honestly thought they were filled. The paperwork . . .'

'I'll need it. And the name of the official at the planning office who provided it.'

Merrick nodded. 'I'll do that.' He looked up at them. 'The other bunkers . . . Have you looked inside those?'

'Not yet,' Marnie said. 'It's next on our to-do list.'

Merrick shuddered. 'You'll tell me if you turn up anything else?'

'If there are questions, we'll be back to ask them. Otherwise, you can follow it on the news, like everyone else.'

When they were back in the car, Marnie said, 'You were right about the bunkers. Six or seven. We'll have to move the whole road out.' She rested her hands on the wheel, looking across the site to where the Thames ran away from them.

'I think he's on the level,' Noah said. 'Merrick. He seemed genuinely gutted.'

'It's going to hit him where it hurts: bad publicity.'

She started the engine. 'Let's see what the planning office has to say. I need to get back for the press briefing. A story this size is going to break soon, no matter how hard we sit on it. Did you get anywhere with the labels from the tins?'

'Yes and no.' He'd done a preliminary search as soon he'd got into work. 'I found a match for the peach label, but it's a huge mail-order firm that ships around the world. They supply some of the bargain-brand supermarkets too. I'll keep digging, but I've got a feeling it's going to be less of a lead than Fran hoped.'

'We'll take whatever we've got,' Marnie said. 'Which means we'd better look into the travellers, too. Cover all bases.'

'After gutless Douglas?'

Marnie pointed the car towards Blackthorn Road.

'After him,' she agreed. 'And the press.'

16

Lawton Down Prison, Durham

Esther is facing the wall where she always sits. You'd think there was something to see, the way she studies it, something other than the new paint job over the old graffiti. The wall's full of lumps and zits, like a teenager's skin. I can't stand it. It's like looking at something I'll never see. Something I can't even remember properly, thanks to the drugs.

Esther takes everything they give us. I think she'd take more, if it was on offer. Me, I'd prefer something old-fashioned and brutal. Like ECT, or a baton to the back of the legs. A woman on the next floor got Tasered the other day. She'd gone for someone with a pair of scissors. They sat on her until she stopped shaking and I swear I could smell her burnt skin, like bad sunburn with a topspin.

Me and Esther . . .

We wouldn't dare touch a pair of scissors, let alone the rest of it. We're too busy being good. Esther with her face to the wall and me with my head stuffed so full of drugs I can't remember what they smelt like, or how long ago they died.

Being good . . .

We'll never be that. They should stop pretending it's possible and get back to the business of punishing us. We're back where we belong, at least. Behind bars. The public-places experiment is over, judged a success. I still can't believe they'd let us out, knowing what we've done. Some things should never be forgiven.

Lyn, the therapist, says, 'The important thing is that you're better now.'

I can't believe she believes this.

The important thing is that we're *punished*.

The important thing is that we're never let out, certainly not where there are children.

'Rehabilitation is possible,' that's Lyn's line.

Yes, but is it preferable? Is anything *preferable* to keeping the likes of us locked up?

If I was ever let out – and I can't believe they're even thinking about it, let alone sitting us in hospital waiting rooms, for God's sake, as if there's a cure for what we did, what we are – if I'm ever let out, there's one place I'll go, and only one place.

One thing I'll do when I get there.

One way to say sorry, and one chance to say it.

I think Esther feels the same; in fact I know she does. You can't live with someone the way she and I have lived – elbow to elbow in this place, sharing everything, sharing even the sounds and smells our bodies make – you can't live like that and not know.

She's the same as me, even if she never says it. If she sits facing the wall and doesn't flinch for anyone, not for that silly sad bitch with the scissors, not even when they brought her down with the Taser.

Esther's become an expert at hiding. And frankly?

That scares me.

I prefer my monsters out in the open, where I can see them.

It's one of the reasons I'm stopping the pills.

I'll take them, but I won't swallow. The pills make everything foggy, and I want to be able to see clearly, to see and to think.

It isn't right that I can't remember how long it is since they died. I ought to have the number of days – hours, minutes – carved into the jelly of my brain. There ought not to be a single second I don't remember. Instead, whole days go by, fog-banked by the drugs, until a crack emerges and a shaft of light stabs through – stabs *me*.

I want to be stabbed, over and over, by the memory of what I did. And by the other memories, the good ones.

How they looked, sleeping. The biscuit smell of their heads . . .

I think, if I stop taking the pills, I'll remember.

I'd hurt more, but I'd forget less.

Lyn says it would be dangerous to stop taking the pills. It was because I stopped taking them all those years ago (how many? It should be carved into the red walls of my head) that the unforgivable, unforgettable thing happened. But I *am* forgetting, and that's worse.

If I stop taking the pills, I'll remember. I'll remember why I must never be forgiven. And I'll see clearly, too. I'll see all my monsters. I'll see *me*.

Lyn is pleased with Esther because she's stopped answering back. She never questions the perceived wisdoms or challenges the platitudes.

'Rehabilitation is possible. You're living proof of that.'

Proof, perhaps, but I question whether we should be living. The lesson, I feel, would be more apposite if we were dead.

I'm almost sure Esther feels the same way. When we're lying in the dark, so close we could reach out and touch hands, I hear so much in her silence. All the shame and pain and *wonder* at the darkness that lives inside a person even when that person looks light, when it seems impossible that cold hard brick is behind that soft face, dim eyes . . .

There's no other darkness than this: what's inside us.

Where we hide; *what* we hide.

Esther hears me sobbing in the night. She hears me ripping at the pillow with my teeth because I've bitten my nails too short to tear at anything. She hears the blood seeping out of me once a month, a constant taunting of what I've lost and can never have back.

She hears when I hold my breath to bring them back, into my arms, into my bed. Even though I lie so quietly and carefully, and try so hard to keep the sounds to myself because I'm afraid of her hearing and holding out *her* arms – tricking them into her embrace instead of mine.

Children drift, like snow, like blossom.

I'm afraid they will drift back to her.

She's got so good at hiding.

Not like me. I'm out in the open, where I want my monsters to be.

Have you heard of Kate Webster?

Women paid to see Kate in her Wandsworth death cell, in 1879. Old women. I don't think they went to gloat. I think it was superstition. They peered into her death cell in the hope of reducing her. She must have looked monstrous hunkered in there, but sometimes fear can be succour. Kate Webster packed her elderly neighbour into a jam saucepan, in bits, and cooked her, and sold the dripping up and down the street. They hanged her, of course. What else were they supposed to do?

Esther is forgiven.

That is what I cannot believe.

After everything, she's forgiven.

How can that be right?

17

London

Commander Tim Welland's tie was skewed to the left and patterned with grease spots. A thumb mark from his breakfast spoiled the collar of his shirt. It was a studied look, one he only ever adopted for the press. His way of saying, 'I've got better things to do than feed headlines to you lot.'

Marnie said, 'Come here,' and straightened his tie, neatening the knot and managing to hide most of the bacon spots. Nothing she could do about the thumbprint.

Welland looked her over, from head to heels. 'You're ready for this?' His voice was a growl: Daddy Bear.

'It could be the fastest way to find out who knew about the bunkers, and the boys.'

He grunted. 'How contained is it?'

'Well, it's not on Twitter yet, if that helps.'

'We're about to put paid to that.'

'Yep . . .' She turned back, giving him a bright smile. 'Put your press face on, sir.'

His scowl was a thing of thunderous beauty.

'There you go,' Marnie said. 'You're ready.'

The press room wasn't packed, because the story hadn't broken properly yet. Welland had been parsimonious with the facts and it was nearly lunchtime, not a journalist's favourite hour for squeezing into an overheated room to hear what might be of only marginal interest.

The hard truth was that the press didn't trust the police to bring them the best stories any more; they'd turned their attention to social media, teenagers on Twitter and middle-aged whistle-blowers. Had Welland broken the Snaresbrook story in any way other than via the official police channel, the press room would have been humming. As it was, a dozen reporters – young and keen, old and weary – were sweating in plastic seats, fiddling with their phones, looking for better stories online probably.

Welland kept the room overheated on purpose, not only because he was immune to the temperature. He knew the press wouldn't want to linger here. He took the chair next to Marnie's. Their audience continued to check their phones, apportioning a fraction of their attention to the stage. Someone took a photograph, blinding them with light.

Blinking, Marnie said, 'Late yesterday afternoon, we found the bodies of two children in a garden in Snaresbrook. It's too soon for the full post-mortem results, but we believe the bodies to be boys, and we believe they were buried four or five years ago.'

Now the room hummed. More flashes of light. Marnie couldn't see any of the faces belonging to the questions that came thick and fast: 'Have you made an arrest?' 'How did they die?' 'How old were they?'

Marnie waited it out. When they paused for breath, she

said, 'We'll know more after the post-mortems have been carried out. Until then—'

'Is this the Beech Rise development? Blackthorn Road?' A man's voice.

The rest of the room fell quiet.

Marnie too. Her pulse slowed, her skin pinched with cold.

That voice . . .

She was quiet for so long that Welland stepped in. 'Further details will be released as and when we have them. Thank you.' He stood, rubber squealing from the feet of his chair.

'What do you know about the bunker?' the reporter asked. His voice was cool, non-combative. 'Or is it bunkers? I'm guessing there's more than one.'

The light from the camera flashes was clearing, and the room came into focus, a slow bleed of colour into what had been whiteness.

Marnie looked for the man who knew about Beech Rise and Blackthorn Road . . .

There, at the side of the room, leaning back in his chair, bonelessly.

Six long feet of slouch.

Fair hair, blue eyes, easy in his own skin.

A smile like smoke from his eyes, just for her.

Adam Fletcher.

18

Noah was looking at the picture of a warehouse the size of an aircraft hangar, stacked with shelves of tins. One shelf alone held what must have been a thousand tins, all with blue and gold labels like the ones they'd taken from the bunker. The same label, chewed by damp, sat in an evidence bag at his elbow.

'Sun-ripe peaches in syrup,' the website said. It offered three purchasing options, the first being a six-month supply. The second was enough peaches to last a year. The third – 'best value for money!' – was three years' supply. Enough peaches to make you sick to death of anything sun-ripened and preserved in syrup.

The website specialised in long-life tinned foodstuffs: 'Apocalypse-proof! I got enough for my family for three years!' They sold drums and saucepans, glass jars and barrels, salt and sterilising kits for home preserving. Everything the paranoid home-provider needed to feel smug in the event of a national disaster or the mass ransacking of supermarkets.

At first glance, Noah thought it was worth asking the site for a list of UK customers in the last six years. Surely, he reasoned, there couldn't be many people who felt the need to bulk-buy as a precaution against a future where the survival of the human race depended on segments of heavily preserved fruit. But he was wrong. The website was peppered with reviews from the UK praising the civic thinking behind the paranoia.

'Coffee.' Ron put a cup by Noah's elbow. 'My round.'

'Thanks.'

Ron peered at the website. 'Shit . . . is that for real?'

'People buy it. Too many people . . .' Noah picked up the evidence bag. 'Fran thought it might be a lead, but it looks like these tins could be all over London.'

'Who'd eat that crap?'

They both winced. Their boys had eaten it. For days, maybe even weeks or months.

'Have you heard of preppers?'

'Nope.' Ron pulled up a chair. 'What're preppers?'

'It's in the review here.' Noah pointed at the screen. '"Perfect for preppers . . ."'

He opened a new window, and fed the word into a search engine.

'Bloody hell,' Ron said.

'"Preparing for the best possible survival in the worst imaginable world",' Noah read. '"You'll want food, water and secure shelter, above or below ground."'

'Below ground . . . What, in a *bunker*?' Ron jabbed a finger at an image on the screen. '*Safe*, it says. Hidden. Just like our boys.' He rubbed at his face. 'Christ, you don't think . . .?'

Noah shook his head. He didn't know what he thought, not right away.

The best possible survival in the worst imaginable world.

'What,' Ron said, 'if this insane fucker thought he was keeping them safe?'

19

'We need to speak with the planning office who sold the land to Merrick,' Marnie said. 'He swears the bunkers were filled in before he started building.'

'Bunkers plural.' Welland looked ominous. 'How did that cagey bastard know about it before we did?' He meant the reporter from the press briefing, Adam Fletcher. 'How did he know? I want that found out, as a priority.'

'He did his homework.' Unlike Marnie, when Adam was around. She'd been sixteen, easily seduced from schoolwork by a single smile. *Crap.* This was going to be hard enough without Adam slouching his way back into her life. She couldn't believe he'd turned up at the press briefing, although heart-slamming surprise was his MO, always had been.

'I'll find out what he knows,' she told Welland.

'Are we going to have to dig up the whole street?' he demanded.

'Yes. That's exactly what we're going to have to do.'

'Well stay on top of it, press included. Especially the one who's doing his homework.' Welland looked disgusted. 'I don't want tripping up by some bloody hack who thinks shaving his chin's too much trouble in the morning.'

Five o'clock shadow. Marnie could feel the burn of it on her skin, even after all these years. Like fingers held too close to a campfire; worth it for the charred sweetness of marshmallow sticking to her lips. Except Adam wasn't marshmallows, or campfires. He wasn't skinned knees in the playground or stolen kisses behind bike sheds. He was . . .

Her shoulders bruised by a brick wall, an ache in her skin that wouldn't go away unless she went back for more. And he was here now, making her job harder, making her afraid of what other homework he might have done, after sixteen years of staying away.

She took out her phone and texted Noah: *I'm going to Blackthorn Road. Meet me there.*

At Beech Rise, she parked under the trees that Merrick Homes had thoughtfully preserved and incorporated into their development. She'd beaten the press pack, but not by much.

Adam Fletcher was waiting at the corner of Blackthorn Road, in the old Levis and dark jumper he'd worn to the briefing. The other reporters were still checking in, getting the address details, playing catch-up, but Adam was one step ahead.

'Detective Inspector Rome.' He managed to make it sound obscene. 'It's been a while. Fancy a coffee?'

'You'll be lucky, around here.'

'I guess I'm lucky, then. Tabitha's Caff . . . It's a three-minute walk.'

They walked without speaking to the café and sat outside, so that Adam could smoke.

She thought: *The last time I did this, they were alive.*

He lit up in the same way, using a cheap disposable lighter with his hand cupped around the flame. Smoking the same brand: Marlboros in a red and white packet. A new warning from the Surgeon-General: 'You smoke, you die.'

She thought: *The last time I did this, I didn't even know Stephen Keele existed.*

Adam lifted the hand with the cigarette and rubbed its heel at his temple. Smoke scuffed the side of his head, greying his fair hair for a second. He was . . . what? Forty-four, forty-five now? He hadn't changed, just acquired a few more hard lines to go with the ones she'd coveted half a lifetime ago. 'So how much do you know about Clancy Brand?'

The question surprised her. She'd expected . . . Not happy memories, that was for sure. But *something*, before he jumped straight into the reason he was back.

'You know the Doyles are fostering him. How much more d'you know?'

'How much more is there? He's fourteen . . .'

'Going on thirty,' Adam said.

'Tell me.'

'Not unless you tell me something in return.' He showed his teeth in a smile. Rakish, offhand and easy in his skin, something Marnie had never been.

'Such as what? You seemed to know as much as we did, at the briefing.'

Tabitha, if it was Tabitha, brought their coffees. The metal table rocked when she set the cups down. When she'd gone back inside, Marnie said, 'You knew about the bunkers.'

Adam took the saucer from under his coffee cup and twitched ash into it. 'Anyone can find out about the bunkers. They're a matter of public record. Try finding out about a fourteen-year-old foster kid. That'll tax your brain. Even yours, Detective Inspector.'

'You knew about the bunkers before we did. How? And why?'

'I'm a journalist. I follow stories.' He thumbed a speck of tobacco from his tongue. 'In this case, big fat gypsy stories.'

'The travellers,' Marnie deduced. 'That's how you know about them?'

He flicked the speck of tobacco to the floor. 'Ask me about Clancy Brand.'

'No. I want to know about the travellers. I want whatever you have, on the bunkers and the dead boys.'

'Zip is what I have. I knew there were bunkers, but I thought they'd been filled in. Don't bother looking for the planning officer who signed the paperwork, by the way. It's a dead end.' He returned the cigarette to his mouth. 'Literally dead. No suspicious circumstances to get excited about, either. Retired and dead of a heart attack within the year.'

'You know this because . . .?'

'I told you, I'm following a story.'

'A story about travellers.'

'It pays the bills,' Adam said.

'Where did the travellers go when they were moved on? Do you know that?'

'Maybe, but you're chasing ghosts. You want to look closer to home.' He finished the cigarette and stubbed it in the saucer. 'Clancy Brand's an evil little shit.' He said it carelessly, without any edge to his voice. This wasn't personal.

Marnie wondered whether anything was ever personal, for Adam.

'Define evil,' she invited, picking up her coffee.

His eyes followed the line of her wrist, up inside her sleeve, then down, across her sternum to her navel. Lower than that. 'That's your job.'

'My job is catching them. Someone else gets to do the defining.'

His eyes stayed on her bare skin. She wondered what he'd make of the tattoos she'd acquired, after his time, but not long after; a palliative for her skin's craving. She could imagine him coming out with some cute crap: 'I can read you like a book . . . By Albert Camus, isn't it?' wrapping the words around the enquiry like a snake up a stick.

They were alive and I didn't know that Stephen Keele existed.

Tears pricked deep inside, nowhere near her eyes.

The cigarette in the saucer was still glowing. Adam pressed his knuckles to it, smothering the ghost of smoke. 'You want to know about Clancy.' It wasn't a question.

'I've got a double murder to investigate. Unless he's connected to that . . .'

'Maybe he is.'

'The children died at least four years ago. When Clancy was ten.'

'And? You're not going to tell me that ten's too young to kill.' He held her gaze.

'I'm not going to tell you anything. Because I think you're winding me up.' She put her eyes on him, coldly. 'You've done your homework. Well done.'

Adam knew. He knew Stephen Keele had killed her parents, five years ago. He knew how, maybe he even knew *why* . . . No. Not even Adam knew why. If he did, he wouldn't sit here and taunt her loss under the pretext of chasing a story about murdered children. Some things she put past him. Not much. But *that* . . . Not even Adam would do that.

She felt the pull of the past so keenly, she had to fight not to lean in its direction. 'If you're wasting police time,' she said, summoning a smile, 'that's an offence.'

His eyes gleamed responsively. He pushed back in his chair, shoving his legs to their full length so that she had to move her feet out of the way. 'You know me,' he said, running the words into one another. 'Anything to cause offence.'

Relieved that she wasn't walking away. That he'd pushed her buttons and she hadn't responded by throwing whatever punches she'd picked up on her way to becoming a DI.

Plenty, she thought. *I know plenty of punches. Push me and you'll find out how many. They'll be written all over your face.*

'So why are you really here?' she asked, matching his careless tone.

'Earning a living, just like you.' He scrubbed a hand through his hair. 'Well, not quite like you.' A rueful grin. He was still good at this, tugging at her skin with his smile.

Careful. Be very careful.

'You've not been earning it around here recently. Where've you been?'

'Abroad.' He shrugged. 'Foreign correspondent . . . When the gig expired, I came home.'

To chase stories about travellers, and teenage boys?

'Who told you about the bunkers?'

'Legwork. The travellers got kicked off-site because of Merrick's development, which, by the way, stinks. I've seen corners cut with more finesse on fucking *Top Gear*. I followed the paper trail to the planning office. Saw the blueprints for the development with all the little boxes, the bunkers.'

'Filled in?'

'According to the paperwork.' He nodded, 'I didn't know it was a scam until I got the call to your press briefing.' He crooked his mouth at her. 'Wouldn't have been out of bed if a mate hadn't called to say it was kicking off on Blackthorn Road. The travellers used to call it the Beach, on account of the number of times the river came close enough to paddle in.'

'So you were following the travellers. How did that lead you to Clancy?'

'He's living on Blackthorn Road, isn't he?'

'So are plenty of other people. Why pick on him?'

'For starters? Little shit keyed my car. Couldn't prove it was him, of course, on account of what a *sly* little shit he is. But I started to watch where he went, and trust me, he's got stuff to hide. Rats don't sneak around the way he does. When I heard about the bunker, I thought you'd found something of his.' He turned his cup until the table tipped on its wonky leg. 'One of his hiding places.'

Marnie put her hand on her own cup, not wanting it to spill. 'What sort of thing?'

'What?' He reached for his cigarettes.

'You said something of Clancy's. What sort of thing?'

'God knows. Drugs. Cash.' He snapped the lighter, pushing smoke aside with his wrist. 'Dead bodies . . . Oh, wait.'

'Don't do that,' she told him.

He raised his eyebrows at her.

'Joke,' she said. 'Don't joke about this. Those children died, in the dark, alone.'

'We're all alone in the dark, dying.' He smoked at the sky, then brought his stare back down. 'That wasn't a joke. You should check the bunker again, make sure he wasn't down there. He's been sneaking around just about every other corner of that dump.'

She waited a beat. 'You really think Clancy had something to do with their deaths? When he was ten years old?'

'Because kids never hurt other kids. Right. I'm telling you . . . you need to look at him.'

'And you need to stop dodging and give me what you've got. Before I start thinking this whole thing is a wind-up.'

'Why would I wind you up, Max?'

Another joke, sixteen years old. Marnie Jane Rome, initials MJR, short for Majority, which got shortened again to Max, because why use four syllables when you could use one?

'Gee, Adam, I don't know. Because you're starting to remember how much fun it was?'

'It *was* fun,' he agreed gravely. He looked at the fresh cigarette as if it irritated him, reaching to grind it out in the saucer. 'I'm guessing you don't have time to fuck about, which is too bad, but neither do I. Being a scumbag journalist with a story deadline.'

'My hearts bleeds for you. I have a double murder to

solve. If you've got information, give it up. Otherwise, stop pissing about and let me get on with my job.'

He studied her with a gleam in his eyes that looked like pride. 'Clancy Brand.' It was the fourth time he'd said the boy's full name. 'Take a look inside his room. You've got access to the house, right? Take a look at how he's living in there, how he's hiding. When you've done that, if you're still not interested? Fine . . .' He stood, putting the knuckles of one hand on the table, making it rock. 'But if you want to put what *you've* got together with what *I've* got? You know where to find me.'

'Nice speech,' she said flatly. 'But no, I don't know where to find you. I never did, remember?' He'd always found her, never the other way around, not even when she needed him so badly it scared her. 'How's your daughter? Tia, wasn't it? She'd be starting college now, I guess. You must be proud.'

'She would, and I am.' Adam flashed his teeth in a smile. 'I'll call the station.'

He took his knuckles off the table, and walked away.

Her phone rang before he was out of sight.

Fran said, 'I've got DNA for you.'

Marnie got to her feet. 'Whose?'

'The boys. I thought we'd caught a break with the swabs from the ladder. We've got DNA there too, and on the underside of the manhole cover. But it's a match for what we took from the bodies. No secondary DNA from anything down there.'

No secondary DNA. That meant . . .

'I'm running more tests,' Fran said. 'They're brothers, like you thought.'

'No secondary DNA means . . . familial DNA?'

'Yes.'

'So . . .'

'They knew their killer. They were killed by an aunt or uncle.' Fran paused. 'Or someone closer: their mum or dad.'

20

Lawton Down Prison, Durham

'Good afternoon, Alison. How are you today?'

'I think I'm doing well,' I say.

I do not say, 'I can't remember how many weeks it is since I saw them.'

I daren't ask Lyn what day it is. I bet she has a name for that, something worse than absent-mindedness or amnesia. A name for my inability to recall details that ought to be etched on my memory, and a way of wielding it that would put back my progress by weeks. Not that my progress exists anywhere other than on her pieces of paper, and the parole board's pieces of paper, but this is my life we're talking about. My freedom; if you can call the imminent release of a dangerous prisoner 'freedom'. I'm not sure I can. I can call it many things – risky, arrogant and fucking irresponsible, for starters – but not freedom.

Freedom isn't for the likes of me and Esther.

Oh they dangle it, of course they do. Just out of reach, in order to get us to take our incarceration seriously, join in with the endless rounds of psychologising, the games we play: Believing in our Rehabilitation; Engaging in the Recovery Process; Role-Playing the Victim, and the other exercises they dream up to justify the idea of a justice system.

'Today,' Lyn says, 'I'd like to talk about your exit strategy, yes?'

To every statement she appends this imperious 'Yes?' as if to imply that only the hard-of-hearing or the foolhardy could fail to see her point. Like a politician's 'Look' at the front of whatever statement they're trying to shove down the throats of the voting public: 'Look at my empirical evidence, my emperor's robes . . .'

I'd like to talk about your exit strategy, yes?

No, I want to say. Let's not talk about exits. Let all doors be shut to me for ever. The way that manhole is shut over their little heads.

I say, 'Yes please.'

Because, forgive me, I do want to get out.

Note that I do not say I want to be *free*.

I do not believe in my freedom. I do not believe it exists, but if it does? I know that I do not deserve it. I think the giving of it to the likes of me and Esther is risky, arrogant and fucking irresponsible, yes?

Lyn's hair is tightly permed and she's skinny but muscular. Her skin is thin over her bones. You can see the veins everywhere on her body. She's an X-ray. She tries to make her face look open, but it doesn't work. It's screwed as tight shut as the rest of her.

She hates us. I truly believe that. She hates every single one of the women in here, because we're weak. Because we fell, we slipped, and worse, we let ourselves down.

Lyn would never let herself down. She's far too wound up for that. She says, 'You've started the process of the outside visits, yes?' Her voice is like this: *rat-a-tat-tat.* She's a one-woman watchtower, gunned, against the barbed wire.

'Yes,' I say meekly. 'Yes.'

The process of the outside visits – she means sitting in the hospital the other night, to see if anyone recognised Esther or, less likely, me.

Alison Oliver, one-time maximum security prisoner, shortly to be on remand because the world isn't full enough of crazy people, child killers, because there's always room for one more, yes? How can this possibly go wrong?

'I think,' Lyn says, 'that the next thing we need to talk about is your accommodation. You say that your mother . . .'

I tune out. She doesn't need me for this bit, her plans for my new place in society. She has a whole life mapped out for me. A bedroom in my mother's place, complete with flowery curtains and a new bedspread, a Gideon bible in the drawer of the cabinet . . .

'. . . mobile home, yes?'

'What?'

Lyn wrings a look of patience from her face. 'Alison, we're talking about your mother, Connie. She's living in a mobile home now. You know this. You've had letters from her.'

Oh yes, the letters. Esther sometimes reads a line or two to me. I don't read them myself. I'm afraid I'll read the word 'forgiven' – or, worse, that I won't.

My mother is a mystery to me. Two small boys died. She loved them. I know that for a fact. She loved them second-best of anyone in the world. If there's anyone who should hate me more than I hate myself, who should be campaigning for me never to be released, it's my mother. Instead, she's offering me a hiding place.

She's told Lyn that she has a room in her mobile home for me. It's one of the reasons they've put a date on my release, because I have somewhere to go when I get out of here.

Esther doesn't have that yet. But she will.

If I'm getting out, there's no way she will stay here.
It's unimaginable.
If I'm getting out, she's coming with me.
That's what scares me the worst.
Esther's coming too.

21

London

No sign of Marnie on Blackthorn Road. Her car was parked at a short distance, under the trees. Noah was about to call her mobile when he saw her coming from the direction of the housing estate; she must've been checking on the house-to-house team.

Noah had the building plans, showing boundaries and the route of the river. Seven neat boxes that looked like garden sheds but weren't. Ian Merrick had told the truth.

Seven bunkers, one per garden.

Marnie's head was down. She was checking her phone, the way Noah had just checked his. She was still checking when she reached his side.

'Hey,' Noah said in greeting. 'Did you get lucky?'

She looked up, her eyes guarded and dark. 'What?'

'House-to-house? I thought . . .'

'No. I've not had the chance to check in.'

She turned to look in the direction of the estate. 'Any sign of the press yet?'

'Not yet.'

'Good. Tell the PCSO to let us know as soon as they get here. I have another house-to-house team coming to speak to the Doyles' neighbours, so that they don't get a nasty surprise when the reporters land.'

'I've got the plans.' Noah unfolded the sheet, showing her the evidence of the bunkers.

Marnie studied it. 'This hatching means – what? That they're filled in?'

Noah nodded. 'According to the planning office. They said the official who signed the paperwork retired a couple of years ago, so it might be a dead end. Ron and I looked at the site selling the tinned peaches. Lots of customers call themselves preppers. Preppers are—'

'Paranoid hoarders.' Marnie cut him short. 'I know what preppers are.' Her stare made him uneasy, too sharp. 'Where are you going with this, detective?'

'I'm not sure. Except that preppers like bunkers, or any secure hiding place. We thought maybe whoever took the boys believed they were keeping them safe.'

'Safe,' she repeated.

Curtains twitched across the street; the neighbours starting to get curious at last?

Noah was surprised no one had come out of any of the houses to ask what was going on. But this was middle-class almost-suburbia; they could take a lot of curtain twitching before they were crass enough to ask questions.

'Let's start with number 8,' Marnie said. 'Douglas Cole.'

Noah shook his head. 'No one's home. I checked as soon as I got here. Tried his phone, too. No answer. I left a message for him to call the station. Do you think he's avoiding us?'

Marnie didn't answer. She stood looking at number 14 before she said, 'I need you in the bunker where we found the boys.'

'What?' He blinked. 'Why?'

'I think I might have missed something. Two pairs of eyes are better than one.'

'Okay.' He tried to ignore the creeping sensation in the back of his neck. 'Now?'

'Let's suit up. We should have done it sooner.'

She moved in the direction of her car, speaking across her shoulder. 'Fran's got familial DNA. The boys were brothers. They were killed by someone close. Their mum and dad, or an aunt or uncle.'

Family killer . . .

'You think we missed something,' Noah said, 'in the bunker?'

'Not evidence, no. But the *sense* of the place, how it might have happened . . . If you're right about safety, about the motive behind this? We should go and take another look.'

Marnie watched the twitching curtains. 'Before the GPR team gets here and we find out what's in the other bunkers.'

22

Noah stood in the dark under the Doyles' garden, waiting while Marnie switched on the police floodlights. She remembered her way around down here. He wondered how long it would take her to forget. It was the first time he'd been further than the forensic tent.

'Did you ever play under the stairs as a kid?' she asked.

Noah shook his head, then nodded. 'Sometimes . . .' And in bathroom cupboards, spying on his mother's obsessive cleaning routine, but he was keeping those memories to himself. This was bad enough without adding seasoning to the spice.

'With your kid brother,' Marnie said. 'Sol, isn't it?'

Sol was short for Solomon. 'Yes.'

Had he and Sol ever played under the stairs? Not that Noah could remember. He remembered Sol setting up a camp bed in their parents' room and sleeping there whenever Dad was away, fetching blankets and a damp flannel for his forehead, everything Mum needed to take care of her sick little boy. Noah couldn't remember Sol ever being sick, not really. But he could remember days and days with Sol in that camp bed, playing at being feverish; his favourite game, and their mother's too. It was a short cut to her affection and attention. Sol had always been good at short cuts.

Marnie finished setting up the floodlights and stood side by side with Noah, facing the makeshift bed. 'You saw the toys they took up top?'

Noah nodded. 'And the books . . .'

What Does a Dinosaur Do All Day? The picture of a Tyrannosaurus rex with a thermometer between his teeth – that was when Noah had first thought of Sol's sickbed games.

'Whoever put them down here,' Marnie said, 'it wasn't intended as a grave. Or not just that.'

'Unless the books and toys were to keep them quiet . . .'

'There are ropes and gags if it was just about keeping them quiet.'

'Distracted, then. Or he wanted to win their trust.'

'Or he already had it.' Marnie picked a flake of rust from her gloved palm. 'The toys didn't look new. They looked like old favourites, well loved.'

The felt eyes had been rubbed flat on the toy monkey, like the face of Sol's favourite lion with its fuzzy mane, a rare present from their dad, who didn't believe in spoiling his kids but who made an exception, sometimes, for Sol.

Noah said, 'Familial DNA . . . Are we sure a family member did this?'

'Would I rather it was a stranger? I don't know if that's better or worse. It depends how they died. If they thought they were safe, if they climbed down here because they felt safe . . .' She turned her eyes away from the bed. 'Maybe that's worse.'

'Of course it's worse,' Noah said reflexively. 'It's betrayal, the worst kind of betrayal.'

'They might not have known that. They might've died

feeling safe. Loved . . . What's the alternative? That they died in fear, terrified, crying for their mum and dad?'

'It's horrible.' Noah buried his fists in his pockets. 'However it happened, it's horrible.'

Marnie didn't speak for a while. Then she said, 'Let's say you brought them down here. How did you do that, without their help?'

It was what they did, how they solved crimes like this. Except that there hadn't been any crimes like this, not for Noah. It was different, for Marnie.

'They were little,' he said. 'They wouldn't put up much of a fight.'

'But there are two of them. You can't carry two at once, down that.' Marnie jerked her head at the ladder. 'I'm not even sure you could carry one if he didn't want you to.'

Noah looked up the ladder with its narrow vertical rungs. 'I drugged them.'

'Post-mortem said no drugs.'

'No *lethal* drugs. This wasn't anything stronger than Calpol in warm milk.' He grimaced as he said it, hating himself.

This was what they did, he and Marnie. Reconstructed crime scenes, acting out the roles of perpetrator and victim, whatever it took to get under the skin of a case. But it felt wrong down here in the dark where the boys had died.

'You didn't mean them to die,' Marnie said. 'Let's go with that theory. You were hiding them. You thought you were keeping them safe.'

'Safe from what?' Noah demanded. 'Daylight and fresh air?'

'Maybe . . .' She crouched by the bed. 'Maybe you were scared of whatever was up there.'

'Daylight and fresh air,' Noah repeated. He didn't understand how she could do it. Treat this like any other crime scene. She'd been doing this job a lot longer than him;

maybe she'd seen worse things than the dead boys. His mind blanked at what that might be.

'So what's up there? What are you so scared of?'

Marnie stayed crouched, not speaking. He counted to thirteen before she said, 'Their DNA was on the ladder, and on the inside of the manhole cover. They climbed up and tried to get out. So I guess you're right. They weren't safe.'

She straightened and he saw her face. Blue shadows under her eyes. With the light bleaching her skin, she looked about sixteen. 'They tried to get out.'

'Anyone would try to get out. Even if it started as a game, as something safe . . . Sooner or later, you'd want to get out. You can't breathe down here.'

Not properly, he meant. Not in a way that let you believe you might survive. The air was a sucker-punch to the lungs. If you were shut down here, with no way out . . . You couldn't breathe the stale air without knowing you were dying. Even if you were only five years old, you'd know. Of course their boys had tried to get out.

Marnie looked at him and her face changed, its lines coming back into focus. 'All right, enough. Let's go back up.'

'No. I'm okay. Let's finish what we started.'

It was important to get this straight in their heads. Noah didn't want to come back at a later stage in the investigation because they'd failed to get it right first time.

He stepped back, careful to keep within the perimeter of Forensics' fingertip search. 'You brought them down here. Drugged, or trusting you. Maybe you bribed them, said it was an adventure. The older boy would want to keep his nerve, show his kid brother he wasn't afraid. And the little one would follow his lead, probably.'

'Only probably?'

'Not all kids look up to their big brothers.'

'All right, but let's say this one did.'

She was remembering the shape they made, curled together, the older boy sheltering the younger with his body. It was impossible to forget a thing like that. Noah hadn't envied Fran the task of separating the bodies. 'Not all the food was eaten.'

'Not all of it,' Marnie agreed.

'So you brought plenty of food. And you organised it.' He nodded to the far corner of the bunker. 'Over there, that was the kitchen. Bucket was there,' he nodded again, 'bathroom. And the bed's here. Kids wouldn't do that for themselves. Not most kids, anyway.'

'Which means what?'

'You were down here with them, keeping house . . .' He stopped.

Marnie waited a minute. 'Why did I leave?'

'To empty the bucket. And to get more food, because there was too much to carry that first time, with the boys in tow. Two boys, some weeks . . . Lots of bodily waste in the bucket, especially if you're feeding them sweetcorn, canned peaches.'

'But then I stopped coming back.'

'Then you stopped.'

'Why?' Her gaze was steady, burning like one of the lamps.

'You . . . had no choice. Maybe you got caught. If this wasn't the first time you'd done something like this.'

'So I'm arrested. But I don't confess to putting two boys down here even when it could save their lives?'

Noah drew a breath. 'All right. Then . . . you'd already killed them.'

She shook her head. 'No evidence that they were smothered, or harmed in any way. They were alive when I left them.'

'Maybe,' Noah agreed. 'But they died because you didn't come back.'

Dead air curled like hands at his shoulders, heavy.

Marnie looked at the whorls of damp on the walls. 'Yes, they did. So why did I bring them down here in the first place? No evidence of abuse, Fran said. Why did I feed them and keep them warm and clean, and then just stop? Leave them to die?'

Noah looked around, trying to see something other than a pit, a grave. 'Maybe you *were* hiding them, keeping them safe.' He couldn't see this as a place of safety. No matter how hard he tried. He just couldn't. 'But what . . . *what* were you hiding them from?'

'Something worse than this. Something so bad it made this place feel safe by comparison.'

Noah shook his head. 'I don't buy it. If you're that scared, you go to the police.'

'Not always, or you and I would be out of a job.' Marnie crouched by the bed again. 'Sometimes the police are scary.' She touched a hand to the shadow left by the mattress. 'We take kids away sometimes. And sometimes . . . we give them to the wrong people.'

The wrong people.

Family killer.

Noah wanted to be up in the fresh air, not down here in the rotten dark. He was starting to feel sick, black puffs of panic in his head. 'Can we go back up?'

Marnie was still searching the space with her stare; the whites of her eyes were the only clean things in the bunker. 'No one reported them missing. No one. Not the schools they went to, not their extended family, or their friends. How does that happen?'

'I . . . don't know.' He couldn't stay down here. He could barely form a sentence, his tongue sticking to the roof of his mouth. 'Ian Merrick said . . . travellers. They don't always send their kids to school, and they close ranks.'

'True,' Marnie said. 'Just be careful how you word that for the press . . .'

She straightened, turning to look at him before taking two short strides to his side.

'All right.' She put a firm hand under his elbow and lowered him to the floor of the bunker, pushing his head on to his knees. 'Noah? Just . . . breathe.'

He didn't think he could, but she held him there with her hand on the back of his neck until the blood began to beat in his temples and the dizziness cleared a little, enough for his chest to register a complaint against the angle she was holding him to. 'I need to . . .'

'All right,' she said. 'But slowly. Take it slowly.'

'I'm okay. Just . . . not great with enclosed spaces.'

She moved her mouth, painfully. 'My fault, and I'm sorry.' She eyed the distance to the ladder. 'Think you can get back up? I could call the PCSO.'

'No. I'll be okay.'

She stepped away, giving him space to climb to his feet. He was glad she didn't offer a hand, embarrassed enough by his show of weakness.

She waited at the side of the ladder. 'After you . . .'

He climbed the ladder easily with the incentive of daylight at the top of it, unzipping the forensic tent and stepping out into the garden, sucking at the fresh air like a surfacing diver.

Better . . .

Marnie zippered the tent shut behind them, standing at his shoulder for a second, looking up at the house. 'You might be right,' she said, 'about the travellers, and the preppers.'

Noah was acutely aware of the bunker at their backs. Standing here with Fran, he'd pictured it as a place of shade, cold. Now, it was like standing six feet from a fire pit.

'I know about preppers,' Marnie said. 'Stephen Keele's birth parents dabbled in it. If you can dabble in post-apocalyptic paranoia. It's more common than you might think, even in the UK.'

Noah nodded dumbly.

Marnie's phone rang and she answered it. 'DI Rome. Beth? Is everything all right?'

She listened in silence before saying, 'I'll come over.'

She pocketed the phone, asking Noah, 'Are you all right to make a start with house-to-house? Julie Lowry at number 12, start there. I'll get back as soon as I can.'

'Trouble?' Noah asked.

'Clancy,' Marnie said. 'And yes.'

23

Lawton Down Prison, Durham

If you were to ask me why we did it, I would tell you a lie. Not because I'm avoiding the truth. I'm a fan of the truth. I rub against it whenever I can, like a bear on a big old tree, satisfying an itch even at the cost of its fur.

I would love a larger serving of the truth. If I could find it in here – a great redwood of truth – I'd ask to be strung up and hanged from it. Believe me when I tell you I hunt for the truth every day, and I do so knowing it's likely to kill me.

So why would I lie to you?

I'd lie for the same reason Pavlov's puppies salivated. Because it's what I've been taught to do, quickly and often. Prison will do that to you.

Some people need a reason to get up in the mornings. In here, it's easy. They ring a bell. Actually, it's a buzzer. (You see, the truth is important to me, even little truths.) I don't lie when I can avoid it, but in here? I'd stand a better chance of getting an extra hour of sleep after the buzzer's buzzed.

Lying is part of prison culture, like a sharpened toothbrush, a melted carrier bag. It's basic self-defence. Because here's the thing about prison: it's all corners. No hiding places.

I'm going to find open spaces a challenge, Lyn says, when I'm out.

It's so close now, just a matter of days away. I can't pretend any longer that they're joking. It's really happening. They're going to let the pair of us out.

Esther won't talk about it.

Lyn tells her the same thing, about challenges.

Open spaces are a big problem, apparently. We've spent all this time getting used to six square feet, less if they've put us in with someone who likes to flex her muscle. You get in the habit of making yourself small. When they kick you out, it's like being thrown from a plane, so much sky thrashing past you and the ground rushing up.

You don't stand a chance.

Of course Lyn doesn't put it like that. Lyn calls free-falling to your certain death 'a challenge'. She talks about 'pastures new' and 'distant horizons', and I swear sometimes I could hang *her* from that tree I was talking about.

What do I think is waiting for us, out there?

Let me try and tell you the truth.

I think . . .

Open space is like outer space. You need a suit, the kind astronauts wear, sealed to stop your blood from boiling and your spine from stretching. Some astronauts grow by five centimetres, because their spines get stretched in space. If Esther grew by even half that much, she wouldn't be able to walk down the street without people staring.

I bet it feels that way when you're first let out.

As if you're growing, out of control.

I don't want pastures new, or distant horizons. The first chance I get, I'm going down, underground. Into tube stations, car parks, anywhere I can feel the ceiling pressing on me and the walls closing in. That and the smell. Dead air, dust and piss.

I'm finding someplace nice and narrow and I'm reaching out my arms to touch the walls either side, my palms flat to the brickwork. Safe. If I get lucky, I can stay that way for hours, like waiting to be body-searched, for someone to tell me where I begin and end, to allocate the space I'm allowed. To tell me how much is too much, where to stop.

And then, when I know where to stop, I'm going deeper underground.

I think you probably know where I mean: the place where we left them.

I'm going down in the bunker.

And I'm taking Esther with me.

24

London

Noah stood at the edge of the dodgy decking, at the back of number 12. The GPR team was testing the place where a trampoline had left indents in the lawn. To his right, over a high fence, the forensic tent breathed with the breeze, its polythene walls shrinking and expanding.

Julie Lowry, the Doyles' neighbour, came out on to the decking in yoga pants and a yellow vest, red FitFlops on her feet, worry eating at her face. 'What've they found?'

'They're still setting up.' Noah saw goose bumps on her arms. 'Shall we wait in the house? I'll make us a cup of tea.'

Her eyes strayed over his shoulder to the circle of shaggy grass where the trampoline had stood. 'The press are saying you found kiddies next door . . .' She pressed her palms together, full of questions, full of horror.

Noah could read tomorrow's headlines in her face. 'Shall we go inside?'

'We all thought it must be drugs, something those gypsies left behind. I'd not put anything past them. Didn't even *think* of bodies, especially not kiddies. Beth must be going spare. It was hard enough on them already, without a thing like this . . .'

'Hard enough on them already?'

'Foster kids . . .' She rubbed at the goose bumps. 'Challenging, that's the word they use, right? *I* couldn't do it. Not that they'd let me, being a single mum. A teenager, too. Don't get me wrong, I think it's amazing what they're doing, but Clancy?' She twisted her lips into a small smile, confidential. 'Between you and me, I'm surprised Terry puts up with it.'

'Puts up with what?'

Her leg jittered, one foot tapping at the decking. 'I used to sunbathe in the back garden, but since he came? I won't even let the kids out here without proper clothes on.' Her eyes slid away then back, more boldly than before. 'I'm not being funny, but I've known plenty of teenage boys. I grew up with brothers. This one? He's not normal. I saw the way he watched your lot putting up the tape and tent yesterday. All afternoon he was at that window of his.'

And you were at yours, Noah thought, *to see him doing that.*

'Everyone's curious,' he said, 'when something like this happens.'

She coloured, and looked away. 'Yes, of course. All I meant was Terry's a saint to put up with it. I've heard some of the stuff that boy shouts at him, and I can't believe I'm the only one he watches. Beth's got a better figure, for one thing. Of course she's not showing yet.' She examined the marks she'd rubbed on her arms. '*I* couldn't do it.'

Noah moved past her, into the kitchen. 'Where are the tea bags? I'll make us a cuppa.'

Julie followed him, bringing mugs from a cupboard and a box of PG Tips. She took a bottle of milk from the fridge, sniffing at it when she unscrewed the cap. Through the window Noah could see the crew at work in the garden, measuring out a plot of earth that corresponded with the plans provided by Ian Merrick.

'Why did you think we might have found drugs?'

'Because of who was living here before the houses went up. Travellers, or are we allowed to call them gypsies again now? I can never keep up.' For the first time since he'd knocked at her door, she flashed a smile. 'Dirty beggars, whatever we call them. I found a condom out there, first week we moved in. Still in its wrapper, but . . .' She stroked at her ankle with her bare toes, watching Noah from the edge of her eye, waiting for the kettle to boil.

He realised, dismayed, that she was flirting with him. 'Did you keep it?'

Her eyebrows climbed. 'Cheeky!'

'It could be evidence.'

His tone deflated her. 'Oh.' She turned towards the garden again, folding her left arm under her chest. No wedding ring on her finger. 'No, I threw it away.'

He saw her bite at her lip. She was nervous. The flirting was her way of trying to keep control of what was happening. Bodies in her neighbour's garden, a bunker under the trampoline where her kids played. 'Mr Lowry. He doesn't live here?'

'What?' Her voice was dull, like her eyes. 'Oh, you mean their dad. We're not married, never were. I didn't see the point. It wasn't like he was ever going to hang around.' She scratched her ankle with her toes. 'Worse than the bloody gypsies, he was. At least they only left johnny-bags. He left two kids.' She winced as she said it, and crouched quickly to smooth a finger at the scratch mark on her ankle, hiding her face from Noah. 'They were just little kiddies, weren't they? Next door. That's what they're saying. Not much older than Beth's two . . .' Her voice swung away from her own worry, gratefully.

She straightened, combing her hair with her fingers. 'How's

she coping? I bet it's knocked them sideways. I'd ring them, if you'd give me a number.'

'You can reach Beth on her mobile.'

Julie nodded, glancing away. Noah wondered whether she knew Beth's mobile phone number, if the two women were friends, or only neighbours.

'So where've you put them? Beth and the kids? Somewhere safe, I suppose. She'll be in a state with the baby coming, and she loved that house, couldn't wait to get settled here.'

'They're somewhere safe, and it's only temporary.'

'Is *he* with them?'

'Terry?' Noah knew that she didn't mean Terry.

'Clancy.' She clenched her teeth around the boy's name. 'I bet he's sorry he's missing this bloody circus.' She nodded at the kitchen window.

'You think he'd want to watch this? It's not terribly exciting, is it?'

'Nobody's in a bikini . . .' Julie took a step nearer, then stopped, shaking her head. 'How much longer, until they know what's down there?' Her face was gaunt and colourless, the ceiling lights finding out every line and furrow. In the garden, she'd looked trim and attractive. In here, she looked old, almost ugly.

Noah said gently, 'I honestly don't know.'

'Have you talked to Carol Fincher yet? Her Lizzie went missing a while back. She must be counting her blessings . . .' She shot Noah a look. 'I suppose you're talking to Doug Cole.'

'Do you know Mr Cole?'

Her eyes slid away. 'I thought so, but then a thing like this happens . . . I mean, *someone* put those kiddies down there. Makes you wonder if you know anything about anyone.'

25

The Doyles' temporary accommodation was as featureless as a prison block. Nothing like the comfortable home they'd been forced to leave.

'It's so hard to stay neat.' Beth stole a look at Marnie, making her conscious of the crispness of her shirt collar. 'It was hard enough in our own home, but here . . .' She reached for an empty carrier bag that'd slipped to the floor. Pulled it flat, knotting it three times in three places, making the bag toddler-friendly. 'Terry's not here. He's working.' She crouched, running her hands under the table before squinting at her fingertips. Something shiny was sticking into the pad of her right finger: a metal staple. She pulled it free and put the finger to her mouth, sucking at the puncture.

'How're the kids doing?' Marnie asked.

'Tommy's sleeping a lot. Carmen's always been a handful. Terrible twos. Now terrible threes . . .' A sound from the floor above made her eyes scare in that direction.

Marnie guessed all the noises in this house were alien. At Blackthorn Road, Beth hadn't been jumpy, not even when the police turned her garden into a crime scene.

'On the phone you said you were worried about Clancy. How's he doing?'

'He hates it here,' Beth said. 'He hated Blackthorn Road, but at least he had his own room. Now he has to share with Tommy and Carmen.'

She allowed that: Clancy sharing a room with her children? Marnie tried to imagine the measure of trust needed to let that happen.

'Do you know how much longer we'll have to be here?' Beth pushed the hair from her eyes. Her hands were dirty, like her hair.

'It's too soon to say. I can promise we're not wasting time. But the investigation needs to be thorough.'

'Of course, I understand. If they were my babies . . .' Her eyes clouded, and she turned her head away. She looked as if she'd lost weight. Perhaps it was morning sickness.

'Is there no one who can come and help out? It's a lot to take on. It was a lot before, but it has to be harder now that we've moved you here.'

'Clancy's angry.' The words burst out of Beth. She put her fingers to her mouth, turned the frightened gesture into sucking at the spot where the staple had stuck. 'He was angry at Blackthorn Road, and he's worse here.'

'In what way?'

'Just . . . you know. Teenage-boy angry.' She bit her lip. 'You know.'

I do know, Marnie thought, *but not in the way you think.*

'Are you worried about his behaviour? Beth? Do you feel threatened by his behaviour?'

'No, no. Nothing like that. It's just . . . I found something, in his room. I wasn't snooping, just cleaning.' She put her hand in her pocket and pulled out a scrunched-up sheet of paper from which she extracted a foil strip of pills. 'I found these.'

Eight pills inside plastic bubbles covered by foil. The name of the medicine was printed across the foil at repeating intervals: haloperidol.

'I looked it up. Haloperidol is an anti-psychotic.' Beth twisted her hands together. 'He's not supposed to be on any medication. We're supposed to be told about stuff like that.'

'You think these are Clancy's pills? Where exactly did you find them?'

'Hidden inside a sock, in the bag he brought from Blackthorn Road. Not his duffle bag, he takes that everywhere with him. This's the bag we packed for him, when you moved us out. It was in the room he's sharing.' Her face creased in pain. 'Tommy could've found those, taken them even.'

The strip was intact. None of the eight pills had been popped from the foil.

'Do you think Clancy is taking these, or that he needs to take them? You said he's angry.'

'Yes, but not . . . not psychotic. He's rude, to Terry especially. I suppose it's a male thing, territorial. Terry's always talking to him, trying to make peace. But Clancy . . . He's testing the boundaries. A lot of it's hormones.' She tried to dismiss it with a movement of her hands, as if she was physically placing her anxiety aside, tying a knot in its neck the way she'd tied the empty carrier bag, to remove the risk of harm to anyone in the house. 'Terry says it's normal . . . I haven't told him about the pills, or the women.'

'What women?' Marnie pulled out a chair and sat at the kitchen table.

Beth sat facing her. 'I've seen Clancy talking with women. Not neighbours. Strangers, and older than him. A *lot* older. At least, I only saw one of them properly, but she was my age, a bit older.' She put her hands on the table. 'They looked . . . *wrong*. Their clothes, the way they were . . .

flirting with him. Who flirts with a teenage boy? *I* wouldn't. *You* wouldn't.'

'Where did you see this? And when?'

'Up on the housing estate. We've told him to stay away from that place. It's not safe, for one thing. You hear these stories about fights, drugs.' She looked at the pills on the table.

'But you saw Clancy there, with these women. When was this?'

'Two weeks ago? That was the first time, and then again the day before yesterday. I tried to talk to him about it, but he got angry. I was going to tell Terry but then all this happened, with the garden and . . .' She turned her hands up on the table, empty.

'Was it the same women, both times?'

'Yes. And they're *odd*. That's why I thought I'd better tell you. The way they dressed, the way they were . . . I've seen lots of women on the estate. They don't look like you and me, but these two? They're odd. Old-fashioned, like they've not bought clothes in about ten years. No make-up, hair all scraggy.' She rubbed at her wrists. 'They gave me the creeps, if I'm honest.'

'They were flirting with Clancy. Was he flirting back?'

'No . . . He was smoking, though. They all were.' Beth's eyes clouded. 'Something else we've banned. I daren't tell Terry right now, not with everything else that's going on.'

'Could you speak with someone in Foster Services? At least find out if Clancy's been given a prescription of any kind?'

'Perhaps, but they're always so busy. And what can they do, really? Except take him away, and that's not what we want. He needs a home.' She said this as if the thought exhausted and sustained her in equal measure, the way a weary traveller will repeat the mantra of how many miles she's come. 'Terry would never give up on him. He just wouldn't.'

'Terry wouldn't want you under stress, especially not at the moment.'

'There's always stress. It's what we signed up for.' She pressed her mouth to a flat line, looking away.

'How did you and Terry meet?' Marnie asked, hoping to steer Beth back into the conversation. She wanted to know more about the women who'd been talking with Clancy; something sounded wrong there. She didn't know, yet, what to make of the pills.

'He did the gardens where I worked. Landscaping, you know. It was just gravel and pots, but then they brought Terry in and he transformed it.' Beth flushed, looking happy for the first time. 'He's got so much energy and focus, but he's quiet too. I had to make the first move.' The flush spread to her neck. 'I'd never done that before!'

'It worked out. Look at the two of you now. Where were you working, when you met?'

'For a law firm in Leytonstone, just an office job. I didn't mind giving it up.' Beth wiped her hands on her skirt. 'Terry misses the garden.'

'We'll put it back together, just as soon as we can.'

'Terry will sort it out. It's hard work, but hard work helps sometimes, doesn't it?'

'Yes, it does.'

'He's always working. Busy. I think it's why he's so good at coping with everything.'

'Even with Clancy the way he is?'

'Terry never loses his temper. He's the most patient man I know. He makes time for Clancy, no matter what. Even when he comes home wiped out after work, he'll go and talk with him about his day.'

'Is Clancy here now?' Marnie asked.

'He went to the park. We let him do that, as long as we know where he is.' Beth looked as if someone had pulled a plug on her face, its features drooping and blurring. 'He should be back soon.' She pushed the pills towards Marnie. 'Would you take these? I don't want them in the house.'

'Of course.' As an afterthought, Marnie nodded at the scrunched-up sheet of paper that Beth had taken from her pocket. 'Was that in Clancy's room too?'

'Just rubbish. School notes, I suppose.' Beth handed it across. 'Or doodles; he's always making doodles.'

Marnie smoothed the page flat, a cheap sheet of lined paper, torn from a notebook.

Scored deep into the cheap paper: circles, joined to smaller circles. Interlinking, repeated at intervals.

The pattern was as familiar as the freckles on Ed's wrist.

Marnie hadn't seen it in five years. But she knew it, instantly and intimately.

The back of her neck clenched.

She folded the page until it was small enough to slip into her pocket with the pills. 'The duffle bag, the one you said Clancy takes everywhere. Do you know what's in it?'

'A change of clothes, money, an Oyster card . . . It's normal, Terry says. They call it a go-bag. So he's ready to leave at a moment's notice.'

'A go-bag,' Marnie repeated. The clench in her neck hurt.

'Lots of them have one, teenagers in foster care. It's an insurance policy. Terry says the day Clancy unpacks the go-bag, that's when we'll know we're doing our job properly. We want him to feel safe. For all the kids to feel safe.'

Beth's face shadowed. 'Perhaps we're asking too much. After what you found in that bunker . . . I've never felt less safe in my whole life.' She pushed the hair from her forehead. 'Perhaps we should all have go-bags. Perhaps that's the best anyone can do.'

26

Five years ago

Kate Larbie stands at Marnie's shoulder, so that they are looking at the diary together.

It should feel comradely. Kate's the same height as Marnie and a good friend, one of the best. But Marnie has grown these spines all over, like a porcupine. She rattles. Even when she's standing still, she rattles, warning people to stay away.

The words of a childhood rhyme keep looping in her head: 'Porcupines are always single, poor old 'pines they must not mingle.'

She knows that the rhyme, like the spines, is in her head for protection, cladding against the cold reality of getting on with her life, but there are times when she wishes she had no protection, when she longs to rub up against that reality, even at the cost of getting cut, because she's sick of feeling numb. Sick, and scared.

What if I never feel anything ever again?

What if I only ever see them as photos, or bloody footprints on the kitchen floor?

She wants her life back.

Not the way it was before; she knows she can never have that. Just the connection, the ability to put out her hand and touch the person standing right next to her, instead of feeling she's inside a torture device with the spikes on the outside.

'I wish I could be more helpful,' Kate says. 'But honestly? The patterns could be anything.'

Circles within circles, interlinked, repeated at intervals.

'They could be anything.'

Kate is a documents examiner. She's subjected the diary to every test she knows, and some she didn't, to appease Marnie's need for answers. She wants to help.

'Not anything,' Marnie insists. 'You've ruled out a secret code, for starters.'

'I have,' Kate agrees. She looks sad.

Everyone around Marnie is sad.

It's something else she's getting sick and scared of.

'He wouldn't need to write in code,' she tells Kate. 'My parents were the last people to snoop in someone's room.'

'Of course . . .' Kate slips a hand through the spines to touch Marnie's wrist, pressing her thumb to the spot where the bone's too prominent.

Now the diary's bathed in white light, but the tears don't fall, drying so fast Marnie's eyes itch from the salt. She presses back at Kate's hand, numbly.

Marnie is wearing a new suit, bought in a panic because none of her other clothes fit properly; she's lost too much weight. The new suit is sleek and expensive, charcoal grey. She's thrown out her black clothes, fearing an extended period of sympathy if people think she's kitted out in mourning. Some people – most people – still can't look her in the eye.

Kate says, 'Have you spoken with Ed?'

Marnie shakes her head, then nods. 'I will, soon.'

As soon as she's figured out a way to separate Ed from his job title.

Victim Support – she grows a spine for each syllable.

Porcupines are always single, poor old 'pines they must not mingle . . .

There wasn't much in her parents' house that belonged to Stephen, but there was this.

A hardback diary bound in manila card, in which Stephen had recorded dates, the start and end of school terms. The date of their murders he had left blank, pristine on the page.

Marnie would have preferred to see the date slashed in black, or ripped from the book. Stephen had marked a date later in the same month, some school trip or other, and this led the prosecution to argue that the killings were unpremeditated, as if otherwise he might have written 'On trial for double murder' after the date in question.

Of course she's not allowed to employ humour in that way, even if it makes her feel better, more human. She must get used to hushed voices when she enters a room, and the shift of eyes away from her. No one likes a victim in their midst. She can't blame them. She's going out of her way to avoid victims. Their loss gets in the way of solving whatever crime is responsible for it, like a hazardous spill holding back a fire crew.

'It's not a logo,' she says to Kate Larbie. 'But I don't think it's just doodling. He's not the type. Everything he does is deliberate. You saw him in court. He doesn't fidget, he doesn't daydream. He's focused. Everything he does is focused. So these,' she reaches through her shield of spines to put a finger on the page, 'mean something.'

Kate has covered the open pages of the diary with a square of magnifying glass.

Marnie's finger leaves a mark, a print. The heat in her eyes paints it red, like the prints in her parents' hallway where he sat waiting for the police to come.

Circles joined to smaller circles, the pattern repeated at intervals.

This is what Stephen Keele drew in his diary in the days leading up to the one when he killed Greg and Lisa Rome.

Circles joined to smaller circles, empty rings, like eyes on the page.

Marnie refuses to believe that the circles mean nothing. She refuses to repeat the healing mantra that says, 'Some crimes are without meaning,' even though she knows it's true and she's been told by everyone from Tim Welland to Lexie, her therapist, that this crime was like that: meaningless. She refuses to believe it.

So she puts out spines and she asks questions, of everyone.

Victims rarely ask questions. That's for detectives to do. She's proving a point, putting distance between her and the crime, another layer of protection like the new suit, but what alternative does she have? Should she stop asking why?

Why and why and why . . .

She doesn't think she can. The questions are all she has and it's not certain, yet, that there are no answers.

He's only fourteen years old.

He can't keep quiet for ever.

People at the secure unit, specialists, are trained in extracting questions from kids who've gone off the rails, even ones who've done it as spectacularly as Stephen.

She doesn't know, yet, that he has spines that make hers look like freckles. That he's as empty of answers as the circles he draws, again and again, in the hardback diary.

She doesn't know that she will see those same circles again five years later, when she's asking different questions but with the same intent.

To heal someone's hurt. To take home answers so that someone can lie down in the dark and weep, until the world comes back upright.

27

Now

Marnie sat in the car outside the Doyles' temporary home, resting her hands on the wheel and watching the street for Clancy Brand. She needed to see the boy in daylight, not hiding behind a curtain or standing in the shadows. She didn't trust her memory not to make a monster out of a normal teenage boy.

Her phone buzzed. 'Noah. What've you got?'

'GPR are just finishing up. They've found six bunkers, none of them filled in.' Noah sounded relieved. Did he?

'Tell me.'

'They're all empty. Nothing with the right mass to be bodies, they seem fairly confident about that. There's a problem, though, at number 8.'

Number 8 was where Douglas Cole lived.

'What kind of problem?'

'Mr Cole is home, finally. And he's unhappy about the GPR team going into his garden. Very unhappy. He's asking for you.'

Marnie held the phone to her ear, tenderly, because her

skin felt thin and hypersensitive, all her nerve endings alert, on edge. 'Have they gone in?'

They had the paperwork, nothing Cole could do about that.

'Only just. It's getting a bit noisy here. The press want an update. They're asking for you.'

'Who's asking, in particular?'

'Hang on. He gave me his card . . .' She heard Noah searching his pockets and she shut her eyes, mouthing the name in synch with his next words: 'Adam Fletcher.'

'Tell Mr Cole I'm on my way. And do what you can to keep the press wide of number 8. I'll deal with it when I get there.'

Through the car's windscreen: a loping figure in a hooded jacket.

High shoulders, narrow build.

His hands stuffed into his pockets, his head down.

Clancy Brand.

28

'Is she coming?' Adam Fletcher rolled an unlit cigarette between the fingers of his right hand.

Noah hoped he wasn't expecting a light. He was surprised the man wasn't self-conscious about smoking so near to a crime scene. But Fletcher didn't look like he cared much what other people thought of his bad habits. He was aggressively good-looking, at least a couple of inches taller than the slouch in his spine suggested, and healthier than anyone with a nicotine habit deserved to look. Clear skin and eyes, athletic build.

'DI Rome?' Fletcher prompted. 'Is she coming?' He nodded at the GPR team. 'That needs a statement, surely.' A drawl in his voice said he'd spent time abroad, in the US maybe.

'It's important you don't get in the way, sir. I'm sure we'll have an update soon.'

Fletcher accepted this with a nod. He snapped a disposable lighter at the cigarette, his eyes on Julie Lowry's house, his free hand shoved into the pocket of his Levis. He wasn't dressed like the others and he was standing away from the crowd, wearing old jeans and a dark jumper, knackered boat shoes on bare feet. If he hadn't presented the press card, Noah wouldn't have guessed he was a journalist. 'Any chance of a scoop?' he asked next.

Noah smiled at him. 'What do you think?'

'I think she's got you well trained.' Fletcher's teeth were too white for a smoker's. Maybe he had them bleached every six months. He shut an eye against the smoke lazing from his mouth, and thumbed a crumb of tobacco from his tongue. 'Where'd you put the kids?'

'I'm sorry?'

Fletcher jerked his head in the direction of the Doyles' house. 'Clancy,' he drew out the name like a splinter from a thumb, 'and the others . . . You moved them all out, right?'

Noah shook his head, sticking to the smile. 'Sorry, I need to get on with my job.' He paused. 'You understand, because you're *just doing yours*. That's right, isn't it?'

Fletcher gave him a dazzling smile. 'All any of us can do.'

He was the second person in the same hour who'd wanted to know about Clancy. As if there was something remarkable about a teenage boy being fostered in a house with a secret burial chamber in its garden, as if the two things had to be connected.

Noah needed to speak with Marnie before she walked into this. Not just the press and Douglas Cole; the rubberneckers had started a cordon of their own. Misery merchants, Ron Carling called them. He'd have tried to break up the crowd if he was here. It was one of the reasons Marnie kept Carling wide of crime scenes.

Noah wondered whether Ron had uncovered anything more about the website selling tinned food. The preppers could be a blind alley. Julie Lowry thought the travellers were a better avenue of investigation. Condoms in the garden . . . Noah couldn't see the connection to their boys. No evidence of abuse, Fran had said. And no evidence that anyone had opened the bunker since the boys died down there, years before the travellers came, and went.

So why was Douglas Cole in such a state?

Noah moved away from Adam Fletcher, carrying the scent of the man's cigarette in his clothes. It reminded him of Sol. When his phone played Dan's tune, Noah knew he was calling about Sol; sensory premonition.

'Where is he?'

Dan said, 'He's here. How did you know . . .?'

'I smelt him.' Noah carried the call away from the crowd.

'You . . . Okay.' Dan laughed, persuasively, like someone who expected the favour he was about to ask to meet with resistance. 'So he's here, at the flat. I said he could stay.'

'Why?'

'To be friendly . . . He's your little brother.'

'No, why does he need to stay?'

'He hasn't said. Just that he wants to crash for a couple of days.'

'Does he have a bag?'

'What? Probably, does it matter?' He heard Dan drop his voice and walk through to the kitchen, where the floors were wood and threw echoes.

'If he has a bag,' Noah said, 'that means he's hiding out. It probably means he's pissed off Mum and Dad. We're his last resort.'

'Because he couldn't drop in on his big brother without an agenda? Look, he just wants a bed for the night. We can do that.'

'Find out if he has a bag,' Noah said, 'but don't open it. Don't even touch it.'

Dan said, 'Seriously? Only I was going to get pizza and Beck's.'

'I'm working. I'll be late. Don't let him smoke in the flat.'
He ended the call and pocketed the phone.
Where was Marnie?

29

Clancy's go-bag was slung across one hunched shoulder. Inside the hoody, his face was pale, pixelated by teenage spots.

Marnie climbed from the car. 'Can I have a word?'

The boy's eyes slid about the street, over parked cars, along the houses, anywhere but her face, her questions. His shoulders were so high they nearly topped his head. Outsized hands and feet, like all adolescents, a width to his wrists that warned her to keep her distance. He was strong. Skinny, but strong; already his shoulders were filling out.

'Can I have a word?' she said again.

'You can have two: piss off.'

Funny kid. Bit of a cliché, but funny. Even slightly reassuring; kids were rude to the police every day of the week. He was just a typical teenager. Except he wasn't.

'I have something of yours. Something I thought you might need.'

She watched for a reaction, but he just shoved his stare away from her, to the other end of the street. 'I don't need anything.' Contempt in his voice, but sullen, the sort kids like this reserved for authority figures.

'Not even your haloperidol?'

'What?' The word meant nothing to him. Why would it? He wasn't a dispensing chemist, or a pharmaceutical technician.

'Your pills,' Marnie said.

He kicked a foot at the tarmac. 'I don't know what you're talking about.' He was wearing beaten-up Converse All Stars, their laces ripped out, caked with dirt the colour of the mud in the garden at Blackthorn Road.

Her neck was hurting her, standing this close to this kid. He stank of pheromones. He wouldn't let her see his eyes. He was stronger than he looked, and *hiding* . . .

The hood, hands buried in his pockets, high shoulders either side of his head; she knew he was hiding something.

'Clancy, when your dad found that bunker—'

His eyes thumped to her face. 'He's not my fucking dad.'

She nearly took a step back, curling her hands in her pockets.

'Terry,' she corrected. 'When Terry found that bunker . . . did you know it was there?'

He didn't give an answer, just stood with his black eyes branding her face before loping away, up the street. Heading to the house where Beth was waiting, where he shared a room with Carmen and Tommy Doyle.

Marnie really hoped she hadn't given him a fresh reason to be angry at the people who were trying to help him.

30

'How's Beth?' Noah asked as Marnie climbed from her car on Blackthorn Road.

'Stressed.' Her quick eyes scanned his face. 'What's happened?'

'The rubberneckers have landed.' He nodded back towards the house.

Marnie's stare swung in that direction, her eyes snagging on something she didn't like.

Noah turned and saw Adam Fletcher standing apart from the other reporters, still smoking. Debbie Tanner was nearby. 'That's Fletcher, the one who was asking for a statement. He thinks you have me well trained . . .'

'Does he?' She looked unimpressed. 'Let's go and see Mr Cole.' She started in the direction of number 8. 'How did you get on with the other neighbours?'

'Julie thinks gypsies had something to do with it. And she doesn't like Clancy much.'

'Julie?'

'Number 12. Immediate neighbour, single mum, lonely.'

Marnie shielded her eyes with her hand to look at him. 'She flirted with you?'

'Okay, that was . . . uncanny. How'd you know?'

She smiled and shook her head. 'What's her problem with Clancy?'

'He watches her from the window when she's sunbathing. And not just her.' Noah shrugged. 'It sounded like she was watching just as much as he was. Maybe he *does* look at her when she's sunbathing, but she was reading more into it, as if he was a bit too interested in the bunker, the boys.'

'You didn't believe her?'

'He's just a kid. The way she said it . . . she made him sound like a psycho.'

'And kids can't be psychos.' Marnie stopped, twelve feet from Cole's house.

'I'm not saying that. But our boys died four, five years ago. Clancy would've been ten. And he wasn't living here back then . . .'

'Do we know that for sure? I don't. I don't know anything about him, only what the Doyles told us, and they don't know much more than that.' She moved so that he couldn't see her face, only her profile. She was watching the press pack. 'Beth found a stash of anti-psychotics in his room.' She put her hand in her pocket, took out a foil strip of pills.

Noah didn't touch it. He remembered his advice to Dan not to touch any bag that Sol might've brought to their flat. 'Clancy's on anti-psychotic meds?'

'Beth doesn't know. She says they'd have been told if he was on medication. That's a basic requirement on the fostering service, to share information of that kind.'

'What did Terry say?'

'I haven't asked him yet. He wasn't at the house just now and Beth says she's not told him about the pills, or about the women she's seen Clancy hanging out with over on the estate. Two of them, much older than him. Odd, Beth said. Old clothes, grubby . . .'

Marnie hadn't taken her eyes off the reporters. Debbie was chatting with Fletcher, her body language making Julie's look demure.

'Surely,' Noah said, 'they wouldn't let anyone foster a kid who needed medication like that. For one thing, how could they be sure he'd take the pills? It makes no sense.'

'Maybe we need to ask the foster service some awkward questions about Clancy Brand.'

He held out his hand for the foil strip. 'Can I see?'

Marnie handed it across.

The name of the strip meant nothing. None of the pills had been popped from their plastic bubbles. 'Eight pills. I wouldn't call it a stash. More like a souvenir.'

'A souvenir of what?'

'I don't know. But eight pills isn't a stash. It isn't even a prescription. Unless he's hiding more pills, in other places.' He felt the weight of his phone in his pocket, and wondered how long it would be before Dan tried calling back. 'He didn't seem psychotic to me. I know I haven't see much of him, but . . .'

'Beth's scared of him. She says he's angry. I saw him at the safe house just now. He was coming back from the park. Something's not right with him. I've seen a lot of angry kids, but Clancy? Something's not right.'

Noah hadn't heard this note in her voice before. Cautious, as if she was feeling her way. No, more than that, as if she was afraid. Of Clancy, or what he represented? Her past had long arms, he knew that much.

'I'll look into it,' he promised. 'Ron's tracing the travellers. Maybe one of them will remember something.'

'Fran should be finishing the extra tests. With luck, we'll finally have names.' Marnie unfolded her arms, shaking the tension from her shoulders. 'Right, let's get this over with.'

They turned in the direction of Cole's house, stopping

when one of the GPR team signalled from the pavement. Serious, a warning in his signal and one eye on the press.

Noah's chest contracted.

Don't let it be bodies. You said no more bodies.

'You'll want to see this.' The man nodded towards Cole's house.

Next door was where the Finchers lived with their little girl, Lizzie.

Protests crowded behind Noah's teeth. He had to lock his jaw to stop them getting out. He couldn't go back inside one of those bunkers, not right now. He couldn't.

Marnie touched a hand to his wrist. 'I've got this.'

Noah shook his head, but before he could speak, a noise travelled from the back garden at number 8, echoing through the hollow walls of the house as it came . . .

A wail, high-pitched and keening, like a child's.

31

A weatherproofed shed stood at the foot of Douglas Cole's garden, its door propped open.

Marnie and Noah crossed the lawn, accompanied by the GPR technician. As they reached the shed, Cole came out. A little man in his fifties, with a thick head of fair hair cut like a monk's, dressed in a pinstriped suit. His round face was pink, small eyes watering, mouth wide with distress that turned to relief as he spotted Marnie. 'DI Rome!'

'Mr Cole. How are you?'

He wrung her hand, shaking his head. Behind him, a second GPR technician emerged from the shed. He nodded at Marnie and Noah. 'You'll want to see this.'

Marnie didn't move straight away, letting Cole cling to her hand a moment longer before she said, 'It's all right, Mr Cole. Let me do my job.'

'It's not,' he stammered, 'what you think.' His eyes were streaming. 'It's *not.*'

'All right. Let me see.' She drew her hand free. 'DS Jake?'

Noah moved to help the man.

Cole turned away, covering his mouth with his hand. 'I'll wait here. I'll be good.'

He stood to attention, like a child.

'In that case,' Marnie nodded at Noah, 'I could use you with me.'

At first glance, it was like every other garden shed Noah had ever seen. It smelt the same too, of creosote and oil. Pots stood along shelves, tools hung from nails around the walls: garden shears; trowels; a pair of iron rods with right-angled ends. An old-fashioned lawnmower was propped in one corner, its blades freshly oiled. The shed was neat and orderly, but not obsessively so. The only striking thing was the open hole in its floor.

A manhole. Like the one in the Doyles' garden. The shed had been built around it, its base a neat cement job, home-made like the shed, leaving access to the manhole cover.

The GPR team had opened the hole.

The smell coming up was squeaky and high-pitched, like the wail Cole had let out.

It'd been opened using the two right-angled rods, Noah guessed, and easily. As if it was done on a regular basis.

Unlike any of the other bunkers in Blackthorn Road.

'Has anyone been down there?' Marnie asked the GPR technicians.

The two men shook their heads. 'We shone a torch to take a look, but we stayed up here. We knew you'd want to be the first ones down.'

Noah tried to read their expressions.

Disgust, but not horror, or not full-blown.

Not small-bodies-buried-alive horror.

Marnie held out a hand for the torch and crouched to peer into the bunker.

Noah did the same, squatting on his heels, sucking a breath at what he saw.

Eyes.

Blue and green and yellow.

Dozens and dozens of eyes, staring back at him from the blackness.

32

Noah said, 'What is that *smell*?'

'Damp course.' Marnie didn't mind the smell so much. It could have been a lot worse.

Inside Doug Cole's bunker, the walls were scratched by shadow, holding off the day's heat. Her body temperature dropped a notch as she stood at the foot of the ladder.

No bodies, so no death stench. No damp, either. Under the chemical top note, the smell wasn't black or green. It was clear and white, like standing water.

The larger dolls wore silk dresses; the smaller ones were dressed in cotton. The baby dolls had been wrapped in shawls, lying in wicker cradles. One or two looked frighteningly real.

Dozens and dozens of dolls. Teddy bears too, and wooden toys, but most of the bunker was filled with dolls.

At her side, Noah exhaled thinly.

Oh Doug . . . why did you have to play down here?

But she knew why. It felt safe. Away from prying eyes. Private.

'Did you know,' Noah pointed his torch around the bunker, 'about this?'

'The dolls, yes. Not about the bunker. He's a toy collector. Most of his house is like this.'

The bigger dolls sat on chairs and hand-painted benches, and around a low table laid with a white cloth and set for tea with doll-sized cups and plates, wooden cakes and candles. In a nursery, it would've looked charming, if a little twee. Down here, it looked sad and creepy. Tim Welland would've called it a freak show. He'd thought Cole's house was bad enough.

Marnie waited to hear what verdict Noah would pass. He wasn't speaking, still shining his torch around the walls of the bunker.

Doug had papered the walls with roses. He'd laid a Turkish rug on the floor and hung pictures. Strung bunting across the ceiling, and fairy lights, which meant he'd wired the bunker for electricity. Marnie looked for the switch and flicked it.

She and Noah stood under the spattering of light that put coloured crumbs on the tablecloth and in the laps of the seated dolls.

'Okay,' Noah said, 'that's . . . worse.'

Marnie knew what he meant. Their boys hadn't had a rug, or lights, or hand-painted furniture. Cole's playroom was a sick satire on the bunker at number 14.

'This took time. The wiring alone . . . He's known about this place for a while.' Noah looked at her. 'Did you search the shed when you were looking for Lizzie Fincher?'

'The shed's new. It wasn't here eighteen months ago.'

'But the house is like this?'

'It's odd,' she admitted. '*He's* odd. But I think he's harmless. I spent a lot of time with him eighteen months ago. And a lot of time with Lizzie Fincher and her parents. Doug was the least of my worries, back then.'

Noah processed this in silence. 'When d'you think he found the bunker?'

'Not recently. You're right. He's been busy down here for a while.'

The fairy lights painted the dolls' faces like chickenpox.

'He should have told someone,' Noah said. 'Don't you think?'

'Hard to say. It's his property, and if it was empty . . .'

'Do you think he knew about the other bunkers?'

'I don't know.' Marnie looked into the glassy stare of the largest doll. 'I hope not. This is going to look bad enough without that.'

Cole's shadow fell roundly at their feet from the open manhole overhead.

Marnie said, 'We're coming up, Mr Cole. Just give us a minute.'

He moved away without speaking. Marnie could sense his misery from twelve feet.

'Does it give you the creeps,' she asked Noah, 'being down here?'

He thought for a moment. 'At first, sure, but now? It doesn't seem so bad.' He took a last look around. 'Either you're right and he's harmless, or I'm getting used to this stuff.'

Marnie switched off the fairy lights. 'Go up.' She nodded at the ladder. 'Make us some tea. I'll be right behind you.'

She wanted a moment alone in the dark and the quiet. Away from the rubberneckers and the reporters waiting on her reappearance. DC Tanner, who'd gravitated to Adam Fletcher as easily as a spider vein to a drunk's nose. They made a handsome couple, Debbie with her curves, Adam with his arrogant height. It made Marnie want to stay down here. A bad instinct, unhelpful. She needed to get on. She'd seen what the GPR team leader had wanted her to see.

Doug Cole's playroom was a nuclear shelter, like all the others in the road. Cold War bunkers built under a field in north-east London by people afraid the atom bomb was coming. It must have been easy to imagine a disaster on that scale after the long years of the Second World War. Marnie's grandmother had spent the war overseas, but she'd often talked about the anxious mood in the capital when she returned to London. Post-Blitz paranoia warring with the country's determination to rebuild. How many people of her grandmother's generation had resorted to measures like this, holes dug underground, the laying-in of precious food supplies? Hiding places.

She climbed the ladder to where the last of the day's light was waiting. Over Cole's fence she could see the perfect lawn of the Finchers' garden, spoilt by the GPR team's exertions.

Nigel and Carol Fincher had spent a lot of money on their garden furniture; it put most of Marnie's indoor furniture to shame. On the other hand, polyrattan wasn't a look she aspired to. The borders were attractive, colourful. Eighteen months ago, the garden had been greying lawn, dead. She wondered whether Terry Doyle was responsible for the new borders.

She rolled the latex gloves from her hands and pushed them into her pocket as a heavy man in a navy suit came through the French doors on to the Finchers' decking.

'Hello,' he said across the fence. 'Carol said it was you.'

Marnie smiled at him. 'Mr Fincher, hello.'

'Quick question,' Fincher said. 'Who's paying for all this?' He gestured at the hole dug in his garden, the open manhole cover. He didn't look at Doug's shed.

'We're investigating a crime. I'm sorry it's spoilt your lawn.'

A blonde girl in school uniform trailed into the garden.

Marnie said, 'Hello, Lizzie.'

The girl looked at her, blankly. She was nearly seven now. She'd grown, but she had the same spacey look she'd had eighteen months ago, returning home with her hand in Doug Cole's, bewildered by all the fuss and questions, her eyes moving between her parents, not quite looking at either one of them, letting them take turns hugging her, taking care to share her attention equally between the two. Defence mechanism; Marnie had recognised it at a glance. Lizzie hadn't changed, just acquired an extra layer of that caution. Her stare went to the hole in the lawn, then retreated, void of curiosity. She'd learned not to ask questions, even when things looked weird. 'Dad, can I go on the internet?'

'What does Mum say?'

'She said to ask you.'

'Fine, but just until suppertime.' Fincher waited until his daughter had gone back inside before he gave a sheepish smile. 'Compromise: the secret weapon of parenting.'

'How's Carol?' Marnie asked.

'Working, she'll be working.' He nodded at the attic. 'Home office. She works from home now. Lucky her.'

Marnie detected a flavour of the old animosity in his tone, but it was neutered. This was a couple who'd raced to report each other to the police when their child disappeared. She had struggled to feel sorry for the Finchers eighteen months ago, and wondered if they were still using their only child as collateral. They'd stayed together. That was surprising.

'We patched things up,' Fincher said, 'for Lizzie's sake.'

'Good for you.' Marnie wondered how good it was for Lizzie.

'You're digging up the whole street.'

'Only this side. The side where the bunkers were built.'

Fincher came up to the fence and peered into his neighbour's garden.

'Doug must be hating this. He loves his privacy.' Sarcasm, but complacent, as if it'd become an easy habit, despising his wife's one-time friend.

'Found anything compromising over there?' His stare sharpened. 'I'm not a nosy neighbour, but Doug? Would make anyone suspicious.'

33

Douglas Cole perched on the edge of his sofa clutching a teacup to his chest. Beside him on the buttoned green velvet sat a doll the size of a five-year-old child, dressed in a frilly white pinafore with a pink sash. Her glass eyes winked every time Doug shifted.

'When did you first find out about the bunker, Mr Cole?' Noah asked.

Doug darted his eyes at Marnie, who said, 'Answer DS Jake's questions, please. That way this'll be over sooner.'

'Eight months ago, when I ordered the shed. They wanted to know about the conditions for laying a foundation. I dug a bit and that's when I found it.'

'You didn't report it?'

He shook his head. 'I didn't think. I mean, it wasn't very exciting. Just an empty bunker, nothing down there.'

'Nothing.'

'Nothing,' he said emphatically.

'You didn't think it was strange, finding an empty bunker in your garden?'

'Well, obviously someone had broken a rule or two.' He drank a mouthful of tea. The movement made the doll rock beside him and he repositioned it matter-of-factly before he continued. 'It was obviously post-war, from the concrete. I know a bit about these things. Disused London is one of my hobbies.'

His other hobby winked her blue glass eyes at Noah.

'So you didn't tell anyone about it?'

'No one.' Doug set his cup down in its saucer, looking at Noah with open apology. 'If I'd thought for a second there might be another bunker . . . I'd have gone directly to the police.' He looked beseechingly at Marnie, who fielded his glance with a nod towards Noah.

'So you thought your bunker was the only one? Was that common for post-war bunkers?'

'It wasn't unusual. I didn't think my neighbours would want to know, if I'm honest. They find me enough of a trial as it is. Most of them won't talk to me in the street, only Terry, and he's friends with everyone. The rest give me a wide berth, but I'm used to that. Par for the course, you might say.'

'Why do they find you a trial?' Noah asked.

Cole blushed to the tips of his ears. 'I'm odd,' he said simply, 'I do know that. But my . . . oddities do no harm. If they did, then I would find a way to curb them.' He looked sideways, at the doll. 'I'm a collector, but I'm not a deviant, much as you might think the two things would be neater hand in hand. Children like the toys. That causes problems, of course.'

He rubbed at the end of his nose. 'I suppose it boils down to this: certain people see me as the Child Catcher, but really I'm the Toymaker.' The corners of his mouth turned down. 'I'm Benny Hill.' He waited to see if Noah would acknowledge the reference, then added, '*Chitty Chitty Bang Bang*. Ian Fleming wrote the screenplay, you know.'

'No one knew about the bunker except you. You didn't tell anyone else.'

'No one.' His ears were still pink, like a scolded child's. 'I'm sorry if that was wrong of me, but I just wanted a little privacy. And the extra space, of course. My collection's getting out of hand.' He looked around, as Noah had done when they entered the room.

Every spare surface was filled with toys and games, spinning tops and stuffed animals. A life-size baby giraffe stood in one corner. There were bears and elephants, dolls with cloth faces or stiff plastic joints, two sets of bongo drums and any number of dented trumpets. A guitar with its strings curling like a walrus's whiskers was propped on top of a DJ's turntable. Moths had eaten dimples into several rag dolls. And toy monkeys, dozens of them, all shapes and sizes. The one on top was holding a pair of cymbals between cloth paws, a red velvet cap set at a jaunty angle on its woolly head.

'You didn't talk to anyone else,' Noah repeated, 'about the bunker.'

'I didn't.' Was he telling the truth?

'You didn't think that one bunker in a field was odd? You say this is a hobby. Disused London. You didn't think there might be more of them?'

'I wondered, of course. But I didn't like to ask questions.' Doug spread his hands. 'Everyone's entitled to privacy, aren't they? If they're doing no harm, I mean.'

'You didn't want to find who built the bunkers? If it was my hobby, I'd want to know.'

'I have other hobbies. And I don't like to stir things up, asking questions, being a nosy neighbour. It's not my style.'

His suit was bespoke. Expensive, like his shoes. A dapper little man, well turned out.

'I know how this looks, of course I do. But I'm harmless. I give you my word.'

'Benny Hill,' Noah said.

Doug nodded, still blushing. 'Benny Hill.'

34

'You don't like him for this?' Noah asked Marnie, as they left Cole's house.

'For the boys? No. Do you?'

'No, but I'm not sure he was telling the truth the whole time. When he said he'd not talked with anyone about the bunker . . . that sounded like a lie.'

Marnie's phone buzzed and she answered it. 'DS Carling, what've you got?' She switched the phone to conference, so that Noah could hear Carling's reply.

'House-to-house have a name.' There was an edge of excitement in Ron's voice. 'A woman. One of the travellers living in the field before Merrick got them moved on.'

'A woman,' Marnie repeated.

'Someone on the estate remembers her having photos of two small boys.'

'You said you had a name.'

'Connie. No surname.'

'What about names for the boys?'

'He only remembers photos. He's an old chap, seemed a bit dozy. But they were brothers, he was sure of that. Little boys, about five and seven. He says Connie called them her angels.'

'We'd better speak with him.' Marnie checked her watch. 'In the morning. Maybe he'll remember more after a night's sleep. Text the details, will you? Thanks.'

'Are you sure you don't want to do it now?' Noah said. 'We're on the ground anyway.'

She could see traces of his earlier claustrophobia, and knew he would keep going until she told him to stop. 'We need some sleep. Let's regroup first thing in the morning. We can start with Ron's new witness.'

She checked the text that Carling had sent. 'Denis Walton, Flat 57 Arlington Court. Get some rest in the meantime.'

'Not much chance of that. We've got Sol staying.'

'Your brother? Have fun.'

'Sol's idea of fun?' Noah shook his head. 'You wouldn't see me first thing in the morning if I did.'

35

'S'up, bro?'

Sol was sprawled on Noah's sofa. Designer jeans and acid-pink hoody, dazzlingly new trainers on his feet. World-beating, shit-eating grin on his face.

'Where's Dan?' Noah asked.

'Bathroom?' Sol shrugged his shoulders. Casual but wired. Had he taken something?

'You can help with supper, if you're staying.'

'Sure.' The pink hoody was like being mugged by Valentine's Day. Sol's eyes were all over the room, shining like his smile. 'Looking good, bro . . .' He'd taken something.

Noah looked like he felt: shit.

He went through to the kitchen. Empty bottles of Beck's by the bin, toast-crumbed plates in the sink. Noah didn't need to be a detective to figure out how Sol had spent his afternoon. He filled the kettle with the idea of making coffee, then changed his mind and got his own bottle of beer from the fridge. Fucked if he was playing the role of designated driver just because his kid brother was sprawled on the sofa off his head on whatever he'd taken to get up the nerve to come here, knowing how warm Noah's welcome would be.

'Hey . . .' Dan appeared behind him. 'When did you get back?'

'Just now.' He checked Dan's pupils when they kissed. Sol liked company when he was on a bender and Dan had been known to indulge, back in the day.

Dan saw him checking and dropped his hands from Noah's hips. 'Seriously? Just because Sol's a bit shiny?'

Noah moved away, to get a bottle-opener. 'Did he tell you why he's here?'

Dan crossed the kitchen to close the door, lowering his voice. 'He just needs a place to crash for a couple of days. I think he misses you. You're his big brother, and yes, maybe he's in trouble of some kind, but can't he come to his brother when he's in trouble?'

'Depends on the trouble.' Noah took a long drink from the bottle. He needed to eat something if he was going to get drunk. And he was going to get drunk.

Dan stood watching him. 'What happened at work? You look done in.'

'Yes, investigating dead kids'll do that to you.' He hated the flippant score in his voice, but couldn't help it. Sol wasn't the only one who reverted to childhood behaviour patterns in the company of his sibling. 'I spent the afternoon standing in a pit where two little boys were buried alive. Sorry if that disqualifies me from membership of the shiny club.'

Dan weighed his mood. 'I'll order pizza.'

'Sorry,' Noah said, meaning it this time. 'I'll be better when I've eaten.'

'I know.' Dan smiled at him. 'I'm sorry about your crap day.'

'We can fix it. We always do.'

Noah took the beer to the sitting room, dropping into an armchair opposite Sol, who looked half asleep on the sofa. 'How long are you staying?'

Sol didn't open his eyes. 'Couple of days?'

'What'd you do?'

'Nothing . . .'

'Nothing would be one night. You did something. Pissed off Dad for starters, otherwise you'd be back home.'

Sol cracked an eye at him. Noah smiled, knowing it would unnerve his brother. Sol had come prepared for anger, expecting it, in fact. The smile caught him off guard.

'Dad's okay,' Sol said slowly, feeling his way. 'He's good.'

Noah lifted the bottle and drank. 'And Mum?'

If Sol was welcome at their parents' house, he wouldn't be here. He went home when his ego needed a stroke, when life made him feel small and he wanted to be bigger. In their mum's eyes, Sol was always a big man. Her little boy, all grown up. When he got too big, out of his depth, that was when he came to Noah, knowing he'd get cut back down to size. It was a pattern, predictable. Noah said again, 'How's Mum?'

Sol attempted a shrug. 'You know Mum, bro. She's always got something going on, always busy with her brushes.'

Which would have been okay had Rosa been an artist. But Sol meant cleaning brushes. He meant brushes and cloths and disinfectant sprays, floor polish and scouring pads.

'How bad is it?' Noah drank, steadily, for his own sake. It was just possible that Sol was here because he was scared to be in the house when Rosa was on one of her cleaning binges.

Sol said, 'It's bad, bro.' He wouldn't look at Noah, searching around the room still. Hiding in plain view. They'd both learned to do that, as kids. The difference was that Sol hadn't learned when to stop.

'Where's Dad?'

'Away on a job. Just me and her, bro . . .' Sol rubbed at his eyes. 'Me and her.'

'Should I go round?'

'Yeah, if you want a shitload of earache.' Sol risked a glance at him. 'Wouldn't, though. Not for a coupla days.'

Wait for the worst of the binge to pass, he meant.

'If Dad's away, that means she's on her own. That's not good.'

'Nothing's good. You know how it goes.' There was a moment when all the world's misery was on his brother's face, but it passed and he grinned at Noah. 'So, pizza, yeah?'

'Pizza,' Noah agreed. He considered his brother's grin, and the misery behind it. 'Do you want to come out with Dan and me?'

'For real?'

'No, I was winding you up. You can stay here while we're out on the razz . . . Yes, for real.'

'Pizza's on the way.' Dan came through from the kitchen, to prop himself on the arm of Noah's chair. 'Did I hear we're going out?'

'Up to Sol,' Noah said.

His brother sat up, rubbing the back of his head. 'Where'd we go?'

Noah drank another mouthful of beer. 'Up West. If you fancy it.'

Sol squinted at his hoody. 'Will I need to get changed?'

'Nope. You're perfect as you are.'

Under the lights in Julian's, the pink hoody blended with everything else on show.

Dan went to the bar, bringing back Mexican beers. Red and gold labels on the bottles, lime wedges in their necks. 'This one's got your name on it.' He passed a bottle to Sol.

'Thanks.' Sol pulled a face as he sucked at the lime, shooting a look at a man in a white T-shirt. The T-shirt showed off the man's tan, and his abs. 'Shit, is he checking me out?'

'Sweetheart,' Dan said seriously, '*everyone* is checking you out. You're not going to have to pay for a drink all night.' He reached for Noah. 'We're dancing.'

'To this?' Noah shook his head. 'I'm all Madonna'd out.'

Right on cue, the DJ changed the track to Sylvester's 'Mighty Real'.

'Sexy disco man,' Dan said. 'Remember?'

He pulled Noah on to the dance floor, keeping his free hand on Noah's hip until the day's tension started to bleed out.

Under the rash of neon from the ceiling, Dan's eyes were the same colour as the beer in the bottles hanging from their hands. He saw Noah glance over his shoulder.

'How's Sol getting on with Abercrombie, or is it Fitch?'

'He looks a bit edgy. I didn't think he'd come out with us. Not his scene.'

Dan danced closer, his fingers inside the hem of Noah's shirt, on his bare skin. 'It'll do him good.'

'Getting hit on by cute guys?'

'Seeing his big brother not-being-a-policeman . . . And you think Abercrombie's cute?' Dan's eyes gleamed. 'Maybe I should go to the gym more often.'

'Oh I think you probably get all the exercise you need dancing.' Noah rubbed their hips together in strict time to the music. 'And shagging.'

'Hold that thought . . .'

36

Marnie sat on Ed's sofa, cradling a mug of coffee. She needed to talk about her day, but she didn't know where to start. With the bunkers, and the Doyles? With Clancy, or Adam, or the Finchers and their blank-eyed daughter who'd been friends with Doug Cole until her parents put a stop to that . . .

Ed was next to her, close but not crowding. The way he'd learned to be when she was like this, wrapped up in her day, too tired to sleep, and inarticulate, struggling to find the words to put enough of the chaos behind her, so that she could face tomorrow.

'Do you believe in too much love?'

Ed leaned forward to pick up his coffee mug. 'Whose love are we talking about?'

'The Doyles . . . They have two of their own, another on the way, but Beth says they have too much love for three kids. So they foster an angry teenage boy. That's not . . . It doesn't seem right. Tell me I'm a nasty cynic.'

'Can't do that,' Ed said. 'I'd be lying.' He touched his thumb to her wrist, moving it in small circles that warmed her skin.

'We hunt in packs.' She nursed the mug of coffee, reluctant to free her hands in case she started to fidget, or make fists. 'Isn't that what they say? Maybe that's what the Doyles are doing. Hiding in plain sight . . . The big family is their camouflage.'

'Maybe,' Ed said.

'I don't suppose Terry called you. I gave him your number.'

'Not yet.' Ed shook his head. 'Give him time.'

'How was *your* day?' She smiled at him. 'You know Noah visited Ayana?'

'Yes, she called me. She's a big fan of DS Jake. We're finally making some progress with Witness Protection for her new identity. So . . . my day was good.'

'I'm glad.' Marnie was quiet for a while, holding on to Ed's news because it was important. 'I don't believe in packs. Gangs come together for a reason. For safety, or to hunt. We're solitary by nature. Aren't we? Even families . . . Fundamentally, I mean.' She leaned in to Ed in case he misunderstood. 'Maybe it's me.'

'It's not you. Everyone has to work at that. Sometimes it comes off, sometimes it doesn't.'

The Finchers were working at being a family; at least that was how it looked if she didn't examine their daughter's hollow stare too closely.

'The Doyles are good people. They're trying to give Clancy a safe place, lots of love.' Beth's hands strangling plastic carrier bags, her fingers hunting down staples on the kitchen floor. 'But you know me, I'd run a mile from that kind of place. Well, I did run.'

I'm still running, she thought, but didn't say. Stifled, not safe, was how she'd felt in her parents' house. Stephen Keele must have felt the same, to do what he did. The idea that she and Stephen had anything in common made her sick.

'The Doyles are into quality time.' She pushed her curls

back from her face. 'Family values, routine. The kids are growing their own food . . . On paper it looks like the perfect model for parenting.'

'But,' Ed said, 'you don't trust them? Terry and Beth.'

'Actually, I do. I like them, him especially. He's a good man. If you'd seen him with the boys . . .' She shook her head. 'He's a good man.'

'And Beth?'

'She's a yummy mummy.' That wasn't quite fair. Marnie thought of the woman's dirty hands tying knots in empty carrier bags. 'No, she's an earth mother, one of nature's real women.' Cave dweller. Why did her mind twist everything maternal into an insult of some kind? 'She's a bit wound up right now, of course.'

'Because of the boys,' Ed said, agreeing with her.

Marnie put down the mug, rubbing the chill from her palms. 'And then there's Clancy.'

'The angry teenage boy? How old is he?'

'Fourteen going on thirty . . . Teenagers are tricky. The Doyles didn't want to accuse Clancy of anything worse than acting up. But I think they're scared of him. Beth more or less admitted it. He has a temper and it's got worse since they left Blackthorn Road.'

'What about their own kids? How're they around him?'

'I don't know. Beth found something of his, though. Doodles.' She reached for paper and a pen. Sketched the shape she'd seen. Circles within circles. Empty eyes.

'Like this.' She pushed the paper towards Ed.

He studied it before shaking his head. 'What is it?'

'For a long time I didn't know. But I've seen it before. In Stephen's notebooks. The ones I kept because I thought I could find a clue, an explanation for what he did.'

Ed looked at the shape she'd drawn. 'Is it some music thing? A logo . . .'

'That would make sense, wouldn't it? Except they're five years apart, Stephen and Clancy. How likely is it they'd have the same taste in music?'

Or the same taste in anything.

Stephen didn't have any tastes, as far as she knew.

Ed studied what she'd drawn; it looked like the cross-section of a maze. 'You said for a long time you didn't know what it was . . . When did you find out?'

'It was Kate Larbie. She knew how much it meant to me, to make sense out of Stephen's diary. She knew how desperate I was for answers – anything . . .'

She turned the sketch sideways, so Ed could see. 'It's a keyhole garden. You plant intensively for small areas with protected access.'

'Protected from what?'

'Trespassers, thieves, rampaging neighbours, starving holocaust survivors . . . You name it.'

Ed searched her face. 'Rome?'

'Keyhole gardens are popular with Doomsday preppers. People preparing for a world-changing event, the collapse of society.'

It was hard to keep the contempt from her voice. The idea of prepping wasn't just crazy, it was anathema. You couldn't prepare, not ever, not fully. Life chucked stuff and all you could do was learn to dodge, be quick on your feet and keep moving, because a moving target is harder to hit. Hunkering down is insane. You'll never be safe, rooted to the spot. It was one of the reasons she wished Doug Cole hadn't made a playroom underground; too easy for people to throw bricks, trash his doll's tea party.

'How do you prepare for the collapse of society?' Ed asked, looking bemused.

'You become self-sufficient. You stockpile food, fuel, weapons . . . It's big business in the US, less so over here although you can spend thousands of pounds on freeze-dried food supplies, if you've got enough cash and the psychosis to match.' She shook her head. 'As if *these* are the people we'd want left alive in the event of an apocalypse, the ones who can't wait to kill their neighbours under the guise of protecting their property.'

She stopped, wanting to be fair. 'The internet means it's spreading. Anyone with access to a computer . . . I've heard of decent people, vulnerable people, buying into it. It's another way of hiding, I suppose, if you're scared. Some people have a good reason to be scared.'

She was thinking of Ayana Mirza, and the other victims that Ed helped.

Ed studied the sketch of the keyhole garden. 'The Doyles?'

'Not the Doyles, but I think maybe . . . Clancy's birth parents? This was in his room. Beth says he has a go-bag. Stephen had a go-bag. He called it a bug-out bag. Everything he needed for a quick getaway. The police found it in his room, packed and ready to go. Six years and he was still ready to go at a moment's notice . . .'

'Stephen's birth parents were preppers?'

'It looked that way, yes. I didn't dig too deep. I know they were paranoid and narcissistic, and that they did untold damage to their only child. Damage they didn't pay for. Damage *my* parents paid for.'

She stopped, waiting for the flare of anger to subside. 'I avoided seeing them after the murders, told myself it was because they couldn't possibly hold the clue I was after, about *why* Stephen did it. He hadn't seen them in six years. I suppose the real reason I avoided contact was because I couldn't stand the idea of them. My parents were dead because *they* gave up on Stephen. I didn't blame them for how damaged he was, but I blamed them for copping out. If they hadn't done that, my parents would be alive.'

Ed reached for her hand and held it.

'I know all about the harm parents can do, but even if they screwed him up so hugely he never had a chance . . . he *did* have one. My parents gave him six years of chances and he still killed them.'

Ed pressed his thumb to her palm until her fingers stopped jumping, until the warmth from his hand bled into hers.

'I don't care how tough his childhood was, how much madness his parents preached, how many tins of peaches they stockpiled . . . My parents gave him six years. Six years of patience and praise and love. That should have been enough. Why wasn't it enough?'

'I don't know. I don't. I'm sorry.'

She turned her hand in his, gripping back for a second before he let go. He always let go before she had to pull free. It was one of the reasons she loved him. 'Of course it wasn't enough for me.' She winced at the sound of her own laugh. 'And I had eighteen years of it.'

Two of those years spent chasing after Adam Fletcher, craving danger, despising the safe option of her parents' house. Those poor boys in the bunker had made her realise, again, how lucky she'd been to grow up in a secure, loving home. And made her feel guilty – again – for running from it. Guilty and ungrateful. Her father had told her once that she'd inherited his mother's rebellious streak, unable to sit still, always on the move. Wherever it came from, it meant she'd wasted what precious time she'd had with them.

Ed said, 'Tell me about these preppers. It's more than just self-sufficiency?'

'Much more, especially in the States. I stopped looking at the websites because they made me want to hurl my laptop through a window. In the UK, it's lower-key. I found some sites that suggest it dates back decades, maybe even to the sixties. So while the flower-power people were partying and swinging, this lot were preaching the opposite of free love. Monogamy, family values, restraint.'

'And you're thinking . . . what? In terms of this new case.'

'I don't know. Except that Clancy is a foster kid, just like Stephen. I haven't found any other kind of connection.'

'But you're looking for one,' Ed said. 'A connection.'

'I don't believe in coincidences, you know that. And Clancy? Creeps me out.'

'In what way?'

'All the time I was in the garden, in the bunker, he was watching.'

'Kids are ghouls. Rome, I don't think . . .'

'I know.' She smiled. 'I do know.'

Ed pressed her fingers. 'Have you heard from Stephen lately?'

It was a fair question. She wanted to give him a straight answer. 'Paul Bruton's called a couple of times. Stephen wants to see me. He's put in a lot of visitor orders, but it's not been a good time, with work the way it is.'

She nursed an ache in her shoulder. 'I'm not sure my visits were helping either of us. I thought a bit of distance wouldn't hurt. We need to move on. It wasn't . . . healthy.'

'Bruton doesn't agree? Or is he following procedure by forwarding the visitor requests?'

'There's more to it than that. He intercepted hate mail Stephen tried to send to the parents of the girl who orchestrated that assault.'

Six months ago, Stephen had been brutally attacked and raped. The nineteen-year-old who'd instigated the attack had slit her wrists shortly afterwards. She'd survived, insisting it was attempted suicide despite having no history of self-harm. Marnie was sure Stephen had cut the girl's wrists in revenge. She couldn't prove it, and Sommerville Secure Unit had closed ranks, shutting her out until Bruton chose to share the story of the hate mail.

Ed said, 'What did Stephen try to send to her parents?'

'Bruton didn't specify, just said he wasn't making it a police matter but he wanted to let me know it'd happened.'

She tidied her hair. 'Bruton's trying to tick boxes because of what I saw in Stephen's room. My dad's glasses, mum's brooch, photos . . . Stephen shouldn't have had any of it. Murderers aren't allowed to keep souvenirs from their victims.'

She heard the cold edge in her voice, and regretted it, and was glad of it. 'Bruton swears Stephen didn't have any of it with him when he arrived at Sommerville. He says a visitor must have brought it in. But what visitor? Who visits Stephen except me? Care workers, psychologists, and me. Not even Bruton would suggest I'd make a gift of my parents' belongings to their murderer. So now he's telling me every little thing that goes down, like this hate mail. To cover his back, I imagine, in case it gets worse.'

Escalates was the word Bruton had used: *in case it escalates*. When she challenged him on how it could escalate from rape and suicide, Bruton sidestepped, repeating that it wasn't a police matter, as if that was a gift in his power of giving.

'The girl who attacked Stephen,' Ed said, 'she's still at Sommerville?'

'Girls,' Marnie amended. 'Yes, they're all still there. Perhaps I should pay him a visit. If it's what he wants . . .'

'What *you* want is what matters.'

'Partly, perhaps. But I can't forget what *they* wanted. Mum and Dad were trying to give Stephen a better life. They believed in second chances, for everyone. And who knows,' she leaned to kiss the corner of Ed's mouth, 'maybe he finally wants to say why, or to say sorry. I should give him that chance, shouldn't I?'

'You've given him five years of chances.' Ed rested his hand in her hair. 'I think I prefer this new strategy, of distance.'

'Last time you came with me.'

'Last time I didn't have so much to lose.' He smoothed her eyebrow with his thumb. 'I don't want to see you upset. Entirely selfish on my part. It hurts too much.'

'It's mutual. This,' she smiled, her mouth against his wrist, 'is the reason I want to move on. Because I like where we're headed.'

Ed put his free hand to her hip, finding the skin under her shirt, the place where the tattooist had inked the words *Places of exile*.

Who apart from Ed had seen the words on her skin?

Only one person: Stephen Keele.

Spying on her at her parents' house, two years before he killed them.

She hadn't known about the spying at the time. Stephen had kept it a secret, only telling her six months ago. He was so parsimonious with his secrets, drip-feeding them to her, his way of keeping her close . . .

Enough.

Marnie stood, holding her hand out for Ed's. 'Let's go to bed.'

37

Lawton Down Prison, Durham

It's night now.

Esther is sleeping. I envy her.

She dreams of them. The boys, the baby.

I think she shuts her eyes and somehow, like dodging bullets, she finds a way through the pain and the guilt and the punishment. A way back to them.

It's not fair.

If one of us should be suffering more than the other, if *one* of us deserves to be in a worse predicament, it isn't me. No corner of my mind, conscious or subconscious, has escaped the therapist's scalpel. They've probed me from every angle, penetrated every defence. I am laid bare, once a fortnight. Twice, at the beginning, until they saw how fast I fell, how quickly I offered up the penance they wanted. My dreams and fears and, God help me, my hopes.

How has Esther been allowed to keep back a private piece of herself, when it was made clear to me that nothing less than wholesale evisceration was good enough?

'All right, Alison?'

It's Beryl, in a white trouser suit that would look natty in an amateur production of a musical about dentistry. I don't know how she stands to wear a uniform that's so man-made it throws sparks when she walks. Her big face, moon-like and pitted, peers in at us through the porthole in the door. I should be grateful for her pretence that we have a little privacy. She won't come into the room unless one of us asks, or yells, for her.

'Just reading,' I say.

'Your last night here,' she says.

I don't want to think about that, so I don't answer. But she's right.

We're getting out tomorrow.

I knew I'd lost track of time in here. I knew I couldn't remember how many days – months, years – it's been since I saw them. But I didn't realise the days were slipping past this slyly. We're getting out tomorrow, me and Esther.

The world has gone mad. The lunatics are being let out of the asylum and no one – *no one* – is going to know what hit them.

Beryl is still in the doorway, watching.

'Lights out soon,' she says.

'Soon,' I agree.

I agree with everything and everyone here. From the senior psychiatric team to the funny little Sikh who washes the floors.

Yes, no, of course.

I couldn't agree more. If I did, they would suspect me of sycophancy. I've tried sycophancy and it doesn't work. Not unless you're lucky enough to get stuck with someone whose ego casts a shadow. I'm good with egos. I know exactly where to stroke and how hard. But they need to know that my subservience is sincere and not just a reflex, a new way of paying homage to the system that, let's face it, has the authority to make or break me many times over. It's strange, but what they want from women like me and Esther isn't humility.

It's more, and less, than that.

They want . . . *modesty*.

How old-fashioned, I thought at first. But now I think, how clever. How clever and cruel to ask for something at once so small (it's only modesty) and so gargantuan.

Do you think that if we had even a fingernail-full of modesty, we could have done what we did? That anyone in any prison passing itself off as a mental institution has anything approaching modesty? It's like asking a wild animal to please keep the noise down when it rampages. If we had *modesty*, we would never, ever have done what we did.

They demand modesty but they hang mirrors everywhere.

Plastic mirrors, but mirrors all the same, where you find your face first thing in the morning or last thing at night.

If you're unlucky, you'll recognise what looks back at you from their mirrors. After what you've done, you shouldn't be recognisable to anyone. You should have a face smeared with ashes and a mouth that's a howl, eyes that bleed and hair coming out in handfuls, because it is, *look*, it's coming out in handfuls.

Their mirrors strip-search your face of all the things you've hidden, everything you've done, until you look like the person you were before. I don't know how it's possible, but I've checked every mirror in this place and they all tell the same sloppy lie that nothing has changed, I'm just an ordinary woman in extraordinary circumstances.

Esther is the same.

Some days, in a soft light, she even manages to look nice.

Harmless.

I want a proper mirror. A hard surface, high shine. I want

to really *see* us. What we've done. Who we are. No hiding places.

If they hung better mirrors in prisons, there would be fewer appeals, I honestly believe that. Fewer appeals and fewer escape attempts, once we've seen for ourselves that we're stuck with the person who did this, as surely as I'm stuck with Esther, and she is stuck with me.

Fuck modesty.

Hang up more mirrors.

Let more of us see how scary we look.

Show us that there's no escape.

Not even when the lights go out and all that's left is an amber prod from under the door, where the corridor bleeds into our room for one last night.

38

London

Dan rolled on to one shoulder, blinking up at Noah from the bed. 'You're dressed.'

Noah smiled at the accusation in his voice. 'Yes.'

'I've got a Mexican headache . . .' Dan rubbed sleep from his eyes as he slid, gingerly, from the bed. 'It's wearing a sombrero and shaking maracas.'

'Coffee,' Noah said. 'I made a pot.' His eyes followed the line of Dan's shoulders, admiringly. He wanted to fill his fist with Dan's fringe and pull until—

'Careful,' Dan warned. 'That suit would never be the same again.'

Noah said, 'Fuck the suit.' But he stepped away, throwing Dan a clean towel.

Dan tied the towel round his hips and glanced at the alarm clock. 'Shit. Eight a.m.? When'd that happen?'

'It snuck up just after 7.55.' Noah picked a feather from Dan's fringe.

Dan leaned into his touch provocatively.

'Careful,' Noah warned. 'That towel would never be the same again.'

In the sitting room, Sol was sleeping face-down on the sofa bed, bare feet kicked from under the blanket, one arm curled around his head.

He'd got as drunk as Noah and Dan last night, ended up dancing with Abercrombie, who'd kept the safe side of groping after Noah caught his eye. Dan was right: it had done Sol good to see his big brother letting off steam. Maybe they should go out together more often.

Noah had called their dad when he was making the coffee. 'Sol's staying here for a bit. How's Mum?'

'She's miles better,' Dad had said. 'New pills doing the trick . . .'

New pills always did, until her body adjusted to them and the trick stopped working.

Sol muttered in his sleep, drawing his arm tighter around his head. Noah twitched the blanket back over his brother's feet, shutting the sitting room door softly.

In the kitchen, he rinsed the coffee cup and dried it, making space in his head for the thought that had been stalking him since last night, seeing Sol's eyes jumping around the room, hearing him dodge the questions about their mum.

Then the phone call with his dad, this talk of Rosa's new pills . . .

He got out his phone and texted Marnie. *Think I might have something. See you on the estate?*

Marnie's phone buzzed as she was parking up in Blackthorn Road.

'You didn't call.' Accusation in Adam's voice, and cigarette smoke. He'd started early.

She locked the car. 'I didn't see your story in any of the papers today. Are you holding out for a higher bid?'

'How about breakfast?'

'You go ahead. I've got work to do.' She ended the call, needing a sugar hit before she tackled the interview on the housing estate.

There was a newsagent's not far from the Doyles' house, so she walked in that direction, glad of the stiff breeze pushing at her face. The crowd had gone from the pavement on Blackthorn Road. Boredom and hunger had moved most of them on when they realised the police presence had thinned to a couple of uniforms guarding the tape.

The newsagent's had a notice: *No more than two schoolchildren at a time.*

Marnie wondered whether the Doyles' kids came here; Clancy, fumbling for mints, sneaking glances at the adult magazines. From a fridge, she took a bottle of Fanta, hideously orange, promising a sugar punch.

'Any for a pound,' the cashier said.

'Any what?'

He gestured at the counter: giant chocolate bars, in sunbleached wrappers.

'Right. No thanks, just the drink.'

The counter was doing a nice line in miniature teddy bears, sympathy cards and fake blue roses with fat plastic raindrops glued to their petals. The teddies had blue bows around their necks. Marnie picked up one of the bears. 'How much for this?'

'Three fifty, or five pounds for two. Most people buy two.'

'Why's that?' She knew why. She wanted to hear him say it, hoping to hear at least a little shame in his voice.

'They found two bodies, in the house up the road.' He nodded at the blue bow around the bear's neck. 'Two little boys.'

'And you just happened to have these in stock?'

'From the Jubilee. We took out the red and white ones.'

Marnie put the bear back. 'Too bad they didn't find more bodies. You'd be raking it in.'

The newsagent looked at her for a second, trying to figure out if she was joking. Then he said, 'Most people only buy one card.'

Outside the shop, Marnie snapped the cap on the bottle and drank three long mouthfuls of the oversugared, undercarbonated orange drink. It was really good. She walked up the road to where the Doyles' house was under siege from cheap toys and sympathy cards.

Bunches of flowers wrapped in cellophane had been fed into the gaps between the railings. A foil balloon was fastened to the railings: Winnie the Pooh and Piglet.

Marnie crouched on her heels to read one or two of the cards.

The messages made her eyes hurt.

Her memory served up a junk pile she'd seen spotlit in an art gallery, years ago. The spotlights had been rigged to pull silhouettes from the junk, conjuring the image of a man and woman seated back-to-back, sipping champagne. The art was just a pyramid of tin cans and broken boxes – a garbage heap – but the artist had posed a champagne glass at its heart and lit the whole thing so cleverly he'd extracted a love story from the mess.

The huddle of toys and flowers left on Blackthorn Road had no champagne glass.

Shivering, shading her eyes, Marnie looked at the houses.

All the same, giving her nothing, their pantiled roofs pink in the early light from the sky. The beech trees were better at this end of the road, taller and thicker. Good cover, if you were trying to hide something. Or getting two small boys to play at climbing trees. Finding a secret hideout, underground. Making a game out of trapping them. Killing them.

She shut her eyes before she refocused on the litter of tributes at her feet. Thinking of another crime scene, a different litter of flowers left by strangers, most of the bouquets inside cellophane which attracted dust and rain so that the patch of pavement outside her parents' house was permanently discoloured and smelt fetid.

Looking for the champagne glass . . .

Was that what she was doing?

'Hello.'

She turned her head so fast her vision blurred.

Terry Doyle was standing next to the railings where the flowers had been pushed. Like his wife, he'd lost weight since he was moved out of number 14. 'You know they're selling those teddies in the corner shop? Beth was really upset when she found out.' He looked down at Marnie. 'Julie Lowry called. She said you found bunkers in all the gardens.'

'We found six bunkers, but no bodies. No other bodies.'

'Do you know yet who they were? In our garden?'

'Not yet. I'm sorry. We're working on it.'

'But you know how they died.' Remnants of shock in his voice, even now. 'How – how much they suffered. You know that.' He moved his right hand, then stopped it, holding it still with his left. 'I'm sorry, I know you can't say. It's just . . . I can't stop seeing them, and I'm not sleeping well.' His face searched for a smile to give her. 'You've got a job to do, I know that. Beth said you'd been round. I'm sorry I missed you. I thought perhaps you had news.'

'It's early days. We're still finding out about them. But I can say that I don't think their death was violent. Our pathologist used the word quiet.'

'Quiet . . .' He reacted to it in the same way she and Noah had, by flinching. 'You haven't found their families?'

'Not yet.' She tried to keep the taint of pessimism from her voice, but his bleak look intensified. 'How're you doing? You said Beth was upset about all this.' She gestured at the teddies, flowers and cards. 'How's Carmen, and Tommy?'

'They're safe. Kids are amazing. Beth . . . Beth's not coping so well.'

'She said you two met at work?'

'Yes. A landscaping job, at her offices.' His mouth twitched into a fond smile. 'Hardly love among the roses, more a case of durable turf and gravel edging, but it was love all right. It happened so fast. One of those times when you don't stop to ask questions of fate.' He drew a breath. 'She said you two talked about Clancy? His temper . . .'

Marnie calculated, decided to be direct. 'Yes. How is that?'

'Much like any teenage boy with his upbringing, I expect. He resents me trying to be his dad. I knew what I was signing up for. It's no worse than I expected.'

'Isn't it? Beth seemed agitated when we talked about Clancy.'

'She worries about him,' Terry said simply. 'The kids who're the hardest to love? Those are the ones who need it the most.'

'Sometimes love's not enough. Isn't that true?'

A frown pinched the skin under his eyes. 'Sometimes, perhaps, but you have to start there. No point going straight to discipline, or drugs.'

'Drugs?'

'Ritalin,' Terry said, 'you know the sort of thing. Often it's the parents chasing the diagnosis, giving up too quickly on kids who need extra help. Jumping to drugs because it makes life easier for them, never mind what it does to the kid.'

'You think someone did that with Clancy? Jumped to drugs?'

He blinked. 'Clancy's not on drugs. Is that what you thought?'

The strip of anti-psychotics was in her bag. She could have shown him the evidence but she didn't, because something here didn't add up. Terry was intelligent, big-hearted maybe, but no fool. If the kid he was fostering was on medication, he'd have known about it.

'I just wondered, after what Beth said about his temper . . .'

'He's a teenage boy. His parents had no time for him. From what I can gather, they were wrapped up in some strange business.' He shook his head. 'Plenty of money, maybe too much, obsessed with security, locks all over the house. Clancy had a personal alarm he was made to carry everywhere. It went through to a private security outfit, if you can believe that. Outsourced parental responsibility . . . Am I allowed to call them neurotics, or is that un-PC?'

'It sounds accurate, in any case.'

'When people talk about neglect or abuse, they don't usually think of kids like Clancy. His parents had plenty of money to spend on gadgets and gear, but they didn't have time to spend with him, or any real interest in being parents.' He looked down at the teddy bears and candles. 'It's not neglect on this scale, I know. Not like what you found in that bunker . . .'

What you *found*, Marnie amended silently. She knew how hard it was to be the first witness to a crime of any kind, let alone one like this.

Every witness suffered. Every witness carried away the stain of what they saw, but the first witness had a special burden not easily, if ever, put down. Tim Welland had been the first policeman on the scene of her parents' death; Marnie still saw the weight of that in his face.

'I'd like to hold a memorial service. If they can't be

identified, I mean, if there's no one else to take care of that for them.' Terry's shoulders came up, self-consciously. 'Does that sound macabre?'

'No. It sounds right.'

'Hard to tell what's macabre and what's not.' He nodded at the fake flowers with the plastic raindrops. 'It hurts us too. Our kids. That's why I thought a service of some kind . . .'

'It's a nice thought. I think it would be a good thing.'

They stood shoulder to shoulder, looking at the litter of sympathy, keeping their eyes wide of the garden at 14 Blackthorn Road.

Marnie thought: *How big is this man's heart, how wide his arms?*

But there was another thought underneath: *What went wrong in his past to make him care this much, about everyone and everything?*

From the pavement, a half-melted candle made a face at her. Her eyes went past it to a small round tin, tucked behind two candles. With a blue and gold label, a ring-pull fitted snug to its lid.

Peaches.

Someone had left a tin of peaches out here.

She crouched, to be sure.

It was the same brand as the ones in the bunker. Not water-stained or rusted. This was a new tin, but the same brand.

Left with the teddy bears and fake flowers and the cards addressed to the dead boys, by someone who knew if not how they'd died then what they ate for their last meal.

Tinned peaches.

A brand popular with preppers.

39

The peaches had been wedged between a teddy bear and a third candle, in a jam jar.

Marnie dug gloves from her pocket, pulling them on before she touched the jar. It was cold. The candle had been out for a while.

They hadn't told anyone about the peaches. The press didn't know. No one knew, apart from Marnie's team, and Fran's team, and whoever had put the boys in the bunker.

'What is it?' Terry crouched at her side.

She'd forgotten he was there.

'I'm not sure.' She reached into her bag for an evidence kit.

Very carefully, she stowed and sealed the tin, scanning the rest of the tributes, checking the cards in particular, looking for messages that didn't ring true. Finding nothing, just sympathy cards like the ones on sale in the newsagent's.

In the end, she bagged the lot, afraid to take any chances.

'Does the street have CCTV?'

Terry shook his head. 'The nearest is on the estate.' He nodded in that direction. 'This was always a quiet spot. Nothing much happened here until now.'

He dropped his gaze to the evidence bags in her hand.

'You think . . . someone was here? Someone connected to what happened?' His voice was low and scared.

'I don't know. But I'm not taking any chances. I'm sorry, I have to go. Will you be okay?'

He nodded. 'Go. Do what you have to do. I should get back to Beth and the kids.'

Marnie waited until he'd walked away before she speed-dialled the station.

Debbie Tanner picked up the call.

'The press who were outside the house yesterday,' Marnie said, 'especially the ones with cameras, I want names and contact numbers. I want to know who was here when the crowd was forming. Specifically, I want to know who was taking photos.'

It was an outside chance, but she had to try.

'What's happened?' Debbie asked.

'Just do it. Please. I'll explain later. Ask DS Carling to help.'

'He's following up on the travellers.'

'Then ask one of the others. This is a priority. You spoke with one of the reporters yesterday. Adam Fletcher.'

'He wasn't taking photos. Not while I was chatting with him, anyway.'

'What were you chatting about, detective?'

A tiny beat, while Debbie caught up with Marnie's mood. 'Just . . . how horrid it was, what we found.'

'What did we find?'

'The boys . . . you know. I didn't tell him anything, of course I didn't.'

'Good. Because that would be a disciplinary matter, wouldn't it?'

Marnie rang off, calling Noah next. 'Change of plan. You'll have to interview Mr Walton on your own. I need to follow up on something else.'

'What's happened?'

'Someone left a tin of peaches outside the Doyles' house.'

'Someone . . .' She heard Noah process the information, knowing that no one outside the team knew about the peaches. 'Shit.'

'I'll call you as soon as I know more.' She rang off.

One more call to make before she took the evidence bags for testing.

'Hey, Max. Changed your mind about breakfast?'

'You have a camera. Were you taking photos yesterday?'

Adam said, 'At Beech Rise? Sure. Nothing that's going to win me a Pulitzer, but—'

'Did you take photos of the people leaving flowers and cards?'

'Those vampires? Yeah, I took a few.' His voice sharpened. 'What've you found?'

'You send me your photos, and any others you can get hold of, and I'll let you know.'

'Exclusive?'

'Depends what you send me. Maybe, yes.' She glanced down at the bags in her hand. 'You were chatting with one of my detectives yesterday, DC Tanner.'

'Your top boy?'

'Debbie Tanner. She was wearing a red shirt . . .'

'Oh right, DC Nigella . . . Yeah, I was. Why?'

'I need to know if she told you anything about what we found in those bunkers.'

Like tinned peaches; a nice scoop for a reporter who knew how to work every angle or, in Debbie's case, every curve.

'You found two dead kids,' Adam said. 'She didn't seem to know much more than that.'

Marnie couldn't tell if he was lying, not without seeing his face and maybe not even then. Could she believe it, in any case? Believe that Adam might have left the peaches? No. He was feckless, and hungry for a story, but he wasn't cruel. Not in that way.

Adam said, 'You okay? Max?'

She rang off.

We all live by leaving behind.

Where had she read that? Somewhere, years ago. Sixteen years ago, probably; Adam and his grappling hook, hauling her back into that past, even when there was work to do.

Connie, the traveller, with her two little angels.

A tin of peaches left with the tributes to the dead boys.

Familial DNA inside the bunker.

Clancy's pills, his rich parents and his doodles, the circles like the ones she'd found in Stephen's diary five years ago, right around the time the boys were being buried alive. She felt as if *she* was turning circles, each one smaller than the last.

The truth is that we all live by leaving behind.

Borges. That was it. Jorge Luis Borges's *Funes the Memorious,* a book about a man who couldn't forget anything, who was driven mad by his memory. Reading Borges had been light relief during her Camus phase, but that line had stuck with her.

We all live by leaving behind.

She couldn't do it. Not with Stephen, not with Adam, or not yet. Certainly not with the dead boys. She needed to put the pieces of the puzzle together – the circles in the notebook, the anti-psychotics, the travellers and the preppers – she needed to piece it all together. Find the champagne glass that made sense of the chaos that had killed those children. Even if it was nothing as graceful as a glass – if it was a rusted pipe or a rotting branch – she needed to make sense of it, and soon.

Before the press caught up with the Doyles, or Clancy's temper got worse, or her team started to doubt her resolve to get this done.

40

'It was outside the Doyles' house,' Marnie said. 'With the flowers and cards, part of the pavement memorial.'

The tin of peaches sat on Fran Lennox's desk, still inside the evidence bag.

'People are ghouls.' Fran was filling in paperwork to fast-track the tests on the tin, in case it matched anything they'd taken from the bunker.

The rest of the evidence bags – the sympathy cards, teddies and candles – were in a plastic crate. Everything would need testing. A waste of time, Marnie suspected, but it had to be done. The peaches weren't left by accident. The tin was unopened, its metal untouched by rust. Nothing like the ones found where the boys died. This tin was shiny-new. Looking at it made her angry.

Fran said, 'Did you skip breakfast? You look peaky.'

The opposite of peachy?

'I'm fine. Just pissed off at the idea that someone's playing games.'

'I could make toast,' Fran offered.

'Really, I'm fine. What I need is fingerprints, if you can get them.'

'Let's take a look.' Fran scooped up the bag.

Marnie followed her from the tiny office to the lab, where they suited up before Fran started work.

In here, behind one of the brushed-steel doors, their boys were lying, waiting to go home.

'No prints,' Fran said. She bent over the tin, concentrating on her tests. 'Sorry.'

'They wore gloves?'

'Woolly gloves, by the look of it.' She reached for a pair of tweezers. 'I've got fibres.'

'It wasn't cold yesterday,' Marnie said. 'Not cold enough for gloves.'

'Wasn't it?' Fran was always cold, layering cardigans over vest tops and T-shirts. 'So the gloves were worn in case of prints.' She saved the fibre for testing. 'By our killer, you think?'

'No one else knew about the peaches. No one outside the team.'

Fran heard the edge in her voice. 'You think someone on the team might've leaked it?'

'Why would they?'

'No reason I can think of . . . Leave it with me. Between this and yesterday's samples from the other bunkers, I'm yours most of the day. Anything else you want to chuck into the mix?'

'Since you ask . . .' Marnie dug out the strip of painkillers from Clancy's room. 'Not prints, but if you could tell me the likely effect on a teenage boy of taking these. He's average build, post-pubescent, mood-swingy.'

'Okay.' Fran put the pills with the rest of the evidence. 'Now clear off, before you think of anything else.' Her phone buzzed as she said it and she beckoned Marnie back, reading a text. 'More results from the first bunker. Might be nothing . . . Hang on.'

She put the tin of peaches aside and peeled off her gloves, reaching for the nearest laptop.

'Soil samples. Okay, this is odd.' She turned the screen so that Marnie could see what she was seeing. 'I've got nitrogen, phosphorus . . . a lot of potassium.'

'And that's odd because . . .?'

'Not your average common or garden soil. This is compost-rich, and not just any compost. Properly organic, peat-free, bark-based, I'd guess. Something like conifer . . .'

She straightened, frowning across the lab. 'This is soil from the *garden*. Not the fields. From the garden, after the Doyles rescued it.'

'Terry found the bunker,' Marnie said. 'He climbed down four rungs before he realised what he was seeing. If the soil's from his boots, it's bound to have bits of garden in it.'

Fran shook her head. 'I tested the boots yesterday, to rule out contamination. This is soil we took from beside the bed, right next to where the boys were lying. It's a match for the soil on his boots, but it was taken from the floor by the bed.'

She looked at Marnie. 'Four rungs down, is that what he said?'

'Why would he lie? He's as desperate as we are to solve this case.' Marnie considered the point. 'Are you sure the soil isn't older? From the killer's boots, or mine? I walked across that garden, stood by that bed . . .'

'You were suited. You took care. Whoever left this didn't. Not the killer, or not from back then, because this kind of compost didn't come from an abandoned field. The boys died long before the houses went up, and long before the Doyles got to work on that garden.'

Fran pressed her lips together, frowning. 'At some point in the last year, after the Doyles put nutrients into the soil, someone walked across that composted garden and down into the bunker. If Terry's telling the truth, then you need to look at who else had access to the garden. Because whoever it was went all the way into the bunker. They stood by the side of that bed, right next to the bodies. They must've known what they were seeing. Why keep quiet? Who keeps quiet about a thing like that?'

'Somebody with something to hide . . .'

'Or someone scared out their wits,' Fran said. 'Or both. Scared *and* hiding. Who do you know who fits that description?'

41

'Tell me what you know about Clancy Brand.' Marnie put her phone on the café table, so that there was no chance of missing a call from Noah, or Fran. 'And edit the bullshit.'

Adam raised his brows at her.

'Edit it,' she repeated, 'because I don't have a lot of time.'

Adam's skin was scuffed by the hot bulb over their heads. Tension just beneath the surface of his face warned her that she wasn't going to like what he had to say.

'Clancy was excluded from his last three schools. Two of them suspended him, one tried to have him expelled, but there were loopholes in the paperwork so he was moved on, made into someone else's problem.' Adam took out his disposable lighter, turning it between long fingers. No nicotine stains on the fingers, and he didn't stink of smoke this morning. 'Three schools in three years . . . I'm betting this new one doesn't stick any more than the others did. Once they find out what they're dealing with.'

'What are they dealing with?'

'He touches kids.' Adam snapped a flame from the lighter. 'Little kids, not his own age.'

He let the flame go out.

'And Social Services know this?' Marnie said. 'Come off it. They would never have allowed the Doyles to foster him, for starters.'

'This conversation isn't going to work,' Adam said, 'if you're going to pretend that Social Services know their elbow from their arse.'

'But *you* do know. You have – what? Privileged information? Evidence, even?'

Adam's smile was empty, and savage. 'Would I be sitting here, dying for a cigarette, if I had evidence?'

Some people died for their countries. Adam Fletcher died for cigarettes.

'I'm talking to the police, though. That's a start.'

Or an act of desperation. If he had a story, he wasn't going to hand it to the police, not before he'd sold it to the press. 'How long have you had this . . . information?'

'Not long.'

'Days, or weeks? How long?'

Adam shook a cigarette from the pack, putting it between his lips. The woman at the counter shot him a look, so he showed his teeth to her, holding up his hands in a gesture that was one part placation and six parts *piss off*. 'A couple of months. Not much more than that.'

'Two months. In other words, you've got nothing.'

'I've got—'

'Nothing. You wouldn't have left the Doyles alone if you had anything worth convincing them with. They've got a little girl about the age Tia was when I found out you had a family.'

Marnie edited the emotion from her voice. 'You'd have warned them if you had anything. So what's this really about?'

Adam leaned forward until the light found his eyes. 'He touches kids,' he repeated. 'Little kids, and yeah, I know about Carmen and Tommy. I know Clancy doesn't give a toss whether it's girls or boys he touches, and he gets angry if he's threatened. That's when he's dangerous.' All the time he talked, he kept the unlit cigarette in his mouth.

He'd wanted to sit outside, but Marnie had made the rules, taking the pair of them to seats at the back of the café. 'How do you know all this?' she demanded. 'He keys your car and you start digging, to this extent? I don't think so.'

'I told you, he gave me the creeps. So I asked around and it turns out I'm not the only one. Lots of people get a bad vibe from this kid. Maybe no one can make it stick, but that doesn't mean anything. Maybe *I* can make it stick. It's a good story. My editor likes it.'

'You're writing a story about a teenage boy now? Make up your mind.'

'Whatever sells.' Adam shrugged.

'You said there was a connection to the bunker. That you could help with the case. How does this help with that?'

'Clancy knew about the bunker. I'd bet money on it. He's a sneaky kid. It's too much of a coincidence otherwise.'

'This is your evidence? *It's too much of a coincidence otherwise?*'

'Don't tell me you started believing in coincidences.' Adam slung his shoulders back in the chair, eyeing her in that old way, proprietorial. 'You used to know better.'

Like finding a child's seat in the back of your car, seeing the wedding ring you forgot to take off, too late to do me any good – coincidences like that?

'Give me what you've got on Clancy Brand, or I'll arrest you for withholding evidence.'

'I'm giving it to you right now. He touches little kids. He knew about that bunker. What more do you want?' He challenged her with a stare.

'How do you know he knew about the bunker? Just because you get a bad vibe—'

'And you don't? Come on, Max. Drop the bureaucratic bullshit for a second, and tell me your skin didn't crawl the first time you met the kid.'

'It's crawling right now. Doesn't mean I can make an arrest that will help my case.' She drank some coffee. 'On the other hand, it would get you off my back.'

Adam leaned back in his chair, looking lazy, looking lethal. His eyes gleamed, as if she'd flashed her bra. He was enjoying this, too much.

'How do you know,' she repeated, 'that he knew about the bunker?'

'I asked the right questions. Something you and your token DS can't manage.'

'Excuse me? My what?'

'Noah Jake.' Adam traced a pattern on the table with his thumb. 'Black, gay and good-looking . . . Nice box-ticking, Detective Inspector.'

Marnie looked at him coldly. 'Your story stinks. I'm not surprised the papers won't touch it, although your bigotry's a good match for a couple of them.'

'Hey.' Adam held up his hands again. 'I've got nothing against your boy. Other than the crap questions he's been asking. If he was half as good as you need him to be, he'd have asked Julie Lowry how often she saw Clancy out there after dark, digging round the bunker.'

Marnie waited a beat before she said, 'You've been talking with Julie Lowry?'

'I've been talking with everyone. Nige and Caro Fincher . . . Did you see that patio furniture? They've got way too much disposable income.'

There were two empty glasses on the table. Marnie wanted to bury at least one of them in Adam's self-satisfied smile. 'And they all said that Clancy knew about the bunker?'

'Just Julie, but she's the one next door. The others said

Clancy was a dodgy kid, they wouldn't want him living under their roofs.'

'Funny, because I can just imagine a couple of warring egotists wanting to give house space to someone else's moody teenager . . . This is crap, and you know it.'

Her phone buzzed. Text from Ed: *Missed you this morning, hope your day's okay.*

He'd been sleeping when she left. She'd taken care not to wake him.

When she closed the text, her phone reminded her of an old message she'd failed to delete: Paul Bruton at Sommerville, again. Another visitor request from Stephen Keele. How many was that now? Four in the last month. Stephen had something on his mind. Or he was playing with her, the way Adam was playing. Snakes and Ladders. Unhappy Families. She still had Clancy's piece of paper in her pocket, the keyhole garden he'd drawn, like the ones in Stephen's notebook. Circles, getting smaller.

A waitress brought their breakfasts: bacon sandwiches and orange juice, more coffee; Adam had ordered before Marnie got here.

He fed ketchup into his bacon sandwich and flattened it back together before taking a big bite. 'The Finchers play golf in matching gear; you've got to see that to believe it . . . You know this part of London's only got one private golf club?'

Marnie looked disbelieving.

'Yeah,' Adam agreed. 'It's a fucking scandal. I'm writing to my MP about it.' He started on the second half of his sandwich.

Marnie should have given him a speech about speaking to witnesses during an investigation, but she didn't, waiting to see what else he was going to say.

Julie Lowry had flirted with Noah while she was telling

him about Clancy's peeping Tom routine. It was hard to believe she'd held back anything more damning, like Clancy digging around the bunker late at night. More likely she'd lied to Adam. As for the Finchers, it was funny how so many people had their eye on Clancy but no one had actually seen anything. Adam had nothing, no real evidence. But Fran did. Soil samples that said someone had walked across the Doyles' garden and down into the bunker. All the way down, standing next to the makeshift bed where their boys died. Who, and why?

'We ever do this before?' Adam licked ketchup from his knuckles.

'Breakfast? No.'

'We had a Chinese.' Adam drank juice, his throat moving smoothly as he swallowed. 'Remember that?'

Marnie remembered. Chopsticks between Adam's long fingers, and then, later . . .

'No,' she said. There was satisfaction in lying to Adam, although admittedly not much.

He finished the sandwich, wiped his mouth on a napkin. 'You're not eating.'

He'd shouldered his way into her dreams last night, while Ed was curled at her back, keeping her warm. 'I'm not hungry.' She pushed her plate towards him. 'Knock yourself out.'

'And you're not asking questions.'

'About London's lack of private golf clubs? No, I'm not.'

'About Clancy Brand.' He eyed her. 'You've got something, haven't you? Something that's telling you I might be right about him.' He balled the napkin and tossed it aside.

'One of us has something,' she agreed. 'But it's not you.'

'You should talk to Nigel Fincher. I bet he's noticed something about that kid. He's a watcher. I know the type.'

'You don't know anything.'

'Trust me. The matching golf gear's a dead giveaway. He's a control freak.'

'Well, you know *that* type,' Marnie conceded.

Adam reached for his second cup of coffee. He dropped his eyes to the table, lifting them to say, 'I was sorry about your mum and dad.'

The apology caught her off guard. She felt her eyes expand with shock.

'Should've said something sooner, sent my condolences as soon as I heard. It wouldn't have killed me to pick up the phone or send a card.'

She was out of breath, as if he'd punched her. 'And break the habit of a lifetime?'

'Yeah . . .' He turned the coffee cup in its saucer. 'I owe you another apology, too.'

'Careful,' Marnie warned thinly. But she was waiting.

'More than one, but who's counting, right?' Adam tried a smile. 'Mostly, though, I'm sorry about your parents.'

The apologies were collateral, she knew that. His way of pulling her back to him. He'd guessed how it was, her better judgement warring with nostalgia. A strange sort of nostalgia, for a place where she'd never been happy. Her parents' house.

Adam moved his coffee cup to one side. 'I know how it must've felt, losing them . . .'

'You don't know anything.'

He adjusted the smile, making it sad. A glass was no good; it wouldn't even scratch the surface of Adam's disguise. What Marnie needed was a chair, or a window.

'You don't know anything,' she repeated. 'Not about then, not about now.'

She pushed back her chair and stood, putting the heel of her hand on the table and looking at him with her face open, hoping he saw every line and shadow on her skin. 'If you fuck up my investigation, I'll bury you. Understood?'

Adam studied her. If he was seeing lines and shadows, he gave no clue to it. Maybe, like her, he couldn't see past the memories. Not just of him and her – of *then* and them. The last time they stood this close, her parents were alive and the only monsters in her life were the ones she chose to chase. She said, 'I won't warn you again.'

'If I have something that'll help, what then?'

'Give it up.'

'To you,' he said. 'I'm not giving it to anyone else.'

'I don't have time to stroke your ego,' Marnie told him. 'But I can make time to have you arrested for withholding evidence, if that's what I think you're doing.'

In the street, she took out her phone and speed-dialled the station.

Debbie Tanner picked up. 'I'm leaving messages, for the photographers. No one's around yet. It's still early.'

'Keep trying. Where's Noah?'

'Waiting for Mr Walton to come home. He was out first thing. Shopping, the neighbours think. Noah's on the estate, waiting for him to get back.'

'Right. I'll call him.'

Marnie put the phone in her pocket, walking in the direction of her car. Her hands were making fists, twitchy with the need to hit Adam, unsatisfied.

What game was he playing? She wished she knew, but she'd never known with Adam. Not even when they were so close her skin carried his scent, like an animal's, repelling all other advances. She'd been glad of it back then, the closeness as well as the repulsion, a sure way of escaping stares in the street when she first started attracting attention, snagging glances from strangers. She'd resented the loss of her anonymity, been grateful for the disguise Adam lent her, his scent worn like armour on her skin.

She stopped by the side of the pavement memorial, reduced to trodden petals and patches of wax, everything else in an evidence tray at Fran's lab. She couldn't get the image of the peaches out of her head. Who did that? Crouched, in woollen gloves, and slid the tin of peaches between the candles and the cards? With what purpose, other than to make her look at her team with suspicion, turning in circles, tying herself in knots . . .

She dug out her phone and called Ed's number, expecting his voicemail.

'Hey,' he said. 'I was hoping you'd call. Meetings were cancelled; I've got the afternoon off, if you fancy lunch . . .'

'Sorry. I need to go to Bristol. I was calling to say I might be late.'

'Stephen?' Ed always knew.

'Yes. Nothing like last time, just . . . questions I need to ask him.'

'You sound pissed off.'

'I *am* pissed off.' She sucked a breath. 'If I'm lucky with the traffic, I might be back for supper.'

'Or I could keep you company. We could stop somewhere on the way back to eat.'

Relief made her shut her eyes for a second. 'Company sounds good. I need to make some calls, then I'll swing by and pick you up. Thanks, Ed.'

'No problem.' He rang off.

Marnie called Noah, reaching his voicemail. 'The peaches are bugging me. I'm going to Sommerville. If my phone's off, call Ed's. I'll catch you later.'

Fran picked up on the first ring.

Marnie said, 'You've finished with the tin of peaches, yes? Can I have it back?'

'Feeling peckish?'

'Not remotely, but I need the peaches. I'm hoping they might get me some answers.'

'They're all yours,' Fran said.

42

In Flat 57 Arlington Court, Denis Walton eyed Noah Jake with the air of a spinster appraising the white elephant stall at a village jumble sale. 'And you're a detective?'

'For my sins.' Noah kept the police ID open in his hand, looking around the flat. 'This is a nice place. Great view . . .' across the pantiled roofs of Beech Rise, the angle hiding the back gardens on Blackthorn Road.

'Better before the houses went up.' Denis jerked his head at the greasy orange sofa. 'Come on then. I suppose you'll be after a cup of tea.'

Noah sat, smiling up at the man. 'If it's no trouble. That'd be great, thanks.'

Denis looked him over again: slim pickings on the white elephant stall. 'I suppose I can show willing,' he said, in a voice that could have begrudged litter to a bin.

He was a thin man with a fat stomach, making him lean backwards like a pregnant woman when he walked to the kitchen at the rear of the flat. His hair leaned in the same direction, growing like a pelt from the base of his bald head. Picking up his feet when he walked, new tartan slippers on his feet.

Noah heard the sound of a kettle being filled.

'Biscuits?' Denis called from the kitchen. 'You're lucky I popped to the shops.'

'Thanks,' Noah called back.

The rear of the flat overlooked the well between this block and its neighbours. Four blocks in total, built around a concreted area where wheelie bins and bike sheds took up most of the space. Unedifying, but Noah had been in worse places. According to the house-to-house team, Denis had lived here twenty-six years. He was seventy-two, single and childless. He remembered Beech Rise being built, and the travellers who'd been cleared to make way for Ian Merrick's men.

Noah was figuring out the best way to ask the right questions when Denis reappeared with two mugs of tea, a packet of Hobnobs tucked under one arm.

'You'll be wanting to know about Connie.' He held out a mug and lifted his elbow so that the biscuits slid an inch in Noah's direction. 'Tuck in.'

Noah rescued the Hobnobs from the man's armpit, putting them on the coffee table as he took the mug of tea. 'Thanks.'

'Connie was a character all right.' Denis stepped over the table to join Noah on the sofa. 'Didn't suffer fools, gladly or otherwise, got up in arms about that development before it even started. The way they threw those houses up . . . I've seen garden sheds with more to them. They've a brass neck calling themselves safety specialists. You know what they specialise in? Panic rooms for rich people who can't take a ring on the doorbell without pissing their pants. And all that bull about the views . . . what about *our* view? That's what Connie wanted to know.' He chuckled, rearranging his stomach in his lap, propping his mug there. 'You should've seen her with the Neighbourhood Watch lot. "Watch this," that was her line.' He tapped the side of his nose. '"Watch this, nose disease" . . . That was Connie. She was a one, all right.' He sucked at his tea. 'Can't say the same for everyone here, but she was a good neighbour. We got on like a shed on fire.'

Noah set his mug down on the table. 'Connie lived . . . here? In the flats?'

'Course she did. Number 55, that's what I told your lass last night. What'd you think?'

'That she was one of the travellers living in the field where they built Beech Rise.'

Denis snorted. He freed his pinkie finger from the mug's handle and picked his nose with it, comprehensively. 'I call that typical.' He inspected the finger, eyeing the nasal hair he'd dislodged with the mucus before wiping the lot on the arm of the sofa. 'Connie would've had another word for it.'

Noah tried not to think about his suit, and the sofa. He said, 'Connie had two boys?'

'Not her.' Denis reached for the Hobnobs, tucking the packet back into his armpit while he worked a biscuit free from the wrapper.

Noah said, 'She had no kids. And she wasn't a traveller. She didn't live in the field.'

In other words, he was sitting on a sofa whose patina was nine parts snot and the other part God knows what, for no good reason.

Denis spoke through a mouthful of Hobnob. 'Her daughter's kids.'

'Her daughter . . . was a traveller?'

'No.' Denis eyed him. 'You have some funny ideas, son.'

'But you saw the children with Connie?'

'I saw *pictures*,' Denis amended. 'I told your lot that last night. Didn't dress it up. Haven't seen Con in five years. That's why I'm surprised you bothered coming back.'

'Connie's grandchildren were boys?' Noah referred to his

notes. He needed to salvage something from this, if he could. 'Aged about five and seven?'

Denis nodded. 'Her angels, she called them.'

'This was five years ago?'

'Give or take.'

'I don't suppose you remember their names?'

Denis looked at him. 'Of course I bloody remember. Christ. Just because one of you lot wrote down the facts half-arsed.' He blew his nose into his fingers. 'Fred and Archie, her angels. Fred was the littlest. Archie was his big brother.'

Fred and Archie . . .

Noah held a breath in his chest for a second. This could still be nothing. Connie hadn't lived in the field, the children weren't hers. It could still be nothing.

'Mr Walton, what happened to Connie?'

'The travellers happened.' He wiped his fingers on the sofa, looking disgusted.

'Did Connie upset them? Get into a fight?' Noah was reaching, wanting a reason to connect Connie to the case. 'Was she afraid of the travellers?'

'Afraid of them,' Denis snorted, 'that's rich. She bloody went with them!'

'She . . .'

'Upped sticks and went with them.'

He flung an arm towards the window. 'When they got cleared out of that field, Connie upped sticks. Sod her friends, sod everything. Overnight, more or less. Left the council to clear her flat. Never came back, never wrote a word about where she was, or why.'

Denis Walton snapped damp fingers in Noah's face. 'Buggered off, just like that. Haven't seen her since, and don't want to. Good riddance to bad rubbish.'

43

Sommerville Juvenile Detention Unit, Bristol

Stephen Keele sat in the visitors' room, skinny in his grey sweats. Black curls, blue eyes, looking like an angel with his shoulders sloped, their blades sharp enough to be hiding wings.

Marnie smiled at the escort, keeping her left hand in her pocket. 'Detective Inspector Rome. I called ahead. Paul Bruton arranged the visit.'

Her escort nodded and left, closing the door behind him.

When it was just her and Stephen, Marnie took her hand from her pocket and put the tin of peaches on the table.

Metal on metal, the sound making the table jump and echo.

Stephen's eyes jumped too. To her hand, and then to the tin with its jaunty blue and yellow label, its ring-pull that counted as a weapon, in this place.

Under Sommerville's rules, Marnie should have surrendered the tin at the main gate. She certainly should not have put it within grabbing distance of a nineteen-year-old inmate, a convicted murderer. 'What is this?' she asked.

Stephen tipped his head, light sliding down the side of

his face. He knew she'd broken the rules, bringing the tin in here; she saw him calculating what it might mean. A dozen recessed bulbs in the ceiling gave him a dozen shadows, in all directions at once. He didn't speak.

This was what he did. How he kept control. By keeping his mouth shut.

'You know.' She waited a beat. 'Don't you? You've seen it before.'

She was tired and angry, and she didn't bother hiding it.

She had always taken care to hide it, in the past.

Stephen registered this change in her, the skin stiffening under his eyes, where it was thinnest, where she could see the blood under the surface.

'I know you've seen this before. You know *how* I know? I read your notebooks. I was looking for clues, some reason for what you did. I found doodles. Gibberish, at least that's what I thought, but it wasn't, was it? It meant something.'

She put her hand on the tin. 'It meant this.'

Still Stephen didn't speak.

'No? All right.' She put the peaches away and took out the torn page from Clancy's notebook. 'What about this?'

Stephen didn't look at the page, keeping his eyes on her face.

Marnie tried to take his pulse from his stare, the fractional changes in his pupils. 'Bruton says you wanted to see me. You've been completing a lot of visitor orders.' She put her hand on the torn page. 'Well, here I am.'

His eyes flickered as if she'd told him a lie.

'Or were you just practising your handwriting, filling in time . . . You must get bored. Bright boy like you, in a place like this. Isn't that what the psychologists say? You're bored.'

Stephen was half the size of the shadows he was casting. Always so much smaller than she remembered him being, when she was away from here. He hooded his eyes from her stare. Looking different. Not scared, not that, but different. Not quite so much in control.

Good.

'You've been getting parcels, too. Things you didn't ask for. Food, mostly. Bruton hasn't passed any of it to you, he says, because that would be breaking the rules. You have to fill in a form if you want someone to send you a parcel. And *they* have to fill in a form. No forms, no food. That's how it works. But you've broken the rules before, haven't you? Smuggling my dad's spectacles in here, and my mum's brooch. Bruton thinks he's too smart to let that happen, but he's not so smart. He thinks you're just a kid.'

Stephen's eyes flickered again.

'Who brought those things in here? The glasses, the brooch? Who's sending you parcels? The same person, that would be my bet. In case you've forgotten, I'm a detective. I find this stuff out for a living. Bruton may not be smart enough to figure it out, but he's not me.'

This time, the only part of his eye that flickered was the iris.

'Then there's this.' Marnie touched the tin of peaches. 'It was left outside a house where two boys died. Most people leave flowers, or toys if children are involved. Cards with messages. Candles. We have to check the messages, in case one was written by the killer. I'm sure you know the kind of thing I mean.'

'What did they leave for you?' Stephen asked.

His voice was the same, too deep and old for a nineteen-year-old.

What did they leave for you?

It took her a second to realise he wasn't talking about the Doyles' house. He meant her parents' house, five years ago. His eyes hadn't left her face.

She wanted to rub at the stain put there by his stare.

When she didn't speak, he filled the silence with, 'Flowers? Or toys, because a child was involved?' He sounded genuinely curious. 'Why do people do that?'

'I don't know, Stephen. Why do people do anything? Why did *you* do what you did?'

He measured her with his stare, stretching the moment thin and taut, until it was in danger of snapping. Then, 'I did it,' he said softly, 'for you.'

Behind them, on the other side of the wall, some kid was playing music in his room; the dead beat of a bass, no rhythm to it and no rhyme.

'You . . .' She didn't want to rub at his stare on her face. She wanted to tear at it, with something sharp. 'Say that again.'

He lowered his lashes at her in a slow blink, dark blue. 'I did it for you.'

'*Why?*' she demanded. 'What's that supposed to mean?'

'Places of exile,' Stephen said. 'It's written on your hip.' He paused. 'Your left hip. I knew what it meant. Places of exile. I knew how you felt.'

She felt beaten, out of breath. 'And the parcels? Who's sending those? Who're you in touch with?'

He shook his head. 'No one. I thought it was you.'

'You thought *I* was sending you food parcels?'

He nodded.

'Why would I do that?'

He shifted the slope of his shoulders. 'Places of exile,' he repeated, as if this answered her question.

'I'll find out,' Marnie said. 'I'll find out who it is.'

'Good,' Stephen said, 'because the fucker's freaking me out.'

They looked at one another across the short distance of the table.

Was he telling the truth? She didn't know, but she doubted

it. Doubted that he knew what the truth was, let alone how to tell it.

'There aren't many people who know you're in here. Your legal team. Your parents.'

That landed. His stare sparked, coldly.

'Theo and Stella Keele,' she said slowly. 'Have they been in touch?'

He didn't answer, reverting to a lush silence she knew he wouldn't break, not this session. He had what he wanted. Her, on the back foot again. He was happy because she'd come here, dancing to his tune. She should have known better.

'You think you can play games with me?'

She stood, so smoothly he blinked. 'I'll play. You'll lose.'

Ed was waiting in the car. 'Home?'

'Home.' She swung into the driver's seat, fastening her belt.

It wasn't yet 2 p.m. If nothing else, this trip had been quick. Plenty of time left in the day for what mattered, checking in with Noah and the team. Just as well.

She'd learnt nothing useful about Clancy's notebooks. She still didn't know who'd left the tin of peaches outside the house in Blackthorn Road. She'd thought there must be a link, a connection, to the preppers perhaps, knowing what little she did about Stephen's past.

Or had she used that as an excuse to break her new rule and come back here? Chasing answers, not for this new case but for the old one. Adam had said he was sorry, about her parents, and she'd hoped . . . she'd let herself believe that Stephen might finally be sorry too. Ready to talk, to give her the answers she needed to make peace with her parents' deaths.

I did it for you.

It couldn't be true. All the way back into London-bound traffic that felt safe, like burrowing into anonymity, she told herself it couldn't be true.

I did it for you.

It was a lie, like everything Stephen gave her. Just another lie, only this time he'd twisted it into such a terrible shape that whichever way she tried to take hold of it, she cut herself on its sharp edges. He was finding new ways to make her hurt. It was what he did. His madness kept moving, so she could never get an angle on it, never second-guess him.

So she could never lose interest.

The traffic thickened, slowing to a crawl.

Ed was watching her, quietly, but with concern. 'What happened in there?'

'I'll tell you. Just . . . Let me try and make sense of it first.'

Ed nodded his acceptance of this.

Marnie rested her head on the door frame and watched the sun strip the metallic paint from the retreating traffic. 'I will tell you,' she promised.

The car fumes helped. She breathed them gratefully, a smell she understood. An honest, overpowering smell, wiping her out.

Her phone, on hands-free, played Noah's tune.

She answered the call. 'What've you got?'

'Names,' Noah said. 'I think I've got names for our boys.'

44

'Connie Pryce was living in the flat next door to Denis Walton, five years ago.' Noah handed Marnie a cup of coffee from the takeaway stand near the station. 'She left when the travellers left. Denis says she went with them, overnight more or less.'

'Why?'

'Denis didn't have any theories. But Connie's daughter had two small boys, Fred and Archie. Connie's little angels . . . I've got Debbie chasing the housing department for details of Connie's whereabouts, and her daughter's.'

'Does the daughter have a name?'

'Denis couldn't remember. He never met her. Something Old Testament, he thought.'

Noah had tried as many Old Testament women's names as he could remember, without hitting on the one Denis half remembered. 'But the boys were Fred and Archie. Connie talked about them all the time.'

'Fred and Archie,' Marnie repeated.

She was trying the names for size, as he had done, to see if they fitted their boys.

'Did you get anywhere,' he asked, 'with the peaches?'

'Nowhere.' A full-stop in her voice.

'There's something else,' Noah said, 'about the daughter.'

Marnie worked the lid from the coffee. 'Go on.'

'Denis is pretty sure that she worked for Ian Merrick.'

Marnie stopped what she was doing and looked at him.

Noah nodded. 'Connie went with the travellers when Merrick moved in to start building Beech Rise. Good riddance, Denis says, but I know he was fond of Connie. Her daughter was different. From what Denis says, they fell out over the housing development. He was pretty bitter about Merrick Homes, said they flattened everything in their way, ruined his views. The travellers lost their home, and it wasn't gentle. The way Denis tells it, the police more or less bulldozed them out.'

'And Fred and Archie?'

'Denis doesn't know what happened to them. Just that when the travellers were moved on, Connie went with them. Overnight. Left everything in her flat, even photos and books she'd liked reading to the boys. The council had to sort it all out. It doesn't make sense that she'd go like that, leaving her grandchildren behind. Not unless something had happened.'

Marnie held the cardboard cup in both hands, not drinking. Steam from the coffee softened the hard line of her jaw. 'Debbie's going after names and addresses?'

'Yes. And Ron's chasing an address for the travellers. In case Connie's still with them.'

She glanced up at him. 'You don't think she is?'

'Denis said it was a snap decision, one he's sure she lived to regret. He couldn't believe she'd move away from Fred and Archie, for one thing. He says she lived for those kids.'

'So if she went, it could be because she knew they were dead.'

'It seems like a leap,' Noah admitted. 'But the way Denis spoke about Connie, and the fact that he's so certain her daughter worked for Ian Merrick . . .'

'Let's see what Debbie can turn up. We need to ask Merrick what he knows. And we need to find these travellers, and Connie. Sorry,' she handed back the coffee, 'I'm all caffeined out.'

Noah emptied the coffee into the gutter, walking to the nearest bin to get rid of the cup.

When he walked back, Marnie was checking her phone.

'Fran?' Noah asked.

'Not yet.' Marnie put the phone into her pocket. 'There was something else, though. From the bunker. Soil that matches the Doyles' garden.'

'From Terry's boots?'

'Not unless he lied to me. We need to look into that possibility. This soil was right by the bed, right by the boys.'

'What are you thinking? Not . . . Clancy?'

'Why *not Clancy*?'

'Because he's a kid, not much older than they were.'

'Not much, but enough. Julie Lowry said she saw him hanging around in the garden.'

Noah shook his head. 'She said he was *watching* the garden, from his bedroom window.'

'She told Adam Fletcher she saw Clancy digging, right where the bunker is.'

'That's not what she told me. Maybe she elaborated, for the press.' Remembering the way Julie had flirted with him, and how good-looking Fletcher was, Noah had no difficulty imagining that scenario. 'You think Clancy found the bunker before we did?'

'Someone went down there. Someone left the tin of peaches, too. Who would do that, unless they knew what was inside the bunker? Only two other possibilities: the killer came back, or someone on our team talked. I'm not keen on either of those options, are you?'

'Debbie was chatting with Fletcher—' Noah was speaking aloud, without thinking. He shut his mouth the second it was out. 'I didn't mean . . .'

'Didn't you?' Marnie cut her eyes away. 'I did. At least . . . I gave the idea headspace.'

Noah processed this, in silence. 'She wouldn't do that,' he said at last. 'None of us would. The boys matter too much.'

Marnie nodded. 'I hope so.' She checked her phone again. 'Let's get moving. As soon as we've got a name for Connie's daughter, we can question Ian Merrick, see if there's something he didn't tell us first time around. And we need to know more about Clancy, and the Doyles. Debbie can get on to that.'

She started walking, then turned back to Noah. 'You thought you had something, first thing. Before you saw Denis Walton?'

'Yes.' Noah fell into step with her. 'About the pills you found. It could be nothing, but I've got Sol staying at the moment. He reminded me that Mum takes pills sometimes, for anxiety, panic attacks . . . The pills usually help to start with, and then she stops taking them, or she builds up a resistance, I don't know exactly.'

Marnie listened, but didn't speak. Her silence made it easier to keep talking.

'When she stopped taking a prescription, I'd sometimes find the bottles, or strips like the one Clancy had, and I'd keep them. I don't know why. It made me feel safe. Anyway, I looked up those pills that Beth found. Haloperidol? It's used to treat all kinds of psychosis in all kinds of people.'

'Go on.'

'That's it. I didn't dig any deeper but I thought it was

worth mentioning. In case we're wrong about Clancy. In case they're not his pills.'

Marnie's silence was sceptical. If he hadn't told her about his mother, he was certain she'd have shot his theory into tiny pieces. As it was, she said, 'Okay. Let's say he found them and hid them. Whose pills are they? And where did he find them?'

'Like I said, it might be nothing. Me seeing connections where there aren't any.'

'Too many connections,' Marnie said. 'That's my problem with this case. Soil by the bed, peaches in the street . . . Someone's playing games.'

Noah heard the flare of anger in her voice, white hot. They'd reached the station steps.

'Find Connie Pryce,' Marnie said. 'And get a name for her daughter, see if she was on Merrick's payroll. I'd like to give him a hard time about that.'

Her phone buzzed. 'Fran? Go ahead.'

Her face changed as she listened, her eyes moving away from Noah, away from everything other than whatever Fran was telling her. 'We'll be there in twenty minutes.'

She shut her phone. 'We need to go. Fran's got something.'

He followed her at a jog, in the direction of the car park.

'You were right. They're Connie's little angels.' Marnie unlocked the car. 'Fred and Archie Reid.'

They climbed in. She fired the engine.

'They weren't in the missing persons database for a good reason.'

Noah reached for his seat belt. 'Why?'

'Someone had decided they were already dead.'

45

'When you told me Missing Persons had nothing . . .' Fran held a sheet of paper between her hands, delicately, as if it was a living thing. 'I didn't want to look for them in the only place I *could* look, but I did.' She surrendered the sheet. 'That's where I found them.'

Marnie took custody of the printout, holding it where she and Noah could read it together. Death records, for two boys.

Fred and Archie Reid.

Fred was a Christmas baby, born 25 December 2005. Archie was the older, by three years, born 20 March 2002. They were five and eight when the report said they died.

Parents: Esther and Matthew Reid.

'DNA confirms it,' Fran said. 'Esther's the mother. The boys you found are hers.'

The printout was black and white, mostly white. Whoever wrote the report hadn't known how the boys really died. It was a sterile summing-up of the horror and sadness that Marnie and Noah had uncovered in the bunker.

Fran said, 'There's someone else.' She passed a second sheet across the desk.

Another death record, for Louisa Reid, just eight months old when she died.

'A baby sister?' Noah's skin felt too tight for his skull.

'Drowned,' Marnie read from the report. She looked across at Fran. 'It says all three of the children drowned, five years ago. We know that's not true.'

Fran turned her laptop towards them. 'They found Louisa's body in the Thames, or rather a fisherman did. Fergus Gibb, poor man . . . I have an address for him, in case that helps.'

She pointed at the monitor. 'The mother confessed. She said she drowned all three children. The evidence supported her confession. The boys' clothing and personal effects were at the scene. She was convicted on three counts of manslaughter.'

Marnie wrote down Fergus Gibb's name and address. 'Manslaughter. Not murder?'

'Diminished responsibility, which brings me to these . . .'

Fran put a foil strip of pills on the desk. 'Haloperidol is an anti-psychotic. Used, among other things, to treat post-partum psychosis. Where did you find these?'

'Post-partum psychosis,' Marnie repeated. 'That was the mother's plea?' She referred to the death records. 'Esther's plea?'

Fran nodded. 'Esther Reid confessed to killing her three children. She was diagnosed as suffering from PPP and ordered to be detained at a psychiatric hospital for treatment.' She touched the foil strip. 'Where did you find these?' she repeated.

Marnie put the pills aside with her hand. 'Forget about the haloperidol for a minute. Tell me about Esther Reid. How much do you know about PPP?'

'Not much, but I did some research while you were on your way over.' Fran pulled up a page of notes on her laptop. 'One in seven women suffers from sudden post-natal depression. One in five hundred gets post-partum psychosis, or PPP. Hallucinations, paranoia, voices inciting them to murder, telling them their baby is evil, or else it's the new messiah and everyone around them wants to harm it. Sometimes they believe the baby has supernatural healing powers and can survive anything.'

She paused, pulling at her fingers as if removing gloves, a gesture Noah had seen before when Fran was upset. 'Suicide due to PPP is the biggest cause of death in new mothers. Every year at least ten die because of it. They were tracking the stats until 2008, when the government decided to cut funding.'

'Is there really no cure?' Noah asked.

'It's entirely curable if it's treated properly. That's one of the tragedies. But so many women are afraid of admitting to their symptoms. Many will have suffered depression as teenagers or young women, so they'll be familiar with that stigma, the way treatment involves judgement. It shouldn't, but it does. And they're terrified of having their children taken away. Suicide starts to look like the only way out, and the worst part? These women never choose a peaceful method. Only in rare cases do they overdose and "go to sleep". Most of the time the deaths are violent. They drink bleach, or hang themselves, or jump from high buildings. They set fire to themselves. These are mostly well-educated, well-off women and they die horrible, agonising deaths.'

'And they kill their babies,' Marnie said.

Fran nodded. 'Sometimes, yes, they do.'

'But there are pills,' Marnie nodded at the foil strip, 'that can treat the symptoms.'

'If you take them. Lots of women are afraid to, especially if they're breast-feeding.'

'But in that case,' Noah protested, 'the symptoms would be obvious, wouldn't they? Someone would notice that something was wrong.'

Fran shook her head. 'Most women learn to hide them. They know that if they're suspected of harming their babies, then the children will be taken away. So the condition becomes entrenched, harder to treat. It's a vicious circle.'

'Vicious,' Marnie agreed. She frowned at the strip of pills. 'Why would someone stop taking her medication if she was aware of the risks?'

'Because she isn't thinking logically or she doesn't understand the risks, or, most likely, because she's worried about the danger to her baby. If she's pregnant again, say, or breast-feeding. Toxic contamination sounds frightening. Nothing like being made to choose between your sanity and your baby's health.'

'Supernatural powers . . .' Noah looked at the death reports. 'You said sometimes these women believe their children can survive anything.'

Fran pulled at her fingers again. 'Yes . . .'

'The way they were put away, Fred and Archie, in that bunker. Hidden. As if to make them safe. Maybe they were never meant to die. Maybe Esther put them down there thinking they could survive, because she thought they could survive anything.'

'She confessed to their murders,' Marnie said. 'She lied about how they died, said that they were drowned like their sister. She drowned their baby sister.'

Noah looked at Fran. 'There's no doubt she did it?'

'None that I could find, but I've only just started looking. You'll be able to get better answers than me. I can't even tell you where Esther Reid is now.'

Marnie looked at her. 'You said she was sent to a psychiatric prison.'

'She was paroled, a couple of weeks ago.'

Noah's skin squirmed in protest. 'Three counts of manslaughter and she's out already?'

'Based on her successful treatment,' Fran said with only a hint of irony, 'yes, she is.'

'And recently,' Marnie said. 'So the prison database must have an address.'

'I looked for a record of Esther Reid in the system, and there's nothing current. Nothing I could find, anyway.' Fran paused. 'The women I read about who survived PPP but served time for killing their children? Ended up with new identities when they were released.'

'So Esther Reid could be someone else by now?'

'Very possibly, yes.'

'Out, and with a new identity . . . She could have left the peaches. She could have been back to the crime scene. Is that what we're saying?'

Fran put her hands up. 'I'm just saying she might not be Esther Reid any more, and good luck getting the new identity from the system. Last time I had to do that – and we're talking about a corpse here – it was like wrestling a greased weasel.'

'Esther's in the Old Testament,' Noah said. 'She was an exiled Jewess.'

Fran looked bemused, so Marnie explained: 'We think we know where to find Esther's mother. Connie Pryce. She was living near Blackthorn Road before the houses went up. A neighbour remembered her daughter having an Old Testament name. He also remembered her grandchildren, Fred and Archie.' She glanced at Noah. 'Denis didn't mention Louisa?'

Noah shook his head. 'Just Fred and Archie.'

'And how quickly Connie left . . . Overnight, wasn't it?' Marnie looked at Fran. 'Connie went with the travellers who were living over the bunkers.'

'You don't think Connie *knew* the boys were down there?'

'If she hadn't gone so suddenly . . . Why didn't she stay

and help her daughter through the trial, the treatment? She ran away, and we need to know when, and why.'

Marnie turned to Noah. 'What else did Walton tell you about Connie's daughter?'

'Just that she worked for Ian Merrick. She and Connie fought about the development.'

'Merrick's the man who built the houses over the bunkers,' Fran said. 'So Esther could have known about the bunkers. Yes, I see. It's less clear why she lied about how Fred and Archie died, although I suspect you're right.' She nodded at Noah. 'She thought she was putting them somewhere safe. Maybe she *did* imagine they could survive down there.'

'The police stopped looking for them because she lied,' Marnie said. 'If she'd told the truth, it might not have been too late. Why didn't she tell the police where to find them? After they'd arrested her, after they'd found Louisa. When it was all over for her and she knew she couldn't get back to the bunker to feed them, or take care of them. Why didn't she tell the police where they were?'

Fran shook her head. 'In that state of psychosis? She wouldn't have been lucid. If she thought the boys were superhuman, all-powerful . . . She was keeping them *safe*, inside the bunker. The *danger* was telling someone else where to find them. I doubt she was rational enough to realise they'd starve without food. She probably believed they didn't even need oxygen. They were her little gods, her miracles.'

But she was cured now, otherwise they wouldn't have released her.

Noah tried to imagine how that must have felt for Esther Reid, the moment in her treatment when she came upright enough to realise what she'd done, burying her boys alive.

'What about her husband. Matthew Reid. Might he know where she is now?'

'I couldn't find him in the system either,' Fran said. 'Hopefully you'll have more luck.'

'What I want to know,' Marnie said, 'is how Esther's pills ended up in a house that wasn't built when she buried her sons down there.'

'If these *are* her pills,' Fran said. 'We don't have a prescription.'

'They were hidden in a bag that Clancy Brand took from Blackthorn Road.'

'You think he found them? Took them from the bunker? We know someone had been down there recently. But why would Esther leave pills she was no longer taking in the bunker with her boys? That makes no sense.'

'None of this makes sense.' Marnie looked angry, and sad. 'There's the tin of peaches, too. Who left those? If it was Esther, why? As a gift, or as a warning? Why risk her parole by going back there? And straight away, within a fortnight of being released . . . That smells like planning to me. What's she up to?'

She stood. 'We need to find Esther Reid.'

46

We took the train to Slough. Right to the edge of our parole perimeter. Any closer and we'd be in violation. That word's playing in my head like violins: *violation*.

We're in violation, Esther and I.

The windows on the train have two layers of glass, giving us twin reflections.

We take up a table seat for four. No one wants to sit next to us, as if we've created our own force field, repelling all boarders.

We're growing, and it scares me. But I'm excited, too.

From the window of the train, we watch the river running away to London. The tracks swing us close then suck us back, as if subject to the Thames's tides. The world's seen a lot of rain since we were last out. The river is swollen all the way to Slough, like a belt that's been doubled into a strap. I think of her little body in that tide, pushed and pulled. The thought brings the strap down on to my back and drives a knife into my chest.

The river looked so gentle that morning. It was like lying her down on a bed of brown silk. If I concentrate, I can see her face, smiling up at me. She doesn't haunt me like the boys.

Fred and Archie would never have gone into the water the way she did, quietly and with a smile. Archie would've dived in after his baby sister. He had bravery in spades. They both did, such fierce boys. Archie would've fought Esther, if I'd let him.

The train runs parallel to the river for a moment, so close I can see my face in its swollen back. I think about the fisherman who found her.

Esther and I didn't just hurt the children, you see. There were so many other people involved. The fisherman who found Louisa. The jury who convicted us. Connie, and Matthew, and all their friends. I sometimes think about that boy, Saul Weller, who fought with Archie until they became best friends. And now this new family, the ones living in the house that Ian built, over the bunkers. The ones who found Fred and Archie.

It's in the papers. It can't be long now before they piece it together and pick up the phone to the parole board. We'll be back inside soon. But not before we've taken our proper punishment. Not before we've looked into the mirror.

Lyn gave us an uptight farewell, one last volley of shots: 'Be-kind-to-yourself-and-take-care.' *Rat-a-tat-tat.*

Be kind to yourself.

Why, I wanted to ask, *with what purpose?*

Perhaps I should feel pity for our plight. Thrown out of the place that was keeping us safe, chucked to the wolves of real life. Sharp objects and tall buildings, rivers and bridges and cheap aspirin and razor blades. The public gaze.

Mirrors, everywhere.

How are we going to survive this?

Perhaps – oh, this is clever, this is brilliant – perhaps *this* is our punishment.

47

Ron said, 'Shit. *Shit.*' He swung a fist at the whiteboard, making it rattle.

Debbie covered her mouth with her hand, eyes glassy with tears.

Marnie said, 'We need a photograph of Esther Reid. We need dates for her arrest, for her confession and her trial. I want the name of the arresting officer, and the psychiatrist who treated her in prison. We need to know where and who and *what* Esther Reid is now.'

'Who?' Ron echoed.

'We think she has a new identity. She's been rehabilitated.'

'Why're we even looking, if she's done her time?'

'Because someone left this,' Marnie set the tin of peaches on the desk, 'outside the Doyles' house, last night or early this morning. If it was Esther, it's a breach of her parole. She lied about the deaths. She said the boys drowned. We need to interview her about that.'

'We're going to charge her with new offences?' Debbie said. 'When she's just been released?'

'If she's committed any, yes.'

'Shit,' Ron repeated. He looked beaten.

'We have names for the boys. Archie and Fred Reid. Put them on the board. And find a picture of Esther Reid.'

Marnie understood the team's despondency. They'd imagined they were chasing a psychopath, a paedophile or worse. All the time they'd been looking for the boys' mother, driven mad by her body's reaction to giving birth; one of nature's sicker tricks. Perhaps the boys had suffered less than they would have done at the hands of the monster they'd all imagined, but it was so desperately *sad*.

Marnie wasn't sure she didn't prefer their earlier theory to this terrible reality.

She tapped the tin of peaches, looking across at Debbie. 'How are you getting on with the press? Has anyone sent in photos they took of the crowd yesterday?'

'Not yet. A couple have said they'll cooperate, but I'm already getting excuses about press freedom thrown at me . . .'

'Stick at it. Noah, you and Ron found a website that sells these tins? See if you can get customer records for recent orders in the London area. What do we have on Connie Pryce?'

'Council records are coming,' Noah said, 'for the flat. I've asked for the date she moved out, and anything else they have.'

'Good. Find out about Esther's other relations, and her friends. Anyone she might have gone to when they let her out. Her parole officer should have what we need. Ron, where're you up to with the travellers?'

'About here.' Carling held the flat of his hand to his eyes. 'They *might* be on a site near Heathrow. I was going to take a recce in that direction this morning.'

'Let's wait until we have a photo of Esther, and some dates. If she was released into Connie's care, then we'll want to come with you.' Marnie nodded at Noah. 'After we've been back to see what Ian Merrick wasn't telling us the first time round.'

The Isle of Dogs was deserted. No workmen on-site, Merrick's mobile office locked and empty. It was like seeing a school playground after dark, the whole shape of the place altered by the absence of people. 'Where is everyone?' Noah wondered.

'UXB stops play?' Marnie stepped out of the way of a chip wrapper breezing towards them. She took out her phone and called the station, asking the team to get hold of Merrick.

'Do you think he lied to us?' Noah said.

'It looks that way. Either Esther found out about the bunkers and didn't tell him, or they both knew the bunkers were never filled in. If he got the land cheap, cut corners . . . Didn't Denis Walton say the houses were thrown up? Then I imagine Merrick knew. If Esther was working for him, and *she* knew?' Marnie shrugged. 'He knew.'

'D'you think he lied about more than just the bunkers? He must've known Esther was arrested, and for what. We told him we'd found the bodies of two little children down there. He could have put two and two together. Maybe he *did* put two and two together.'

'And decided it was best to keep his mouth shut? Maybe.'

They were quiet for a moment, standing in the empty chill of the site.

Noah broke the silence by asking, 'Does it matter?'

Marnie pushed her hair from her face, knotting it at the nape of her neck. 'Because Esther was punished? Because her children are dead and there's no killer to catch? It matters.'

'The tin of peaches,' Noah deduced. 'If Esther left them . . . Why? Why would she go back? There's nothing there for her.'

'Nothing obvious,' Marnie said. The wind whipped her hair loose again. She narrowed her eyes against the sting of it. 'Come on. Let's talk to Fergus Gibb.'

'The fisherman who found Louisa? Can he give us anything we don't already know?'

'Maybe not, but if I was Esther Reid? I'd want to go back to where I last saw my children alive. We've been concentrating on the bunker, but perhaps she's been to the river too. The place she put Louisa. The place she *said* she put the boys. I want to see it.'

48

The river moved reluctantly, resisting the tug of the tide. A long bank led to the road where Marnie had parked.

Slippery mud hauled at their boots as she and Noah made their way to the water's edge. She didn't know how the fishermen stopped their camping stools from sinking into it. Three men were fishing, their lines in the water, hooded yellow oilcloths worn to keep the damp out. The mud was like the river, hungry, belching at their boots. The sound rose from deep inside the wide muscle of water coiling across London, carrying God knows what out to sea.

Fergus Gibb hadn't been down here by the water in five years. Not since he found the body of a baby girl floating in a polystyrene box.

'The kind they pack fish in,' he'd told Marnie and Noah, 'for market. You find all sorts washing up there. It wasn't the first time I'd found something that shouldn't have been in the river. But it was the worst time. She was so,' he framed a foot with his hands, 'small.'

'We're sorry,' Marnie said, 'for making you go through this again.'

'Never stop going through it,' Fergus replied. 'Not a day

goes by. I gave up the fishing, can't even walk the dog by the river now.' The dog was at his feet, grizzled chin tucked into its paws. 'Time was I'd have said you couldn't lose anything in the river, not for long. The mud's like a magnet, but it sends everything back up eventually. We used to joke it was the best place to lose a pound, and the worst place to bury a corpse. The river sends it all back up.' He leaned to put a hand on the dog's head. 'Not the boys, though.'

The river had sent back Louisa Reid. It hadn't returned her brothers, Fred and Archie, because it'd never had them.

Esther had lied to the police, to everyone. She'd put Louisa into the water, but the boys . . .

The boys she hid underground, as if they'd be safe there.

Marnie tried to put herself in Esther's shoes, she really did. Tried for empathy, some thread of connection to the woman's madness, her pain. From what Fran said, it was likely that Esther had suffered from depression as a teenager. Maybe she'd felt she didn't belong. Maybe all this started with an escape. Running away . . .

Marnie could understand that.

She watched the city guttering in the water's edge, London's landmarks reflected in the turning tide. Everywhere around, the mudflats were fired by orange street light into abstract sculptures, as if the city's salvage was being thrust up from the shore.

The river's breath sat wet and slick on the yellow oilskins of the three fishermen.

Tamas, Fergus Gibb had called the Thames, giving the river its old name. Father Thames. Some father, taking the body of Louisa Reid, only to return it, shrunken and grey.

'They say the river can carry a body a mile a day,' he'd told them, 'but it didn't carry her.' He walked the dog in another direction now, away from the river to a scrub of parkland, one of London's meaner green squares.

At Marnie's side, Noah shivered. His shoulders were hunched, in a bid to keep the cold from creeping into his ears.

Marnie felt a pang of guilt for bringing him here. Maybe Noah didn't need this nearness in order to do his job. Maybe it was just her who needed to rub up against the sharpest corners of the crime, the tragedy.

Esther Reid had smothered her baby and wrapped her in a blanket. Put her in a box, and put the box into the Thames. Crime scene investigators had discovered a neat pile of clothes on the bank. Not just Louisa's clothes. Fred and Archie's, too. They searched for days with police divers and dogs, but they couldn't find the boys. Esther said she'd drugged them and put them in the water. She said they drowned.

Empathy was impossible.

Marnie doubted that Esther Reid, wherever and whoever she was now, could feel empathy for the woman she'd been when she killed her children. She doubted Esther would want empathy, or sympathy, for the woman who did that.

Standing at the water's edge, all Marnie felt was sadness. Desperate, soul-corroding sadness – and fear, for what a woman waking up to that nightmare might do.

'Christ, it's cold.' Noah tipped his head back at the sky. 'But at least it's out in the open.'

Not underground, in other words.

'Yes.' Marnie looked upstream, the heels of her boots sinking in pleats of mud. The police had dragged the riverbed for more than a mile. No sign of the boys, anywhere.

How easily would she have given up the search, had she been in charge? How long did you decently look for lost children? Five years, alone in the dark. Would she have looked for them that long? Would she have found them if she had?

Noah's phone played the theme from *The Sweeney.*

'DS Jake. Yes . . . Hang on.'

He turned on the speaker, holding the phone so Marnie could listen at the same time.

'Beth Doyle just called.' Debbie Tanner's voice was strained. 'Her kids are missing, Carmen and Tommy. She's in a right state.'

'When was this?'

'Just now. She's on the other line. I wanted to call you right away. She doesn't know how they got out of the house, only took her eyes off them for five minutes, thought they were with Clancy, maybe at the park, but she went to look for them and there's no sign. Anywhere. I'm on my way over to her. I wasn't sure how quickly you could be there.'

'Forty minutes,' Noah said, 'if the traffic's not too bad.'

He and Marnie started back towards the car.

'It's only been an hour, I know.' Debbie's voice broke up for a second, from static or stress. 'But I thought *these* kids . . . that family . . .'

'You're right,' Marnie told her. 'We'll be there as soon as we can. Stay with Beth until we get to you. And put in a report on the missing kids. Let's not take any chances, or waste any time. If you get push-back, send it my way. We've got grounds for worrying about these kids, given what's happening in Blackthorn Road.'

'It couldn't be Esther,' Debbie said. 'Could it? I mean . . . she wouldn't do that. Take someone else's kids?'

'We can speculate later,' Marnie said. 'Clear the line. We're on our way.'

PART TWO

1

Five years ago

She's upstairs. You can tell by the creak of the floor, and the heat over your head when you stand in the hall, listening. A hot spot in the house. Dangerous.

She's in the nursery, with the baby.

You're a coward. You don't go up straight away. Instead, you look for Fred and Archie. To be sure they're safe.

They're on the sofa in the sitting room, in their pyjamas. Archie's playing on his DS. Lolling at his shoulder, Fred's got his thumb in his mouth and his eyes are glassy, the way they were when he was a baby. He's nearly five now, but he's regressed, gone back behind the barricades of baby-speak, whining when he doesn't want his food.

'Archie?'

'What?' Archie's angry. His version of Fred's regression; the pair of them hunkered down, in defence mode. It's a bad sign. It means it's been a bad day.

'Have you eaten?'

Archie rolls his eyes as if you should know this, as if you

fed the pair of them yourself. He jabs at the game console with his thumbs, killing stuff. He's eight years old.

The heat shifts overhead, away from the nursery, towards the bathroom.

Your throat makes a fist. You put everything away, didn't you?

Razor blades and pills, make-up bags with metal zips; you even changed the light switch from a pull cord to a presser in case she found a way to make a noose of the nylon cord.

'Esther?' You climb the stairs two at a time, breathless by the time you reach the top.

The bathroom door's shut, but not locked. You took out the locks, after the last time. The shadow's still there on the join between the tiled floor of the bathroom and the carpeted floor of the landing: the place where the blood leaked. You cleaned the tiles, but the carpet sucked up the stain and put down a shadow you can't shift.

The heat coming from the other side of the bathroom door is horrible, as if someone's lit a fire in there.

You reach your hand to the door, half expecting the handle to burn you.

You're scared now, bile at the back of your throat. 'Esther . . . are you okay?'

You'd smell smoke if there was a fire.

It's not a fire. It's just her.

Esther.

You made a pact, the two of you. After you took the locks from all the doors. You promised to always knock when the door was shut, and wait for her to answer. A pact to preserve her dignity. Yours was lost long ago. Given up for dead, like your courage.

You turn and go down the landing to the nursery.

Louisa's not in her cot. Just the covers, pulled neat. That's bad. Neatness is bad.

It means Esther's on a binge.

You've tried explaining this to the doctors, the midwife, anyone who'll listen. They say it's a good sign that she's noticing things, taking care of housework. You know better. She's trying to fend off the flood. It's the first sure sign that chaos is on its way. Again.

You have to go into the bathroom now, you have to.

For Louisa.

You make up a story in your head, a version of what you'll find. Something safe and normal, so that you have the courage to go in there. She's changing Louisa's nappy. She's washing her hands. She's on the loo. She's having a bath, like she used to with Archie, the baby sitting on her stomach, the pair of them perfectly happy. No, not the bath, that's where she did it last time . . .

You're sick, shaking. Your thighs are sweating.

'Esther . . .' You turn the handle, push at the door.

The first thing you see is the mirror, the plastic one you put up in place of glass.

Your feet prick at the sight, remembering the broken pieces on the tiles, a splinter that went deep into your heel. Your face is in the mirror, crowded out by hers.

'Esther . . .'

You flinch at the sight of her reflection, the newly alien familiarity, like an over-realistic Hallowe'en mask. You shift to one side so the two of you are sharing the mirror, your faces sliced in two; a bad Abba video.

She's standing there naked, all her scars and welts on show, and you know . . .

She's doing an inventory, looking for a place to put some new damage.

Her fists are clenched. You're afraid she's got hold of something sharp.

You put it all away, didn't you?

Your eyes scare to the tooth mug (plastic). Prisoners make weapons out of toothbrushes, and carrier bags. They melt them down and make them into sharp objects.

Fred and Archie's toothbrushes are in the mug. And yours, Esther's . . .

Your eyes jump around the room, looking for what she's hidden.

'Where's Louisa?'

She doesn't look at you.

She's breathing low and deep, like an engine, like a furnace.

Her shadow stretches up the walls, falls into the bath and paints the cupboards black.

You know that if she fought you, you'd lose.

She's holding all the power. She's holding . . .

'Where's Louisa?' There's a whine in your voice, like Fred's when he doesn't want his food. Like the puppy, Budge, until she had to go; too many things to worry about.

You're losing this fight. Like all the others.

'Please,' sobbing now, 'Esther, where is she? Where's Louisa?'

2

Now

Beth was in the kitchen at the safe house, pacing back and forth, touching cupboard doors and chairs. It reminded Noah of his mum's rituals, when she was in the grip of one of her cleaning compulsions.

Debbie whispered, 'I think we should call a doctor. She's been like this since I got here.'

'Where's Terry?' Marnie asked.

'She says she called him, but he's working on a garden somewhere. She can't remember where. From what she said, there's no signal on his phone, or he's switched it off.'

Marnie nodded. She didn't take her eyes off Beth. 'Check that, would you? You have Terry's number.'

Debbie looked surprised. 'Yes, but you don't think . . . she's lying?'

'I think she's understandably agitated and distressed. We need to do everything we can to help her. Terry needs to know what's happening, and he'll want to be here with her.' She watched the woman's pacing. 'You're right about the doctor, but try and get her GP, or her midwife. Someone she knows and trusts.'

Debbie nodded, leaving the kitchen to make the phone calls.

Beth had stopped to pick up pieces of the children's washing from a laundry basket, pulling creases from the little clothes.

Marnie went to her. 'We're here to find the children. Can you tell me what happened?'

'I don't *know*!' Her voice was high enough to climb walls. She pulled at a tiny vest, twisting it with her hands as if she was wringing water from it. 'They were in their room, playing. Clancy was here. I thought he took them to the park. But they're not there. They've *gone*. I don't know where . . .'

'How long since you realised they weren't in the house?' Marnie asked.

'An hour ago, more than an hour,' her eyes ran to the clock, 'at eleven. Clancy sometimes takes them to run around in the park so they'll be hungry before lunch. But he has to bring them back by twelve. He *knows* that.'

It was 12.37.

'This is the park just up the road?' Marnie said.

The police had searched the park as soon as Debbie called in the location. No sign of Carmen or Tommy, or Clancy.

'Yes.' Beth wrenched at the child's vest. 'I won't let him take them any further than that. He's always . . . he always brings them back on time.'

'Did you see them leave the house together, Clancy and the children?'

Beth shook her head. 'He told me he was going out, but I assumed he meant on his own. I thought Carmen and Tommy were upstairs.'

'Clancy told you he was going out,' Marnie repeated. 'What time was that?'

'At eleven. I told you. That's the last time I saw them. I went upstairs just afterwards, and their room was empty. I looked all over the house, in case they were hiding, then I thought he must've taken them with him, to the park, that I must've misunderstood what he said . . .'

'So that I'm clear, Clancy didn't say he was taking the children?'

'Just that he was going out.' Beth's hands twisted, putting creases back into the vest she'd straightened. 'Maybe he didn't shut the door properly. Maybe they went after him . . .'

'Was the door shut properly when you were looking for them?'

'Yes . . . but Carmen knows how to close it. She could've done that, when they left.'

'You didn't hear the door close? When Clancy left, or later?'

Beth shook her head.

'The last time we spoke,' Marnie said, 'you told me you were worried about Clancy's temper. You said he was angry, missing the house . . .'

'You think I shouldn't have left him alone with them.' Beth's stare was blind, moving about the kitchen, avoiding Marnie. 'You think if I *knew* he was angry . . . what was I thinking, letting him look after them?'

'No, I'm not saying that. I just wondered if there'd been a fight of some kind. If Clancy left the house in a bad mood . . .'

'You don't have kids.' Beth flung the vest into the laundry basket. 'You don't know what it's like trying to keep an eye on all of them, every minute. Clancy wanted to help. It made him happy, it made *them* happy, and it meant I could get on with all . . . this!' She gestured around her at the washing, the dishes in the sink, breakfast mess on the table, an overflowing pedal-bin. 'Half an hour, that's all I needed, half an hour . . .' She reached for a chair and sat, abruptly, as if someone had kicked her feet from under her.

Marnie nodded at the kettle, and Noah moved to make tea.

'Why wasn't Clancy at school?' Marnie pulled out a second chair and sat facing Beth. Noah saw Beth surrender her hand to Marnie's steady grip.

'He's been suspended, for fighting with another boy, but that doesn't mean . . .' Beth's eyes were huge. 'He's *good* with Tommy and Carmen. He really is.'

'Have you tried calling him?'

'His phone's broken. That's what the fight was about.'

'So he doesn't have a phone right now?'

'We were going to get him a new one at the weekend. Clancy *knows* . . . He knows to bring them back from the park in time. Tommy gets too tired otherwise and then he won't eat his food. It can't be Clancy who's taken them. He *knows* the rules.'

Beth's face hollowed. She pulled her hand free of Marnie's to wipe at her eyes.

'What mood was Clancy in when he set off?'

'The same as always.' Her voice broke. 'He was angry with me!' She started to weep, quietly, not proper grief, not yet.

Debbie came back into the kitchen, shaking her head in response to the question Marnie asked with her eyes. 'Gillian's on her way,' she told Beth. 'She'll be here very soon.'

'Gill . . .?' Beth looked lost. 'Why?'

'To make sure you're okay.' Debbie nodded at Marnie and Noah. 'Gill is Beth's midwife. I'm afraid Terry's got his phone switched off. If we knew where he was working . . .'

'Landscaping, that's where he is. Putting in trees today. Willows and birch . . .' Beth's eyes closed, as if she was able to relax now that Marnie and the others were in charge.

'The kiddies will be hungry.' Debbie sat in the spare chair at Beth's side. 'Do they have anything with them, like snacks? Does Clancy have anything?' She used a chatty tone, as if she was making small talk at the school gates.

'Don't know.' Beth rocked in the chair. She looked nearly comatose.

Noah set a cup of sugary tea at her elbow.

'Did he take his duffle bag?' Marnie asked.

Beth shook her head. 'I don't know . . . Probably. He takes it everywhere.' She bit her lip. 'They love him, especially Carmen. He's the only one she'll listen to sometimes. He's got a way with them . . .'

'If they wanted to be naughty,' Debbie said, 'give you a fright, where would they go?'

Marnie kept quiet, watching for Beth's responses. Not just verbal; she was watching the woman's body language, trusting Debbie to keep Beth talking.

'Is there somewhere they might go? Just as a game, without thinking . . . You know what kids are like.'

Beth's head nodded. 'The estate,' she murmured. 'Clancy knows we hate it there. We tell all the kids to stay away from the estate . . .'

Marnie met Noah's eyes and he took out his phone to text the station, telling the team to check the housing estate for any sightings of Clancy and the children.

'They can be terrible places, can't they?' Debbie matched Beth's sing-song intonation; it was hard to believe they were discussing missing children. 'Like mazes, one wrong turn and you're muddled. What's the one like near you? It's up behind Beech Rise, isn't it?'

'Arlington . . . It's horrible. Dirty. Drug dealers, smashed windows, we tell the kids to stay away, but Clancy . . .' Beth's voice died. She rocked in the chair, not reacting to any further questions, even when the midwife knocked on the door.

Noah wondered if it was a defence mechanism, her body shutting down in order to safeguard her unborn child.

Debbie stayed sitting with Beth as the midwife started to check her over.

Noah went with Marnie, up the stairs to the bedrooms.

It wasn't hard to tell which bedroom belonged to Carmen and Tommy. Soft toys padded the room like a cell. Against one wall: a travel cot for Tommy and a camp bed with pink bedding for Carmen. A navy nylon sleeping bag was unzipped, kicked to one corner of the room.

'She lets Clancy sleep in here,' Marnie said, as if she couldn't quite believe it.

The room smelt of sugar and mushrooms, the aroma of teenage boy slogging it out with the sweeter scent of the children.

'No duffle bag. That means he took it with him.'

'That's significant?' Noah asked. 'What's in the bag?'

'A change of clothes, money, an Oyster card. It's a go-bag.'

'And now he's gone . . . Do you think he's dangerous?'

'To them?' Marnie looked at the sleeping bag, the cot, the camp bed. 'I don't know. But he's damaged, and he's hurting. Put that together with the anger . . . He's not safe. That's assuming the kids went with him.'

No cupboards in the room, no hiding places.

Everything was in plain sight.

'Beth trusts him with her kids.' Noah followed Marnie's gaze as it swept the room, seeing piles of unwashed clothes, the smear of fingerprints on the walls. Neglect.

It wasn't like the house in Blackthorn Road, nor was Beth the same woman she'd been there. Something had broken between then and now, running like a crack across the heart of this family. What they'd witnessed in the garden, in the bunker . . . No wonder they were coming apart.

'If you were Clancy,' Marnie said, 'would you trust a stranger? A woman.'

'Esther Reid? You think she took them *and* Clancy?'

'Beth saw Clancy with two women on the estate. Dressed as if they hadn't bought new clothes in a long time. What if one of them was Esther Reid?'

'With Clancy? Why?'

'Because she knew where he lived. Maybe she wanted a way back into the house, or into the garden. She needed him to trust her . . .'

'Why would he do that?' Noah asked. 'If she was a stranger?'

'Teenage boys have their own criteria for trust. Beth says all three of them were smoking. Perhaps they gave him cigarettes. That might have been enough to swing it.'

Marnie looked at the sleeping bag kicked into the corner of the room. 'He's only fourteen. We have to treat this as three missing children, at risk of harm.'

'If it's Esther,' Noah said, 'and she's taken them . . . what's she going to do?'

'I don't know. I don't want to guess, either. We need to look at the evidence. Let's get that photo of Esther, in case Beth recognises her as one of the women from the estate.'

A sound from downstairs made them move in that direction.

Terry was standing on the mat in his gardening clothes, a red jumper unravelling at one wrist, ancient jeans, blue socks. Seeing Noah and Marnie, he came to a standstill.

'What's happened?' Fear wiped his face blank. 'Where's Beth?'

'She's in the kitchen.' Marnie went down the stairs towards him. 'Gill's with her, and DC Tanner. If we could have a moment to talk, before you go through . . .'

Terry wiped at his face with the crook of his elbow. He

smelt of earth and leaves, his hands caked and ruddy. 'Tell me,' he said.

'Carmen and Tommy are missing. So's Clancy, but—'

She wasn't halfway through the sentence before he started moving.

Not in the direction of the kitchen; back out of the house.

Marnie and Noah followed, staying close.

In the porch, Terry was pulling on his wellingtons. His face was fierce, mouth thinned to nothing, shoulders shaking as he struggled with the boots.

Marnie wanted to hold him still. 'We have a team looking for the children.'

'Where?' He stood with one boot on and the other in his hands, eyes haggard with hope as he searched their faces. 'He'll be on that housing estate . . . Christ!'

His feet were swollen from the day's work. He couldn't get the remaining boot on, nearly falling sideways until Noah's hand stopped him, holding him upright until he'd got his balance back. 'I know where he is. He'll be on that estate. Arlington . . .'

'We have a team on the way there. You should stay with your wife. She needs you.'

'My kids need me. Tommy and Carmen,' his eyes blazed with distress, 'they need me. They're just little kids. Little, little kids . . .'

'We'll find them.' Marnie touched his arm, feeling the fizz of his shock through the sleeve of his jumper. 'Come back into the house. Please.'

Terry wiped at his nose. 'Clancy's playing games. He wouldn't hurt them.' The words jerked out of him, defensively. 'He wouldn't.'

'That's good. I'm sure you're right. We're doing everything we can to find them. Come back into the house and tell us where you think they might have gone.'

They took Terry to his wife. When his arms were tight around Beth, Marnie nodded at Debbie to stay with the couple.

Noah followed her out of the house, pausing to move the wellington boot that Terry had abandoned in the porch. 'Will he be okay? He's in a worse state than she is . . .'

'I'm on it.' Marnie had her phone to her ear.

Ed picked up on the third ring. 'Hey.'

'I need a victim care officer.' She gave Ed the address. 'Terry and Beth Doyle. Can you come?'

Ed didn't waste time on questions. 'I'm twenty minutes away.' He rang off.

Marnie's phone buzzed almost immediately. 'Ron, what've you got?'

'A crap picture of Esther Reid. You're right, she's got a new name. I'll text what I've found. You're going to want to talk with her psychiatrist, because it's worse than we thought.'

'DC Tanner's here with the family,' Marnie told him. 'Victim Support's on its way. You're on house-to-house. I want all eyes on the Arlington estate. Someone must have seen those children, and Clancy. We can't assume they're together. Where can we find Esther's psychiatrist?'

'Lyn Birch. She's in London for a conference at the Barbican. She treated Esther in Durham, out of Lawton Down Prison, but right now she's in the Holiday Inn on Old Street.'

'How is it worse than we thought?' Marnie asked.

At her side, Noah tensed, watching her face.

'Put it this way,' Ron replied, 'if I said they were off their rockers letting her out? I'd be making the understatement of the fucking century.'

3

Lyn Birch was wound like a spring, one heel tapping on the floor, her face tight enough to bounce pennies off. 'Patient confidentiality . . .'

'Doesn't apply,' Marnie said, 'where there's a breach of parole. Or a risk to the public. So please don't waste our time, or yours. I'm sure you're very busy. Tell us about Esther Reid.'

'Alison Oliver,' Lyn corrected.

As if they'd made a fundamental error. Got their facts back to front. Named the wrong suspect.

'What?'

Lyn Birch repeated, 'She's Alison Oliver now.'

A beat, before Marnie said, 'You mean she has a new identity.'

The woman's lips pursed. 'It's rather more complicated than that.'

'In what way is it more complicated?'

'Alison stopped being Esther when she . . . faced up to what Esther had done.'

'Stopped being Esther . . . How is that possible?'

'You need to understand the psychology.' Lyn smoothed

her clothes with her hands. 'But trust me, she's Alison Oliver now. Esther is . . . someone else. Someone she's not.'

Marnie looked at her, waiting. She was willing to bet that Esther Reid didn't think she was Alison Oliver. Not if this woman had done even a fraction of her job properly. It wasn't a job Marnie envied, waking women to the chaos wrought by their illness.

'Esther was a very sick woman,' Lyn said. 'How much do you know about PPP?'

'Enough to know that each case is unique. We're not after a broad understanding of Esther's condition. We need to know *specifically* how ill she was when she came to you. And how she was when she left.'

'I hope you're not suggesting I discharged a sick woman.' A sharp voice, stark syllables, like listening to the pinging of a black box. Dressed in a dark suit that showcased her bones. Against the impersonal white of the hotel room, she was like an expensive X-ray.

Marnie said, 'You've seen the papers. You know what we've found in Snaresbrook.'

The woman moved a hand in protest. 'You're not saying . . . Those children . . .'

'Were Fred and Archie Reid. DNA tests proved it. The timing's odd, wouldn't you say?'

The woman blinked, showing the taut lids of her eyes. 'You think it's significant? A risk to the public, you said. Surely you can't mean . . .'

'We think it's a strange coincidence. You discharge Esther at the same time we discover she committed perjury. Doesn't that seem odd to you?'

'She was ready to be discharged. I wouldn't have signed the paperwork otherwise.'

'Esther was ready to go back into society. She was well enough for that.'

'She'd made huge progress, yes?'

'Are you telling me,' Marnie said, 'or asking me?'

'What?' The flush ran like water across the woman's face.

'You said "yes", but it sounded like a question. *Did* she make huge progress?'

'Yes, she did.' Lyn opened both hands. 'Huge progress. What you have to understand is that these women don't know what they're doing when they're in the grip of PPP. They don't realise how very ill they are, or how dangerous.'

'We understand that,' Noah said. 'But when she *did* realise it, when you'd helped her to realise it . . . what happened then?'

'She retreated, to begin with. That's natural, yes? But as you say, we helped her to understand her illness and to see that in order to get well, she had to stop hiding.'

'Hiding how? What were her symptoms?'

'She hid behind Esther.'

Silence, underscored by the whine of the air-conditioning unit.

Noah said, 'I don't understand. She *is* Esther . . .'

'She's Alison,' Lyn corrected. 'That was an essential part of her rehabilitation. She was horrified, revolted really, by what she'd done as Esther. That's normal. We worked to help her regroup,' forming a circle with her hands, 'as Alison. To see that she could move beyond what she did. Start over.'

Start over with what? She'd destroyed it all. Her family, her life, all of it. The Doyles' family was different. Unless Esther didn't see it that way.

'She hid behind Esther,' Marnie repeated. 'You're describing what, exactly? A split personality? Schizophrenia?'

Lyn's face rippled with professional distaste. 'Nothing as . . . clinical as that. It was a question of who she was, and who she *could be*. Surely you believe in second chances?'

'Right now? I believe in plain speaking.' Enunciating every

word very clearly: 'What do you mean when you say that she hid behind Esther?'

'Alison would sometimes talk about Esther in the third person, as if she was someone else, apart from her. But she got past that stage, yes?'

Or she got better at hiding.

Marnie didn't imagine it took a genius to trick Lyn Birch, with her rhetorical questions and her nervous energy that looked very much like professional insecurity.

A briefcase sat on the hotel desk under the window. Paperwork for the conference she was attending. Next to the briefcase, a lanyard was laid out like an expensive necklace.

'Did she talk about where she would go,' Marnie said, 'when she was paroled?'

'To her mother, Connie Pryce. That was agreed. The parole officer will have the address. It might not be conventional, but . . .'

'In what way is it not conventional?'

'Connie Pryce lives on a travellers' ground in Slough.'

'And that's a stable environment for a woman like Esther?'

'Alison,' Lyn insisted, but with less conviction now. 'It wasn't ideal, but her mother wanted it. She wanted her daughter to have a second chance, a safe place to go.'

'Connie had forgiven her?'

'Absolutely.'

'In all the time you spent with her,' Marnie said, 'all the sessions, Esther never once admitted what she really did to the boys? She never mentioned the bunkers?'

'Never.'

'But she demonstrated remorse. Enough for you to recommend her release.'

Lyn's face thinned into a smile. 'She was *consumed* by remorse. I don't think I've ever treated anyone more completely filled with it. To the brim.'

'And that's . . . healthy. To be so consumed by remorse.'

Lyn bristled. 'I do know my job. Without remorse, there can be no recovery.'

'But remorse in itself isn't a guarantee of recovery, is it?'

'Of course not. There are no guarantees. But in Alison's case, it was a first step. An extremely indicative first step.'

'She stopped hiding behind Esther?' Noah asked.

'Yes she did.' Lyn tided her face to a smooth sheet. 'She put that part of her life behind her, and moved on.'

'To Slough,' Noah said.

Lyn nodded. 'To her new life.'

'Back to her mother. The grandmother of Archie and Fred, and Louisa.'

'Forgiveness is a process, like everything else. Alison is extremely fortunate to have Connie in her life. If, as you believe, she's breached the terms of her parole, then it's a great shame. A very great shame. I had high hopes for her complete rehabilitation.'

'She lied about the way in which her sons died. She lied to the police, and to the courts. She lied to you. That doesn't give me much confidence in her rehabilitation.'

Or your skills as her psychiatrist, Marnie thought but didn't add.

'Do you consider her a danger,' she said instead, 'to young children?'

'What? No. Absolutely not.'

Angry at the suggestion; her name on the paperwork.

'Two young children are missing, in Snaresbrook. Children who were living in the house where Esther buried her sons.'

Lyn recoiled. 'That's . . . It's horrible. But why would you assume Alison is involved? Do you have any evidence that she is?'

'Not yet. But we have reason to suspect that she's been back to Blackthorn Road since her release. She gave no indication she was planning to do that?'

'None whatsoever.' Her heel tapping the hotel carpet. Nervous, or just impatient?

Marnie said, 'I'm going to ask you again if you believe she's a danger to small children.'

'Of course not. I would hardly have supported her parole were that the case. Every sign pointed to her recovery. *Every* sign.'

The air conditioning in the hotel room was grey, like breathing through a hole in a tin can. Lyn Birch spent a lot of time in air-conditioned rooms. It showed in the lined skin of her face, nowhere for her age to hide. Did she prefer guest-speaking at conferences to spending time with patients? Marnie would put money on it.

'Hypothetically speaking,' she said, 'if Alison wasn't fully recovered, or if she was only pretending to be recovered . . . what then?'

'Then,' Lyn said tartly, 'I don't deserve to hold on to my job.' She bit her lip. 'I'm sorry, but I had such high hopes of Alison. When you talk about her like this . . . it's distressing.'

'Hypothetically speaking. If her prognosis was different, if there was any room for doubt . . . would you consider her a risk to children?'

Lyn looked across the room, at the empty view from the window. Muddy sky, stuffed with clouds. Her face contorted, painfully. 'Of course. If she wasn't recovered, I would be seriously concerned for her welfare and that of others. As I said at the outset, PPP is a serious illness with severe consequences for everyone affected by it. I would take every possible precaution to keep her away from young children.'

'If she has taken these two missing children, what are we looking at? What sort of danger are they in?'

'I can't say. She was so full of remorse. I can't picture the scenario you're describing.'

'Try. Two small children. Living in the same place where she buried the boys. Are we talking about a re-enactment? Penance of some kind? Sacrifice . . .'

Lyn shook her head. 'She was *better*. None of what you're imagining makes any sense. It's all hypothetical, in any case.'

'The missing children are real. We need to know how much danger they're in.'

'PPP is a serious illness,' Lyn repeated. 'I'd have taken every possible precaution to keep her away from young children. But that was implicit in the terms of her parole, wasn't it?'

She made a movement with her hands as if she was wiping her patient away. File under Failure. This was Marnie's problem now. Hers and Noah's.

'One last question. If we were talking about Esther Reid and not Alison Oliver. The Esther Reid who revolted Alison, horrified her, you said . . . If it was *Esther* and not Alison at large, with two small children missing, what would you be thinking?'

Lyn shook her head, flatlining her mouth.

'I'd be praying that you find those children, and fast.'

4

Tommy was sleeping. He was always sleeping. Babies were boring.

Carmen kicked her feet on the floor, because it made a funny noise, thick. She wanted her pink carpet, in her own room. This floor was horrid and hard.

She picked up Baggy and hugged him, then turned him over in her lap and smacked him until the beans inside him rattled. 'Naughty, Baggy, naughty. Go to your room.'

She threw him and he landed face down against the wall, his ears stretched out in front of him, his tail in the air. Tommy was sleeping like that, face-down, the way he did on the blow-up bed when they went on holiday. Mummy blew it up with a hairdryer. Carmen liked to bounce on the bed, but she got told off because it wasn't safe.

Tommy had his red blanket and his thumb in his mouth. If she listened hard, Carmen could hear him snoring. She was in charge, his big sister, but she was bored. There was nothing to do here. They weren't allowed to touch anything and she didn't like it. It smelt funny. 'What if I need a wee?' she'd said. 'What if Tommy wakes up?'

'Play with him. You're the big one. You're in charge.'

Carmen crawled across to where Baggy had landed, stroking his ears. 'There, there, Baggy, honey-bee, s'all fine now.'

She pulled one of her plaits to her mouth and sucked on it, even though she wasn't supposed to because you could choke on hair. It wasn't safe.

Maybe when Tommy woke they would bounce on the bed.

There was no one here to tell them to stop.

5

'Holy rolling Christ.' Tim Welland washed at his face with his hands. 'Run that past me again. We've got a schizophrenic child killer with a new identity, and three missing kids, one of them an angry teenage boy. Which red-top's wet dream are we trapped inside, exactly?'

'Not schizophrenic,' Marnie said. 'Lyn Birch was insistent on that score.'

'You're not telling me you believe in Esther's reincarnation as Alison Oliver?' Welland eyed her and Noah. 'I've heard more convincing miracles coming out of Mormons.'

'Her psychiatric assessments say she distanced herself from what she did as Esther. She talks about her as a separate person, someone *other*. Calling her a child killer isn't helpful.'

'I wasn't trying to be helpful,' Welland said. 'I was pointing out – and correct me if I'm wrong here – that they let *Esther* out of prison when they released Alison Oliver.'

'Yes, they did.'

'So it could be Esther who left the peaches outside our crime scene. And Esther who's taken these children.'

'Yes,' Marnie agreed, 'it could.'

'We have to operate on that principle. You can bet your

life the press will. Bad enough when they thought she'd put her kids into the Thames. When they find out she buried two of them alive, and lied through her teeth about it? Tricked them into dreaming up headlines about drowning when they should've been writing about underground torture chambers? If you think they were tough on her five years ago, wait until they get started on this new story.'

Marnie and Noah accepted this in silence. Wherever she was – whoever she was now – Esther Reid was going to wish she'd stayed hidden, lost in the system.

'She's not with her mum, I take it.' Welland studied the photograph that Ron had unearthed. 'At this travellers' ground in Slough?'

'We sent a team to look. No sign of Esther or Connie. Her neighbours didn't know she had a daughter, that's what they're saying. No one was prepared to tell us when they last saw Connie. Local police are keeping an eye on the place.'

'So the mum could be in on this?' Welland pulled at his lip. 'Two kidnappers? Plenty of places they could hide kids on a travellers' ground . . .'

'We'll need a warrant,' Marnie said, 'and the press will be all over it. We'd better have a good reason for thinking Carmen and Tommy are there, before we move in. We're looking at CCTV in Slough. Nothing so far. It's a long way to take two small children without help, or a car. Neither Connie nor Esther can drive.'

'How about the place she was living when she killed them?'

'Alperton, the other side of London. If she's gone there, that's another breach of parole. But I can't imagine she'd go back. The house was sold, her husband hasn't lived there in five years. We sent a team, on the off-chance, and we're checking CCTV. No sightings so far.'

'What about this boy Clancy? Where does he fit in?'

'It's unclear. We're asking Foster Services for anything that might shed light on why he'd abscond with the children. Beth says he's angry, but she trusted him with Carmen and Tommy. I don't think she'd do that without good reason, and from what I saw of Carmen, she wouldn't have gone quietly with someone she didn't trust.' Marnie stopped.

'Spit it out,' Welland said.

'Beth saw Clancy with two women on the housing estate. Old-fashioned clothes, odd-looking, one of them about Esther's age. The three of them were smoking together.'

'When was this?'

'Two weeks ago. Around the time Esther was paroled. And more recently, a day or so before Terry found the bunker.'

'In other words, Esther could have made contact with Clancy?'

'In theory. It's possible, yes.'

'No other sightings of her since she was paroled?'

'None so far.'

'So all we've got right now is this bad photofit.' Welland tossed the picture on to his desk. 'Which could be anyone . . .'

It was a photograph of Esther Reid, but Welland had a point. Grief or pills had stripped the colour and features from her face, dulling her eyes and drawing her mouth as a crooked line, faltering, above her chin. It wasn't a face you'd remember, even if you concentrated. Out of focus, as if someone had used a soiled cloth to rub her out.

'Why did she leave the peaches?' Welland said. 'I don't like that, makes her look like all sorts of a loony from where I'm sitting.'

'*If* she left them,' Marnie said. 'I don't know. Maybe she meant well, maybe she was trying to be kind, or it was penance of some description. I can't imagine what's going on inside the head of someone who's been through what she has.'

Nor could Noah. A child killer and a bereaved mother, perpetrator and victim rolled into one. How would you begin to unravel the pain and punishment, loss and loathing?

'She's broken the terms of her parole,' Welland said, 'by going back to the crime scene. Not to mention the perjury from five years ago. So we find her and arrest her. Hopefully before the press launch in. We've got all the crap-quagmire we can wade through right now.'

Noah checked his watch. 'It's not been four hours since the children went missing. If they're with Clancy, he might bring them back.'

He shook his head as he said it, because they had to prepare for the worst. Hope for the best, but prepare for the worst: that Esther had gone back to the place where she'd buried her boys and taken two other children as replacements of some kind. What was the word Marnie had used?

Sacrifices.

Welland tapped the photo with his thumb. 'You'll need a better picture than this to show to the public. I don't like using prison mugshots for that, but . . .'

'Ron sent the photo to Debbie's phone,' Marnie said. 'You're right, it's not a great picture, but the Doyles didn't recognise her. Beth's adamant she wasn't either of the women she saw smoking with Clancy on the estate, so that could be a false lead. House-to-house is ongoing. We're checking all the places Terry told us Clancy liked to go. We could use extra hands . . .'

'You've got them.' Welland nodded. 'I'll sort out the warrant for Slough. I want these children found, and soon.'

'What've we got?' Marnie asked the team.

'Paperwork coming out of our arses.' Ron gestured at a

pile of printouts. 'No sightings of Clancy or the kids. Debbie says the Doyles are going spare.'

He was at the whiteboard, marking the names of the missing children, pinning pictures of Carmen and Tommy, and Clancy Brand.

'What's the paperwork?' Marnie asked.

'Merrick Homes. Places they developed, land they bought, planning permissions, you name it.' Ron smoothed his thumb over the photos of the missing children, making sure they were secure on the board. 'Not sure it's relevant any longer.'

Marnie's phone rang and she took the call. 'Ed. How's it going?'

'Have you got a minute to talk?'

She knew he wouldn't ask unless it was important. 'Yes.' She carried the call away from the whiteboard where the team was gathered. 'You're with Terry and Beth?'

'Out of earshot, but yes. Beth's sleeping, or trying to. DC Tanner's keeping an eye on her.' Ed paused. 'I'm more worried about Terry.'

'It's why I wanted you there,' Marnie agreed. 'I'm not sure he's recovered from seeing the dead boys, and now this.'

'It's been a while since I've seen someone this stressed. Given what I do for a living, that's . . . not good.'

'Does he need a doctor?'

'He says not. I backed off from suggesting it, because it wasn't helping. He's making the kids' supper, cleaning the kitchen, washing windows . . . I can't get him to stop. It doesn't sound like the end of the world, I know, but I'm usually pretty good at getting them to stop.'

She hadn't heard this level of worry in Ed's voice since they were driving back from Sommerville. 'Do you need backup?'

'No. I think that might make it worse. I'm going to stay

with him for a bit, see what I can do. I'm guessing there's no news about the kids?'

'Nothing yet. We're looking for Esther Reid.'

'Debbie showed me the photo,' Ed said. 'Poor woman.'

Where Welland had seen a bad photofit, Ed had seen a woman in pain.

'Debbie says Beth and Terry are sure they haven't seen her on Blackthorn Road,' Marnie told him. 'We didn't tell them who she was, or what she'd done. I don't want them thinking the worst. We need a better photograph, I do know that.'

She looked across at the whiteboard, to the faces of Terry's children. 'Ed . . . have we got this wrong? Something doesn't feel right. What if the kids were with *Clancy* . . .'

A beat of silence in her ear, before Ed said, 'I can't get Terry to talk about Clancy. He keeps saying Clancy wouldn't hurt them, but the *way* he says it . . .'

It took a lot to unnerve Ed, she knew that from personal experience. But his voice was worn with worry for Terry Doyle.

'I'll come over,' she decided. 'Maybe he'll tell me what's going on with Clancy. If we've got this thing wrong, I want to know what we're up against. Can you stay with them? I'll be there as soon as I can.'

'Of course.' Ed rang off as Ron and Noah came across to where Marnie was standing.

She read their faces. 'You've got something. On Esther?'

'On Clancy,' Noah said. 'But you're not going to like it.'

6

'The Foster Service,' Noah said, 'has no record of Clancy Brand.'

'No record,' Marnie repeated. 'What does that mean, exactly?'

'It means the Doyles aren't fostering him. They can't be. Plus we found this, in the paperwork that came through.' He handed her a sheet of paper. 'Merrick built a panic room for a couple in South Kensington. The planning must've been a nightmare because we're talking about a listed house, so I'm guessing Merrick cut corners, or bribed someone. The couple who wanted the panic room? Scott and Christina Brand.'

'Clancy's parents?'

Ron nodded. 'Don't ask us why he ended up with the Doyles instead of at home with his parents. Unless there wasn't enough space in the panic room for a moody teenager . . .'

'You didn't find a link between the Doyles and Clancy's parents?'

'Other than Ian Merrick?' Ron shook his head. 'Nothing. We're still looking.'

Noah said, 'I don't understand why Clancy would take the children. *If* he did. They're hard work, apart from anything else. If he's not even their foster brother, if the Doyles lied about that . . . why was he looking after them in the first place? Why were they *letting* him look after them? It doesn't make sense.' He shook his head. 'I don't feel like we have a handle on who Clancy really is, do you?'

'No,' Marnie said. 'But I know a man who thinks he has.'

She nodded at Noah. 'Call DC Tanner, and tell her we need to interview the Doyles. Send a car for them. Ed's there too. Bring everyone back here.'

7

Adam Fletcher stretched his feet under the interview table. 'So he's taken them. Clancy Brand.' Anger lifted off him in a solid wave. 'He's taken those little kids. Your lot were all over the estate, asking questions . . .'

'If you have information that would help the police,' Marnie told him, 'this is your last chance to give it up.'

'They're not on the estate. I looked.'

'You looked.'

'I've been watching him. You know that.'

'A shame you weren't watching him four hours ago, when it's possible he went to the park with Carmen and Tommy Doyle.'

'Yeah, well there's only so much hanging around playgrounds you can do before someone reports a pervert to the police . . . He's not on the estate. Who told you he was?'

'Terry Doyle. He's been living with Clancy for months. What's your qualification?'

A flash of something – the truth; was he about to tell her the truth? It was gone so fast she might have imagined it, his blue stare coming up like shutters.

'What do you know about the Doyles? I don't mean the kids. I mean Terry and Beth.'

'I know they took a huge fucking risk having that psycho under their roof, as witnessed by this shitstorm.'

'You could've warned them. Why didn't you?'

'I warned *you*.'

'Not really. You pussy-footed around, pretending you had evidence that patently you don't or you'd have handed it over. Now that Tommy and Carmen are missing, I mean. I appreciate you had to honour your bullshit code of silence earlier on—'

Adam kicked the leg of the table so hard it shook. 'You don't know what the *fuck* you're talking about.'

'And you wouldn't know the truth if it was standing in front of you wearing a shiny hat and waving pom-poms.'

His eyes gleamed appreciatively. 'Good to see you showing your true colours.'

'Yes? Unless black and blue are the colours you have in mind, you'll stop kicking the furniture and start answering my questions.'

'Police brutality?' He nodded at the tape recorder, then scrubbed at his scalp suddenly, as if he'd had enough of the game.

Marnie looked at him sitting there smelling of cigarettes, smelling of *her.* All the rotten ripeness of her teenage derailment, her mistakes and cravings, self-loathing and hard-snatched happiness. *God help me,* she thought, *I was happy. Causing them hurt, staying out all hours, making them sick with worry – I was happy,* hating *them.*

'Where on the estate did you look for Clancy Brand?' she demanded.

'Everywhere the kids hang out. I've seen him there before. I know the places he goes.'

'You can't possibly have been watching him twenty-four

hours a day.' She thought of something. 'Did you have anyone else keeping an eye on him? Women. Smokers, like you.'

The women Beth had seen with Clancy, up on the estate.

Marnie had been afraid one of them was Esther Reid, but now she was remembering the easy way Adam had flirted with Debbie Tanner, and Julie Lowry.

'You have mates on the estate keeping an eye on Clancy. That's right, isn't it?'

The flicker in Adam's eyes said she'd guessed correctly. He didn't answer right away, looking at the tape recorder. Finally he said, 'People get worried when there's a dangerous kid around. Parents get worried. Even the police give a shit, eventually.'

'So you had people watching Clancy. Watching where he went.'

'Just a couple of drinking friends. Women, like you said. He's not on the estate. We looked.'

'Terry made him promise to stay away.'

Adam scoffed through his teeth. 'Doyle couldn't extract a promise from a politician. I suppose you think he's a hero for taking in a kid like that.'

'You clearly don't. Why not?'

'Doyle's the last person a kid like Clancy would trust.'

'The last person . . . Why?'

'He's too straight for one thing, too *decent*. Mister green-fingered salt of the earth . . . I'll bet he's never lost his temper with anyone. A kid like Clancy needs someone who won't take his shit at face value. He won't have told Doyle the truth about anything that mattered.'

Marnie thought of the boy's eyes thumping at her face – *He's not my fucking dad* – so full of hate she'd wanted to take a step wide of his rage.

'So what's this about?' Adam asked. 'Really?'

'The Doyles aren't fostering Clancy. But you knew that, didn't you?' Marnie met his stare head-on. 'You know about Clancy's parents and the panic room that Ian Merrick built. You know why he isn't living at home, why the Doyles took him in. All of it. You know.'

Adam looked at her for a long moment before he nodded.

'For the tape,' Marnie said inflexibly.

He moved his mouth as if it hurt. 'Yeah,' he said. 'I know.'

8

'Have you spoken with the travellers?' Adam asked Marnie. 'They'll tell you about Ian Merrick. "He hasn't got a heart, he's got a swinging brick," that's what they told me back before they found out I was a scumbag journalist.'

'What did they think you were?'

'A traveller. I told you, I was chasing a story. Undercover. I talked with everyone who lived on the site before Merrick bulldozed them out. Not just Beech Rise. He's got sites right across London. Always places with a history, when you start digging. And I started digging. My editor wanted a story about travellers, but I found something better. I found *preppers*.' He said it like an obscenity. 'Merrick specialises in safety, and storage. He finds disused tunnels, bunkers, abandoned drainage plants, septic tanks, you name it. *Subterranea*, he calls it. The kind of unfilled landfill that no one'll touch because it's a planning nightmare. Health and safety have a fit if they get within fifty feet of it, but Merrick makes money out of it.'

Adam curled his mouth. 'According to Merrick, you used to be able to make money from architecture, *spectacle*. Now it's all about the buildings you can't see, rather than the ones you can.'

'Subterranea,' Marnie repeated. 'Like the bunkers on Blackthorn Road.'

'Like that, yeah.' Adam pushed the heel of his hand at his right eye.

How long since he'd slept? He looked dead on his feet.

'You're saying Merrick is breaking the law?'

'No. He's too slippery for that. He's just got a gift for exploiting paranoia.'

'Tell me about Scott and Christina Brand. Clancy's parents.'

'Rich, scared, controlling.' Adam shifted the length of his legs under the table. 'They were going to be the stars of my story. Guess I can kiss goodbye to that now.'

'How do they know Terry Doyle?'

'Through Merrick. Doyle's a gardener, isn't he? He does landscaping for Merrick. He sorted out the garden for Scott and Chrissie after their panic room was finished.'

'And Clancy. Why's he living with Terry and Beth instead of with Scott and Chrissie?'

'You've seen Doyle. He's a do-gooder. Clancy ran away from home, more than once. His parents are control freaks, and he was out of control. He'd have ended up on the streets if it wasn't for Doyle.'

'The Doyles told me they're fostering Clancy. You told me more or less the same thing, gave me a lecture about Social Services not knowing their arse from their elbow. What was that, misdirection? To keep me wide of your real story?'

'If you're asking whether I lied to the police,' Adam looked at the tape recorder, 'the answer's no. I don't have the full facts of the arrangement. Most of it's guesswork. Hunches, you ever get those?' He rubbed his eyes. 'I told you to look into Clancy. I gave you that.'

'You told me he was excluded from school for touching small children. Was that guesswork too? Or was it a lie?'

Adam put his hands in his pockets, legs at full stretch,

spine low in the chair. His eyes were diamond-bright. 'It was a story doing the rounds. I told you I follow stories. It's what I do.' Something wasn't right with his gaze, the studied way he was slouching.

He was holding something back. Something big.

He leaned forward under the light, showing her the shadows in his stare. 'The point is this, Detective Inspector. Clancy Brand is an evil little shit who's taken two small children fuck-knows-where and on *your* watch. Because you chose to think that all the warnings I gave you were me pissing about for the fun of it.'

'You haven't given me any evidence, at any point. You've given me guesswork and hunches and *smoke* because you're protecting your story, whatever it is.'

'Trying to help.' He looked away from her, a muscle twitching in his cheek. 'I really was.'

'You got it wrong, in any case. About Clancy, probably. Definitely about the Doyles. They're not who you think they are. For starters, they lied to the police . . .'

'What about Stephen Keele?' Adam said softly. 'Am I wrong about him?'

Her heart thumped in her chest. 'What?'

'Stephen Keele. The kid who killed your mum and dad. His parents were preppers. You think it was a coincidence, me going after this story?'

'You . . .'

His mouth hardened. 'No coincidence. I knew what I was doing.'

'This . . . was about *Stephen*?' She couldn't believe it.

'I wanted to help.' Adam looked at her. Something was wrong with his eyes; they were too dark, too hot. 'I wanted to give you peace because I know what it's like to live without answers. To have your whole world wiped out, and not know who or *why*.'

'You . . .'

Adam shook his head. 'At least you know *who*, Max. At least you have that.'

'What happened?' She felt ill asking the question because she half knew the answer; it was there in Adam's eyes, the grief he was letting her see for the first time. 'Not Tia?'

He moved his mouth but didn't speak. After a beat, he nodded.

Tia. His daughter. Dead.

'When?' Marnie asked.

He glanced at the tape recorder. She thought he was going to ask her to switch it off, but he didn't. 'Five years ago. Nearly . . . five years.'

When Tia was fourteen.

'How?'

'Coach crash. School trip. Not anyone's fault, that was the verdict.' He pushed the heels of his hands at his eyes. 'Two dead kids and no one to blame. So . . . yeah. My marriage broke down. I was a wreck, a cliché. Too bound up in my own misery to care about anything else.'

'That's when you went abroad?'

'I tried running, yeah, but guess what? You can't outrun crap like that. I guess I don't need to tell you . . .' His mouth wrenched. 'I lied about Tia. All those years ago, when she was just a kid and we were . . . I lied. Pretended I wasn't a dad. Not hers, not anyone's. Pretended she didn't exist. Nothing like appreciating what you've got after it's gone . . .'

His eyes blazed with unshed tears. 'I let that drive me crazy for a bit. Then I found out you lost your mum and dad around the same time. I found out about that *shit* Stephen Keele. What he did to you, how he wouldn't tell you *why*. It was different with Tia, there wasn't anyone to blame, but Keele? There's something there. A story. I could smell it a mile off.'

'You smelt a story,' Marnie repeated, sick with disbelief.

'I didn't want it for myself,' Adam said angrily. 'For *you* . . .'

'This is penance? For what we did? Because you lied to me, pretended she didn't exist?'

'I wanted to bring you *peace*—'

'By investigating Stephen's parents.' She cut him short. 'What did you find?'

'They're preppers, just like Clancy's lot.'

'Do they *know* Clancy's parents? Do they have *any* connection to this case?'

'Maybe. Look.' He leaned in, drawing a line on the table with his hand. 'Merrick's a crook. That's why I followed the travellers.'

'You followed Clancy too. Or you had him followed. Why?'

'Something's up with that kid. You saw it, I know you did. His parents are whack-jobs, just like Keele's . . .'

'And he's the same age Stephen was when he went off the rails.'

'Yes. *Yes.*' Adam looked relieved, as if she'd finally got it.

'Fourteen. The same age as Tia when she died. Clancy's dropping out of school, getting into trouble, running away from home . . . . What a waste of a life. He's throwing it away.'

Not like Tia, who would have made her dad proud, had she lived.

Adam moved his head, adjusting his focus. Listening to what she was saying.

'Believe what you like,' he said at last. 'I know what I was trying to do. I wanted to find you *answers*. It's what I'm good at. So yeah,' he nodded at the tape recorder, 'go ahead and call me on my redemption bullshit, but Clancy led me to Scott and Chrissie Brand, who led me to Merrick and his merry men. To preppers. And back full circle to Stephen Keele.'

'How, exactly?'

'What if Keele's parents knew Merrick? What if he built *them* a panic room?'

'Did he?'

'Ask me when I'm done digging.'

'No, in other words. Even if they knew Merrick, they don't know why Stephen did it. No one knows that except Stephen, and maybe even he doesn't know. Do *you* know why you did the things you did when you were fourteen? I don't.'

'But you *want* to know,' Adam insisted. 'Why he did it. Why they died. I want to help. I can find the answers you're after. I may be a scumbag, but I'm a nosy scumbag. I get results.'

She recognised the light in his eyes. Obsession. She'd been like that once.

'Adam . . .'

'These preppers,' he said furiously, 'they're psychos. Scott and his fucking panic room like a padded cell . . . He's got a gun, d'you know that? Scott Brand. He's got a gun. With a licence, but so fucking what, frankly. They had a teenage boy in that house doing whatever he wanted because there was no one telling him to stop and there's a fucking *firearm* in the house . . . So he's acting up, trying to get Mummy and Daddy's attention and guess what? They don't take him to a psychiatrist, they don't sit him down and talk to him about why he keeps getting into fights at school, why he's being excluded, why the other kids are accusing him of being a pervert even if the teachers never *see* anything . . .'

'Adam . . .'

'What'd they do? They fitted him with an alarm. Did Doyle tell you about that? An alarm, like a dog. They'd have had him microchipped if they could. Hey, if this was America, that's *exactly* what they'd've done. Microchipped the little bastard, so they knew where he was whenever he sneaked off.'

'A personal alarm system,' Marnie said. 'Yes, Terry told me about that. Do you know the name of the security company that provided the alarm?'

'What?' Adam looked baffled by the question.

'Forget about Stephen Keele,' she said. 'I need to find Terry's kids, and Clancy. Do you know the name of the security company that provided the personal alarm system the Brands gave to their son?'

'He stopped using it when he went to live with Terry . . .'

'All right. But if they kept the data, they might know where Clancy used to hang out. They might know his old hiding places. Do you have the name of the firm?'

'No.' Adam thought for a moment. 'But I could find out.'

A knock on the door made Marnie look up.

Noah was outside the interview room, holding a phone.

Something had happened, it was written all over his face.

Through the glass he mouthed, 'Front desk. You'll want to come.'

9

At the front desk, two women were waiting.

One was in her sixties, five foot four, with silver hair and a softly creased face, grey eyes that chipped to ice as she saw Marnie and Noah. At her side, in a loose-fitting dark tracksuit, was a fair-haired woman about Marnie's age and height.

Thin-faced, prematurely aged; the ghost of someone pretty hiding behind her eyes.

Barely recognisable.

She stood completely still, resting her stare on Marnie. The stare was intense, transfiguring her face. She had bad skin, pale and blotchy.

Prison pallor.

'I'm Esther Reid,' she said. 'I'm the monster you're looking for.'

10

Alison Oliver – Esther Reid – folded her hands in her lap. Her eyes were dry, her lips parched. She repeated the first words she'd used when she came into the station: 'I'm the monster you're looking for.' Her voice was like her lips, cracked and thirsty.

'Can you give your name, please, for the tape.'

'I'm Alison Oliver.'

'And you don't want a solicitor present at this interview.'

'No.'

Marnie said, 'Have you ever gone by any other name?'

'You know I have.'

'For the tape, please.'

'I was Esther Reid. Before that, I was Esther Pryce. Now I'm Alison Oliver. It doesn't matter what name you use. I'm your monster. The one you've been looking for.'

Marnie could smell remorse leaching from the woman's skin, a sweet-sour smell like a nursing mother's. The dry eyes were a lie. Unless she'd cried all her tears in prison.

'Why did you come to the police station today?'

'To save you the trouble of coming after me. Or going after Connie, my mum.'

Connie Pryce had gone with Noah into a second interview room.

'She calls me Alison now. She's forgiven me. Can you believe that?' The woman made fists of her hands and laid them in plain sight. 'I murdered her grandchildren, but she's forgiven me. She won't even call me Esther. She believes in my rehabilitation.'

Slowly she uncurled her fists. Her hands were knotted with scar tissue, her nails bitten to the quick. Each time she moved her head, the strip lighting found another patch of damage: old scars on her neck and under her chin, a bruised indent where she'd pressed the end of the tracksuit's zip into her throat. It was hard to look at her.

'You came here because you knew we'd be looking for you. Why would we be looking?'

'Because of Blackthorn Road, the bunker. I saw the papers, I know you found them. Fred and Archie. My boys.' She blinked her eyes. 'You've found my boys.'

'You knew they were in a bunker on Blackthorn Road,' Marnie said.

Alison leaned forward until the light found the cracks at the corners of her mouth. 'I put them there.' It wasn't a boast, but nor was it simply a confession.

It was a demand: *Look at me, your monster.*

'You told the police they drowned.' Marnie referred to the woman's statement from five years ago. 'You said you drowned your daughter Louisa, and your sons Fred and Archie.'

'I lied. I didn't trust the police. I didn't trust anyone.'

'You were sick, we know that. You were suffering from hallucinations, paranoia . . .'

'I murdered my children,' she thrust the words at Marnie, 'my baby daughter and my boys. They died a horrible death, at my hands. It's on me.'

'You served a prison term.'

'I lied about the way they died. I shouldn't be out. It's not safe. We're . . . I'm not safe.' She licked at her lips. The tip of her tongue was an ugly mass of scar tissue.

'This is why you came here,' Marnie said, 'because you feel unsafe.'

'I came after I saw Connie. After she wouldn't look at me, at Esther. All that forgiveness and I *knew* . . . I knew she wouldn't ever look at me. At what I'd done . . . Have you ever felt remorse?'

'Of course,' Marnie said lightly. No ammunition in her voice, nothing the other woman could twist or use.

'Hurts, doesn't it? Real remorse, the proper realisation of what you've done . . . But you've never killed anyone. You've never felt remorse for anything as terrible as murder.'

'No, I haven't.'

'If I was devising punishments, ways to make people suffer, that would be top of my list. Remorse, *real* remorse, is the best weapon. If you could inflict it. Administer it, say, in a not-quite-lethal dose.' She was watching Marnie's face and perhaps she saw something there, because her next words were stinging, intentionally or otherwise. 'If there was someone you wanted to punish, someone who'd hurt you personally, that would be the way to do it. Make them feel remorse. Inflict it on them in whatever way you could. There's no pain like it.'

She sat back in the chair, her face grieving for a second before she stiffened it into the mask she'd worn when she walked into the station.

Marnie took a photograph from the folder at her elbow and placed it on the table, facing towards the other woman.

Alison Oliver blinked. 'Who . . .?'

'Do you know him?'

She shook her head, but her eyes snagged on the photo as if she couldn't look away.

'Clancy Brand. He's fourteen years old.'

'No . . .'

'You've not met or spoken with this boy. Are you certain of that?'

'Yes. Who is he?' She blinked at the photograph. 'He looks . . .' Her voice dried up.

Marnie waited, but the woman was silent.

'Have you been to Snaresbrook in the last fortnight?'

'Of course not.' Reflexively. 'That would be a violation of the terms of my parole.'

Marnie took two more photographs from the folder and placed them on the table.

The other woman leaned close, her mouth twisting in recognition.

Recognition.

'Why are you showing me these?' Her voice was a whisper now, scared.

'They're missing. Carmen and Thomas Doyle. Carmen is three and a half years old, Thomas is just two. They live at number 14 Blackthorn Road. The house where the bunker was found.'

Alison sat like a carving in the chair, her face frozen, her gaze on the missing children. 'I don't know them,' she said, but her eyes blazed with recognition.

Marnie's thumbs pricked, hotly. 'Where were you between 11 a.m. and 1 p.m. today?'

'With Connie. I was . . . with Connie.'

'Where?'

'In Slough. Then we caught a train here.'

'Which train. I need times, please.'

Alison recited the train times. She hadn't taken her eyes off the photos. The look on her face made Marnie clench her hands under the lip of the table.

Alison Oliver knew something. About the missing children.

It was all over her face, spilling out of her eyes.

'Did you take them? Alison? Did you take Carmen and Thomas?'

'No . . .' The woman looked stricken.

'Then . . . Esther. Did Esther take them?'

Alison shook her head, but she said, 'Yes. Yes. Yes.'

She put up her hands and dragged at her hair.

It made Marnie wince. 'Tell me.'

'Esther,' Alison said. 'Esther did this.'

11

Connie Pryce's stare was so direct and unapologetic that Noah wondered whether it wasn't a disguise, her way of keeping questions at bay. She stated her name for the tape, speaking in crisp syllables that didn't belong in a travellers' ground, or a police interview room.

'Your DI Rome . . . does she understand about my girl in there?'

'We spoke with Lyn Birch, Esther's psychiatrist.'

'Alison's psychiatrist,' Connie corrected.

Commander Welland hadn't believed in Esther's re-incarnation as Alison Oliver, but Connie did, fixing on her daughter's new name insistently. 'Lyn talks a lot of nonsense, but she's right about one thing. Alison's not the one you want to worry about.'

'Esther . . .' Noah began again.

'It killed her,' Connie said. 'The business with the boys, with the baby . . . It broke her. That's the truth. Broke her heart, and the rest of her along with it.'

She delivered the speech briskly, as if sympathy was the last thing she wanted. The soft face was a disguise; she was hard as nails. Was she?

'You collected Alison on the day of her parole, two weeks ago. Is that right?' He watched the woman nod. 'And she's been with you, at your home in Slough, since then?'

'Every day. Just as we agreed.'

'Today, between 11 a.m. and 1 p.m., where was Alison?'

'With me, in Slough. Then we caught a train here.' She recited the train times without being prompted, picking up the mug of tea that Noah had provided.

He put the photograph of Clancy Brand on the table. 'Do you recognise him?'

Her ice-chip eyes scanned the photo. 'No. Am I supposed to?'

Noah added the photos of Carmen and Tommy, turning them so that Connie could see their faces while he watched hers for a reaction.

'What's this?' she said sharply.

'Carmen and Thomas Doyle. They're missing. From number 14 Blackthorn Road.'

Connie leaned closer to the photographs, her mouth pursed in concentration. And something more . . . Alarm? She was scared of what she was seeing.

'Mrs Pryce? Do you know these children? Carmen and Thomas Doyle. Do you know where they are? Do you know anything that can help us to find them?'

Alison's mother put down the mug of tea. Her hand was shaking.

'Your DI Rome needs to leave my girl alone,' she said. 'And I need my handbag.'

'Mrs Pryce, if you know *anything* that can help us find Carmen and Tommy . . .'

'I need my handbag!' Fiercely, with tears in her eyes. 'Fetch my bag! You want to see missing children? Fetch me my bag.'

When the handbag arrived, Connie pulled out two photos,

both crumpled, and put them on the table next to the pictures of Carmen and Tommy.

'There,' she said, sounding out of breath. 'There. Do you see?'

Two little blond boys, one older than the other. Solemn, mischievous faces under rough-cut hair, high cheekbones, long eyelashes.

'That's Fred,' Connie said, pointing to the smaller boy. 'And that's Archie.' She touched their faces in turn with the tips of her fingers. 'Do you see?'

'Well?' Ron asked Noah when he broke the interview with Connie. 'What's she's saying? Did she do it? Take the kids?'

Noah shook his head. 'She's not saying anything that helps. Just that the boss needs to leave her daughter alone . . . What's the news from house-to-house?'

'No one saw anything.'

'Where're the Doyles? We sent a car for them, didn't we?'

'Debbie says they're waiting for Beth to wake up. The midwife's a bit of a guard dog, she says.' Ron rolled his eyes. 'Ed Belloc's over there, so I figured we'd better not get too heavy-handed . . . I'll find out what's happening.'

Noah walked to the whiteboard, where Ron had pinned photos of Carmen and Thomas Doyle. He added the crumpled photos of Fred and Archie Reid.

'Finally.' Ron moved close enough to study the faces. 'Good-looking kids. Archie's a proper tyke . . .' He touched a finger to the photo of Esther's older boy. 'Poor little sod.'

Both boys were fair like Esther, but with determined chins and bright eyes. Fred's hair was a shade paler than Archie's, and his eyes were a lighter blue. Archie had a wicked smile, but his eyes were serious under very straight brows.

'She's going to confess, right?' Ron dropped his hand to

his side. 'The boss is working on her. She'll get a confession, a location for the kids. Carmen and Tommy . . .'

Carmen Doyle wasn't smiling in the picture, her chin pointed up at the camera. Tommy was in his mother's arms. He had Beth's eyes. Both children had their father's nose and brows, arrow-straight.

'Noah.' Marnie carried a cup of water to where they were standing. 'How's Connie?'

He shook his head. 'Worried about her daughter. Otherwise, not much help.'

The phone rang, and Ron went to answer it.

'Photos at last. From Connie?' Marnie studied the white-board.

Up close, Noah could see how tired she was. Her eyes burned in her face, and she looked strung together with wire.

'Nothing from house-to-house,' he told her. 'Not yet, anyway. The Doyles are on their way, once Beth's been given the all-clear by the midwife.'

Marnie was studying the whiteboard, not speaking.

'She's sleeping. The midwife wants to wait for her to wake up . . .'

'Noah . . .'

Marnie reached up and unpinned the photographs from the whiteboard, one after the other. Four photos of four children. Fred and Archie Reid. Thomas and Carmen Doyle.

'Look.'

She put the photographs side by side on the desk.

Noah peered at the children's faces.

'Are they . . .? Shit. They look alike. Are they *related*? They have to be related.'

He straightened and stared at Marnie.

She was looking towards the interview room, where Alison Oliver was sitting.

Noah said, 'They're not *her* kids. Carmen and Tommy can't be hers, she was inside . . .'

'Terry,' Marnie said.

She touched the photos of Fred and Archie Reid. 'They're his boys. Look at their noses. And their eyebrows.'

All four children had the same noses and brows, more defined in Archie because he was the oldest, but even little Tommy had the start of Terry's straight nose.

'*Shit* . . .' Noah breathed.

'We know their father was given a new identity, just like Esther.'

Marnie's hand stayed on the photos. Her fingers were twitching.

'Their father . . . It's Terry Doyle.'

She lifted her eyes to Noah. 'He's Matthew Reid.'

12

Five years ago

You hide in the kitchen. You're getting the boys' supper ready, that's what you tell yourself, but what you're doing is hiding.

Esther doesn't come into the kitchen any more. It used to be her favourite room in the house (the oven, the knives), but since you made it safe, she's lost interest.

It's hard to cook without knives or heat, but you manage. The boys like cold stuff anyway, bananas and ham rolls, oranges and crisps. Fred used to like grated cheese, but you got rid of the grater when you disconnected the oven. Now the cheese is pre-sliced, like the ham.

Their favourite food comes in tins. You bulk-buy, decant the contents (sweetcorn, ravioli, peaches) into plastic containers. Feeding Louisa is harder, because you're supposed to heat her bottles, but you hide the kettle between feeds. Esther's good at finding stuff; you have to be so careful. She could find a needle in a haystack. She's got a sharp eye for sharp things.

The wire coat hanger was the worst.

You'll never forget the coat hanger.

Blood on the bathroom tiles.

Her handprints, red, everywhere.

She'd straightened it out, somehow. The hanger. It must have taken her hours.

She unwound the hook so that she had a sharp end. A weapon.

You tried to replicate what she'd done, to fill another gap in your understanding, but you couldn't do it, not without a pair of pliers. She did it with her bare hands.

The things she can do with her bare hands . . .

It makes you wonder if you're kidding yourself, hiding the cheese grater, switching off the gas. You can't switch off the electricity; the boys like TV too much.

There's only so much you can do.

'I can't watch her every second of every day,' you told them.

You have to go to work. You have to work up the courage to leave in the mornings, not knowing what you'll come home to.

The coat hanger was bad, but she's capable of worse.

You can see it in her eyes.

It's your job to keep them safe. Louisa and the boys. They discharged Esther into your care. You have a job to do. You're a husband and a dad.

The man of the house.

You're hiding in the kitchen making soft rolls for supper because you daren't have anything sharper than a spoon in the house.

All your suits are on plastic hangers now. The armpits smell of sweat. You can't stop sweating and it stinks. Fear, a hundred per cent proof. At work they've started avoiding you. You've stopped taking the lift in case someone remarks on the smell. And anyway, you can't risk being stuck in there. You might start punching the walls.

Who would take care of the kids if you got carted off like a crazy person?

You missed your tube stop that day, because you hadn't slept and you dozed off. You ran all the way home, but when you got there you stood like an idiot (coward) for a full minute before you went inside.

Fred and Archie were in the living room, watching TV.

Louisa was sleeping in her cot.

Esther . . .

Esther was in the bathroom, lying on the floor, with the coat hanger.

You could see the wire bent double in her fist, but you couldn't see the rest of it because she'd buried it inside herself, out of sight.

Blood, thick, all over her thighs and the floor.

Ever since that . . .

Every time she goes into the bathroom, you start sweating.

You count the seconds, minutes, until you can't stand it any longer and you tap on the door with your knuckles, out of respect. She's on the floor. Nine times out of ten, she's lying on the floor, staring at the place where the light bulb used to be.

Bile burns in your throat. 'Esther?'

She rolls her head at the neck and looks at you.

She's fine. Not dead. Not bleeding.

You let the breath out of your lungs and realise, with a fresh wave of self-loathing, that you were hoping for something else.

The kids are fine. The kids are safe.

And you'd allowed yourself to hope that it might be over.

13

Now

'Beth's here, but Terry's gone.'

'Where?' Marnie asked. At her side, Noah tensed, listening to the phone call.

'I don't know.' Debbie's voice thinned to static. 'The squad car was waiting. I thought it was okay because he was with Ed Belloc . . .'

'Let me speak to Mr Belloc.' Marnie waited a beat. 'DC Tanner? Put Ed on.'

'He's not here. Boss, I'm sorry.' Her voice dropped. 'I thought they were in the squad car, that's where they were headed. I was waiting with Gill for Beth to wake up, and Terry and Ed went out to the squad car, but they didn't get in. The driver didn't see where they went, said he was checking his phone and didn't see—'

Marnie cut her short. 'They're both missing, is that what you're saying?'

'Both of them, yes.'

'Bring Beth back here.' Marnie ended the call, speed-dialling Ed's number.

It didn't even get the chance to ring, because the phone was switched off.

Ed never switched his phone off. Noah was speaking, but she couldn't hear past the scrabble of panic in her skull. *Ed . . .*

'The children,' she said, when she was able to speak. 'We need to find the children.'

'I'll organise a second search team,' Noah said. 'For Terry, and Ed.'

'We need to find Carmen and Tommy.' She was glad her voice didn't shake. 'That's our priority. Let's stay focused. Two young children are missing. We need to get them back.'

14

Marnie put the photographs of the four children in a line on the interview table.

'Carmen and Thomas Doyle. You recognised them, didn't you? You knew they were Matthew's children.'

'I *didn't* know . . .' Alison twisted her hands on the table. 'About Matt. About his new family. I didn't know he was living in that place. I didn't know he was the one . . .'

'The one who found them? It was him. He found Fred and Archie in the bunker where you left them.' Marnie put a fifth photo on the table. 'He's Terry Doyle now. He has a new family. His wife is pregnant with their third child.'

Alison put her hand over the photo of her ex-husband's face. 'Where is he?'

'We don't know. We saw him this morning, when his children were reported gone. He was with a victim care officer. Matt and the VCO went missing forty minutes ago.'

Alison didn't speak. She kept her hand over the photo of her ex-husband's face.

'You said Esther did this.' Marnie touched the photos of Matt Reid's new children. 'When we asked if you'd taken Carmen and Thomas, you said yes. What did you mean?'

'I'm responsible. It's my fault. I . . . broke him.'

'Matthew, your husband.'

'They'll have told him I was getting out. They gave him a new identity but they'd have told him, because of what I did. To him. I destroyed his family. I broke him.'

'You broke Matt.'

'Into a thousand pieces,' Alison said. 'A thousand tiny pieces.'

She looked up at Marnie with terror in her eyes.

'He's not safe. You have to find him. You have to *help* him. If he's the one who found Fred and Archie, and now these new children . . . *his* children . . . He's not safe.'

'You said it's not Esther we should be worried about.' Noah sat opposite Connie. 'What did you mean?'

'It broke her,' Connie said, 'clean in two. But their father . . . He's the one I'd be watching, if I were you. Esther was in two, but him? He was in pieces. Still is, I should say.'

'This is Matthew Reid. Matt.'

Connie nodded. 'He doesn't go by Matt now, I imagine. The papers were cruel. No one could believe he didn't see it coming. You should've heard them . . . He was *less than a man*. Or else he drove her to it. An animal. Couldn't keep his own kids safe . . .'

'Matt has a new identity too. You knew that?'

'I assumed it,' she said crisply. 'He needed a new life, almost more than she did. At least they sent her somewhere to get well, to *try* to get well . . . There was no help for him, none at all. Not that I'm saying a new name makes a difference, but he deserved a second shot. He was a good man, Matt. He did his best by her, and he *loved* those children. Oh, he loved them. Nothing was too much, until she was.' Connie looked away from Noah. 'She was too much for all of us.'

'Did you know his new name?'

She shook her head. 'I didn't want to know. I couldn't help him. I thought he'd moved away, like I did. Made a fresh start. I didn't keep in touch because what was the point? We were no use to one another. Barely any use to ourselves.'

'He didn't move away. He was on Blackthorn Road. He's Terry Doyle now.' Noah touched the photos of Carmen and Tommy. 'These are his children, and they're missing. So's Matt, and a victim care officer who was trying to help him.'

Connie closed her eyes, then opened them on his face. 'I suppose . . . he couldn't stay away. He needed to be close to them. Fred and Archie. I was the opposite, couldn't bear to be anywhere that reminded me of them. There's not a thing of theirs doesn't drag me back to that hell. But maybe Matt had to be near them. He loved them almost too much.'

Too much love.

'They'll have told him she was coming out,' Connie said. 'They had to do that. He was her victim too. He'll have known she was coming out. That'll have scared him. It put the fear of God into me, and she's my own flesh and blood.'

'Do you think he's dangerous?'

'I have no idea. I only know he was devastated by what happened and that he got no professional help whatsoever. They don't help the husbands of PPP sufferers, did you know that? He saw the worst of her. Heaven only knows what he lived through in that house.'

'He knew where Fred and Archie were buried,' Noah said. 'He must have done. How else was he living in that house?'

'I imagine he did the job the police failed to do.' Matter-of-factly, no accusation in her voice but plenty in her stare, like black ice. 'He looked for them, and he found them.'

'Why did he look for them? When she said they'd drowned . . .'

'Neither of us believed that. We told the police we didn't believe it, but she was convincing. She could be very convincing.'

'How did Terry find the boys?'

'Through Ian Merrick, I imagine.' Connie's eyes sparked coldly. 'He hated her working there as much as I did.'

'Why did the pair of you hate that so much?'

'Because of the sort of man Merrick is. Immoral. He preys on people's weaknesses, their need for security. Builds cheap, sells high. He's repulsive. And he was poison for *her*. Toxic. Always whispering about safety, about panic rooms and hiding places. If she wasn't mad before, he helped drive her there.'

'I spoke with your neighbour, Denis Walton. He said you and Esther fell out over the development at Beech Rise.'

'We fell out over *Merrick*. That man? He hasn't got a heart, he's got a swinging brick.'

'Why did you leave so suddenly after Esther's arrest? Denis said you went overnight, with the travellers.'

Connie shrugged. 'I'd made friends, people who knew the sort of man Merrick was. I couldn't stay, could I? The press were all over us. *She* was gone. There was nothing left of her until they got to work with the pills. You're too young to have children, but imagine looking at someone you love and finding them gone. Right there in front of you but *gone*. No trace left. You'd have upped sticks too, if you had any sense.'

She drew a breath. 'I went back once she showed signs of getting better. Of course I did. I'm not heartless, but right at that minute? When they were gone and with the press slavering everywhere? I couldn't bear it. So yes, I ran. I saw a quick way out and I took it.'

'Matt was living in that house for a year before he called the police.' A year before he opened the bunker, if Fran was right about the manhole staying shut as long as it did. 'Why?'

'Why did he live there, or why did he wait so long to call you? Perhaps it was enough for him to be near them. Then I imagine he panicked when he heard she was coming out. *I* panicked, and as I say, we're flesh and blood.'

The timing made sense. They were called to Snaresbrook just after Terry would have been told that his ex-wife was being paroled. What didn't make sense was why he'd lived for so long next to his sons' graves without reporting it.

'These children . . .' Connie moved her hands to the photos of Carmen and Tommy, stopping short of touching them. 'He loves them. Whatever else you might think of him, you can be sure of that.'

She looked up at Noah. 'Matt was the best father I ever knew. I never met a man with a bigger heart. Until she broke it.'

15

Carmen and Tommy were safe. You'd seen to that.

You knew you couldn't take any risks, not with the children. Especially not now, with Esther out of prison. You had to move them, just like you had to move Fred and Archie.

No one's safe from Esther, not ever.

You knew she'd come straight back, if they ever let her go.

She never left, not really. Like you. You never left them. They were safe with you for a while, but you're a coward, the same as always. You tried so hard not to be.

You tried to be something new, something *more*.

For Beth and the babies. Carmen and Tommy, and the new one on the way. A second chance to prove you could be more than the coward who let them down, let them die.

Be a man.

You wanted to be that.

You were a good dad, everyone said so.

Just not when it mattered most.

You were good with Carmen and Tommy. Patient, careful. You kept them safe.

Clancy too, except he didn't want it. Looked at you as if

you were a threat. As if *safety* was a threat. You had to show him. You had to explain.

If he'd known the things you knew . . .

'You could have someone's eye out with this!'

A wire coat hanger. He'd brought a wire coat hanger into the house.

After everything you'd told him, all the warnings.

'Look at it!'

You straightened the thing the way she did, the sharp end of the hook refashioned as a point, something that could stab holes in anything, anyone.

You wrapped the rest of the metal around your fist and showed him – *'Look at it!'* – what a weapon looked like.

16

'We need someone who knows Terry Doyle,' Marnie said. 'Where he might have gone, and what he's capable of.'

'He was at the house *after* the little ones went missing.' Debbie shook her head. 'He stayed with Beth for over an hour, then he was cleaning, making supper . . . Ed Belloc was with him. I honestly thought everything was all right. I mean, it crossed my mind that he might go *looking* for the kids, but I never thought he'd *taken* them. I never thought for a second there was any chance of that.'

'None of us did,' Marnie told her. She was very calm.

Too calm, Noah thought. He tried to imagine how he'd cope if it was Dan who was missing, but his imagination short-circuited.

'Why did he come back to the house,' Debbie said, 'if he'd taken them? Where *were* they while he came back to the house? With Clancy?'

'He was terrified,' Noah said. 'When we told him the children were missing. He was absolutely terrified. I don't think he was faking that. Do you?'

Marnie said, 'I don't know. It didn't look like it, but this is a man who was living with the bodies of his dead boys for twelve months before he called the police. A man who received no treatment for what he went through five years ago. Esther had Lyn Birch, and medication. Matt didn't have anything, as far as I can gather.'

They all looked at the whiteboard, the new photographs pinned there.

Connie had given Noah a family portrait: Matt and Esther Reid with Fred and Archie and baby Louisa. Esther had been a striking young woman. Alison was an inch shorter and eight pounds heavier, her hair thin and brittle. Matt, too, had changed. Terry Doyle was still handsome, but Matt's eyes were brighter, his face softer, unlined. There was nothing left of Esther and Matt Reid. There was only Alison Oliver and Terry Doyle, two half-people who didn't really exist, their new identities purchased for the price of a passport.

Ed Belloc's photograph was on the whiteboard too.

Commander Welland was organising a hostage negotiation team. They were trying to trace Ed's phone, and the phone registered to Terry Doyle. Nothing was in Matt Reid's name. Not the car that Terry drove, or his credit cards. Welland's team was trying to locate the car.

'One thing we can clear up,' Marnie said. 'The haloperidol that Beth found in Clancy's bag was part of a prescription for Esther. She stopped taking the pills when she was pregnant with Louisa. We have to assume Terry kept the pills and Clancy found them.'

'Terry kept his wife's pills?' Debbie said. 'Isn't that a bit weird?'

'Perhaps he hoped she'd start taking them again. Or he wanted something to hold on to, a memory of when she was well, or the hope that she might be made better.'

'Clancy's a sharp kid,' Debbie said. 'Won't he have found out what the pills were for? He could've googled the name . . .'

'Maybe he did. Maybe he asked Terry awkward questions, which Terry couldn't answer without giving away the secrets he was keeping.'

'How did he know where his boys were buried?' Ron asked. 'That's what I want to know. If he went looking, that means he knew they weren't drowned. How? When the police didn't have a clue? How sure are we that he's a good guy?'

Marnie said, 'Esther's medical records, the police reports . . . There's no evidence at any point that Matt was anything other than a victim. He tried to keep his family together. Social workers said the children were safe with him. Doctors discharged Esther into his care. We might think that was a wicked thing to do, but they clearly had faith in his ability to look after her, and the children.'

'Until he didn't . . .' Ron shook his head at the whiteboard.

'Connie doesn't miss a trick,' Noah said. 'She said Matt was the best father she'd known. She wouldn't have said that if there was any chance he had a hand in their deaths.'

Ron conceded, rubbing at his face. 'Poor bastard . . .'

'He wouldn't hurt them,' Debbie said, 'would he? Carmen and Tommy. He wouldn't hurt them. I saw them together, when I took that bag to the safe house . . . The kiddies love him to bits, and he loves them. I'd swear to it.'

'Connie says the same thing. She thinks he panicked,' Noah said, 'when the parole office got in touch. Maybe he was scared of Esther going back to where she left the boys. He might've taken the children to a safe place . . . Beth said the house we put them in didn't feel safe. If I was Terry? I'd be paranoid about safety.'

'We should check inside number 14,' Marnie said. 'The PCSO says the house is secure, no one's been inside since we sealed the garden, but there might be clues of some kind to Terry's state of mind.'

'You think Belloc went with him voluntarily?' Ron asked. It was the first time anyone on the team had referred directly to Ed's disappearance.

Marnie threw Ron a look. 'His phone's switched off. But that doesn't mean he's a hostage. It's possible he's trying to help. He was worried about Terry, I know that much.'

'What's Beth got to say? Did she really not know?'

'That Terry was Matt Reid? No. She's admitted they lied about Clancy being fostered. She says he's the son of one of Terry's friends, but she's insisting Terry put their names down to be foster parents, that they *would* have been fostering Clancy officially, once the paperwork went through. Terry was handling all of that. Even after we told her about Matt and Esther Reid, she believes what he told her.'

'Dozy cow,' Ron muttered.

'Terry said Clancy's parents were wrapped up in some strange business. Those were his words. They had too much money and were obsessed with security; Clancy had a personal alarm he had to carry everywhere. The alarm went through to a private security outfit.'

Marnie nodded at Colin Pitcher, the team's data analyst. 'I've got the name of the security firm. There might be a lead there.' She looked at the others. 'Beth said Terry wanted to live on Blackthorn Road because of the views and the space. He said the garden at number 14 got more sun, despite the beech trees. He loved the trees.'

'He knew,' Ron said, 'about the bunker. He must've known. If he made a fuss about *which* house . . . He knew where the kids were buried. Maybe the trees were a clue. My two love climbing. If Fred and Archie were the same . . .' He shook his head.

'Terry did the gardens in the whole road,' Noah said, 'isn't that what Beth told us? He was looking for the right bunker, but how did he know *any* of the bunkers were there?'

'Ian Merrick,' Marnie said. 'Esther worked for Merrick, and Merrick was a builder, which meant land, secure hiding places . . . As Terry Doyle, he got a job with Merrick doing landscape gardening. Odd jobs, so his name isn't on the paperwork, but it's possible he was part of the team that put down the show gardens on Blackthorn Road. If that's the case, he had plenty of opportunity for digging.' She paused. 'There's another connection we need to look into. Merrick built a panic room for Clancy Brand's parents. Terry worked on the Brands' garden. That's how he met Clancy.'

'Which means that shonky bloody builder knew exactly what was going on.' Ron scowled at Merrick's name on the whiteboard.

'Where *is* Merrick?' Noah asked. 'Did we track him down?'

'We left messages,' Ron said. 'And we sent someone to his house. No one's there.'

'Let's find him.' Marnie nodded at the paperwork. 'And let's find out about his sites. If Terry persuaded him to give up the location of the bunkers, perhaps he persuaded him to share his other hiding places. That could be where Terry's gone with the children. Find out which of Merrick's sites have CCTV we can access.'

She straightened up. 'We need someone who knows Terry, and Matt. Someone who knows what's going through his head right now, and what he's capable of.'

'Esther,' Noah said. 'Esther knows.'

17

Alison Oliver folded her scarred hands on the interview table. She was still refusing a cup of tea, or even water, despite her cracked lips. 'I won't ever forgive myself,' she said. 'In case you think that's on the cards, it's not.'

'What about Esther?' Marnie said. 'Connie's forgiven her. Have you?'

'You've been speaking with my therapist, Lyn.' Dry humour in her voice, before she extracted it. 'Esther's different. It's been a long time since she spoke to me, or anyone. It's a shame. She was always much better at talking than I am.' She moved her mouth. 'I know I sound crazy. I do know that. But it's Alison I can't forgive.' She touched her chest. 'Me. I can't hide behind Esther any longer. I did, for years, but not now.'

From the speech, it was easy to imagine that she'd made peace with her past. But Marnie could smell it on her. Grief, and pain. Bone-deep, with-you-forever pain.

'Why did you come back?' she asked.

'For the same reason Matt did,' Alison said simply. 'To be near them.'

'Knowing it was breaking the terms of your parole?'

'Where else could I have gone? There's no *starting over*, whatever they tell you. There's only what happened, what you did. That thing, that place. You can't ever *let it go*, any more than you can let go of your own skin. It's always with you, because it *is* you.'

'Didn't it hurt, to go back?'

'Yes,' Alison said emphatically, as if Marnie had named the silver lining.

'Lyn Birch told us you were ready to move on. Is that not true?'

'Move where? Where would I go? I murdered my children.'

'Manslaughter,' Noah said. 'It was manslaughter on the grounds of diminished responsibility.'

Alison looked at him with a terrible pity, the kind that came from staring too long into the pit of the past. Noah had seen his share of frightening people. Psychopaths, sociopaths and stone-cold killers. Alison Oliver – Esther Reid – was in another league. She wore her damage like armour. No wonder Terry had panicked at the idea of her parole.

'You've forgiven Esther . . .' Marnie began.

'Because she loved them. She was their mother, and they loved her back. Her arms . . . it was *her* arms that held them. Can't you understand? All the memories, including the good ones, the best ones, the ones that keep me going, are hers. I can't be without Esther, or I'll be without *them*. I can't hate her. If I cut her out, I'll lose what's left of them.'

She looked at Marnie, but didn't ask again whether Marnie understood.

Instead she said, 'I'm in two minds . . . How many times have you heard that expression? Connie uses it all the time. I'm in two minds . . . I'm to blame. *Alison*. Let Esther keep them safe. The memories. How soft their faces went when they slept. How sweet they smelt. Esther heard their secrets.

It was *her* who put plasters on their skinned knees and kissed them better. She was a good mother.' Her voice hardened for the first time. 'She was a *good mother*.'

Until she wasn't. Until she got sick and couldn't look after anyone, including herself.

'We need to know where Matt might have taken the children. He's with a victim care officer who may be a hostage. We need to know what's going through Matt's mind. We think you understand him better than anyone else.'

'I wanted to see him,' Alison said.

'Why?'

'He's my mirror.' She withdrew her stare, looking down at the old damage on her hands. 'I don't expect you to understand that. Connie . . . won't look at me, not properly. She calls me Alison. But Matt knows. Matt knows Esther.'

'You wanted to see him, but you came here instead. Is that right? You didn't go to Blackthorn Road, or try to contact Matt in any way?'

'No. I came here instead. Connie persuaded me. She said it was too cruel to Matt. I know she's right. I do know that.' She knotted her fingers, her voice faltering for the first time. 'How were they when you found them? You saw them. Fred and Archie . . .'

Marnie said, 'They were together. They seemed . . . quiet. As if they were sleeping.'

Alison's face twisted to accommodate this version of the truth. It'd sounded brutal when Fran first said it, and it was brutal now. How must it sound to the woman responsible for it?

'What was it like,' Noah said, 'in the bunker? When you first took them down there . . . Did they think it was a game, or were they scared?'

It was a cruel question, but they needed Alison to focus on Carmen and Tommy. Perhaps if they could get her to remember Fred and Archie, she'd snap out of this self-punishing apathy and start to help.

'To begin with, we were happy. Then . . . I don't remember.' Her voice was cracked from side to side. 'I don't.' She lifted her fist of fingers and knocked at the side of her skull, raising a hollow sound. 'Too many pills . . . Esther remembered some things, little things. How good they were about getting into their pyjamas, brushing their teeth . . . Archie taking care of Fred, being such a good boy, taking charge when she had to go away.'

'Why did she have to go?'

'Louisa.' Her voice shrank to nothing. 'For Louisa.'

'You . . . She couldn't tell the police, about the boys?'

'She didn't. I don't know why. She was scared. She was insane,' shaking herself, 'she was cruel and hateful. How many excuses do you need? Lyn has a hundred. More.' She made her hands into claws. 'She took everything the pills didn't get, wrote it all down. You'd think I'd be grateful for that – the pills, the *not remembering*. But I'd rather have pain, and truth. I *hate* not being able to tell you the truth. I want to know what their last days were like. I want to know whether they knew how loved they were, how *huge* they were, in my heart.' She stopped, emptying her hands, sitting under the dull stew of light, looking lost again.

'They were together,' Marnie said. 'Archie was holding Fred, taking care of him. They were together.'

Alison turned her face away, as if the image Marnie had given her couldn't compete with the pictures in her head. Or as if it made the pictures worse.

At Marnie's side, Noah was silent, watching the woman.

Marnie said, 'Tell us about Matt.'

'I can't tell you anything, not really. I don't remember the worst of what I did, just . . . Sometimes I remember his face, seeing me. The horror on it. Fear. He was afraid of me. Desperately afraid. He was the only one who saw what I was capable of. Not the police, not Connie, not Lyn. Only Matt. He saw how . . . inhuman I was. Beyond help. Beyond anything.'

Desperately afraid.

This was the man who'd taken his two small children into hiding. The man Ed Belloc had been trying to help.

'He didn't visit you? Connie said she did, after the medication started to help.'

'She never saw me the way Matt did. She never saw Esther. Matt stayed away because he knew there was no help. No *getting better*. He knew what I was.'

'I don't believe that,' Marnie said. 'I've met Matt. He believes in second chances. He rebuilt a life for himself, and I think he would want the same for you.'

'If you were right, he wouldn't have taken his children into hiding. You wouldn't be afraid. I can see you're afraid, of what he might do and where he might have taken them.'

'Where might he have taken them?'

Alison shook her head. Then she said, 'You had another photograph, of a boy . . .'

'Clancy Brand.' Marnie took the photo from the folder and handed it over.

Alison studied it. 'He looks like Matt.'

'What?'

'When I first knew him, when he was seventeen, Matt looked like this. A little.'

Alison stroked the photograph with her thumb. 'It's the eyes . . . Trying to look tough, but he's not. He wasn't ever tough, just a bit careless. And happy. Perhaps if he *had* been tough, he'd have been able to stop me. No, not *stop*. No one could do that. He could've let me die, though. He could've done that. But he wouldn't give up. Not on anything. Poor Matt.'

Was that why Terry had taken on Clancy, because the boy reminded him of Matt? Of the person he'd been before Esther got sick? Careless, pretending to be tough when he wasn't, not really, not enough to stop this woman destroying his family. And Clancy was around the age Archie would have been had he lived. Was that in Matt's mind too?

'What do you think he felt,' Noah asked, 'when he heard you were being released?'

'Scared,' she said, 'to death.'

Silence in the room, just for a second.

'Tell us about Ian Merrick,' Marnie said, 'and the bunkers.'

It took a moment for Alison to answer, as if she was struggling to remember who Merrick was or why he mattered. 'He knows all the safe places,' she said finally.

'Did he know about Fred and Archie? About the safe place you put them?'

'I didn't think anyone knew.' Her mouth thinned. 'Not even me, not properly. Not then.'

'But Merrick knew about the bunkers. He knew they weren't filled in. He built family homes on ground that wasn't safe.'

Alison glanced at Noah in surprise. 'It was safe. Those bunkers were solidly built, better than the houses some people might say. People wanted them.'

'People wanted the bunkers.'

'They were safe,' Alison insisted. 'Hidden. How many places are like that? Don't tell me you've never wanted a place you could go, away from everyone else. Quiet. *Safe*. Everyone wants to feel secure, and Ian knew all the best places. He helped to build shelters, special rooms . . . Everyone's scared of something nowadays. Ian understood that.'

'Your mother didn't like him. She thought it was unhealthy for you, working with him.'

'She was right. Look what happened. I found a bunker and I buried my children alive.'

A phone was ringing, somewhere in the station. Noah held his breath, praying for news of the children and Ed, but no one came to interrupt the interview.

'Did Merrick know you'd been inside the bunkers on Beech Rise?' Marnie asked.

'No.'

'But he knew you were aware of the existence of bunkers on that site.'

'Of course he knew. He told me about them. He knew all the best places, and the people who wanted them. Supply and demand. He could've sold that land six times over if he'd held out for the right people.'

'Why didn't he?'

'Sometimes you do a straight deal to stop people looking too hard at the crooked ones.'

'He said that to you?'

'He didn't need to. I was a grown-up. I knew how the world worked.'

'You weren't well,' Noah said. 'That was why Connie didn't want you working there.'

'I was a grown-up,' Alison repeated. She looked wiped out with the questioning. 'Worse things happen in other places. He was just making money. We're supposed to make money, aren't we? Ian was good at his job.'

'Which people would have paid over the odds for the bunkers on Beech Rise?' Marnie asked. 'You said he could have sold the land six times over. To whom?'

'They call themselves preppers. They want safe places, underground. They'll help you make the place nice, lay in provisions, tinned food, water . . .' Alison's voice faded.

'Tinned food. Sweetcorn and . . . peaches. Provisions like that?'

Alison nodded. Her eyes had gone far away.

'We found tins of peaches, with the boys. And somewhere else. Was that you? When you came back?' Silence. 'Alison?'

The woman retrieved her focus with difficulty. 'What . . .?'

'Did you leave a tin of peaches on the pavement outside the house in Blackthorn Road?'

Bewilderment. 'No. Why would I?'

'I don't know, but I don't see who else would have known to do that. Leave a tin of peaches where Fred and Archie died. Unless it was Matt. And if it was Matt, that scares me. It makes me wonder what's going on inside his head. And it makes me scared for the children, Carmen and little Tommy. So I need to know. Was it you who left the peaches?'

'It wasn't me. How could it be? That's . . . horrible, hateful. How could anyone do a thing like that? How could *I* . . .?' She went away again, behind the glass wall in her eyes.

'It was you, wasn't it?' Marnie made her voice hard, unforgiving. 'You left the peaches because they needed to eat and peaches were their favourite food. You had to leave something. Other people left soft toys and candles. You left peaches.'

Shock tactics. Marnie was trying to make her connect to what was happening.

Alison blinked slowly, as if the lids of her eyes were heavy. 'It wasn't me. I know you need this to make sense, but it doesn't. It will never make sense. I killed my babies, Louisa, and my boys. I put them in a bunker and left them to die. I did that. But I *did not* leave a tin of peaches five years later.'

'So it was Matt. You said it was a horrible, hateful thing to do. This is what we're dealing with. A man who would do a thing like that, whose children are missing. Together with a victim care officer and a teenage boy who's the same age Archie would've been had he lived.' Marnie held the woman rigid with her stare. 'You need to put away your pain and your punishment, or whatever you imagine this is, and help us find him.'

Alison said, 'Thank God for Matt. Thank *God* for him. He knows what I am. He knows what I did and he will never lie about it, never pretend it was less terrible than it was. He'll never forgive me. I *need* that. I need to remind myself what a monster I am.'

She looked at Marnie and Noah with appalling pity in her eyes.

'Who asks for help from a monster?'

18

Tim Welland was waiting in Marnie's office. 'I spoke with Belloc's boss. He says it's not the first time Ed's been in a hostage situation.'

Marnie shut the door, coming across to her desk, where Welland was propped.

'We don't know for sure that this is a hostage situation, sir. There's been no contact. If Matt Reid had demands, wouldn't he have made them by now?'

'So where're his kids? Where's Clancy Brand?'

'We're looking for them. Two teams. We'll find them.'

'I should stand you down.' Welland studied her. 'Personal connection to the . . . hostage.'

Victim. He'd been about to call Ed the victim.

Marnie said, 'I'm looking for the children. You're in charge of the team looking for Belloc and Reid. I'd like to be allowed to do my job.'

'No one's questioning your professionalism, detective. They'd have to come through me if they did.' Welland lightened the growl. 'Belloc's boss wants to know why he was alone with Reid, or Doyle, whatever he's calling himself now.'

'That was my call,' Marnie said directly. 'Ed phoned to say he was worried about Terry. I was on my way over there, but I got distracted, asking questions about Clancy.'

'Was there any reason to suspect Doyle of being a danger to himself or others?'

Welland was covering their backs, Marnie's and his. Maybe he was trying to salve her conscience, too.

'Ed was concerned. I asked if he wanted backup, but he said no. He was worried it might make things worse. He wouldn't have said that if he thought Terry was dangerous.'

It was the thread she was holding on to, the fact that Ed was a great judge of people and situations. His voice had been full of worry, but he'd been certain he didn't need backup.

Welland nodded. 'So what now?'

'We've got CCTV to check from Merrick's sites. We're going to start with the places Terry worked as a gardener. DS Jake and DC Tanner are taking a look inside number 14, in case he left any clues there. And I'm going to interview Beth.'

'I thought she didn't know anything about her husband's past, about Matt and Esther?'

'That's what she says. She's pregnant, so we need to tread softly.'

'And quickly,' Welland said. 'It's been eight hours since those kids went missing.'

Ed had been gone less than three.

Marnie had two clocks in her head, counting down.

'His boss said Belloc was a natural, last time around. Defused the situation. Kept his head.' Welland put his paw on her shoulder. 'Don't lose faith, detective.'

Marnie shook her head. 'Of course not, sir.'

19

The housing estate was a pit of shadows, high-rises blocking out the sun, litter blowing from one corner to the next, never escaping. Noah handed the photos of Terry Doyle to the officer in charge of house-to-house. He didn't envy the team their task, imagining the accusations, the fear on people's faces: 'You just found two dead kids and now you've lost three more?'

Debbie didn't speak as they walked to Blackthorn Road, but when they reached number 14 she said, 'How could Beth be married to him and not *know*? He lost his whole family. How could she not know about a thing like that? And all the time he's *searching* . . . looking for his boys, for Fred and Archie. How did he keep it a secret?'

'We don't always know the truth about other people, even the ones we're closest to.'

'And then he finds them and he moves his new family here. It's horrible.' She shivered. 'They're living over those little graves and he *know*s and he doesn't say anything? And she doesn't *suspect* anything? How can he play at being Terry when he's Matt Reid?'

'I don't think he's playing,' Noah said. 'That's the thing

with new identities. Ayana Mirza told me that she's already thinking of the person she'll be when she has her new name. She says it's as if that person isn't her, she's finally shrugging off all the terrible things that happened to Ayana. Not *forgetting,* but it means she can lock the bad stuff away and start over. Maybe it was like that for Matt, when he became Terry.'

At number 14, a solitary PCSO was guarding the tape. He'd been standing a long time; rain from earlier in the day was slicking the shoulders of his jacket.

Behind him, the house was silent. Keeping its secrets, all its windows unlit.

Noah and Debbie ducked past, up the side alley to the garden where the forensic tent was still pitched over the bunker they'd opened.

The garden smelt of wet earth and vegetation. Two days ago, it had been bright and well tended, full of colour. Now it was ragged round the edges, weeds making the most of the hiatus from Terry's care. The rainwater drums were overflowing, dripping on to a margin of mud by the kitchen wall.

Aware of being watched, Noah glanced in the direction of the house next door.

Julie Lowry was standing at the upstairs window. She gave a little wave of her hand when she saw him, then moved away.

'Neighbourhood Watch,' Debbie said. 'But not one of them saw what was really happening here.'

The kitchen was just as he remembered: messy, lived-in, comfortable.

Nothing like the rest of the house.

Upstairs, in the bedroom belonging to Carmen and Tommy, the furniture was fastened to the walls and the windows were nailed shut.

Safety windows, the kind that could be broken with a rock hammer in the event of a fire.

They found the rock hammer in Beth and Terry's room, together with a rope ladder and a fire extinguisher. Out of reach of the children, but readily to hand. The windows in this room were nailed shut too. The mirror above Beth's dressing table was made of plastic.

Debbie and Noah searched for something with sharp edges, and failed to find it.

In the bathroom Debbie said sadly, 'He was scared of everything, wasn't he?'

Cabinets, out of reach of the smaller children, and locked.

Plastic mirrors, and plastic walls to the shower unit.

Another window that wouldn't open.

'Look at this.' Debbie touched the door to the bathroom. 'No lock.'

Just a raw hole where it'd been torn out. As if someone had taken a car wrench to it. Someone in a panic, desperate to open the door. Or desperate for it not to be locked.

'Who takes the lock out of a bathroom door?' Debbie said. 'Unless one of the little ones got trapped in here, by accident . . .'

'Wrong side of the door,' Noah said. 'If Carmen or Tommy got locked in, then the lock would've been removed from the other side . . . The police report said Esther cut herself in the bathroom. On purpose, and more than once. It was always Matt who found her.'

They looked at the bath and the shower, seeing pictures of what that might have been like for Matt Reid. Nothing Noah could conjure was bad enough.

'It's spooky.' Debbie shivered. 'Even if you didn't know about Esther, this house is spooky. The windows, the doors. It's weird. I mean, it's so . . . *safe.*'

The way a prison was safe.

Terry had built a prison for his new family.

No locks on the doors meant no secrets.

The whole house felt oppressive. Threatening.

Was Terry so scared that he couldn't see the huge shadow his fear was casting? And if he was this scared *before* Esther was released, what was he like now?

What had seeing his dead boys done to that fear?

'I couldn't have lived like this when I was a teenager,' Debbie said, 'with no privacy, nowhere that's just mine. I'm not surprised Clancy ran off.'

'And if Clancy took the kids?'

'We don't know what Terry was like, not really. Maybe Clancy was looking out for them . . . But we think it was Terry, don't we? We think it was *Terry* who took the kids.'

'We don't know,' Noah said. 'That's the problem.'

The house was holding its breath, silence packed solidly up the stairs. They checked the other doors in the house. The locks had been removed from every one, even the door in the attic where the pantiled roof was pitched like a tent.

Clancy's room.

The bed, shoved back against the far wall, had collected a puddle of sun from the skylight. No posters on the walls, no iPod or speakers, nothing to say the room belonged to a teenage boy. A low chest of drawers was fastened to the wall like the cupboards in the kids' bedroom downstairs. The round mirror above the bed was plastic, in a rubber frame.

Windows and skylight nailed shut.

Noah turned a slow circle, looking for evidence that Clancy lived here. No TV, no computer. Not even any bookshelves. Just the bed and the chest of drawers.

Debbie crouched and opened the drawers, one after another. 'Underwear and T-shirts.'

The view from the skylight was non-existent. If you added

blue, put fluffy clouds up there, it would still be depressing. There was nothing to see. No wonder Clancy spent all his time at the window, with its clear view to Julie Lowry's garden and, further up the road, the shingle roof of Douglas Cole's shed.

'Look at this.' Debbie had found something at the back of one of the drawers.

A china doll in a silk dress with green glass eyes.

Noah said, 'Doug Cole collects those.'

'So what's it doing here?' Debbie turned the doll until it shut its eyes.

'Let's ask Mr Cole,' Noah said.

They were back downstairs when Noah's phone played the station's tune. 'DS Jake.'

'We're going through Merrick's paperwork,' Ron said. 'Remember Gutless Douglas?'

'Cole.' Noah glanced at Debbie, who raised her eyebrows at him. 'What about him?'

'He's right here, on our list.'

'Because he bought number 8 from Merrick Homes. Everyone living on Blackthorn Road is on the list . . .'

'Forget Blackthorn Road. Cole and Merrick are mates.'

Noah looked at the doll in Debbie's hand, his skin creeping. 'Define mates.'

'They belong to the same society,' Ron said, 'and guess what? It's all about underground hiding places. Holes. Old tunnels. Bunkers. They call themselves "Buried".'

20

Douglas Cole answered the door to number 8 before Noah and Debbie could knock on it. He was wearing his bespoke suit and his face was pinker than ever.

'I was about to call you. I just got home.' He swallowed. 'You'd better come in.'

He led them in the direction of the kitchen at the back of the house. 'I didn't know, really I didn't. I only just got back. I've been at work all day.'

The kitchen was neat and orderly, no sign of the toy collection that sprawled around the rest of the house. A big table, scrubbed clean, against one wall. Fitted units, showroom-shiny. The door into the sitting room was shut tight, like the back door leading into the garden.

From where he was standing, Noah could see the shed Cole had built over the bunker.

Something moved under the table.

Pink and yellow, hunched over.

A shuffle of shoes, the huffing of breath through small teeth.

Noah crouched on his heels and peered under the table. 'Carmen?'

She scowled back at him, all plaits and duffle coat, a crayon in her fist, a sheet of paper under her heels, covered in scrawls. She was dirty, but she didn't look hurt.

Noah felt a flood of relief; he propped a hand to the tiled floor. 'Carmen, I'm DS Jake. I'm a policeman. I was with your mum and dad the other day, remember?'

'Go 'way.'

Debbie crouched next to him. 'Carmen, love, where's Tommy? Where's your brother?'

'Go 'way.'

'Ooh, can we see your picture?' Debbie held out a hand.

Carmen shoved the sheet at them. She'd been chewing at the crayon; there was red wax on her mouth. A half-eaten banana was turning brown on the floor at her feet.

'This is a great picture,' Debbie said. 'Is this your dad?'

'No,' scornfully.

'Is it Clancy?'

Carmen nodded. There was mud on her shoes, and on the hem of her pink duffle coat, a leaf in her yellow hair. She sucked on the crayon, looking sleepy, her eyes glazed over.

Debbie said, 'Did Clancy bring you here?'

The little girl was unresponsive.

'Or was it your dad?'

Nothing.

'Did they bring Tommy too?'

'Go 'way.'

'Where's Tommy now, love? Is he with your dad, or Clancy?'

Carmen kicked her foot at them. 'Go *'way.*'

Debbie said, 'Okay. But first we're going to call your mum and let her know you've drawn this great picture. She's going to love it.'

Carmen's scowl darkened. She hunched away, keeping

under the table when Noah straightened, nodding at Debbie to stay with the girl.

'I don't know how she got in here . . .' Cole was blushing to the tips of his ears.

'We're looking for her brother, Tommy. Is he here in the house too?'

'I know Tommy.' Cole shook his head. 'I haven't had the chance to look. I only just this second got home. The front door was locked. I've no idea how she got in.'

'Is this yours?' Noah held out the doll they'd taken from Clancy's bedroom.

'Yes.' Cole looked bewildered. 'Where did you find her?'

'At number 14. You said your door was locked when you got home. Who else has a key?'

'No one.' Cole hesitated, shifting inside his suit. 'Well, only Terry, but that's for the garden. It's a back door key.'

Noah crossed the kitchen to the back door, testing the handle.

The door was locked.

Carmen was cuddled in Debbie's lap, her eyes filmy with sleep and the secret of what had happened in the hours since she disappeared with her brother.

'Call the station,' Noah told Debbie. 'Let them know what's happening.'

He nodded at Cole. 'Let's look for Tommy.'

No sign of Thomas Doyle in the sitting room, where the dolls and monkeys stared back at Noah empty-eyed. No sign of the boy in any of the rooms downstairs.

They climbed to the first floor, Noah keeping Cole in his sights.

'Terry does your garden. Does he know about the bunker under the shed? You told DI Rome and me that no one knew, but did Terry?'

Cole hesitated, then nodded. 'I didn't want to get him into trouble. He's the only friendly face on this road, the only one with any time for me.'

'Have you seen him today?'

'No, not in a few days. He's at the safe house, isn't he? The one you put him in.'

'He was,' Noah said. 'Now he's missing. Like his children.'

Nothing in the rooms on the first floor.

They started up the stairs to the attic.

Cole said, 'Where did you find her?' He meant the doll.

'In Clancy's bedroom.'

Cole shook his head. 'I don't understand.'

'You didn't give the doll to Clancy?'

'No, of course not. Why would I?'

'Why would you . . .?'

They reached the attic room.

The door was open, letting out a dim slice of light.

Silence from inside.

'That's not right,' Cole said. 'I keep this door shut. There are valuables in here . . .' He started towards the room.

Noah put a hand on his arm to stop him. 'Wait here.'

He pushed the door wide, and went into the attic.

Cole's valuables were stacked neatly and obsessively everywhere in the room. On shelves built into the eaves and in crates on the floor. Pristine action figures in unopened boxes, dolls behind cellophane, untouched, never played with.

'Oh dear. Oh no . . .'

Behind Noah, Cole started to sob softly.

He'd seen what Noah was seeing.

Curled on the floor among the torn packaging from printed boxes, clutching Obi-Wan Kenobi in a small fist, sleep sticking his hair to his forehead: Tommy Doyle.

21

Ron punched the whiteboard with a broad grin. 'About time we had some good news!'

'Both children? And they're unhurt?' Marnie held the phone to her ear, listening to Noah. 'What about Clancy, and Terry?' *And Ed.*

'No sign of anyone else,' Noah said. 'Sorry . . . The kids are okay. A doctor checked them over. They're a bit dehydrated, but that's all.'

'Who took them to Cole's house, have they been able to tell you that?'

'Not yet, but Debbie's with Carmen. She'll find out what happened, I'm sure of it.'

'Good. Meanwhile we need to find Clancy, and Terry.' *And Ed.*

Marnie glanced at the interview room, where Adam was still sitting, waiting for her to tell him he could go home.

'Bring Mr Cole to the station,' she told Noah. 'We need to ask him some questions, starting with what it's like to be Buried.'

Under the yellow light in the interview room, Douglas Cole looked jaundiced, all trace of pinkness gone from his round face. He sipped at the cup of tea Marnie had handed to him. 'I didn't know. About Carmen and Tommy being in my house. I didn't know.'

'You knew about Ian Merrick,' Noah said. 'You were part of the same society.'

'Buried.' Cole nodded. 'It's an historical society. We're interested in derelict parts of London. I told you about it the last time we talked.'

'Where does the society meet?'

'Different places. Usually in the library, after hours. We met in the church once, and in the community centre up on the estate. Just wherever we can get together.'

'Who else is in the society?'

'Oh there's quite a few of us. Some of the older gents from the estate who've been there donkey's years . . . Ladies, too. But it tends to be men. Me and Terry, and Ian Merrick. Anyone who's interested in history, and London.'

'The trouble is,' Marnie said, 'we don't think Ian Merrick's much of an historian.'

'He was interested in the places we were recording. Really interested. I thought he was a kindred spirit.' Cole shook his head in defeat. 'But you're right. He isn't an historian.'

'He was looking for sites to buy and sell. Underground sites. Places with tunnels and bunkers. Like Beech Rise.'

Cole nodded miserably. 'Yes, he was.'

'How many sites like that exist across London?' Noah asked.

'No one knows for certain. We keep finding more all the time. We know some of the numbers, for instance the bunkers built by the Royal Observer Corp, mostly during the Cold War, although some much earlier than that.' He sat up straight. 'There are one thousand five hundred and sixty-four ROC bunkers across London. That's the tip of the iceberg, really. So much of this building was secret, you see. And a lot of it's managed to stay secret.'

'Did you know about the bunkers when you bought number 8?'

'Not then,' Cole said. 'Ian told me just after the sale went through. He pretended I'd known about them all along, but I hadn't and he *knew* I hadn't. I suppose . . . he was blackmailing me. He wanted to find other sites, places the society knew about. He wanted to know before anyone else.' He neatened his hair with his hand. 'Once I realised what he was up to, I wanted it to stop. He wasn't doing anything illegal, but I wanted him out of the society. He said if I did that, he'd tell people about the bunker in my back garden. People would draw their own conclusions, he said, as to why I wanted a house with a ruddy big cement tomb in the garden. Those were his exact words.'

Cole's mouth turned down like a child's. 'He called me "the Collector", said the papers would call me worse. I knew he was right, because of what happened with Lizzie Fincher. Even your boss thinks I'm strange. I wouldn't be surprised if he had me down as a suspect for those poor little boys Terry found . . .'

'They were his boys,' Marnie said.

'What?'

'Terry's real name is Matt Reid. He knew about the bunkers when he bought the house. His ex-wife worked for Ian Merrick.'

'His boys?' Cole looked dazed, distraught. 'Terry's boys?'

'He changed his identity after his wife killed their children. She was suffering from post-partum psychosis. She put the boys in the bunker, meaning them to be safe. Terry spent years looking for them. We think he followed the trail from his wife's job with Merrick; that he found out about the underground sites Merrick was selling.'

Marnie paused, watching Cole's face. 'You didn't know any of this?'

'No, no . . .' Tears made Cole's stare swim. 'Poor Terry. That poor man . . .'

'We think he panicked when he heard his ex-wife was being paroled. That's when he opened the bunker and called the police. We think he was scared she was going to return to the place where she put the boys, not knowing that he was living there with a new family.'

'The woman in the other interview room,' Cole said nervously. 'That was his wife?'

Marnie didn't answer the question.

'Then,' she said, 'Carmen and Tommy went missing. With Clancy, or at least that's how it looked. But then Terry went missing, too. With a victim care officer. We don't know how the children ended up in your house, Mr Cole. Can you help us make sense of that?'

'I . . . can't. I had no idea they were there, or how they got in. I'd *never* have left children alone in there, especially not the attic. Tommy's made a terrible mess of it. Not that it matters as long as he's safe, but you have to see *none* of it was my idea. It's not a safe house for children to be alone in. Some of those toys are very old. They have sharp edges, lead paint . . . Thank goodness he didn't find any of those.' His hands flustered then settled around the cup of tea. 'It's why I took Lizzie on the tube. Because I knew it wasn't safe inside the house. I know it sounds funny, with all the toys and whatnot, but they're not to be played with.'

'Did Terry know about your collection?'

'Yes, he'd seen it. He wouldn't have let the children play in the house, I'm sure of that. He was extremely safety-conscious. Extremely.'

'But he had a key to the back door.'

'Yes, so he could make himself a cup of tea when he was doing the garden.'

'The doll,' Marnie said, 'that we found in Clancy's room. Can you tell us about that?'

'Her name's Sophie and she's French.' Cole's smile crumpled. 'But you don't mean that, of course. You mean can I tell you how she ended up in a teenage boy's bedroom. No, is the answer, I can't. I wish I could. She went missing about three months ago.'

'From where?' Marnie asked. 'The house, or the bunker?'

Cole swallowed a mouthful of tea. 'From the house.'

'And only Terry has a key.'

'Yes.'

'So you must have assumed that Terry took it. Her.'

'No.' Cole shook his head emphatically. 'I never thought for a second that it was Terry. He wouldn't do a thing like that. I assumed it was the boy, Clancy. He came round sometimes, with Terry, to help in the garden. Terry tried to get him interested in doing some hard work. The boy didn't want to know, not really. He's at that age, I suppose.'

'You didn't challenge him about the doll? Or speak to Terry about it?'

'I didn't want to make a fuss. I could see how he was trying with the boy. Fostering's hard enough without worrying about things like petty theft. Poor old Sophie isn't worth anything to anyone else but me. She's just a pocket-money toy.'

'Why would a teenage boy take a doll?' Noah asked.

Cole shook his head. 'You've seen my house. There's not much else to take. I expect he wanted a souvenir. It's how I started collecting. Buying souvenirs from the strange places my parents used to take me.'

'Buying,' Marnie said, 'not stealing.'

'He's a strange boy. But I don't think he's bad, not really. Just unsettled. Feeling a bit unloved, in spite of Terry's best efforts.' Cole put down the tea. 'He's ever so good with the little ones. They worship him, Carmen and Tommy. He's like their big brother. Of course,' he added, 'I didn't see them together all that often, and never without Terry there. He's always so careful with them. He must've been out of his mind with worry when they ran off.'

'What do you think happened? You have a theory, I'm sure. Can you share it with us?'

'I don't know anything for certain, really I don't. I'd help if I could. That poor family . . .'

'But you have a theory.' Marnie smiled encouragement at him. 'You've seen the children with their father, and with Clancy. You've seen the family. Terry's a part of your society.'

'Yes . . . he joined as soon as they moved to Beech Rise.'

'Did he and Merrick get on?'

Cole sipped at his tea, considering the question. 'I can't say they did, and I can't say they didn't. Ian was always a bit funny around Terry. A bit . . . careful, I suppose you'd say. I suppose it was because he gave Terry some gardening work from time to time. And on Blackthorn Road, of course, when the houses were first going up. Terry did all the gardens in the road, except Ian wouldn't pay extra for decent soil or plants. That's why most of us asked Terry to sort out the gardens properly, after we moved in.'

'It doesn't sound as if they got on very well,' Noah said. 'Ian and Terry.'

'That's one way of looking at it, I suppose. I'm not terribly good at judging social situations. I'm much happier taking the minutes, keeping accounts, that kind of thing.'

'Did you meet Clancy's parents?' Marnie asked. 'Scott and Christina Brand?'

Cole shook his head. 'But I heard Terry talk about them a couple of times.' His brow creased. 'Or it might've been Ian, since he built a panic room for them. He was very proud of that. Personally, I'd have opposed the planning permission. They live in a listed house, early Georgian, lots of original features by all accounts. But Ian was happy to tear up the cellars and run ventilation pipes around the place.' He shook his head. 'That was when I first challenged him about what he was up to, using Buried to find places he could exploit . . .'

'You didn't think it was odd that Terry was looking after Clancy? The Brands obviously have a lot of money. More than the Doyles.'

'Money's a funny thing,' Cole said. 'Look how I spend mine . . . What that boy needed was a proper home with people who cared for him. You can't fault Terry on that score. He worked so hard to make Clancy feel wanted. And they got on well, the little ones and Clancy . . . It was harder for Terry, with the discipline and everything.'

'Discipline?'

'Rules and boundaries, you know the sort of thing. I imagine teenagers need a lot of that.'

'Was Terry very strict with Clancy and the other children?'

'He was . . . careful, I'd say. Always very careful with all the children. He wanted them to learn life skills. Grow their own food, fend for themselves . . . He taught Clancy to look out for the little ones, be a good big brother. It paid off, too. I never saw a teenage boy so protective of babies, never mind how typical he was in other ways.'

Fend for themselves.

The way Fred and Archie Reid were made to, in the last days of their lives.

Marnie said, 'What do you think happened earlier today? How did the children end up in your house? We realise you don't *know*, but what's your theory?'

Cole sat up straight in the chair, feet together, like a schoolchild wanting to give the right answer. 'I think Clancy brought the children to my house. I think he borrowed the key from Terry and let himself in, and left the children there. I don't know why. I don't know where he is now, or where Terry is. I wish I did.'

'If Clancy did that . . . if he was hiding the children . . . what was he hiding them from?'

'I don't know. I can't imagine. I can't think of any family that's closer or happier or *safer* than Terry's. That's why it makes no sense.' Cole spread his hands. 'It just makes no sense.'

22

You can smell him.

You smelt the same once. Scared. Leaking sweat and fear.

You're sorry for him, somewhere under everything else.

But if he's hurt them, you'll kill him.

After everything you've done, all the lessons you drummed into him, the chances you gave him, the love.

Too much love.

He's had enough from you. Enough chances to grow up and *be a man.*

You trusted him, because trust is important. You opened your home to him when he was a stranger, someone else's problem. What were you thinking, really?

Did Esther teach you nothing?

You were trying to be a better man, a better father than you were for Fred and Archie, and Louisa. You were trying to be strong, to take care of them. To prove you could do that this time. But if they're not safe, what's it all for?

If he's hurt them, you'll kill him.

No more chances, no more lessons.

'You could have someone's eye out with this.'

Doesn't he know how dangerous the world is?

He cuts up apples and leaves the knife on the draining board.

He takes the safety covers off plug sockets and forgets to put them back.

The wire coat hanger was the worst, though.

A *wire* coat hanger.

After everything you'd taught him. As if he was deliberately trying to provoke you, the way he does with his words, his eyes. You tolerated that, but this?

You had to show him enough was enough. You had to make him understand, in the way *you* never understood, before Esther. It's for his own good, as well as theirs.

If he's hurt them, you'll kill him.

You wouldn't hit a woman (couldn't hit a woman), but he's nearly a man and he can take care of himself, in a way you never could at his age.

You taught him to do that.

They send boys as young as ten to prison. He's nearly fifteen, and he's not been a child in years. You saw it in his eyes, the first time you met.

You cut him slack, a lot of it, because of those parents of his, but this is different.

This is your family.

If he's hurt them, he's dead.

23

Beth Doyle came into the station with Debbie Tanner. Carmen and Tommy were at their auntie's house, with Beth's sister. Neither child seemed traumatised, although Carmen still wouldn't talk about what had happened between the park and Douglas Cole's house, not even to confirm whether it was Clancy who took them to number 8.

Beth came to a standstill in the corridor, her eyes fixed on the windows of the interview room where Alison Oliver was sitting with her mother.

'That's her, isn't it?' she said. 'That's Esther Reid.'

Her stare was one part curiosity, nine parts terror.

Debbie said, 'Come on. I'll make us both a nice cup of tea.'

In the second interview room, Beth sat opposite Marnie. Her face was swollen by the stress of the last few hours. 'I didn't know,' she said. 'About Esther, or Terry, or the children. The dead boys . . . I didn't know.'

'We're trying to find Terry,' Marnie said, 'and Clancy. And Mr Belloc, the victim care officer who was with Terry at the safe house. We need your help.'

'How *can* I help?' Beth's voice rose in pitch. 'I didn't *know* anything! He didn't tell me anything!'

'It's been very hard on you finding out like this. I am sorry.' Marnie used her steadiest voice. 'But I do think you can help, and we do *need* your help.'

Beth focused her eyes on Marnie, with difficulty. She jerked her head in a nod.

'How was Terry when you first moved into the house? I know it was a busy time. Tommy was very little. Can you remember how Terry was?'

'Happy. He was happy.' Beth started to cry quietly, tears sliding from her eyes.

Marnie thought of Alison's dry eyes in the room next door. She wondered what had attracted Matt to Esther, and then Terry to Beth. Was it simply that Beth was physically so different? Esther had been lovely once, and she was sharp, clever. Beth was pretty, but plain. Uncomplicated, at least on the surface. The two women had nothing obvious in common, other than that they'd married the same man.

'He can't have been happy,' Beth said, 'can he? That can't have been any truer than the rest of it. He kept *everything* a secret from me . . . He can't ever have been happy.'

'I don't think it was like that,' Marnie said. 'He'd changed his name. Sometimes that helps people to get better. You were helping him to get better. You and Carmen and Tommy.'

'All that time he was looking for his boys . . .'

'And he found them. Perhaps there was peace in that.' Marnie picked up her mug of tea and drank, waiting while the other woman mirrored the action. It was hard to take this slowly, knowing what was at stake, but there was nothing to be gained by rushing Beth. 'A fortnight ago, Terry heard from the police that Alison was coming out of prison.'

'Alison. That's what she calls herself now?' Beth wiped at her eyes.

'Yes. Do you remember anything that changed about Terry's mood a fortnight ago? Was he was more . . . anxious, perhaps?'

'Terry's never anxious,' Beth said mechanically, as if she was speaking by rote.

'And when you were moved to the safe house, how was he then?'

She shook her head, not answering.

'You told me Clancy was angry. Was Terry angry too?'

Beth didn't look at her. 'Terry's never angry.' Rote again.

'Did he ever mention a man called Ian Merrick?'

'No.' Beth pressed her mouth shut.

'Ian Merrick,' Marnie repeated. 'He built the houses on Blackthorn Road. He employed Terry as a gardener sometimes.'

'Terry never mentioned him.'

Marnie picked up her tea. The tannin set her teeth on edge, but it was a useful prop. Beth copied her, relaxing a fraction. 'Tell me about Clancy. When did he come to live with you?'

'Just after we moved to Blackthorn Road. His dad's a friend of Terry's. They were struggling with Clancy, he was acting up at home. He'd run off a couple of times. Terry offered to take care of him for a bit, to see if he could help him to settle down. He's so good with kids.' Her neck stained red. 'We were going to foster him.'

'But you're not fostering him at the moment?'

'Terry said it was best to tell people that was what we were doing, so we wouldn't be asked awkward questions. He said Clancy was unsettled enough without that and we were *going* to foster him. Terry had organised the paperwork and everything. That's what he said.'

'Did you meet Terry's friend, Scott? Clancy's father.'

'No . . .'

'What about his mother, Christina?'

'I never met either of them.'

'Even though Scott was Terry's friend?'

'He didn't have time for friends,' Beth said. 'To spend with friends, I mean.'

'But he had time for Clancy.'

'He made time. He wanted to help. It's what he does. It's *all* he does.' Beth shut her eyes. Tears ran down her cheeks. 'He's a good dad. He *is*.'

'He is,' Marnie agreed. 'Everyone tells us that. I'm sure it's true.'

'He was good with Clancy. He *tried*, he really did. Talking to him all hours. Making time for him. Teaching him about the garden, helping him at school . . . Some days Clancy would come home in a state because of something that'd happened, a fight or just a bad day, and Terry would go up to him, spend hours giving him a quiet talk. Talking him down. He didn't have to give him so much time. He had our two, but he was always up there talking with Clancy, till all hours some nights.'

She wiped her nose with the back of her hand. 'I told him to give up once. I said it was killing him, giving so much time to someone who didn't appreciate it, but Terry wouldn't give up, not on anyone. It's the kind of man he is. He said Clancy reminded him of himself at that age. *Irresponsible*, that was the word he used. He said he wanted to help him be a better person. Stronger, more responsible. It was like . . . a *mission*. I left him alone after that. I could see he needed to help Clancy, even though I thought it was a lost cause. I *missed* him. Terry. All the time he spent up there in the attic . . . I wanted him back down with us.'

She moved her hands. 'Not that he neglected us. It was never like that. It was usually after the children were in bed. It was only *him* who was neglected. There was nothing left of him, some days. It was burning him up, being a dad to that boy on top of everything else.'

'At the safe house,' Marnie said, 'earlier today. Did Terry tell you he was going to leave?'

'I was sleeping. I didn't know he'd gone until I woke up and they told me.'

'Did you get the chance to speak with Mr Belloc, the victim care officer?'

Beth shook her head. 'I slept through the whole thing.' She dried her nose on the cuff of her sleeve. 'I'm sorry. Thank God Carmen and Tommy are safe . . . I was so *sick* with worry. We both were. I've never seen Terry like that . . .'

'Angry?'

'Scared,' Beth said. 'He was scared to death, the same as me.'

24

'Terry was on a mission to make Clancy a better person.' Marnie held the side of her neck as if it hurt her. 'Beth says he devoted hours to talking with Clancy about the need to be less irresponsible. Less like Matt, in other words. I think I understand why Clancy ran, maybe even why he took the children to Cole's house. But why didn't he stay there? If he's scared of Terry . . . why didn't he go into hiding too?'

'It wasn't a great hiding place,' Noah said. 'That close to number 14, and somewhere Terry had a key to? I'm guessing he panicked.'

'So where is he now? Why are they both missing? And why take Ed?'

'I know you think the Brands are a dead end, but could Clancy have gone home? They have a very secure house, with a panic room. If he was trying to hide . . .'

'Would you go back there? If you'd run away, more than once? If they'd had you fitted with an alarm as their idea of security? I wouldn't. I'd take my chances in the open air. I think Clancy's running. What I don't understand is why Terry's running too. If he is . . .'

She shook her head. 'Consider *missing* as an indicator, not just an event in itself, isn't that what they tell us? Terry was scared stiff when the children went missing. There's been no activity on his credit or Oyster cards. No signal on his phone suggests he's gone underground. Until we get a sighting of the car, our best bet is looking at the hiding places he knew about from Merrick.' She looked at Colin Pitcher. 'What's Cole given us so far?'

'Merrick has seventeen sites under development in the Greater London area. Fourteen have bunkers or tunnels, or similar. Do you want us to widen the search?'

'Not yet. How about the security firm that was tagging Clancy? Any crossover between Merrick's sites and the places where Clancy used to go?'

'Possibly, but the firm won't release the data without parental consent, or a warrant.'

Debbie said, 'Mr and Mrs Brand aren't answering calls.'

'They won't.' Marnie studied Colin's list. Adam had told her about the Brands. 'They'll lawyer up before we get within fifty feet of our first question, but there's no reason to think they know where Clancy or Terry went, so I'm not in a hurry to waste time there.'

'Security nuts,' Ron said disgustedly. 'But they let their only kid go missing. What's the point in making your home into Fort Knox if your son isn't safe?'

His phone rang and he moved to answer it.

Marnie looked at Colin. 'How're you getting on with Mr Cole?'

'Very well. He's meticulous, and he really wants to help.'

'One thing,' Noah said. 'We could check the soil types at Merrick's sites. The last time we saw Terry, he had red hands. From soil, or clay. Beth said he'd been at work, but this was *after* the children were first missing. His boots were stained red too.'

'Alluvial,' Colin said. 'That's reddish brown.' He looked

at the list of sites. 'Most of the subsoil at the Isle of Dogs is alluvial. Perhaps we should start there.'

'He's looking for Clancy,' Debbie said. 'That's my bet. He was scared stiff when he heard the kids were missing and *he* wouldn't have left them at Cole's place. He's after Clancy.'

'He doesn't know,' Marnie reminded her, 'that we've found Carmen and Tommy. He's not answering his phone, and we don't have any easy way to get that message to him. We have to assume he's looking for all three children.'

'Or he's hiding from us. He saw the photo of Esther. He must've known we'd find out he was Matt Reid. The secrets he kept from Beth . . . it's all come out now.'

'He wouldn't run without knowing the children were safe,' Noah said. 'Not after what he went through with Esther. He *must* have gone looking for them.'

'With Ed?' Marnie kept her voice light. 'Ed would have told him to keep his phone switched on, for news of the children. Ed trusted us to find them.'

Noah nodded, but he said, 'We've got a man who lost his first family in a way that would drive anyone insane. And an angry teenage boy whose parents are obsessed with everyone's safety but his. I wouldn't want to bet which one's more dangerous.'

Ron came back from his desk, bright-eyed. 'CCTV sighting.'

'Terry, or Clancy?'

'Merrick. At one of the sites Cole told us to look out for, off the M25. Artificial caves. They used to take young offenders down there as part of some bollocksy programme to get them used to controlled spaces. Site's been closed for donkey's, but CCTV's got Merrick heading in there at 1.35 p.m. He didn't come back out.'

'Good work. Noah, we'll take this one.' She nodded at the others. 'Keep looking for Terry and Clancy.'

'What d'you want to do about the press, Fletcher? He keeps demanding a fag break.'

'He can wait,' Marnie said. 'We're busy.'

'Detective Inspector.' Connie was in the doorway to the interview room. 'My daughter needs a doctor. We've been waiting hours.'

In the interview room, Alison was sitting with her hands pressed to the table, silver patches of sweat on her face. Her eyes were fixed on the wall so intently that Noah half expected to see words written there.

'Why does she need a doctor?' Marnie asked.

'Why do you think?' Connie snapped. 'She's not well. Do you imagine it's been easy for her coming here, talking about what happened? She needs to see someone. She needs pills.'

'Is she asking for a doctor?'

'No.'

'Then—'

'Don't give me that,' Connie said. 'You know as well as I do that she's sick.' She blinked tears from her eyes, looking ferocious. 'She'll never ask for help, because she doesn't think she deserves any. But I'm her mother and I'm telling you she needs a doctor.'

Marnie nodded at Noah. 'Go. Take DS Carling. Bring Mr Merrick back here so we can ask him some questions.'

She looked to where Connie's daughter was sitting with her face to the wall.

'I'd better stay and deal with this.'

25

You're crying. It's pathetic.

You did what you had to do. You didn't want to, but there wasn't any other way. You'd tried everything else. Patience. Questions.

There comes a point, doesn't there, when you have to stop waiting and hoping and biting your tongue. You did enough of that with her, and look where it got you.

Everyone said you should have been able to stop it.

You were in charge, you should have been in charge.

You were trying too hard to be gentle, considerate.

That's not what a man is. You needed to take charge.

Man up.

You did what you had to do.

You shouldn't be snivelling about it.

You should be glad.

It's done.

26

'Your mum thinks you need to see a doctor.' Marnie sat across from Connie's daughter. 'Is that something you want?' She waited for a response. 'Alison?'

'It's Esther.' The same cracked, thirsty voice as before, but now it came from deep inside the woman's chest. 'My name's Esther. Let's bypass the bullshit, shall we?'

'Do you want to see a doctor?'

'No.' She stared at the wall as if she believed she could break it with her stare. Or burn it. Burn a hole right through the station wall, into the world outside.

Marnie had told one of the desk officers to take Connie to get some fresh air. She'd wanted time alone with Esther Reid.

'We found Carmen and Thomas. Terry's children. They're safe and well.'

Esther turned her head at that, dragging her stare to Marnie's face. 'You're lying.'

'Why would I lie?'

'To make me feel better.' Her lips thinned. 'Or to make me feel worse.'

'It's impressive,' Marnie told her.

'What?'

'Your self-loathing. Your determination to be a monster. It's impressive, but it's getting on my nerves. You could be helping, if you weren't so busy chasing after punishment.'

'How could I help? You said you found them.'

'I said we found Carmen and Thomas. Matt's missing, and so is Clancy, who was living with the family. He's fourteen years old. We don't think he and Matt got on very well. We think it was Clancy who took the children and hid them, because he was scared of Matt. He saw a side of Matt that no one else saw. And it scared him.'

She stopped, holding Esther still with her stare. The woman's eyes wouldn't keep quiet. It was like trying to hold a boulder in one hand.

'You can understand that, can't you? How Matt might be frightening to a teenage boy. You were right when you said they looked alike. Matt said Clancy reminded him of himself at that age. *Irresponsible*. That's the word he used. He was trying to teach Clancy to be less irresponsible. He'd made it a mission.'

Esther pressed her lips together, not speaking.

'Every window in the house was nailed shut. Every one. Matt nailed the windows shut and he ripped out the locks in all the doors inside the house. Even the bathroom door. There was nowhere in the house where anyone could be private, or alone.

'You think you belong in a prison. Matt was living in one. He *built* one, to keep his new family safe. To make sure nothing terrible could happen to them. But it had already happened, hadn't it? They weren't living with Terry Doyle, they were living with Matt Reid.

'I think Clancy saw Matt. I think he's Matt's mirror, the way you say Matt is yours. And Matt saw himself in Clancy. It scared the pair of them, to death.'

Esther said, 'No.'

'No?' Marnie echoed. 'No what? No, he didn't build a prison? He didn't rip out the locks and nail the windows shut? No, he wasn't Matt when he was trying to be Terry? He wasn't scared to death? No what?'

'No, I can't help you.' Her voice was buried behind her teeth. 'I can't.'

'You can tell me what you think Terry would do to a teenage boy who took his children and hid them.'

'He'd kill him. I think . . . he'd kill him.' She clenched her face. 'It's what he should've done to me.'

'Murder's not that easy,' Marnie said. 'Not for most people. You, for instance. You'd never have been capable of it if you hadn't fallen sick.'

'I . . .'

Marnie leaned closer to the woman. 'You would *never*,' she repeated, 'have been capable of it if you hadn't been sick.'

Esther shut her eyes. Her shoulders shook. 'I want to tell him,' she said. 'Matt. I want to tell him about the boys. How it happened, what their last days were like . . .'

'You said you didn't remember.'

'I don't remember *enough*. But I can give him something. Not the nightmares. The stories I read to them, the games we played in the dark, how they laughed when I tickled them . . . the way they looked sleeping. Their *courage*. I want to give him that.'

'You can,' Marnie said. 'You just have to help me find him.'

'This boy . . .'

'Clancy.'

'Clancy. He took the children. Carmen, and Thomas.'

'That's what we think.'

'He didn't hurt them.' Esther's eyes searched Marnie's face. 'They were safe and well when you found them.'

'Yes, but we've not had the chance to tell Matt. He ran before we could let him know.'

'Did he have any reason to think the boy would hurt them? To see him as a threat?'

'Everyone we've spoken with says Clancy was careful with the children. He took care of them, and they loved him . . .'

Not everyone, Marnie realised as she said it.

Adam Fletcher had insisted that Clancy was a risk to the children.

She'd asked him why he hadn't warned Beth and Terry if he was so sure their family was at risk. Had he done that?

Had Adam warned Terry about Clancy?

Because Marnie had guilt-tripped him into it?

Esther was saying, 'If he had no reason to see the boy as a threat—'

'Hold that thought.' Marnie stood up. 'I'll be right back.' She paused, looking down at the woman's drawn face. 'With a doctor.'

'Who are you trying to save?' Esther asked. 'Matt, or Clancy?'

'Both,' Marnie said. 'I want to save them both.'

Adam was still kicking his heels in the other interview room. Marnie didn't bother switching on the tape. 'Did you warn Terry about Clancy?'

'Did I . . .?'

'You think he's a predator, a danger to small children. Did you warn Terry about him?'

'It's what you said I should do. If I thought those kids were at risk.'

'So you did.' Fear put its fist into her stomach. 'You told a grieving father that his new family was at risk from a teenage boy.'

'Grieving? What the fuck are you talking about?'

'Terry Doyle. Those were *his* boys, in the bunker. Buried by his first wife when she lost her mind to post-partum psychosis.'

Adam moved his jaw as if she'd hit him. 'No.'

'Yes. You told a grieving dad that his children were at risk from Clancy Brand. You put a kid in the firing line because it made a good story. Predatory teenage boy with security-obsessed parents . . . God forbid the truth should be allowed to get in the way of your *scoop*.'

The skin under Adam's eyes thinned to nothing. 'Have you found them? Carmen and Thomas. Jesus. Are they . . .?'

'Alive. Thanks to Clancy. He took them out of range of Terry's fear and pain and whatever else he's going through. Your *evil little shit* saved those children. And now he's missing, and so's Terry. Who thanks to you thinks that boy was a threat to his children.'

'You haven't met his parents,' Adam said, 'or talked with anyone at the schools he got kicked out of. He was a psycho, everyone said so. Sooner or later he'd have snapped—'

'You're out of your mind . . .' Marnie drew a short breath. 'I get it. I do. She died. Tia died and everything else is just a long shadow thrown from that loss. *Your* loss. But you can't live like that. Not usefully. Not in any way she would have wanted. You have to—'

'What?' Adam demanded. 'Let it go? Move on? Let's hear it, Detective Inspector, your platitude of the day. What is it I *have* to do?'

'Stop,' Marnie said. 'You have to stop. Stop being scared of the shadows. Stop chasing, stop digging. He's a fourteen-year-old boy, for pity's sake.'

'Yeah?' Adam shoved his stare at her so hard the floor tilted under her feet, the last sixteen years stripped away, all of her past here and now, in his eyes.

'So was Stephen Keele.'

27

Noah wasn't a fan of caves, or any enclosed space for that matter. The fact that this cave was man-made and had been used to teach young offenders about controlled environments didn't make it any less of a dank, dark hole in the ground.

What kind of man looked at an abandoned hole in the ground and saw money?

Ian Merrick.

Merrick raided London's catacombs, exploiting the city's secret subterranea for profit. Concrete tomb raider in a hard hat.

Unconscious from a suspected skull fracture.

Paramedics were doing what they could to stabilise him, but by their best estimate, Merrick had been unconscious for some hours. In the cave, in the cold. It didn't look hopeful.

'Attempted murder?' Ron said. 'Or GBH?' He was looking at Merrick's wrists, at the way they'd been tied and with what. 'Someone put him into the recovery position . . .'

Merrick was wearing steel-toe-capped boots, and a business suit.

'He knew he was coming on-site,' Ron said. 'When he

set off here, I mean. Why wear the boots otherwise? He wasn't snatched, in other words.'

Noah looked around the cave. It had a hard clay floor and cemented walls, one of which had been made into a climbing wall, painted orange and plugged with hand grips. A vertical ladder, sunk into a concrete base, climbed to the ground level above.

The paramedics were going to have to try and get Merrick up the ladder, once he was stabilised. Far easier if he was in a body bag, but they had to hope it wouldn't come to that.

'If Terry did this,' Ron stepped out of the way of a paramedic, 'he's dangerous. That doesn't look good for Belloc . . .'

'I'm going back up,' Noah said. 'No phone signal down here.'

Ron nodded. 'What're you going to tell the boss?'

'That someone attacked Ian Merrick,' Noah said, 'and he might not make it.'

In the dead space above the cave, he dialled Marnie's number.

Funny how these sites all felt the same. Restless, wrapped in litter, as if they'd sucked in all the debris from the surrounding area . . .

'Noah.' Marnie's voice was crisp. He could hear traffic in the background and guessed she was in the car, on her way to the site. 'What've you got?'

'Ian Merrick with a suspected skull fracture. Someone tied him up and hit him and left him in the cave. He's alive, just. Paramedics are trying to keep him that way.'

After a beat, Marnie said, 'Tied him up how, and hit him with what?'

'No weapon on the scene. Whoever did it took whatever they used away with them. Paramedics think it was something blunt, maybe a rubber torch. One blow, a lot of force behind it. Not a frenzy, in other words. But his wrists were tied. With a wire coat hanger.'

'A wire coat hanger,' Marnie repeated. 'Do you think he was meant to die down there?'

'Hard to say. He was in the recovery position and his wrists were tied in front of him. If he'd come round, he could have climbed back up. It wouldn't have been easy, though.'

'I'm assuming no sign of Clancy, or Terry.'

'Or Ed. Sorry, no. Nothing that Ron or I could see. We've put a call through to Forensics.'

'Stay where you are. I'm taking Esther to St Thomas's. Lyn Birch has contacted the psychiatric team there, in case she needs a prescription. I'll meet you at the cave site.'

'She's Esther again now, not Alison?'

Marnie said, 'She was always Esther.'

'A coat hanger,' Esther said. She was sitting next to her mother in the back of Marnie's car.

The traffic lights were red, again. At this rate it would take them an hour just to cross the river. Marnie turned in her seat to look at the two women. 'I'm going to drop you at St Thomas's, where a female police officer is waiting. She'll stay with you while I'm gone.'

'Someone's been tied up and hit,' Connie said. 'Was it Ian Merrick, or is that wishful thinking on my part?'

'You said a wire coat hanger,' Esther repeated. 'What was it used for?'

The traffic lights changed to green.

Marnie turned on to Westminster Bridge Road. She didn't answer either woman's question, watching them in the rear-view mirror from the corner of her eye.

'It was Matt,' Esther said. 'If he used a coat hanger . . .

it was Matt. And he's dangerous.' She stared out of the window at the passing traffic. 'Very dangerous.'

Connie clicked her tongue, holding her daughter's hand in her lap.

Esther said, 'I hope he's dead.'

'Matthew?' Connie sounded shocked.

'Ian,' Esther said. 'I hope he's dead. I hope Matt killed him.'

'He'd go to prison,' her mother said.

Esther watched the traffic through the window. 'He's there already.'

Marnie's phone buzzed. She used hands-free to take the call. 'DI Rome.'

'Marnie . . .' Ed.

Ed.

'Where are you?' Marnie slowed the car, watching the traffic.

'Merrick . . .'

'We found Merrick. Where're you?'

'Isle . . . of Dogs.' Ed's voice was fractured, uneven. 'Sorry . . .'

'Isle of Dogs. Merrick's site?'

'Y-yes . . .'

'You're hurt. How bad is it?'

'Just . . . N-no. I'm okay. My fault. Is Merrick . . .?'

'He's alive. Carmen and Tommy are safe. Is Terry with you?'

'He's . . . somewhere. Here. Yes . . .'

'Are you safe?' A frenzy of static. '*Ed.* Are you safe?'

'I'm . . .' Struggling to breathe, in shock, hurt. 'Okay . . . I'm okay.'

'Leave your phone on. We're coming.'

28

Ed's hair was grey with dust, his clothes filthy and full of creases, but he was in one piece. Thin-faced, hollow-eyed, but alive.

Paramedics had found him soon after Marnie's emergency call. By the time she reached the Isle of Dogs, Ed was sitting in the back of an ambulance with a foil shock blanket around his shoulders, answering questions from a uniformed officer. From the way he was holding himself, his whole body hurt. 'I'll take it from here,' Marnie told the PC.

She sat facing Ed until he held out a hand for hers. 'Sorry . . .'

'Don't.' She moved to his side. 'Where's Terry?'

'He was here.' Ed turned his head to look out of the back of the ambulance. His pupils were shot wide, but responsive. He was badly shaken up, a bit bruised and dehydrated, but the paramedics had given him the all-clear.

Wind whipped at the site, with enough force to rock the ambulance in the shallow trench where it was parked. 'Clancy,' Marnie asked. 'Is he with Terry?'

Ed nodded. 'Yes, I think so. He . . . ran.'

'You didn't see him?'

'I was in the boot of the car.' He tried for a smile. 'My choice, more or less. He's . . . panicking.'

'Terry.'

'He's . . . not Terry, is he?' Ed's hand was cold under hers. 'He wouldn't tell me . . . enough of it. But those boys . . . were his?'

'Yes.'

'Damn . . .' Ed looked at her. 'You need to find them. He's . . . You need to find them.'

'What did he do?'

'He gave me a choice, to stay at the house with Beth. I said I wanted to go with him, to try and find the children. That's what I thought he was going to do. He wasn't thinking straight and I thought if I stayed with him, I could help. Stupid of me. Next thing I know, I'm in the boot of the car. He took my phone. You must've been . . . I'm sorry.'

She smoothed a thumb at his cold fingers. 'You said Clancy ran?'

'When we got here . . . He was in the back of the car. He'd been with Merrick, I think.'

'Clancy was with Merrick?'

'I think so. I couldn't follow much of it.' Ed rolled his shoulders. 'Boot of the car's a rotten way to travel. He had his gardening kit in there. I've got spade-shaped bruises . . .'

'How did you get out?'

'Through the back seat. He'd left my phone in the glove compartment.' Ed managed a proper smile. 'You said Carmen and Tommy are okay?'

'Safe and well. Thanks to Clancy, we think. Any idea which way he ran?'

'Into the site,' Ed said. 'I could hear gravel . . . He ran into the site, and Terry went after him. You need to find them. Terry was . . . out of his mind. Clancy wouldn't tell him where he took the children and Terry was shouting about Merrick . . .'

'What was he shouting?'

'That Merrick was dead, and they were next.'

'They?'

Ed rubbed brick dust from his eyes. 'He meant the two of them, him and Clancy.'

29

Ian Merrick had put up a new sign at the Isle of Dogs: *Danger UXB*.

His way of keeping trespassers away, Marnie guessed. Hardly subtle, but his on-site security detail wasn't in evidence, and he hadn't fitted the new locks he'd talked about.

She walked across the gravel, towards where Ed had heard Clancy and Terry running. The site sprawled away in all directions. In the dark, it looked bigger, badly lit and full of potholes and scaffolding; any number of hiding places.

Where had they gone? Underground?

The local police unit were shivering on the sidelines, like supporters at a football match, waiting for the kick-off. Marnie had told them to wait for Noah and the others.

'We're looking for a man in his mid-forties who goes by the name of Terry or Matt. And a fourteen-year-old boy, Clancy.' She shared the photos around the team. 'Either or both might be dangerous, but the man especially. He lost his family.'

'Missing, or wanted?' the unit leader asked.

'Missing,' she said. Hedging her bets. 'At risk of harm. Both of them.'

Esther, at least, was out of harm's way. At St Thomas's Hospital, with Connie and a female DC. One less thing to think about.

Her phone rang: Colin Pitcher.

'There's a condemned tunnel system,' Colin said, 'under the Isle of Dogs. It connected to the Greenwich foot tunnel at Island Gardens, but they closed a section off just after the main tunnel was opened because it kept flooding. They blamed it on tidal corrosion. The rest of the tunnel's been repaired just recently, but the section they closed hasn't been touched in years. DS Jake's bringing the plans.' He paused. 'We were glad to hear about Mr Belloc.'

'Thanks, me too. How's Merrick?'

'Hanging in there, by all accounts. DS Carling's with him.'

'How long until DS Jake and the team gets here?'

'Half an hour, in the current traffic.'

'We'll need a hostage negotiator, and a dive team. MPU will have the skills and equipment to track bodies down there. Can you make a start on the calls?' The Marine Policing Unit could get here quickly, by water. No trouble with traffic for them.

Colin said, 'Will do.'

'You'd better get on to Bomb Disposal too.' She kept walking, glancing back at Merrick's home-made UXB sign. 'On the off-chance there really is a bomb here, although I suspect I'm looking at a piece of cut-price security to keep trespassers off-site . . . And there's CCTV. Let's find out what secrets that's keeping. Private security footage, I bet, but see if you can't persuade them to be helpful for once.'

'Got it.' Colin rang off.

Marnie reached the mobile office with its dead straggle of fairy lights.

Hard to see inside, because the windows were caked with

dust and dirt. She remembered filing cabinets, a girlie calendar, red sleeping bag . . .

Merrick had lied, well enough to convince Noah that he was a decent man. 'On the level,' he'd said, after their first visit to the site.

Marnie wondered whether Merrick would live. From what Noah had told her, it hadn't looked hopeful. Wrists tied with a wire coat hanger, hit once but with enough force to fracture his skull, and left in an abandoned cave where no one was likely to find him.

Esther was certain that was Matt's work, because of the coat hanger. Marnie had read the medical reports from the woman's trial. She understood the significance of the hanger. Esther had attempted to abort a child she wasn't carrying. The foetus was a hallucination, like so much else from that time, at the height of Esther's illness. Matt had found her in the bathroom, haemorrhaging from self-inflicted internal injuries. He'd stuffed towels between her legs, kept her alive until the ambulance came. If he hadn't done that . . .

His children might still be alive. Fred and Archie, and Louisa.

By saving their mother's life, he'd signed their death warrant.

Was that how he saw it? Hard not to see it that way.

Grief and guilt was a toxic mix, as bad as it got . . .

Marnie licked a finger and cleared a spot on the grimy window of the office, to see inside.

What she saw was her reflection, and someone else's.

Standing right behind her.

30

Buzzing woke her. And the cold creep of something at her wrist.

A bluebottle.

She shook it away with a shudder, coming awake to rough stone under her cheek and against her back.

Underground . . .

She was underground.

She pushed herself into a sitting position, her head throbbing from lack of air.

Dark, it was too dark. She couldn't see anything. Not the stone floor, not the fly droning at her feet. No other sound, just the fly. The floor raw under her hands. The smell . . .

Red, and black. Everything was red and black.

An echo from the dizziness, from not being able to breathe because of a hand over her nose and mouth. She'd passed out. Up there, by the mobile office.

Pockets, check your pockets.

Wallet, badge, phone. All here.

No signal on the phone and no display, as if the battery was dead, or faulty.

'Hello?'

No answer, not even an echo. Nothing. There was nothing down here. Just the bluebottle buzzing in time to the red and black throbbing in her head.

Time to get out.

She felt for the wall at her back and pushed herself warily upright, a hand above her head in case the ceiling was low.

It wasn't. She couldn't reach it, even when she stretched.

She waited for her eyes to adjust to the lack of light, but it was taking too long so she started to feel her way around, arms out in front of her like a drunk, expecting to hit something at every step. A wall, or a ladder.

She was looking for a ladder. A way out.

It took her under a minute to work her way around the small square space.

Empty floor, blank walls.

No ladder.

Just four walls, stone like the floor, and a ceiling she couldn't reach.

She was shut in on all sides.

This was a big stone-lined, breath-stealing box of stale air.

Panic ate its way up her spine, a brute pressure that had her lungs labouring and her hands curling into fists. Her throat burned with wanting to scream.

She made herself sit down on the stone floor, and breathe. Slowly.

Okay. All right. Think.

Her phone was here, her hands were free. She wasn't in the boot of a car. She didn't have a skull fracture or a wire coat hanger wrapped around her wrists. She was in a bunker, under Merrick's site on the Isle of Dogs. She hadn't been unconscious long enough to be anywhere else, not unless he'd drugged her, and if he'd done that, she'd be able to taste it.

Matt Reid . . .

It must have been Matt who put her down here. She hadn't had time to recognise the face in the dirty glass of the mobile office. Too fast, the face and the hand in the same second, closing over her mouth, cutting off her air. But it must have been Matt Reid.

How had he got her down here, without a ladder? He hadn't dropped her. She didn't ache enough for that. Her pride was bruised, but she wasn't hurt.

So there had to be a way in, and out.

Worst-case scenario . . .

Noah and the others would find her. No signal on the phone, but it was switched on, even if the display was faulty. That would be enough for them to get a location.

Colin Pitcher had the plans for the tunnel system; he'd given them to Noah, who was on his way. Ed would be able to tell them where she'd headed, across the site.

She should have stayed with Ed, in the ambulance. Waited for the rest of the team. It wasn't like her to be reckless, but she'd thought . . .

She'd been scared for Clancy, and Terry.

For Matt.

How had he got her down here?

She must have missed something.

There had to be a way in and out.

Setting her teeth, she pushed upright again, ignoring the sucking panic, the dead air.

Searching again, with her hands out in front of her.

One step at a time, every square inch of the box she'd been put in.

31

The unit leader nodded at the sign Ian Merrick had nailed to the gate.

'Unexploded bomb. Your boss a bit gung-ho, is she?'

'Not remotely,' Noah said. 'She just knows a piece of improvised artwork when she sees it. We checked with Bomb Disposal, and nothing's been reported in this area.'

'So who put the sign up?'

'Most likely the man who owns the site. Ian Merrick.'

'And you've got his permission to search here?' The man was a pedant, or possibly just lazy; easier to stand here arguing with Noah than to put in the work required to sweep the site for signs of unlawful entry to the tunnel system under their feet.

'Clancy Brand is fourteen and at risk of harm. Any more questions, or can we get on?'

The light was going and everyone was tired. It was the end of a long day. Noah had hoped to check on his mum on the way home to Dan and Sol, but . . .

They had to find Clancy, and Terry.

At least Ed Belloc was safe.

He walked to where Ed was sitting in the back of the ambulance. 'How's it going?'

'I'm good.' Ed gave a lopsided smile. 'Feeling like a first-class idiot, but good.'

'Don't beat yourself up.' Ed looked like the car boot had done that job for him. 'You didn't know what we were dealing with. None of us did.'

'How's Beth?' Ed asked. 'And the children?'

'They're safe. I think they'll be okay.'

Noah looked across the site to where the team was rigging extra lights. 'I'd better find the boss and show her these plans . . . Catch you later, Ed.'

32

The box was thirty square feet of stone. The same size as the bunker where Esther had buried the boys, but no ladder, no manhole. A box, shut in on all sides.

Marnie crouched in the darkness, picking grit from the stinging palms of her hands. She'd searched every inch of the floor. No bucket, no bed, no tinned food. Just raw stone that took the skin from her fingers as she searched.

No ladder. How could there be no ladder?

The bluebottle didn't like it any better than she did. She could hear it knocking about in the dark, hitting the walls, searching for a way out. It had got in, so it had to be able to get out. The same went for her.

Air was getting in too, no matter how quickly she fried it by breathing too fast and moving too much. Air was getting in.

Logically, she knew there was a way out. But logic wasn't getting much of a look-in just at the moment. She remembered Noah's panic in the bunker under Blackthorn Road, and thanked God he wasn't here to witness this new dimension of hell.

Try it without the manhole or the ladder.

This wasn't a pit. It was a tomb.

She'd tried shouting. Tried it until her throat felt flayed. Shouting for Matt, and for Terry, even for Clancy. It didn't do any good. The box just absorbed her noise. When she finally shut up, the bluebottle was there, droning, knocking about in the dark.

Why had Matt put her here? It made no sense. He was after Clancy. Wasn't he?

All the reasons she'd dreamed up for his actions – worrying about the children, wanting to teach Clancy to be more responsible, hiding from the police – none of those reasons led here. He could have asked her if the children were safe, and she'd have told him. He could have stayed hidden from her, up on the site. She hadn't spotted him until he appeared behind her.

What did he want? Why was she here? Why put her in an airless box (not airless, not quite; slow down; breathe) and leave her? The way Esther left his boys . . .

Out of harm's way. Except they weren't. The harm was right there with them, in that hole in the ground. Was this revenge?

Slow down. Breathe.

Noah was coming. He'd be on-site by now, with the team and the plans to the tunnel system, except this wasn't a tunnel it was a tomb, and what if she wasn't under the site at all? What if he'd taken her somewhere else? How far . . .

How far could he have taken her? How long since he shut off her air with his hand, up there by Merrick's mobile office? An hour? Less, surely. She couldn't see her watch face, no illuminated dial.

He hadn't drugged her; she'd be able to tell if he'd drugged her. Wouldn't she?

Her head ached, black and red, and there was a metallic taste in her mouth, but it was thirst. She was very thirsty.

That wasn't good.

The bluebottle bumped off the walls, an angry buzzing.

Marnie sat with her back to the wall, counting her blessings, such as they were. If she was under the river, at least it was dry down here, no danger of flooding. She wasn't too cold, or hungry, yet. She was thirsty, but she could stand it, for a while at least.

Ed was safe. Carmen and Tommy were safe. Noah was coming.

Clancy and Terry . . .

Her mind blanked. She didn't even know for sure that it was Terry who'd put her down here. It'd happened too fast. She pressed her lips together, trying to taste the hand that had covered her mouth. A large hand, but Clancy had big hands. Strong wrists . . . .

Her lips tasted of metal, dry.

Terry had put Ed into the boot of his car before Ed knew what was happening. He was fast. The gardening had given him strong arms, all that digging . . .

She saw his spade, silver-edged, lying on the lawn at number 14.

He'd found his sons buried alive.

What had that done to his mind?

Clancy knew, she was sure of it.

Clancy had looked at Terry Doyle and seen Matt Reid. On a mission to make him more responsible, less like Matt at that age. Talking to him all hours, up in the room at Blackthorn Road where Noah said the windows and skylight were nailed shut and there was nothing to show that a teenage boy lived there, no trace of Clancy in sight.

Like Stephen's bedroom, at her parents' house.

They'd moved him into Marnie's old room, waiting for Stephen to show an interest in redecorating. He'd not shown an interest in anything, other than her skin, and their deaths.

Clancy wasn't like Stephen. Was he?

Both boys had a go-bag, their lives packed, ready to run. Prepared for anything, because that was what their parents had taught them. To be afraid of the world and everything in it, prepared for the worst possible scenario. Paranoia, taken to its outside extreme.

She would have been able to fight off a fourteen-year-old boy. If it was Clancy who'd grabbed her outside the mobile office, she'd have been able to fight.

Wouldn't she?

33

No sign of Marnie with the search team, and her phone had no signal.

Noah called Ron at the hospital. 'How's Merrick?'

'He'll live, by the look of it. How's things on the Isle of Dogs?'

'It's going to be a long night . . . Has the boss been in touch?'

'Nope,' Ron said. 'But she's got better things to worry about than whether this bastard pulls through. We all have.'

Noah didn't argue.

He called Colin at the station. 'Have you heard from the boss?'

'Yes, about an hour ago. I told her you were on your way, with the tunnel plans. I take it there's no news yet? Of Terry and Clancy?'

'Not yet.' Noah rang off.

A hard breeze was blowing up from the water, chilling the back of his neck.

Where was Marnie?

34

Searching the walls, again. Fingertip search, the kind they taught her years ago. Cyclical fingertip search. Round and round. It made her wonder whether the boys had done this; not Fred perhaps, but Archie, the big brother, the one in charge.

How many times did Archie climb that ladder and try to get them out, before he became too weak to climb? How long was too long? When did you give up trying, and accept that there was no way out and no one coming to rescue you? She wanted to believe the boys didn't die like that, in despair. But it was frightening how quickly despair crept up on you.

Noah was coming.

This wasn't like the bunker where Fred and Archie died. She was in part of a tunnel system, she had to be. It was marked on the plans Colin gave to Noah. Right now, they were looking at the plans, figuring out how to find her. She had no reason to give up hope.

Had Archie given up? Or had he gone to sleep with his arms around his brother, believing he would try again tomorrow, or that tomorrow his mum or dad would come?

A false hope, but better than the alternative. Better than despair.

Ed was safe. Carmen and Tommy were safe. Noah was coming.

She was near water. She could smell the Thames, finally.

Not red or black, but brown.

She was under the river, in the tunnel system. There was a way out, into the tunnels. She just hadn't found it yet. She'd figured it out, though.

An opening, high up on one of the walls. Like an inlet pipe, but wide enough to let a body through. When she had the energy, she'd search again.

She'd been concentrating on the floor, and the walls within easy reach. What she needed to do was stretch *up* the walls, maybe jump, high enough to find the opening.

It couldn't be that high, or she'd have fallen when they pushed her through, broken something or picked up bruises at least. Her phone had taken a knock, but she was okay.

The opening had to be above the place where she'd been lying when she came round. She'd lost her bearings, though, no longer sure whether she was facing east or west.

Too easy to give in to the voice in her head whispering: *trappedtrappedtrapped.*

How had Archie got beyond this point, enough to take care of Fred the way he must have done, to keep them both alive as long as he had? Brave, brave boys.

She wished she could have saved them. That she hadn't been too late, the way she was always too late . . .

Enough. Get up. Get out.

Start looking. East, or west, it doesn't matter. Cyclical search, remember?

Just work your way round . . .

It took twenty minutes, by her best estimate.

Twenty minutes of stretching as high as she could reach, inching the ends of her fingers across the stone for as long as she could stand the pain of gravity pulling at her shoulders, her hands protesting the lack of blood circulation.

Inch, inch, inch.

Rest, let the blood back into your fingers, ignore the pins and needles.

Inch, inch, inch.

She sobbed when she found it.

A high ledge where her fingers caught and hooked, cooled by the slow curl of air from above.

A way out.

Seven or eight feet up the wall, nearly too high to reach. But she reached it, hooking her fingers there for a second before she started measuring.

Four feet wide, and flat. Easily wide enough for her to climb through, if she could get a grip and pull herself up. Assuming the gap was deep enough.

One way to find out.

She touched the ledge once more, for luck, then retreated to the other side of the box, keeping her stare fixed dead ahead, on the spot her fingers had found.

Ran, and jumped, fingers scrabbling for the ledge, slipping, not enough strength in her arms to drag herself through the gap. She ended up back on the floor, knees bruised where they'd smacked into the wall.

Picked herself up. Retreated again. Wiped her hands on her clothes to get rid of the sweat. Got her breathing under control. Measured the distance to the ledge. Visualised the gap as a letterbox but one large enough to fit her body through, out to the other side.

Ran and jumped, grabbing hold of the ledge with both hands and hauling her body up the wall, head down, chin tucked tight to her chest.

Her grip held.

She dragged herself on her elbows through the neck of

the aperture, until only her feet were still inside the box, for the few seconds it took to wriggle deeper into the pipe.

Six, seven feet of pipe, then a short, sharp drop down the other side.

Into the shallow, fetid water of the tunnel system.

35

She was looking at a microcosm of London, all the city's litter and stink packed into fifty, sixty feet of subterranea. Enough light leaking through the brickwork here and there for her eyes to prick with returning vision.

The tunnel snaked ahead of her, each curve scaly with shadow, the last holding the light in its jaws like an egg. It had been used by people sleeping rough, or taking drugs. Litter was kicked into gutters, the walls burnt to black at intervals. Empty carrier bags and cardboard boxes lay in leaking layers.

Water was running to her right. She could feel the tidal path of the Thames, responsible for the flooding that had closed off this part of the tunnel system. Except it hadn't, not properly. People had been down here. Not just Ian Merrick. And recently; the floor was hazardous with broken glass and bricks, cigarette packets, empty bottles of Smirnoff Ice.

A sound made her look dead ahead, to the last curve in the tunnel, where the dark fell away like dirty water down a drain. 'Hello?'

The air in here was flat and empty. If she shouted for help it would fall at her feet; no echo to bounce it about. Cement overhead, cement underfoot. She was out of the box, but she was still stuck between layers of London, like the city's dead, stamped all over the city.

Bones on bones on bones . . .

Nice. But enough. Move.

She started down the tunnel. Her brain didn't like it, hissing at her to stop, to wait for the rescue team. But she'd had enough of sitting around, waiting to be rescued.

She pushed on, stooping to go into the space where the tunnel curved away.

Damp ran down the walls. Her feet splashed in standing water. She retreated to where it was dry, relying on the dull bleed of light through the bricks to show her what lay ahead.

The shallow water swallowed the light and spat shadows on the walls.

A square space, set to one side of the main track of the tunnel. Standing room for equipment in the event of repairs, she guessed.

She wished she had Colin's map of the condemned tunnels. She was at the outer perimeter of the site, close to where the river passed overhead. Was she?

Damn, she was thirsty.

The blood beat blackly in her head and she reached for the wall, working her way down it until she was sitting. Easier to fight the sudden flush of dizziness down here.

That noise again . . .

But it was empty. The tunnel was empty.

Just her and the dark.

Wrong.

Someone else was down here.

Two crouching yellow points of light.

Eyes, watching her.

She could smell him, through the blackness.

A heady mix of hormones and hate.

36

'Clancy?'

'Shut up!' A hiss, like gas escaping under pressure. All it needed was a match and the whole tunnel would be alight.

'Where is he?' She kept it low, a whisper, but he moved at her, fast, angry. She kicked backwards, her feet slipping in the slick from the flooded storage room.

He was quick, getting in behind her at the last second, clamping a hand across her mouth so that she could taste him. Bitter and metallic, like a fired gun.

She twisted, trying to get free, trying to say his name.

'Shut up!' Clancy's hand tasted of soil, and sweat. He was strong, easily holding her still with one arm across her chest.

He dragged her towards the wall, away from the trickle of light, dropping them into the dark so suddenly, Marnie yelped.

She fought the instinct to bite down, to find his eyes with her nails, because there was something scarier than Clancy down here. Something worse than a teenage boy with his dirty hand across her mouth. The pain was a footnote to the fear.

The fear paralysed her.

'Be quiet,' Clancy hissed. His body was rigid against her. 'He's coming.'

He's coming . . .

Terry Doyle. Matt Reid.

She strained to hear above the beating of the blood in her ears and the thud of Clancy's heart against her shoulder blades.

Light, first.

Yellow, from a torch searching like a dog's snout, sending shadows scattering ahead of it, making the graffiti leap and scuttle up the walls.

Her head churned, sickeningly. She fought Clancy's grip on her, but he held harder, his breath hot at her cheek. *'Be quiet!'*

The shadows stopped, squatting at their feet.

Behind the shadows, torchlight ate everything, like looking into the sun.

Marnie strained against the boy's hands.

Whatever was behind the shadows and the light, whatever was making Clancy's palm sweat acid into her mouth . . .

She had to see.

37

Noah and the unit leader stood at the newly opened neck of the tunnel system, listening for sounds from inside. Their torches swept the empty space for eighteen feet or so.

No sign of DI Rome, or anyone else.

Colin said, 'The tunnel runs south, under the river eventually. Lots of boxes and junctions. You'll need to stick to the map. If she's lost in there . . .'

Noah straightened, stepping back from the gap. 'We'd better assume she's with Terry, or Clancy. Or both of them. We need to get a rescue team together.'

'DS Jake!'

Another member of the search party was coming at a jog from the south side of the site.

In his hand, a blue canvas duffle bag. Muddy, with scratches up the sides.

Noah took the bag and checked the contents.

Oyster card, cash, bottled water, a change of clothes . . .

It was Clancy Brand's go-bag.

'Where did you find it?'

The man pointed, and Noah started in that direction, until Debbie Tanner called him back.

She was running, out of breath. 'Esther . . .'

'She's at St Thomas's. Isn't she?'

Debbie shook her head. 'DC Barrow called from there. Esther gave them the slip.'

'*Shit.* At this rate we'll be organising search parties for half of London.'

'Her mum thinks she's headed back this way.'

'What?'

'Esther heard the boss talking on the phone, when they were in the car. She knows we're at the Isle of Dogs and that we're looking for Terry. For Matt, I mean.'

Debbie got her breath back. 'Connie says it's what she's been wanting for the last fortnight. The chance to see Matt. She says Esther's coming this way.'

38

The torchlight sat on Marnie's feet.

Cold white light, like lymph from a wound, carving a hole behind itself where a boulder was wedged. Except it wasn't a boulder, it was a man.

Terry Doyle.

Matthew Reid.

Marnie knew him by the shape of his right wrist, the unravelling red jumper he'd worn the last time she saw him. She was trapped, held hard by Clancy's hands at her mouth and chest. She recognised the taste of the boy's hand. Clancy was the one who'd put her in that box, just like he'd put Carmen and Tommy in Cole's house. Out of harm's way.

'Where are they?' Weird acoustics fractured Terry's voice, the words falling like spears into the shallow light at their feet.

Clancy was shaking at her back, his hand so wet it slid across her lips, her teeth.

'Where are they?' Another volley of spears.

Marnie cringed into the boy in a bid to shield him from Terry's wrath.

'*Where?*'

The torchlight flushed up Marnie's thighs, to her face.

She blinked through it, shaking her head at Terry to stand down. Her head was bursting with pain.

Clancy let her go, suddenly. He was going to make a run for it, she knew. There was nowhere to run except straight into the wall of Terry's anger.

'Terry . . . Mr Doyle . . .'

He swung the torch away from her, hitting Clancy with its beam.

Marnie heard the boy hiss in terror.

'Terry!' She snapped it, needing the man's attention on her. 'Carmen and Tommy are safe. They're with their auntie. Beth's sister.'

The words didn't reach him, no echo to bounce them past the wall of his rage.

If she put out her hand, she'd feel it. His rage. Solid, impassable. It would bruise her fingers. Words wouldn't help. She could snap all she wanted. Nothing was getting past.

'Stay still,' she told Clancy. 'Stay still.'

The boy whimpered, his anger eclipsed by Terry's.

Not good. She needed him angry.

Angry kept you alive.

Torchlight hit her face like a hand, cold. Her chest was cold too, where Clancy had taken his arm away. She wanted it back. The boy's anger and his heat, the way he'd held her hard against him, keeping her upright, keeping her quiet.

'Where are they?'

No echo. The words didn't bounce, but they jarred enough to put cracks in the cellar walls. Something was going to break, bury them . . .

She reached behind her for Clancy's wrist, holding the boy still, and stared into the dark behind the torchlight, the place where the man was standing. 'They're safe. Carmen and Tommy are safe. They're with their auntie and their mum—'

She'd used the wrong words.

Light cracked so savagely that for a second she was sure he'd hit her, her head snapping to the left, but it was just the beam from the torch.

Was that what he'd used to fracture Merrick's skull?

Where are they?

She wasn't even sure he was asking about Carmen and Tommy. She didn't recognise this furious man, not as Terry Doyle. But she knew him. Knew his rage and loss. Gut recognition, like looking in a mirror. He was the father of their boys. Esther's husband, broken into a thousand pieces. He was Matt Reid.

She kept hold of the boy behind her, wanting Clancy wide of the man's retribution.

Matt smashed the torch at the wall, cracking the glass so that light leaked out everywhere before it slunk back to his feet.

He was nothing like the man she'd left at the safe house.

Safe house.

What a joke. Life was just limping from one disaster zone to another, decamping, taking your dead and injured with you, blowing bridges as you went, if you had the ammunition, and the sense, to spare.

Anger flooded her sweetly, like relief.

'What?' she demanded. 'What're you going to do? Beat us up? Bury us here? You can't dig in cement, and in case you've forgotten, I'm a detective inspector. You'll be in prison for a long time. Your kids won't recognise you when you get out.' She winced as she said it.

'What do you know?' Matt's voice was in the pit of his throat. 'What do you know about my kids?'

'I know you loved them, the way you love Carmen and Tommy. That's why we're getting out of here. All of us. Back to the children. They're waiting for you—'

Smash of the torch into the wall.

Light guttering on the ground again, before crawling back to his feet like a wounded dog.

He keeps this up, he's going to break the torch, and then it'll be him and me in the darkness, and how the hell can I keep Clancy safe . . .

'They're waiting for you,' she repeated. 'Carmen and Tommy are waiting for their dad.'

Like Fred and Archie, waiting for five years until you found them, God help you, you found them . . .

'We need to go back up. Back to Carmen and Tommy . . .'

Clancy said, 'You can't let him. He's crazy. He was crazy before and he's getting worse.'

Matt made a hard sound. 'Get out here.'

He pointed the nose of the torch at his feet. 'Hiding behind her . . . Get out here!'

Clancy would have done as he was told, from bravado if not obedience, if Marnie hadn't held him back.

'I'm not scared of you.' The boy's voice shook as he said it.

'Get. Out. Here.'

Each word colder and harder than the last, like rocks coming loose from the walls.

Marnie had to get them out. She had to get Clancy out.

She pushed the boy behind her, moving to the left in a bid to prompt Matt to do the same; hoping it would clear at least a little space between him and the only exit.

Not much of a chance, but better than nothing.

Matt stayed standing, his shoulders squared, his shadow like a cobra's hood, death in his eyes.

So much of it that Marnie couldn't see a way past.

39

Esther had taken a high-vis jacket when she absconded from the hospital. That should have made her easy to spot on the site, but it didn't. She'd gone to ground.

'She said she knew this place,' Connie Pryce told Noah. 'There are tunnels here, that's what she said.' Her face was set in hard lines, made harder by the site's artificial lighting. 'She knows a way in, one of Merrick's hiding places.'

'We've found it,' Noah told her. 'We're looking for DI Rome. And Matt and Clancy.'

Debbie was holding the boy's duffle bag.

'He wouldn't have left that behind,' Noah said, 'if he was in charge of what was happening. Beth Doyle said he never let the bag out of his sight.'

'Terry,' Debbie said. 'He's down there too?'

'Matt,' Connie said. 'He's Matt. No point pretending otherwise.'

She looked at Noah. 'That's what you're dealing with. I hope you're prepared.'

40

Shadows shrank the exit to a pinhole behind Matt's head.

Marnie forced herself to focus on the broken torch in the man's hand.

It was the only weapon he had, if you discounted the death in his eyes. A broken torch. Rubber, not metal, which probably meant it would hurt more when it hit her, but at least it wouldn't cut. A broken torch wasn't a knife. He didn't have a knife. But he'd managed to fracture Merrick's skull.

Eyes, ears, throat. Those were his weak points. Not his balls – men expected that – but she could go for his ears, or his knees.

He was out of his mind, she could see that.

Out of his mind with grief and guilt and the need to know what Clancy was hiding. She didn't want to hurt him; he was hurting enough. But she was damned if she was getting bounced around a condemned tunnel by a madman with a torch.

She hissed behind her at Clancy, 'When I tell you, you're going to run. You're not going to fight. You're going to get out of here and fetch help. Understood?'

She never got the chance to find out whether Clancy understood or not.

Matt swallowed the shadows in two strides, sweeping her out of his way, grabbing Clancy by the scruff of his neck and swinging him at the nearest wall.

Clancy yelled in pain, hitting out, some of the blows connecting but with no effect other than to drive Matt harder, pushing Clancy ahead of him into the wall, the boy's head thumping against the bricks.

Marnie tried to sweep Matt's ankle, a move she'd perfected in the self-defence classes with Kate Larbie. It was like trying to swat a bull with a feather. Matt just thrust an elbow back and she ended up on the floor again.

'Matt! Matthew!' A shout, from behind them. 'Matthew!'

Footfall coming up the tunnel, someone running towards them, calling out. 'Matt!'

Matt froze, his forearm jammed up against Clancy's windpipe, his whole body jumping in response to his name, and the voice that was calling it.

Esther.

Marnie got to her knees, tears wrecking her vision so that what she saw coming through the cellar's mouth was a blaze of white, stuffing the entrance as if something solid was being shoved into place, trapping them inside.

'Matt!' The shout, whip-hard, made all three of them jump.

Matt's arm dropped from Clancy and the boy kicked out, shoving Matt off as he slid down the wall, hugging his knees, his mouth bruised blue by lack of air.

Esther was dressed in fiery yellow. Fluorescent; a high-vis jacket.

Marnie forced herself to her feet, moving to where Clancy was heaped, touching careful fingers to the boy's neck. He was icy with shock, sucking breath between his teeth.

She lifted her head and looked at Matt Reid and his ex-wife, spotlit by the yellow of the borrowed coat, her face fiercely haggard.

Matt couldn't look at her. He stood cowed, all the fight wiped out of him.

Marnie could smell his fear from where she was crouched at Clancy's side.

It was sweet and rank, like death.

41

Connie Pryce stood watching the last of the light as it clung to the polythene sheeting of Merrick's stalled development. 'So much,' she said, 'for keeping her safe.'

Noah glanced at her. 'She chose to run. She was told to stay in the hospital.'

'Your boss should've stayed with her. She knew she was sick. Now she's down there.' She jerked her head. 'Down in the dark with God only knows what . . .'

'My boss is down there too.' Noah's jaw ached where he was clenching it.

He was waiting for word from the specialist unit that was making the area safe. However much he might want to drop down into the hole that had swallowed Marnie, he couldn't. Not without backup. It could put her in more danger.

At his side, Connie shivered.

'Esther was always on about site safety. She was obsessed with it. She wouldn't let anyone go anywhere without hard hats, steel-toe shoes, the full rig-out. She was responsible, she said.' Connie shook her head. 'You wouldn't know it now, but she was such a happy girl, once. And *funny*. She could win a laugh from anyone. That's why he fell in love with her, I expect. That and her common sense. Of the two of them, she was the sensible one. And so conscientious. If anyone got so much as a scratch it would be on her conscience and she couldn't live with that. She said she couldn't live . . .'

More floodlights came on, drowning the site in white.

Noah and Connie blinked, blind for a second.

'Health and safety,' Connie said. 'What a joke.'

42

Esther filled the mouth of the tunnel, her face wet with the slick light jumping from the torch in her ex-husband's hand.

Matt looked like someone had skinned his face to bone. Seeing the murderer of his children, his worst nightmare. His monster.

Behind Marnie, Clancy shuddered, nearly as scared as Matt. What had he witnessed to make him so afraid of the man he'd known as Terry Doyle?

Esther said, 'Matt,' gently now.

He cringed as if she'd struck him.

Their eyes locked, a fused stare that stretched from terror at one end to pity at the other. A terrible pity, almost pitiless, and *surely* he could see . . . surely Matt could see that Esther had not forgotten or forgiven the woman she was when she destroyed their family.

Clancy was holding on to Marnie. How was she going to get him past Esther and Matt? She couldn't leave them down here like this. Too many ways it could end in disaster.

'Esther . . .' She wanted the woman to look at her, give some sign that she was here to help, not for punishment or retribution, or because her mind was lost again.

Esther's stare was locked to Matt. Thirsty. Drinking him up, his fear and all.

What had she called him, back at the station?

Her mirror.

Marnie said, 'Esther, we need to get out of here. *Now*.'

The torch hung from Matt's hand, swinging a little as he shook, marking stripes on the floor that hurt Marnie's eyes.

'I wanted to be back with my boys.' His voice was pulled inside out by grief. 'I just wanted to *be* . . . with them.'

Esther didn't speak. Her shadow swallowed half the tunnel.

Matt smashed the torch at the wall, screaming the next words: 'You buried them alive! You buried my boys!'

Clancy cringed into Marnie. She held him still, her eyes on Matt.

'Fred and Archie. My boys!' White spittle flew from his mouth. 'Louisa . . . little Louisa. That wasn't enough? You had to take them too? Down in the dark for years and years and years. Bones . . . they were just bones. I saw them like that, the way you left them!'

'Matt . . .' Esther's face was a mask, rigid with remorse.

'You warned me you'd do it.' He moved his arm in Marnie's direction. 'She kept saying she'd kill herself and the children. No one but me believed her.' A laugh cracked his voice in two. 'The doctors said to keep sharp objects out of sight, as if that was all it took. I was always hiding stuff and *she* . . .' his arm swung back to Esther, '*you* were always finding it, hoarding it, like a sick game we were playing. You were only happy when you were hiding pills and razor blades and pencils . . . But not *them*. I didn't think you'd hide *them*. Not like that, not in the dark. They *hated* the dark. You know they hated the dark . . .'

'I know. I do know. Matt, I'm so sorry . . .'

'I kept some of your pills, did you know that? After they took you away, when they started asking why I hadn't *done* something. *Anything*. I wanted proof that I'd tried to get you help.' Across his shoulder to Marnie: 'She wouldn't take the pills. She said she couldn't, when she was expecting Louisa. I put them out of reach of the children, on a high shelf . . .'

Not too high for Clancy to reach. The boy's fingers clutched coldly at hers.

'Matt . . .' Esther tried again.

'She sharpened pencils all the time, to stab at herself . . . Holes in both ankles where she tried to find veins.' He shivered, staring at the woman in front of him. 'You have holes in your ankles, but nothing hurt you. Nothing stopped you. *I* didn't.'

His voice dropped abruptly. 'I didn't stop you.'

He started to sob, his chest heaving. 'I *saved* you. I saved your life. It's *my fault* they're dead. If I'd just let you do it . . . let you *die*. They would be alive. It's my fault, *mine*.'

'Oh Matt, *no* . . .'

'*Yes*.' The torch smashed at the wall. 'I should've let you *die*. I should've *killed* you!'

His anger took up too much space; it was hard to breathe down here.

'I should've killed you!' he screamed again.

'Yes,' Esther whispered. 'Yes, you should.'

The torch smashing at the wall; Matt closing in on the woman.

'Carmen and Tommy need their dad,' Marnie snapped. 'Carmen and Tommy and the new baby. Beth can't raise that family on her own, Terry. She needs you. *Terry!*'

Matt's head moved in confusion.

'Tell me,' Marnie said. 'Tell me what she did. I'm listening. I want to know.'

'She killed my family! My boys, my baby, my *wife*.' A staggering sound in his chest. 'Everyone. She killed everyone . . .'

He put his free hand blindly to his face, as if the light was burning him.

Marnie knew that feeling. How bereavement laid you bare, made you raw. Everything hurt – daylight, other people's eyes on you – as if you were missing a layer of skin. She remembered the fellow feeling when she stood at this man's side by the pavement memorial to the boys. Grief, coming off him in waves. She should've recognised it sooner.

'I should have died. I *wanted* to die. When I saw Louisa, when I saw my baby girl . . .' He gripped at his face until his fingers turned white. 'I wanted my boys back, wanted them *safe*.'

'You knew they hadn't drowned,' Marnie said. 'How? How did you know?'

'Archie . . . would never let that happen to Fred. They could swim. I taught them.' He uncovered his face, flinching as he looked at his ex-wife. 'The police said you drugged them, but I didn't believe it. I could see in your face they were dead. I didn't have any hope, not really, not when I started looking. I couldn't ask easy questions, because I wasn't *Matt* any more. It took a long time. I went to the places you used to go. Then I thought about *Merrick*,' his voice spat again, 'the fact that he was building everywhere, all those sites, derelict land he'd bought. I made him tell me about the places you'd been.'

Which was more dangerous, his rage at Esther or his rage at himself? Grief, or guilt?

'Merrick gave me a list of all the places you'd been, while you were working for him. I worked my way through the list, but it took time. I had a job, bills to pay. I couldn't spend all my time searching. *Terry* took up a lot of time, all the rules I was supposed to follow . . .'

'And you met Beth. You started a new family.'

'*I* was responsible. That's what they said. Matt was

responsible. I didn't want to be *Matt*. Matt was pathetic, useless. Responsible for you . . .' He bared his teeth at Esther. 'They locked you up for a month. Do you even remember that? They locked you up with violent schizophrenics, people who were out of control . . . Then they discharged you,' his voice flooded with bitterness, *'into my care.'*

No follow-up care, no diagnosis or treatment for Matt Reid. Just an instruction to take care of his wife when she was judged fit enough to be sent home to her young family. And later, an instruction to move on, get over it and get on with life when how could you move on? After everything had stopped and your life had been ripped out of you?

When he spoke again, his voice was a snarl over his shoulder at Marnie. 'I was *scared*. Of what she'd do, what I *knew* she was going to do. She didn't even try to hide it. If I went to work, she'd phone to say she was going to kill herself, and the kids. Can you imagine getting that call? Not once, but day after day? I lived in fear of what I'd find when I got home. She *terrorised* me.' The snarl swung back towards Esther. 'You . . . *exulted* in it. Hoarding whatever you could get your hands on. Razors, combs, anything. The only time you were happy was when you were stockpiling weapons.' He shook with rage, and terror. 'I couldn't watch you and the kids 24/7. How could I? How could anyone?'

Esther didn't speak, didn't move.

'They couldn't,' Marnie said. 'No one could. But now . . . you're married to Beth.'

'Yes.' The word emptied out of him, a small word made huge by his distress.

'And you have a new family.'

'Yes . . .'

'Tell me what that's like.'

Keep talking, focus on what you have, *not what you've lost.*

'It's like . . . being dead. I'm Terry, and Matt's dead, and that's *good* because I stopped hurting, for a bit. But I was scared of getting it wrong all over again. When Tommy was tiny, and Carmen, with her tantrums. Never anything like that with Fred and Archie. Carmen and Tommy are so . . . different.' He spoke about the children as if they were strangers. Maybe they felt like strangers. He was mourning his lost children. That hole was impossible to fill, no matter how hard he tried, how much love he had left to give.

'You bought the house with Beth,' Marnie said gently, 'knowing the boys were there?'

'Not *knowing*. Hoping . . . I wanted to be close by. Back with my boys.' He wiped at his eyes with his free hand, the other still full of the broken torch. 'I thought it would be enough, to be close to them. But it wasn't. I had to see them. I had to *know*. Then the parole office told me *she* was getting out. They gave me a date and I had to do something. I wanted them out of that hole. Safe.'

'You must've known that finding them and reporting it would spark an investigation. You must have known we'd find out you were their father.'

'I didn't care about that!' His voice rose. 'I only cared about making them safe. From *her*. I had to see Fred and Archie. I saw Louisa,' grief pulled at his face again, 'they let me hold her. But the boys were gone. Washed out to sea, everyone said, but I *knew* it wasn't true.'

He pointed the torch at Esther. 'You took their things. Nothing of Louisa's, just Fred and Archie's favourite toys and books. Fred's monkey, and Mister Squirrel . . . Archie was growing out of toys, but he still took Mister Squirrel everywhere. That's when I knew. I knew you'd put them somewhere, hidden them. You were *always* hiding things.'

A fresh lick of anger in his voice. 'I started going through Merrick's list and I found Beech Rise, the field that was there before he started work. You used to take the boys walking in fields, before you got really sick. They'd come home covered in mud, leaves in their hair. Beech leaves. You kept them in a bowl . . . As soon as I saw those trees, I knew. They loved to climb . . . I knew that was how you tricked them.'

He turned raw eyes towards Marnie. 'I *tried* to give up. Get over it. But I couldn't. Seeing Carmen and Tommy, watching them sleep, it just made me want my boys more. It *hurt*, it physically hurt. My arms *ached* for them. I pretended it was work, but it wasn't. I wanted to hold my boys. I'd held Louisa, but not them. My arms ached all the time. If I'd just been able to say goodbye . . . If I only knew where they were . . .'

'I wanted to tell you,' Esther whispered. 'I did want to tell you. Before the pills took hold. Before I was Alison who couldn't remember anything . . . I wanted to tell you, but I was scared. They said you had a new life, and you deserved that much. I knew it was true. I hoped you were happy, that you'd started over. It was one less thing I'd destroyed . . .'

'You destroyed *everything*! And you *lied*. You lied about what you'd done, how they died, where you'd hidden them. The other side of London, miles away! You took them miles away. I had to search for months and months . . . I dug those gardens until my hands were raw. You have no idea what that was like, not knowing, wanting them *found*.'

'You didn't give up,' Esther whispered. 'You never gave up.'

'How could I? On them? Our boys. I had to know where they were and what you'd done. I couldn't stand the thought of them alone out there. I *had* to know.'

Marnie said, 'You dug the gardens at Beech Rise for Merrick. That's when you were able to check the bunkers, eliminate the empty ones. But you didn't open the bunker at number 14, not until two weeks ago. How could you be sure the boys were there?'

'I couldn't, of course I couldn't, but have you *any* idea how much courage it took to open those bunkers? I was terrified.' His mouth drew into a fresh snarl. 'Just like old times. Right, love? Me, being a *coward*. Too scared to look and see what you'd done. Hiding from the truth. Making up stories to make myself feel better. Maybe they did drown, maybe they felt nothing, maybe they were safe somewhere . . . *Lies* so that I could face whatever you'd done this time. The same as always. Stupid, careless, *cowardly* Matt.'

'But you opened the bunker,' Marnie said. 'Two weeks ago.'

'I had to make them safe when I heard she was coming out. There was no choice then. It wasn't about me any longer, it was about *them*.'

His face burned white, feverish. 'I stood by that . . . bed. With my boys, what was left of my boys. I couldn't bear it. Their little hands, their feet . . . I wanted to cover them up. They looked so *cold*. I knew it would mean the police, that Beth would find out I'd lied and I'd lose everything I had left, but none of that mattered. I just wanted them not to be *alone*. And I wanted to give them a proper burial, with their baby sister, somewhere I could go and sit and talk to them . . .'

He broke off with a barking sob. 'God forgive me, I left the peaches. I don't know why. I wanted to leave *something*. I saw the tins down there and I recognised them. The Brands had a catalogue of provisions for their panic room . . . I knew where to buy the peaches, so I did. I shouldn't have left them outside the house, but I wasn't thinking straight. I wasn't . . . myself.'

'All right,' Marnie said. 'It's all right. I understand what you did. Shall we get out of here? We can talk more, but—'

'No. *No.*' Smashing the torch again. 'We're staying here. It's not safe. I know what's up there. Police. Doctors. People who'll tell me it's *my* fault. Who'll take away my kids . . .'

'I'll explain what's happened. I'll make sure they understand.'

'No! We're staying *here.*'

Clancy was rigid with hostility at Marnie's side. She squeezed his hand in warning, needing him to stay quiet. She had to make Matt understand what was at stake here. More than his pain, and Esther's punishment. A fourteen-year-old child, entrusted to his care, scared out of his wits.

'We need to go, Matt. I don't feel safe down here. Nor does Clancy. Beth and the children are waiting—'

'He's safer down here than he was with *them.*'

'Scott and Chrissie Brand?'

Matt's face twisted in a new direction. 'He wasn't wanted. They let him know that. Not just once, in the heat of the moment. Night after night, told that he was unwanted and unloved . . .' He clenched his fists. 'It shouldn't be that easy to give up kids.'

'You wanted to help. You wanted him to feel safe. So let's go where it's safe.'

'I couldn't have fostered him,' Matt said. 'Beth didn't know that.' His stare found Esther, through the darkness. 'No one believed it was just *you.* No one believed I couldn't stop it. I should've been able to do something, that's what they all thought. Beth thinks it, too. Whenever there's anything on the news about women who kill their babies, she'll ask about the dads, as if they should have been able to do something. She can't understand the women, let alone the men.'

Homely Beth with a toddler on her hip, making motherhood look easy, on the surface at least. Had Matt picked her for that reason? A good wife and mother, content in her domestic role. Whatever the reason, her apathy had put the children at risk. Never once had she questioned the way her husband ran the household. It was left to Clancy to do that.

Even so, Marnie's chest ached with empathy for Matt Reid. It was a form of blindness, her wavering recognition for this grieving man, the way a seared retina always sees the last thing that lit it. 'You wanted everyone to be safe. That's what I want now. Not down here. We need to go back up.'

'No! I can't! You know what I did to Merrick. I'd had enough of his lies. When he started on the boy . . . I'd had enough. I hit him and left him in that pit he was hoping to sell. I hoped he'd rot there.' He flinched as he said it.

'You made sure he was breathing, then you tied his wrists in front of him so that he could climb out of there when he came round.'

'I hoped he'd *rot* . . . That's attempted murder!'

'You turned him on to his side, into the recovery position.'

'I tied him up.' The same insistence in his voice as Esther's when she refused to be allowed excuses for what she'd done, but the anger was slipping now, into something else.

'You fastened his wrists in front of him,' Marnie repeated. 'That's a very poor attempt at attempted murder. I don't think the CPS will be very impressed.'

'I didn't know I was capable, of that.' His stare searched behind her, for Clancy. 'Is he . . .? I'm sorry. I didn't think I was capable of sinking so low, being that person. I thought I was in a dark place before, but that? It was like no other darkness I've ever known.'

He was slipping into despair. Only one way this could end if he lost hope or decided there was nothing left to salvage from this nightmare.

Marnie was running out of words, afraid of sliding into

platitudes about loss and redemption. Thirst was making her dizzy, dry-tongued. She thought of all the ways you could push past this point, find a way back from grief and loss. By reaching for anger, like Adam, or for exhaustion in the guise of work. She'd opted for numbness, but Matt Reid had wanted to *feel*. He'd wanted to fill his arms and his heart, take responsibility for a new family, even for a lost boy unloved by his parents. That took extraordinary courage. She wished she could find the words to tell him how brave he'd been, how extraordinary.

The tunnel stank of the four of them.

Too human, too hurt.

Trying to find a way back.

'Thank you,' Esther said softly.

Matt's head jerked in her direction.

'For finding them. For never giving up. Thinking of them every day, all the days when I couldn't because the pills . . . wiped them out. Thank you for being with them all that time, never forgetting or giving up. Their dad, their brave dad, who never stopped loving them.'

Matt shook his head, but he was watching her. Hearing her.

'I took them into the fields,' she said.

Her voice was low, steady.

'Fred couldn't climb the fence, but Archie helped him. He was always helping him. You remember. When Fred was funny about his food, when he wouldn't go to sleep at night. Or brush his teeth, or get dressed. Archie was his big brother. Fred would do anything for him.' She stopped, sounding out of breath.

Matt hadn't moved, hadn't spoken.

Esther said, 'It started out such a nice day. Sunshine. Then the rain came and they were happy . . . They were happy to get into the shelter. It was a shelter.'

Her voice frayed, drawing echoes into the dead space.

'It was a game. We were playing a game. I don't know how . . . I don't remember where it went wrong. I was sitting with them in the shelter. They were shining their torches on the walls and I was making shadow puppets. Archie wanted me to make a blackbird, like the one outside their window. I tried, but I was never very good at shadow puppets. You were best. Fred said, "Daddy's best at shadows, Mummy," and I said, "He is," and then Archie made a shadow puppet and said it was you, and we laughed. We wanted you there with us.'

A smile fractured her face. 'In the shelter. With us. We wanted you there.'

Marnie could hear the thin scratch of Matt's breath in his chest.

At her side, Clancy was quiet, watching Esther, watching Matt.

'Louisa was with my mum that first day. I wanted her with us too. All of us together. It was never about me and them, shutting you out. They'd never have stood for that anyway. They wanted their dad. Archie wanted you there. I think he understood I wasn't well. He was such a bright boy, and Matt . . . he was so *brave*. They both were, but Fred thought it was a game. Not just that first day, but later. When I took the sleeping bags and the books down there, Archie knew. I think he knew. But he would never have left his brother.'

Her face twisted in self-reproach. 'I suppose I counted on that . . .'

The torch creaked in Matt's fist, but he still didn't move.

'They were your boys.' Her voice was swollen with grief. 'They were your boys and I stole them from you. I killed Archie and Fred, your brave boys. I didn't go back for them, and I didn't tell anyone, and then I couldn't remember, and

I don't know *why*. I don't. Matt . . . I can't remember. Only one day . . . There's only one day that's clear. The day the rain came and we took shelter, playing shadow puppets.'

In the torchlight, her face shone with tears.

'And Archie wanted you there with us, so he made a shadow puppet of you and we laughed because we were happy, all together.'

43

It was like walking into a wall of floodlights.

Outside the tunnels, Merrick's site was filled with police. Squad cars, their sirens circling, were parked between potholes, with an ambulance. Paramedics.

Marnie pointed Clancy in their direction. She was stumbling, clumsy, gutted by exhaustion. But she'd got them out. All of them. Esther and Matt reduced to silence finally, faces ruined by tears, but out.

Someone caught her, a hand under her arm saving her from falling on her face.

'Got you . . .'

Noah.

'Esther,' she managed to say, 'and Matt . . .'

Noah nodded. 'We've got them too.'

44

Later

Clancy Brand sat with his big hands dangling from his knees. His appropriate adult was a thin man in spectacles who didn't look much older than Clancy.

Marnie pulled up a chair to sit facing the boy, catching the sharp smell of the tunnels on his skin. 'How are you?'

He nodded before moving his stare away from her.

'I need to ask you about what happened earlier today, but before that too . . . With Terry, and Beth.'

'Okay.'

'Why were you living with them, perhaps we can start there, instead of at home?'

'Home was a head-fuck. Locks, alarms. I didn't think it'd be worse with them.'

'With Beth and Terry.'

Clancy nodded.

'How was it worse?'

'At least at home I could *see* the fucking locks.'

The appropriate adult shifted in silence, as if he disapproved of the bad language.

Clancy shot him a look of contempt.

'Was Terry a friend of the family? Is that why you went with him?'

'He wasn't a friend. My lot don't do *friends*. They do *associates*. People who can be counted on in an emergency. Terry was one of those. *Reliable*. He heard about me running off, and he offered to let me bunk down at his place for a couple of nights. I thought that was okay. I mean, he's not a pervert or anything, and it was raining a lot back then. I didn't mind the streets, but I hated the rain. So I went with him. It was okay for a bit. Then he gave me my own room, made a big deal out of it. I wouldn't have stayed except the little kids liked having me there. Later . . . I wanted to be sure they were safe.'

'Carmen and Tommy.'

He nodded. 'I'd have been better off on the streets.'

He put his hands together, wedged them between his knees. 'I knew this girl, Josie. She ran away from home, ended up on the streets. I saw her this one time, living rough, eating junk from bins, even the stuff they spray with dye to stop people eating it. She was better off than I was in that place.'

He'd had his own room with the Doyles, a warm bed, decent food. He would rather have eaten ruined food from bins, on the street.

'I should've run as soon as I saw the head-fuck.' He hugged his hands with his knees, all elbows, spiky as a cactus.

He reminded Marnie of someone she'd not seen in a long time: the girl who'd let Adam Fletcher take over her life.

'Why did you take Carmen and Tommy to Doug Cole's house?'

'I could see where it was headed. *He* was getting worse. *She* couldn't cope.'

'But why Cole's house, why take them there? Why leave them alone?'

'Because it's safe there. I thought they could play with the toys, it'd keep them happy. He's okay. He's a weirdo, but he's okay.' His shoulders shrugged. There was something else under the pretence of not caring. Bewilderment.

'You took Esther's pills and hid them in your room. Why did you do that?'

Clancy wiped his nose with his hand. 'Dunno. I wanted something of theirs.' He put his chin up, daring her to dispute what he said next. 'I thought I could sell them.'

His first answer sounded more like the truth: *I wanted something of theirs.* Like Noah, taking his mother's medication. Clancy wanted Marnie to think he was a tough nut. Empathy made her shiver. 'You were excluded from a couple of schools. What happened?'

He bit his lips together. 'The usual . . . I got a ton of crap because I didn't have any mates, because I was a loser, and because I got on okay with the little kids and that was *weird.*'

He raised his chin again. 'Little kids think I'm a laugh, and they trust me. But that's weird, apparently. That's perverted. So yeah. I got kicked out because I punched some kid in my year for saying shit about me.' He clenched his fist and looked at it.

Marnie wondered how she'd ever imagined a likeness, however fleeting, between this angry boy and Stephen Keele. Clancy wore his anger as armour. On the surface, even at fourteen years old, Stephen was cold. All his rage driven down, hidden away. The only way to understand him, if that was what she wanted to do, was by sticking her hand in that cold fire of hate and misery and memory, for however long it took.

'What happened earlier today, with Terry?'

'He was freaking out. Ever since you moved us out of

that house . . .' Clancy's eyes went to the window, then to the wall. Tracking a line of shadow, smaller now, knotting his body tighter against the questions. 'He's off his head. You saw him. You know.'

'I know . . . some of it. You took the children to Mr Cole's house because you were scared of what Terry might do. Is that right?'

'He was talking about taking us all somewhere safe. It was doing our heads in, not just me. *She* was stressing out. Carmi and Tommy . . . I just wanted to stop him doing anything worse.'

'Why didn't you stay with them, in Mr Cole's house?'

'I wanted a burger,' he answered quickly; too quickly. As if he'd prepared the reply. 'There was nothing decent to eat in the house. I got some bananas for the kids, but I was hungry. I wanted a burger.' Nicotine stains, faded, on his fingers.

'You didn't want to smoke in the house, with the children?'

Clancy flushed, but he nodded.

She would warn him, later, about the two women on the estate who'd been feeding him cigarettes: Adam's unofficial spies.

'Then what happened?'

'Then it all kicked off.' Clancy curled smaller in the chair. '*He* came home. I saw his car. I couldn't go back then, could I? Your lot were everywhere. So I ran.'

'To the Isle of Dogs?'

'Not then. Later. When he came after me.' He lifted his head quickly. 'He had a guy in the boot of his car. In the fucking *boot*. Did you know that?'

'Yes. He got out. He's okay.' She paused. 'How did Terry know where to find you?'

'Merrick,' Clancy said through clenched teeth.

'Ian Merrick? How did Merrick know where you were?'

'He found me. I was hiding on one of his sites. I knew all about the stuff he was into, because my dad was part of it. Buried. All that shit . . . That's how they met. They were all going on about this new place Merrick had bought, where they used to teach kids how to climb. It sounded pretty cool. Safe. I knew where it was, knew it'd be dry . . .' He looked at his hands. 'Didn't think the fucker would call *him*, did I?'

'Merrick called Terry?'

'Told him I was trespassing. Said he should call the police. He backed down, though. Next thing I know, *he's* there.'

'In the man-made cave. That's where you went?'

Clancy nodded. 'Where you found Merrick.' He put a hand to his mouth, chewing at his thumbnail. 'You found Merrick, right?'

'Yes, we did. Can you tell me what happened? Between Merrick and Terry?'

'He stuck up for me.' Clancy rubbed at his face in confusion.

'Terry?'

'Yeah . . . Merrick was bitching about what a fuck-up I was, how everyone said so, even my mum and dad. Terry told him to shut up. They were yelling at each other. Merrick was coming out with some crap about Terry being a soft touch, a bleeding heart; said he only took me in to fill the hole in his life . . . That's when he said he was going to show me how *men* solved problems.'

'Who said that?'

'Terry. Matt. Whatever the fuck he's called.' Clancy shifted in his seat. 'That woman from the tunnel . . . she killed those kids.' He wore the knowledge, everything he'd witnessed in the tunnels, like a stain on his skin. 'His kids.'

'She was very ill,' Marnie said. 'It's called post-partum psychosis . . .'

'I know. She had pills for it, but she stopped taking them. She should've kept taking the pills.' He chewed his nail, sounding like an adult, looking like a child. 'It fucked him up. He blamed Merrick for the bunker, said Merrick must've known.'

'What did Merrick say?'

'He said he didn't know. He kept saying it. Like I kept saying I didn't know where Carmi and Tommy were.' He sucked blood from the cuticle he'd torn with his teeth. 'That's when he hit Merrick, with the torch. I thought he'd killed him. But he said he was breathing, he checked. He tied his wrists with a coat hanger.' Clancy cringed. 'He was always going on about the fucking coat hanger, yeah? It came with my uniform, I didn't *want* it. But it freaked him out. He said you could kill someone with it. I mean, *as if*. But maybe he meant *he* could kill someone.'

He stopped, looking lost for a second. 'I thought he was going to do it. Kill Merrick. Put the hanger through his eye, into his brain. I saw that once, on a DVD. He looked like he'd do it. I got scared. He was always angry when I was scared. Not angry like most people. He never shouted. He never hit stuff. He just . . . went quiet.' Clancy rubbed at his eyes. 'He had this *voice*, when he was mad. Very quiet, very *fuck-you*. He said we were going somewhere we'd be safe. He wanted to talk to me, he said, make me see what I'd done. I thought he meant Carmi and Tommy. I told him I didn't know where they were. I was too scared to tell him. He was off his head.'

'So you went with him, to the Isle of Dogs?'

Clancy nodded. 'I knew about the tunnels. My dad was all over that. But I didn't want to go down there. I managed to lose him on the site. And *you*. I tried to get you out of the way, like Carmi and Tommy. I didn't know what else to do. I had to go down into the tunnels; there wasn't anywhere else to hide.'

'And Terry came after you.'

'Yeah. You saw. He'd have killed me, and maybe you too, if *she* hadn't come.'

He started chewing his thumb again. 'That's it. That's everything that happened.'

He looked like a child. At fourteen, Stephen Keele hadn't looked like a child. But he'd been brought up by parents like the Brands, who believed the world was a dangerous place where you had to prepare for the worst.

'Tell me about your mum and dad. You've said you don't want to go home. Why?'

Clancy was quiet for a bit, then he said, 'Josie, my mate, she told me why she ran. Her dad was having an affair, only she called it *playing away from home*. She said she didn't feel safe knowing what he was up to.'

'Like you,' Marnie hazarded. 'You didn't feel safe at home.'

Another laugh, too old to be coming out of a kid this young. She'd never heard Stephen laugh, but plenty of times he'd sounded older than his years. Cynical, because he'd been taught to expect the worst? The way Clancy had been taught.

'They're *safe*. If that's what you're worried about. That house is the safest place on the planet. It's a fucking fortress, thanks to Merrick. Nobody's going in or out.'

'But you didn't feel safe there. Like Josie didn't feel safe.'

'Not like Josie.' He blinked, looking away. 'There's no *playing away from home* in that place. Fuck that, there's no *away from home*. That place is *everything*. Mum and Dad's perfect world. "Everything you need's here." That was their favourite line. Food, water . . . Like the whole universe is in that house and you'd better fucking like it. You'd better not complain it's making you sick being stuck in there day in, day out. You'll take your turn with the chores and laugh at their jokes and pretend to be part of their perfect fucking *nuclear* family, because if you don't? If you don't . . .' he was crying now, 'they'll wipe you out.'

Wiped out. Was that how Stephen had felt when he came to their house?

'They'll look right through you,' Clancy said, 'like you're not there. Like you were never there in the first place. Like you're *nothing*. I got sick of being nothing. No one can live like that. *You* couldn't.'

'I couldn't,' she agreed.

I did it for you.

Was that what Stephen had meant? Did he think he was saving her from a fate like the one Clancy was describing? Places of exile . . .

I did it for you.

Clancy wiped his nose again. 'Terry gave me grief about growing up, what it meant to be a man, but at least he never did *that*, never made me feel like nothing. You'd better not be thinking about sending me back to them, because I'll run. I'll fucking *run*.'

He looked at Marnie, eyes blazing. 'You'd run too. If it was you . . . No matter how much stuff they gave you, if you had to live like that? You'd run too.'

45

Connie Pryce wore the rain on her face like a veil.

Debbie said it was only right and proper that it rained. Funerals needed rain, she said, as if the earth was going to put up flowers. Perhaps it was; perhaps it would.

Connie's coat was fire-engine red, the boys' favourite, she said. Ron wore a black nylon mac over his suit. Fran Lennox looked frozen, wrapped in a sheepskin jacket. Everyone was in black, except Connie, and Marnie. Maybe she should have replaced one of the black suits she threw out after her parents' funeral, but with Connie in her red coat it didn't matter that Marnie wore grey. She had no trouble crying at this funeral. No one did.

The rain meant they all could weep, even the men.

Ron had come up to Marnie before the service. 'I was wrong.' He was gruff, apologetic. 'When I called this a cold case, said we couldn't do anything that mattered. We did. The boys are with their sister now, and their family has a place to come, to be with them. You were right. I just wanted to say that.'

Marnie had nodded, digging up a smile before the tears came.

Ed held her hand throughout. She was grateful for his body heat, hadn't been able to get warm since coming out of the tunnels.

Adam was at the service, staying at the back of the church. When they filed out into the rain, he was standing under a tree, smoking, no one to tell him it was a nasty habit, to complain about the stink in his clothes. Marnie caught a glimpse of the child, Tia, crinkling her nose against the smell, refusing to hug him until he'd washed. 'Daddy!'

Matt Reid was at the service with a minder; he'd volunteered for psychiatric treatment. The CPS was still deciding whether to charge him, and with what. Marnie hoped it wouldn't come to that. Tim Welland was doing his best to talk the CPS down. Ed had offered himself as a witness in Matt's defence.

The rain had wiped out Matt's face. Beth held his arm, staying close. Her sister was taking care of Carmen and Tommy, but there was hope for his new family.

Marnie had to believe that.

Esther had stayed away. For Matt's sake, she'd said.

She didn't believe he would ever forgive her, or even that he should, but Marnie was holding on to the memory of his remorse in the tunnel, his realisation of the harm he'd done unthinkingly to Clancy, to a child in his care. He'd known a little of the darkness that had consumed Esther.

Marnie hoped he could forgive Esther, and himself, enough to find peace.

Ed pressed warmth into her hand. 'My place or yours?'

She smiled at him, weak with gratitude. 'Yours. Please.'

46

Sol was sleeping on the sofa when Noah got home, his face squashed by the pillow, profile smudged and soft as a child's. Maybe Dan was right and this was Sol's safe place now.

Noah was glad. If that was the case . . . he was glad.

He stood and watched Sol for a long time, grateful for the end of the day, and the end of this case. Glad of the fact that his family wasn't broken, that his brother had come here when he needed help. Clancy Brand had been forced to run to strangers. Sol had run to Noah. He still didn't know why, what Sol was hiding from, but perhaps it didn't matter.

Sol cracked an eye open. 'S'up, bro?'

'Nothing . . . Go back to sleep.'

'I was gonna cook.' Sol swung his bare feet to the floor. 'Dan said you had rice and shit . . . I do a mean risotto.'

'All right. Let's cook. But let's do it at Mum's. She could use a decent meal.'

Sol pulled a face. 'For real?' Then he grinned. 'You're doing the washing-up.'

'Fine. I'm doing the washing-up.'

Sol reached for his bag, but Noah shook his head. 'Stay, for a while. Or longer, if you'd like.'

'You're not kicking me out?'

'I'm not kicking you out,' Noah said. 'You're my brother. Stay as long as you want.'

47

St Thomas's Hospital, London

Rain wipes the mirror from my window, washing my reflection clean.

I want to say, 'It's over,' but I can't.

Not quite. Not yet.

The truth takes up too much room in my mouth and its taste is strange, leaving splinters between my teeth, under my tongue.

I'm not Alison any longer.

I'm more, and less, than that.

Esther . . .

I'm trying to be Esther again.

The way she was before.

Matt's wife, the mother of his children, loved and loving.

The boys are with Louisa now. Matt and Connie can visit whenever they want. If I stick with the pills, they say that I can visit too.

One day.

The rain won't stop, but it's soft, bringing the green scent of leaves through the glass, washing London clean.

I sit and watch it coming down, and I think of Matt standing by their graves, with the peace of the rain on his face.

Fred and Archie and Louisa and Matt.

All together. At last.

Author's Note

No Other Darkness is a work of fiction, but I found the following to be particularly relevant and/or inspirational when I was writing and later editing the book:

- David Emson's experience of PPP which appeared in an article by Lois Rogers, published in the *Sunday Times*, 13 January 2013
- The Joe Bingley Memorial Foundation, a charity which aims to help women and their families by raising awareness and providing help and information about postnatal depression: www.joebingleymemorialfoundation.org.uk
- *Derelict London* by Paul Talling, published by Random House, April 2008 (978-1-9052-1143-2)

Acknowledgements

For helping me to navigate the choppy 'second novel' seas, I'm indebted to my terrific agent, Jane Gregory, and her team. For her nerves of steel, I thank my brilliant editor, Vicki Mellor. Special thanks to Elizabeth Masters and Emily Griffin at Headline, and Emily Murdock Baker at Penguin.

For everything else, I thank my family. I could never have written a book about broken families had I not come from such a safe and happy one. The same goes for my friends, especially Anna, custodian of my sanity and Keeper of the Gin.

For the Max posse, Anne-Elisabeth, Becca, Claudia, Elaine and J – see what I did there?

For my daughter, Milly, whose courage every day amazes me – never stop being You.

To everyone who read *Someone Else's Skin* and cheered for Marnie and Noah, and asked for more – my thanks, and here it is.